E. J. SWIFT

PARIS
ADRIFT

SOLARIS

First published 2018 by Solaris
an imprint of Rebellion Publishing Ltd,
Riverside House, Osney Mead,
Oxford, OX2 0ES, UK

www.solarisbooks.com

ISBN 978 1 78108 593 6

10 9 8 7 6 5 4 3 2 1

A CIP catalogue record for this book is available from the
British Library.

Designed & typeset by Rebellion Publishing

Printed in Denmark by Nørhaven, Viborg

E. J. SWIFT

PARIS ADRIFT

for Dominique Larson and Björn Wärmedal
and for friends in far away places

Montmartre, Paris

THE ANOMALY IS waiting. It has been waiting for a long time, although the anomaly's sense of time differs from a conventional understanding, given the peculiarities of its nature. It does not know exactly what, or rather who, it is waiting for, but it will recognise them when they come. The anomaly is ready. Its hunger grows.

The anomaly has one desire, and that is to expand. With the right incumbent, it can push its feelers out through the centuries, backwards and forwards, producing new shoots which will emerge into unexpected temporal gardens. Like all of its kind, the anomaly has neither knowledge nor understanding of where, when, or what the consequences of these shoots may be. It wishes only to expand. The chance of discovery by a matching incumbent is approximately one in a hundred thousand, but the anomaly does not know that, either. All it can do is wait.

Every now and then, the anomaly has a squatter. This state of affairs makes it—as far as it can experience emotion—deeply unhappy. It is impossible to evict the squatter, because the squatter has no physical substance. It is impossible to communicate with the squatter, because the anomaly's intelligence, if it can be called that, is not human. And so the anomaly must endure this hostile presence.

Time passes.

Weeks.

Months.

Years.

And then, at the very edge of the anomaly's awareness, a disturbance.

Something—someone—is approaching.

PART ONE

The End of the World

CHAPTER ONE

Prague, 2318

THE EXPLOSIONS HAVE stopped, and in their absence a raw quiet unfolds. The bunker feels empty and cold, as if the people it harbours are already dead and have been for some time. Outside, what looks like snow is falling. It is not snow. Figures lurch past the cameras, sudden ghosts, there then gone. Inga breathes out. Breathes mist. In the confinement of the underground space, she listens to her thoughts detonating one by one.

This is the calm before the storm.

This time—this storm—will be the end.

There is a chance to fix this, but it means breaking everything they believe in. All that they've worked and sacrificed to preserve.

"The heating's gone."

That's Toshi, the eldest of them.

Inga looks about the bunker, observing her depleted crew. Only a handful of history's incumbents remain. Some have died during their travels through time, or have taken their own lives. Most have been buried never knowing the truth about their nature—perhaps they are the lucky ones. Others are yet to be born. Might never be born, now. Those too, she envies. What is left of the House of Janus is a world-weary collective, traumatised by experience and the implausibility of what has happened to them. They are addicts, although they had no choice about that. Over the years they have suffered relapses. Most returned to Janus, acknowledging the importance of their mission. Because they are survivors. But what they have survived will be meaningless if this is the end of humanity.

She shivers, hugging herself inside her coat. The war feels as though it has always been here, yet compared to most wars it has been short. A matter of weeks. Wars are rarely about what their perpetrators profess them to be about; Inga has seen enough conflict to know that. This one has seen entire continents reduced to nuclear wastelands. The fact is, it no longer matters how the war started, unless they stop it.

She turns to her analysts.

"What do you have?"

Efe clears her throat. She sounds nervous.

"We've worked back from the Marceau address and identified two turning points which should cause minimum disruption to the timeline. The building of the Parisian basilica Sacré-Coeur, and a twentieth century woman called Rachel Clouatre."

"Show me."

The analyst waves her hands and a scroll of mathematical code gleams into being: banners dictating action and reaction, probability and consequence. The randomness of the universe reduced to a set of equations. Looking at those digits gives Inga a strange feeling; at once childish and omnipotent. Like a field biologist who may observe but never intervene, she has dedicated most of her life to preserving history. Now she is preparing to do what she swore she would never do.

"This Rachel... she's an ancestor of our man?"

"She starts the Marceau bloodline."

"And the Sacré-Coeur—"

"Was where the April address was made. The catalyst."

"You're certain about this?"

"We've scanned every source."

It is an unavoidable fact that by addressing the Marceau bloodline at its root, they will be condemning several generations before their instigator is born. Inga supposes that's the penalty of acting for the greater good. She glances around. The others nod their agreement.

"How do we get there?"

"We've identified an incumbent who was a near miss. She passed very close to the dormant anomaly in the north of Paris, but never discovered it."

One of the lucky ones, thinks Inga. A map of the French capital unfolds, and the four people present in the room form a circumference around it. Efe moves a finger through the projection, pointing to a site on the right bank of the river Seine.

"This one."

"Do you have a lock?"

"Twentieth, twenty-first century—I'm trying to narrow it further—"

"Don't try. Do."

The analyst sits back, defeated.

"Early twenty-first century. Somewhere between the year fifteen and twenty-five. That's the best I've got."

Inga folds her arms, psyching herself up to face the person she needs. Of course it would be Léon, she thinks. Léon, who is closest to the brink, who of all of them has the fewest travels left before the anomaly claims him for good. She hears him exhale.

"Léon."

When she looks up, his gaze is locked upon the map.

"Léon, we need you."

"I can't." He speaks softly.

"If there was anyone else… you're the only one with a European anomaly."

"I can't... go back there."

Efe focuses intently upon her projections. Toshi moves aside, giving Inga and Léon the illusion of privacy.

"I know." She steels herself. She knows what it means to return to something you had overcome; that you thought you had escaped. "And I know the danger. I know this could be your last travel. It could even be the tipping point, there's no point pretending otherwise. But we can't trust the chronometrist to do this alone. Even if we could trust her, she hasn't got the range. We need someone on the ground to identify the incumbent and steer her to the anomaly. We have to oversee the mission."

His gaze drops away. They all agreed on the course of action, but that was before they knew what it would entail.

"How will you get me into Paris?" he says at last.

"We'll take the hopper."

"You might not get out again."

There is no denying this. The European mainland is gone. Paris is ripe with radiation.

"Then you'd better make sure you succeed." She raises her voice, bringing the others back into the conversation. "Time to get the chronometrist in here, before everyone outside is a goner."

THEY WATCH ON the cameras as the chronometrist selects her body. Through the white flakes Inga catches glimpses of Prague, a once beautiful city reduced to skeletal buildings and the burned out carcasses of vehicles and people. Civilians lie at odd angles in the street, slowly being covered in ash. Inga doesn't know who bombed Prague. In some ways she'd rather not. She's fifty-six, older out of time, thought she'd seen everything there was to see. She was wrong.

As they watch, one of the wounded raises himself from the ground and gets awkwardly to his feet. He begins to shuffle towards the bunker. As he draws closer, Inga can see that half of his face is missing, the white of calcium exposed.

"For fuck's sake," says Toshi. "That one's practically dead."

"Her idea of a joke, no doubt."

"Some joke."

As far as they know, the chronometrist was the first incumbent. When the anomalies began to appear, sometime around the twelfth century, she was a young woman growing up in the Southern Song dynasty in China. Like all of them, she discovered her anomaly by accident. She liked what she found, and the power it bestowed upon her. The chronometrist travelled without restraint, further and further away from her home time, and as she reached a tipping point the anomaly began to hollow her out, like a cockroach wasp taking over its host. She faded, and faded. She exists now only as a consciousness, one whose sanity is dubious at best. Tied to the timestream, she can travel through and pass between any anomaly in the world, but can communicate only by using a body within a few hundred metres of an anomaly. If she remembers her name, she has never revealed it.

The chronometrist's host enters the tunnel to the underground bunker. Previous members of the House of Janus constructed the bolthole centuries ago. It is the site of an anomaly whose incumbent was killed in the Battle of Vítkov Hill. Out of time. Inga supposes technically there is no difference, but it seems worse, to die out of time, when in a sense you are not really living at all. Occasionally she has the impression of ghosts surrounding her, traces of the doomed incumbent coming and going. They all feel it.

A knock on the metal door. Inga feels the atmosphere in the bunker shift. No one likes dealing with the chronometrist, even under normal circumstances.

"Let her in."

As he staggers inside, the dying man's injuries make themselves known. It is impossible to ignore the smell of rotting meat. The man stands, clad in makeshift combat gear, swaying from foot to foot. He is a patchwork of blood, grime, ash and gangrene. Multiple gunshot entries mark his jacket.

His lips move; the chronometrist's voice comes out in a parched croak.

"Oh—my dear Janusians—how delightful—to see you."

Toshi fetches a glass of water, but the chronometrist ignores it. Inga pushes a chair towards the man.

"Could you not have let this one die in peace?"

"I'm doing—him—a favour—don't you think? Taking his mind—away—"

"All right, all right. You know why you're here."

The injured man giggles.

"Stop the war, stop the war, stop—the—war…"

"Exactly. Or we're all dead."

"Don't know—if I *can* die."

"You'll find out soon enough, if you don't help us." Inga's words float back to her. This is what it has come to: they must put their trust in the psychopath. She pushes the thought aside. "It's all up to you and Léon now. We've found an incumbent."

"A new one?" The man's voice squeaks with the chronometrist's excitement.

"You will have to engage her. Influence her. But she mustn't know what's she's doing. It's best she thinks it's an accident, at least until the mission is completed. We don't want her getting any ideas. Once it's done, Léon will induct her into the code of practice. Do you understand?"

The man's eyes slip away. His fingers poke at one of the entry wounds. Fresh blood begins to ooze through the synthetic material of his jacket. Toshi's frown deepens.

"Ye-es…"

Inga speaks sharply.

"Then listen carefully. This is what we're going to do."

LÉON SAYS NOTHING as he straps himself into the co-pilot's seat, and Inga does not attempt to instigate conversation. The landscape says it all for them. As they rise into the ash and then break above its veil, the blitzed city reverts into a maze of tessellating shapes until it blurs again, a blackened smear on a blacker land. Léon watches in silence as the earth falls away and she points the aircraft west.

It takes them two hours to reach northern France. Everything below is the same: grey rivers, grey country. Some cities appear almost untouched, but stand still and silent, monumental sculptures carved upon the land. Paris will not be like that. Paris was decimated. She was one of the first cities to fall. On the approach, Inga begins a slow descent. This whole region was underwater once. Perhaps it will be again, with the seas rising. Perhaps that would be better. She wonders what is going through Léon's head, seeing the ruination of the city. It's not where he grew up, but the anomalies make themselves the centre of your heart. Once you have answered that call, everything that came before is meaningless.

Inga dreams about Mexico City every night.

"I'll need your help to navigate," she says.

"South of the river."

He directs her. Inga spirals in slow circles and touches down in what must once have been a wide boulevard, busy with department stores and brasseries. Léon's anomaly is located deep inside the catacombs beneath the city. She lets the hopper's engine wind down. Léon unstraps and stares out of the windshield.

"That's the last of our fuel," he says.

"Yes."

He doesn't elaborate, and neither does she. It is what it is.

They step outside. The silence strikes her. No living thing stirs here, no birds or insects, or even the slow creep of plants. A breeze moves black dust about their feet.

"This way."

Léon leads her through what is left of the streets. There are bodies, inside cars or lying in the road, all covered in that fine black dust. It gets into her nose, her mouth. Her throat thickens. She can't swallow. She is reminded of Pompeii, the way the lava made sarcophagi for its victims as it cooled.

She had assumed they would have to blast their way into the tunnels, but luck favours them. The glass dome that housed the entrance to the catacombs has collapsed, but when they clear aside the debris they find the stairway down to the tunnels is intact. A mouth in the earth, as if it has been waiting for them, the way the anomalies wait for their incumbents. She hands Léon a torch and follows him below. There are six million dead buried down here, stacked in immaculate constructions of tibia, fibula and skulls. And now another three million above, preserved in dust.

"How far in do we go?" she asks.

"All the way."

The skulls observe their passage, the grinning masks alive in a way the dead above are not. They have been walking for twenty minutes when Léon stops. Inga sees the problem at once. Part of the tunnel has caved in. She glances overhead. Impossible to tell how stable the ceilings are.

They work together to clear the piles of rocks and dirt. Léon's movements are precise, methodical. He shows no sign of anxiety or fear, though he must feel both. She sits back on her heels for a moment, watching him.

"How old were you, when you found your anomaly?"

"Twelve."

"No child should have to deal with that."

"I don't know. Perhaps it's easier that way. To accept. Your views aren't so rigid."

But the damage is worse, she thinks, in the long term.

"You know, when you go through it will feel like none of this could possibly happen."

"I know."

"You'll be centuries away. It would be very easy to immerse yourself in a new life. To forget about us. About the future. I know there will be side effects, but—"

"I won't forget."

"We're counting on you, Léon."

He looks up, just once.

"I know."

There is nothing more she can say. They have almost cleared enough space. She helps Léon enlarge the gap until his shoulders can fit inside. He pushes through without hesitation. On the other side, he stops.

"The roof is unstable. There's no point us both going on."

"All right."

"What will you do?"

"I'll wait. In the hopper. If it works—I don't know. I suppose all this will vanish."

"I suppose so."

They stand for a moment.

"You never know," she says. "The twenty-first century might suit you. In a quaint kind of way."

He grins reluctantly. She has a glimpse of the person he could have been, should have been, if it were not for the anomaly.

"It'll be something," he says.

"Good luck, Léon."

"And you."

He makes his way down the tunnel. Inga follows his progress, trying to imagine how it must feel, this return. What it would be like if it were *her* anomaly, back in Mexico City, back in—no. Don't think about it. But she does. It rushes up. The exhilaration and the terror. The desperate urgency to meet the flare, the feeling that this and only this can make you whole. She has tried not to indulge those memories; the grief is too much. At times it is almost unbearable. A terrible jealousy overcomes her at the sight of Léon's receding figure. She can feel it gripping her, thinks perhaps she should follow him, as though by being close when he travels, she might recapture some of that lost joy—

A rumbling overhead causes her to look up in alarm. Trickles of dust are beginning to skitter down the walls and over the bones.

"Shit—"

She backs up, turns, runs; stooped, with her arms cradling her head. She hears the rush as the crawlspace they cleared caves in again. When she looks back, she sees plumes of dust. Then rubble.

The way is blocked.

"Did he make it through?"

From the interior of the hopper, she watches the bunker on her transmitter screen.

"Looks like it. His anomaly lit up like a star."

"And the chronometrist?"

"She's all set."

The wounded man is lying on the floor. His eyes open, staring up at the ceiling. Inga leans closer to the screen, knowing the chronometrist can see her too.

"You know what you have to do and you know the stakes. For all our sakes, behave yourself. No detours. Remember the code of practice."

The man's lips tremble.

"As if—I would do anything else, my dear Inga…"

He draws in a single rasping breath. Then the air sighs out of his lungs, his head lolls to one side and he goes still.

"She's out."

They wait nervously.

"Okay, Prague's lighting up. She's in. And there goes north Paris. She's crossed."

How strange, she thinks. Somewhere, not far from here if you measure in distance, the chronometrist's spirit is floating. If you can call it a spirit. Inga isn't sure *what* she would call the chronometrist.

"She's left us a corpse," says Efe.

"She always was a generous sort."

"Inga, how can we trust her?"

"We can't. But it's not as if we have another option."

"So what do we do now?"

"We wait."

"Are you all right there?"

"I'm all right. It's quiet. It's… peaceful, I suppose."

It's the end of the world.

She sags back in her seat. When she returned to the aircraft, she attempted to wipe the black dust from the windshield, but already new drifts are piling up, slowly obscuring her view of the silent city. Soon she will not be able to see out at all. A fit of coughing takes her. She tries not to think about the radiation levels, or getting sick, or how long it takes to die alone of radiation poisoning.

If history changes, will all this be redacted? Or will it be something only they have lived through, trapped forever in their memories? Will they even be born?

"South America's gone," says Toshi over the comm.

"Just like that," she murmurs.

"Just like that."

I shouldn't be surprised, she thinks. In all the centuries she visited, she never failed to be amazed by humanity's capacity for destruction. One crazy person with their finger on the red button. That's all it takes. She wants to ask Toshi about Mexico, but doesn't dare, and surely she would know, would feel the death of her anomaly like the loss of a lung.

Their hopes now rest with the twenty-first century incumbent. Inga wonders who she is and how she will respond to the events to come. It will be wondrous at first, and Léon's job is to contain it at that, ensure she completes the mission and then get her the hell out of Paris. But if it continues, travelling will become impossible to resist. Incumbents who swore on their lives to adhere to the code of practice have gone to terrible lengths to return to their anomalies. They have escaped incarceration, deportation and exile. They have lost themselves in time. Eventually, the incumbent becomes like the chronometrist, a thing of air but no mass, disembodied, perhaps immortal, without sensory experience or ties to the physical world. It was the fear of that fate that led the first incumbents to form the code of practice. That led them to where they are now.

"Good luck," she whispers. "Whoever you are, good luck."

PART TWO

Millie's

CHAPTER TWO

Paris, 2017

I'VE BEEN IN Paris for three weeks when I find myself outside Millie's, the bar next door to the Moulin Rouge, the bar I am told will employ anyone with a pulse. Gathered at my back is the neon riot of boulevard de Clichy. Together with boulevard Barbès, Clichy cordons off the eighteenth arrondissement from the rest of the city. Noisy, congested, segmented with sex shops and kebab kiosks and tourists in fur coats queueing for the cabaret, spilling out drinkers from midnight until morning, its central aisle is riddled with addicts, dealers, sightseers and the homeless—whose ranks I am shortly to join, if this afternoon doesn't go as planned.

I approach the entrance, then swerve away, my hands sweating. On the pedestrian concourse in the centre of the boulevard, two girls are taking a selfie on the Marilyn Monroe air feature, skirts billowing up around their thighs. I turn back. I've already wasted thirty minutes wandering up and down, trying to summon the courage to go inside. Something keeps drawing me back.

This is ridiculous, Hallie—even by your standards.

I set my shoulders and walk towards the double doors. This time I'm ready. As I reach for the handle, someone pushes from the other side; the door moves towards me faster than I anticipated, and next thing I know I'm flat on my arse.

"Fuck!"

"Putain—"

I scrabble back. A slender boy dressed entirely in black appears from the other side of the door. He extends a cautious hand.

"Don't you look where you are going?"

He sounds amused by the situation. I am not, and my nose is beginning to throb painfully. My voice comes out taut and high pitched.

"You opened the door on me!"

"Ah, I did not see you..."

"Probably because you're wearing those fancy shades," I snap. "Indoors."

He lowers the sunglasses and winces.

"Putain, your nose."

I touch it tentatively, and encounter blood.

"Come inside, I'll get you a drink," declares the boy, as though this will fix the swelling in the middle of my face. I give him a proper appraisal. Dark hair and brown skin; a sculptor's dream of a face with perfectly symmetrical features. He is wearing a leather jacket, slim fitting jeans, a pair of patent, pointed shoes and the aforementioned sunglasses.

"Do you work here?" I ask. He gives me a slight bow.

"Angel, at your service. And you?"

"H-Hallie."

It's out before I can catch myself. All this time I've spent trying out alter egos and now, when it matters, I've reverted. How amateurish.

"Hallie. Enchanté."

"Angel?" I repeat dubiously.

"The Americans love it, they think I am a slayer of dark forces. You're anglaise, yes?"

It would be rude to ask if he's French, so I don't, but Angel evidently reads the question.

"Algerian, darling."

"Oh." I feel the heat rising to my face.

"Not that I would be *allowed* in Algeria today."

He doesn't expand upon this statement and its exact meaning is left unclear—is he gay? Does he have a criminal record? Embroiled in social awkwardness, my meticulous planning is unravelling by the second.

Angel takes pity on me.

"I'm from Marseilles," he says gently. "Come on, come inside. Millie's boudoir awaits you."

Angel ushers me through the doors before I have a chance to explain the purpose of my visit. The interior of the bar is dimly lit, and extends back into the building further than I expected. When we enter I hear a high-pitched keening noise, almost tinnitus, putting pressure against my ears. I hang back, worried it might prompt an attack, but then the noise and my head clear. I reassure myself: it's going to be all right.

We go up to the bar, where an elfin woman with a blunt, heavy fringe and a dragonfly tattoo at her collarbone is the only visible staff member. She is stripping mint leaves from their stalks with brutal efficiency and tossing them into a plastic box. Seeing Angel, she frowns, as though indecisive about how his return should be greeted. Angel hoists himself up onto the bar and kisses her on both cheeks.

"Eloise, ma chérie, mon coeur, this lovely Anglaise here needs a tissue and a shot."

Eloise gives me a cursory glance.

"Why, what did you do to her?"

"It was an accident," I say, then wonder why I'm defending him. He could have broken my nose.

Eloise relinquishes her bundle of mint with a ponderous sigh. Slowly she walks to the other end of the bar, and returns equally slowly with a single piece of tissue. I dab at my nose, wincing. Eloise trickles vodka into a shot glass and inches it over the counter with a gladiatorial stare. I look from her to Angel. It's five pm, respectably into l'heure verte, but I haven't eaten anything since breakfast.

"I'm not—I mean—I'm looking for a job," I say.

Angel spreads his hands delightedly.

"Our redemption! There you go, Eloise. You needed a new girl for tonight, here is one right here, looking for a job."

Eloise looks pointedly at the vodka.

"I was not looking for some harlot you bring in from the street."

"Eloise," purrs Angel before I can protest.

"Well, maybe. I guess we could do with some more people tonight. I suppose. I'll have to see if Kit's about. You leave everything to the last minute, Angel, and why is there only one bottle of Grey Goose on the top shelf? One! We had ten last week. Don't tell me you've been giving it out to the Moulin staff?"

"Um, if it helps, this guy—"

"No, no, no, no. Kit gave it out, most definitely it was Kit. Now where's that planning for tonight? You're my favourite poussin, you know, Eloise."

"Everyone's your favourite poussin," snaps Eloise. "And anyway I'm your manager, I get to say who is the favourite, poussin or no poussin."

"This guy called Léon sent me," I say, when I can finally get a word in. Angel and Eloise exchange looks. "I mean—" I stumble on. "I said I was looking for a job—he said to try here—he said to say he recommended me."

"Did he now," says Eloise. Her voice is loaded with indecipherable meaning. She turns away. I'm beginning to regret taking the advice of some random guy who happened to be sitting next to me in the brasserie. If it hadn't been for that smile...

"Eloise is one of the night managers," Angel explains, when Eloise has stepped off the bar. "She does not like girls. Dutch," he adds, thoughtfully.

"What's she got against girls?"

"She doesn't trust them."

"Well, I'm not like that."

"Like what?"

Flustered, I say, "Whatever she thinks they're like. Should I not have mentioned that guy? Léon?"

"Oh, *Léon*," says Angel, as though this should explain everything. I change tactic.

"Who's Kit?"

"Kit is the top manager." Angel leans over and plucks a few mint leaves from the box. From the other end of the building, Eloise glares and Angel blows her a kiss. "This mint is brown. Brown mojitos, that is revolting. It was Kit who hired me."

"Not Millie? The website—"

"Oh—no. Millie doesn't work what you would call regular hours."

"Okay." I digest this. "What's the worst thing you've ever had to do?"

"When I worked the nights, I had to clean up vomit all the time. Now I am days. You would start with the nights."

Vomit, whilst far from pleasant, does not scare me. I doubt Angel has ever had to clean up after his mother decided to siphon her own blood for an art installation. I push the thought of her—of back there—aside.

Eloise comes back and says Kit will see me. I wipe the rest of the blood from my nose and follow her into the back room, where two boys are unstacking armchairs and arranging them into lounge seating. Steps lead down to a wide dance floor and a second bar, smaller than the first. From a DJ box, a guy in a tight T-shirt and cargos is checking the lights.

I pass up my CV, an uneventful affair which I have embroidered with a few industry relevant jobs. The manager, Kit, inspects it.

"Geology?"

"That's right." I wait. He doesn't say anything. "I studied mineral compounds, that kind of thing. It's kind of like mixology. I mean, obviously the fields are different, but there are definitely parallels. Intersections." *Stop talking.* "And I'm a very hard worker. I apply myself. You won't regret hiring me, I promise." *Just stop.*

"We take bartending very seriously here," says Kit. I restrain myself from saying that it is unlikely to be taken too seriously anywhere else, and offer a chirpy smile. "Your CV says you started university two years ago," he continues. "So you haven't finished."

I clasp my hands together tightly. *Remember the octopus, Hallie. The octopus avoids detection through its faultless camouflage, and you—you are the octopus.*

"I'm on a gap year," I say.

"How's your French?"

"Très bien."

The manager's expression suggests it is far from that, but he says, "Can you do a trial tonight?"

"Whenever you need."

"Fine. You start at eight."

I emerge provisionally employed, and tell Angel the good news. He tells me I have just missed his dear poussin Gabriela, who he swapped shifts with for tonight, but never mind because it is now the perfect time to go for a beer and meet the staff at the bar down the road. In the hour before my baptism, Angel gives me a short but unsparing run down on all of the staff, most of which I forget instantly. One pint turns into two pints plus tequila and by the time we amble back up the road I am feeling quite light-headed. Again it occurs to me that I have forgotten to eat.

This is about all the training I will ever need to work at Millie's.

CHAPTER THREE

ELOISE TAKES ME down to the girl's vestiaire. She presents me with an oversized T-shirt, a bumbag and a cash float. "You'll be working the front bar for now," she says. "We may move you into the back bar later."

"Okay."

"And don't loiter. Keep moving."

"Okay."

Like Angel, Eloise's English is immaculate. I am already ashamed of my French, which owes its paltry existence to a C-grade GCSE and recent eavesdropping on café terraces. She shows me the ice machine ("If you're asked for ice you get it straight away") and the keg room, a dank concrete cavern stacked with kegs and crates. A line gurgles as lager is pumped upstairs. Again, I hear that keening noise emitting from an invisible source.

"Don't leave anything down here," says Eloise. "I want it tidy."

"Of course."

"One time I found a peacock in here."

I stare at her, assuming she must be joking, but Eloise continues.

"It had shat everywhere. Those boys think they're so funny with their little jokes. They didn't find it so amusing when I made them clean up its shit."

In the moment Eloise turns away, I feel an inexplicable shift in the atmosphere. There's a flush of heat, a thickening in the air around us that acts like an opiate. I breathe out, struggling to shake the dizziness. Blink. A figure stands before me. Or something close to a figure. Its presence isn't fully formed, but nebulous, composed of wisps and eddies, flecks of cirrus cloud. I can make out a head, a torso and limbs. Then the features of the face begin to emerge, contracted in alarm. Equally startled, I take a step backwards and bump into Eloise.

"Sorry, sorry—"

She gives me an irritated look. I glance back, but of course there's nothing there. I can feel the residual heat in my face. I hope this isn't some new permutation of the attacks—hallucinations are the last thing I need.

Our tour concluded, Eloise escorts me back upstairs. The place is beginning to fill up. After the unsettling experience of the keg room, it feels reassuringly normal, and I'm eager to get started. Angel is behind the bar, juggling limes. He gives me an exaggerated thumbs up. On the floor, I begin a meandering circuit, and am accosted with my first order. From then on, I don't stop. I take orders for burgers and bloated chips and ferry trays of cocktails. After the first linguistic mix-up, I carry a menu with me.

The bar grows steadily busier. From around half past nine the night team begin to trickle in. They form a huddle around the coffee machine, nursing their espressos, blinking soporifically. With their swaddling coats and the caldera shadows beneath their eyes, there's something of the gothic about them. Not sinister, but separate, as though they have been set apart by their shared experience of the night. They stir only with each new arrival, which requires an enactment of ritual kisses: two, three, sometimes four.

A customer taps me on the shoulder.

"Hello-o, can we get some drinks here or what?"

"Sorry, yes, I'm coming."

The group want shots and cocktails. One of the night team takes the order, a tall, angular blonde. She doesn't volunteer her name, but I overhear it: Dušanka. She has a beautiful, truculent face, studied in its blankness. I wait while she begins making the drinks but she catches me staring and waves an impatient hand. Remembering my first and only instruction—*don't stand still*—I melt back into the floor.

When I return, the bar is three deep and Dušanka is standing with hands on hips, long neck strained, completely ignoring any other demands for her attention. Catching my eye, she lifts one hand in a gesture that is purely French but in Dušanka's body language I can only assume means *get your arse over here now.*

At eleven o'clock the back room opens and a stream of people flow inside. Men hunch over the balcony, staring at the first pioneers of the dance floor. Swivelling lights blink through the colour spectrum with the gathering ravers.

I fight my way around the dance floor, collecting empty bottles. I can feel my make-up sliding down my face, the sweat gathering in every crevice. From his position of sanctuary behind the bar, Angel waves at me. I roll my eyes.

At midnight I am dispatched on break with the other newbie Mike, a skinny black guy from Chicago.

"They said we should go to the pub down the road," he says.

"Oh, yes, I was there earlier," I say, feeling knowledgeable. We go to the other pub, which is also heaving, but where our sloganed T-shirts act as passports to discounted drinks.

"What brought you to Paris?" yells Mike over the music.

"I'm travelling," I yell back. "Paris is the first stop. Then I'm going to Rome. My boyfriend's out there." The lies roll easily off my tongue. "How about you?"

"I'm having a pre-career break, you know?"

"What did you study?"

"Math."

"Why did you come to Paris?"

Mike embarks on a convoluted story. There's something about Europe, he says. It's the age of it, the antiqueness. His great-grandfather was sent here after the Second World War and he wrote letters home; it was a tragedy, he wrote, that so much history had been lost in the bombing, the liberation, though of course now *that's* history, the letters, and isn't that cool? And now he's seeing what his grandfather saw.

Mike gestures. I lean closer, straining to hear.

"Everything here is old," he yells. Old, and so small: the streets, the parks. It's cute. The food isn't bad either, though he can't deal with this steak haché bullshit. Fire was invented for a reason and besides, it's fucking expensive.

"Do you know what we get paid?" I ask, realizing this is the one thing I have neglected to find out.

"Like shit," says Mike. "And the French don't tip, have you noticed that?"

Break over, we walk the hundred-metre stretch back to Millie's. The cold air against my face is a blissful respite until we duck back into the bar, the sauna of seething bodies. I pummel my way from one end of the building to the other. Someone's shoulder knocks my nose and a fresh wave of pain assaults me. It stays frantic until I get a second fifteen-minute break, at three-thirty in the morning.

In the girls' vestiaire I find Dušanka lying on her back with her shoes and socks off and her ostrich legs extended against the metal lockers. In one hand is a cigarette, in the other a volume of poetry by Anna Akhmatova, bent at the spine. Her combat trousers fall in soft folds around her thighs. She inhales a maximum of smoke and tips ash onto the tiles beside her. I sit for a few minutes in silence, wishing I had thought to bring a book.

"All the translations are shit," says Dušanka morosely.

"What?"

"The translations." She waves the Akhmatova. "Only the original retains its elegance."

The obvious response would be to ask why she is reading Russian poetry in French if it is so terrible, but I'm not sure we have reached this level of rapport.

"How long have you worked here?" I ask instead.

"Too long," she spits. "But next year I finish my research masters. Then..."

She blows smoke upwards.

"What do you study?"

"Philosophy."

"That's cool."

"They are morons. The professors."

She lights one cigarette from another, and angles the box towards me.

"Have one."

"Do you have a lighter?"

Dušanka raises one eyebrow as though it is inconceivable that anyone should not have a lighter on their person. Grudgingly, she produces a tab of matches.

I rarely smoke, have only ever done so in situations like this, where conformity—camouflage—demands it. The first draw goes straight to my head. My body feels preternaturally light, suspended in the plane between adrenaline and the pending crash that is bound to follow.

"This is not a real life," Dušanka says. Smoke seeps upwards from between her teeth. The confines of the locker room lends an air of intimacy to the conversation, but it is clear that my role is to be a receptacle for Dušanka's musings. I don't mind. I'm happy to have a role.

"Every morning I wake up and I know this is not real," Dušanka continues. "This is not what real people do. Real people see daylight, and they eat breakfast. Cereal, or some shit. This—this is a dream life."

The bass thuds dimly on the ceiling. I nod, privately unconvinced. The odour of my own sweat, the heat, the bruises from passing elbows—it all seems real enough to me.

"What happened to your face?" asks Dušanka.

The vestiaire door bangs open before I have a chance to respond.

"You—new girl—"

I jump. It's Eloise, and she looks angry.

"What are you doing down here? Your break was up five minutes ago!"

I scramble to my feet, but the face disappears before I can respond. Dušanka gives me an ambiguous smile.

"The fifteen-minute break? You can count it by two straights or one roll-up. For the future, smoke faster."

There is no time for a retort along the lines of why Dušanka has decided to enlighten me now, or why she herself hasn't been hauled out for the same transgression. I race upstairs. No sooner have I reached the bar than someone yells at me to go and get ice. Back down I go. I find a roll of sacks but no scoop. I look everywhere around the ice machine. Nothing. Seconds are ticking away. Upstairs, the bar staff are waiting. I can imagine them talking, the derision in their voices.

That new girl's useless—

Took half an hour just to get the ice!

My legs start to tingle. I feel the telltale pressure squeezing my chest, my ribcage winching tighter, smaller, with every breath. Blackness speckles my peripheral vision. I put out a hand to steady myself. I lasso my mind. *No.* Not here. Not now. I need this job. If I can't find a way to make money, then England is back on the agenda. And I will not—I *cannot* go back.

Breathe. Start counting. One to ten. One to ten. I plunge my hands into the ice machine to bring down my body temperature and there's the scoop, buried under a mound of cubes. Reprieve! I fling shovelfuls of ice into the plastic sack. As I sling the straining bag over my shoulder, Dušanka emerges from the vestiaire, yawning.

"My god, it is so boring tonight. These people have no joy."

Upstairs, Kit calls all the staff to the bar and hands out shots. I drink what I am given. The first taste is of tart apple, then it explodes against the back of my throat.

Buoyed by alcohol, I fight my way into the back room. Ahead of me I see a black-clad girl shouldering expertly through the crowd. I follow, using the path she is forging to ease my own, and notice we are wearing the same boots—classic purple Doc Martins. I push forward, and see a flash of yellow at her heels. I stop. Glance down at my own left heel. Pikachu's round face beams up at me. My brother George put the sticker there years ago, no doubt to annoy me, but I never had the heart to remove it. I look again for the girl, glimpse her ahead, but she's moving too quickly, and a moment later I've lost her. So now I'm projecting. For the second time tonight I curse my delinquent brain.

When I return to the front bar Eloise is blending frozen margaritas, her head rotating in all directions as she scans the crowd. She spies me and her eyes narrow.

"Where's the jet?"

"What?"

"The jet I asked you for, where the hell is it?"

I stare mutely. Is this some kind of test? Eloise glares.

"Get down and get it before I fire you!"

I daren't ask for clarity. Trembling now, I head back to the stairs, hoping I'll meet someone who can tell me what the hell I'm supposed to be bringing back. I check the vestiaire but it's empty. The clang of metal steps brings me out in time to see a familiar pair of Doc Martins heading round the corner towards the keg room.

"Hey—"

I run after the girl, who must be another of Millie's staff. The keg room door is open. I go inside. The air feels strangely thick again and a lurch of vertigo blurs my vision momentarily. I look for the girl, but there's no one in here. Where did she go? I remember the ghostly figure from earlier, remind myself I don't believe in ghosts. Then I see, stood on a keg, a frosted-glass bottle of spirits. The label reads Get 31. Get. *Jet*. Either someone is helping me, or this is a practical joke, an initiation. Right now I don't care which. I grab the bottle and sprint upstairs.

By five o'clock the place is finally beginning to empty. Mike and I stack up the empties. The bar staff begin a seemingly endless cycle of the dishwasher. The last song plays. The lights come up. The effect is immediate and awful. Now you can see the cracks in the foundation, mascara entrenched around dissipated eyes. Circling couples of a moment ago stare at one another like absolute strangers.

Whilst the bouncers evict the stragglers, we wax the woodwork and sweep the floor. Mike sees me picking up chunks of broken glass.

"Just kick it under the booths," he mutters.

Finally, the doors close. There is a yell I don't understand until it is followed by an avalanche of breaking glass. My ears ring. The non-glass bins overflow with black sacks. One of the boys climbs into the bin and jumps on them.

At quarter past seven Kit pronounces us done. About twenty people are sitting in the back room, half of whom I haven't seen until now. By the time staff drinks arrive, I am barely conscious. I've been up for almost twenty-four hours. Angel is chatting to one of the bartenders in French, and I can't understand a word. Très bien.

Angel introduces us.

"Ah oui, 'Allie," says the bartender, Simone. Her hair sits in tight braids against her scalp, the extensions falling to her waist. "We met earlier."

"Yeah…" I smile brightly, hoping to mask my lack of memory.

I've met so many people tonight. My cocktail arrives. It tastes just like a chocolate milkshake.

I stagger out into the morning sunlight, red-eyed and blinking. It feels as if I've been entombed for days. Cars sweep past, a horn blares. I almost fall into the road. I squint to left and right, trying to remember which route will take me back to the hostel in Barbès. Angel grabs my arm.

"This way, this way."

"Where are we going?"

"To Oz, mon poussin. To see the wizard."

Oz proves to be the only bar that stays open later than Millie's: smaller, darker, the little remaining clientele comprising bartenders from other parts of Clichy. Our entrance is met with whoops of delight. A young woman in jeans with long dark curls shouts Angel's name.

"Gabriela, ma poule! You handed in?"

She pumps her arms in a victory gesture.

"It is done!"

They exchange high fives. Angel draws me over.

"Gabriela, meet Hallie, our new Anglaise."

"Welcome!"

She jumps up and kisses me on both cheeks. Her eyes are the colour of rich coffee, large and expressive in a smooth olive face. For a moment I just stare at her.

"Oh, but you're beautiful," I say, which wasn't what I meant to say at all. Then I remember I must stink of sweat and I have a lump in the centre of my face, and cringe. Then someone hands me a drink and I no longer care.

"She's a bit peculiar," says Angel. "But aren't we all, chérie? Santé! To Millie!"

"À Millie!"

The clink of glasses fills the room. Everyone drinks vociferously. I lean against the bar—or at least, the bar keeps me vertical. From the other side of the taps, an amused voice issues over my head.

"I see you made it out alive. Félicitations."

I lower my drink before I choke on it. I recognize the bartender's voice. I recognize it because I heard it earlier this afternoon—yesterday, technically—whilst perusing job adverts on a terrace in the seventeenth arrondissement. There I was, minding my own business, enjoying my espresso, when the same voice said, "You know, your French will never improve if you're thinking about teaching English." I recall the voice's owner: a guy in his mid-twenties, mixed race, athletically built and unfairly handsome.

Léon.

I reply without turning around.

"You know, I'm not sure your name did me any favours."

"Harsh, Hallie, very harsh."

"Eloise didn't seem impressed."

"Ah, *Eloise.*"

"Right."

"Yet here you are, a valiant survivor of the first shift. Drink?"

My fingers itch. It's tempting, so very tempting, to accept. But earlier this evening, Angel opened a door on my face. I deem it best to stay outwards facing.

"I'm good, thanks."

"Suit yourself, chérie."

I sense him grin. I paid witness to that smile earlier, and now I find I can conjure it without effort. It's a smile that could charm armies out of warfare. A smile that says this is a man who sails through life, for whom the complex highway of obstacles and emotional crises and impossible decisions will always be easy, because who could resist responding to that smile? Just looking at him makes you want to be a part of that warmth, to luxuriate in it: knowing everything will be all right if you stick by his side.

And for this reason, I force myself to move away from the bar and rejoin Angel and Gabriela.

"Ma poule, I read the synopsis of episode nine. There are such twists..."

"I'm not listening!" Gabriela puts her hands over her ears.

"Truly, you will not believe what happens with Samira—"

"Arrêt!"

The mention of Samira has a revitalizing effect upon me.

"Are you guys talking about *Transfusion*?"

A science-fiction show where the main character can jump into the head of her blood relations, revealing their secrets and (inevitably scandalous) desires, *Transfusion* has claimed hours of my life. It's also the kind of show you don't admit to watching if you want to retain credibility among your peers. But I was never very good at that.

Gabriela's eyes light up.

"You know it?"

"Yeah, I bloody love that series. We haven't got the new one in the UK yet, though. I'm dying to see it."

Gabriela leans over and squeezes my hand excitedly. Her fingers are warm and dry.

"Series three is the best yet. Ignore Angel, he does not even watch it. He likes to threaten me with spoilers."

"The conceits are dated and poorly executed," says Angel. "The actors have been pulled from the garbage cans of Los Angeles. What more is there to say?" Gabriela and I glare at him, but before either of us can defend our addiction, he throws up his hands in mock surrender. "That is, it is the most amazing television since *Breaking Bad*."

"I have the new episodes. We can watch them together," Gabriela tells me, smiling. I smile back idiotically, aware that other people want to talk to Gabriela, Gabriela being the kind of person that people gravitate towards, the way I have gravitated towards her, and that I have no idea how to extricate myself from the situation, or even if it is a situation. Across the room, Léon lounges behind the bar, charming everything with legs. I angle myself away from his line of sight. It's a relief when Dušanka appears, intent upon finding someone to lecture about the vagaries of Nietzsche. I listen, confused but surprisingly content, until the bar announces last orders and the remaining drinkers disperse one by one.

My feet take me back to the hostel in Barbès. The number of refugee tents under the métro arches has already doubled since I arrived. A man wearing a hooded jacket and jeans stands outside, his face drawn and wary, smoking. Our eyes meet briefly. I look away, shaken by the insignificance of my exodus in the face of his. I am wearing my T-shirt inside out. My tips and a bottle opener clank in the pockets of my jeans. I pass a bakery. The smell of warm bread drifts outside, and my stomach contracts with hunger. But I cannot face the prospect of having to appear human in the harsh light of morning.

The crack dealer sitting outside the hostel laughs visibly as I shuffle past. I'm too tired to give him the finger. I slink upstairs past reception, collapse onto the bunk in my clothes, and sleep.

CHAPTER FOUR

I LURCH AWAKE. For a few, merciful seconds I have no idea where I am or how I got here. It doesn't last. As if on cue, every muscle in my body shrieks in chorus. I move my head and become aware of a raw, throbbing lump. My stomach is a seething pit threatening to advance back up my throat.

There is a loud rattle which I realize is the blind going up. *What arsehole has let the blind up?* And then: a strange sensation, cold and fluid, as if I am being immersed in oil.

I feel something enter the room.

I say 'something' because I know—I just know—it isn't some*one*. Behind my eyelids, I feel the thing drawing slowly closer.

I half open my eyes and stare at the window, straight on. Nothing. But that sense of presence remains. Experimentally, I press one side of my face into the pillow and let my exposed eye drift across the room.

A bird is perched on the windowsill. Not a pigeon or a songbird, but an older, more predatory outline: some species of falcon. Too small for a peregrine. A merlin, perhaps. It stands side on, a quizzical expression in its round black eye.

As I stare, little hooks of pain digging inch by inch into my skull, the falcon's beak dips. Just as if it is nodding to me. Or preparing to gut its prey.

I groan.

"Please, go away. This is no time for hallucinations."

"I'm—sorry," says the falcon. "Do you imagine—I have a choice in the matter? Do you honestly think—I don't have better things— to be doing than addressing you, latest—in the line—of befuddled expatriates? Look—at the state of her!"

"I have no idea," I say. "Birds aren't my area of speciality."

The falcon gives me a stern look. "Your area of speciality is—at this stage—irrelevant."

I put the pillow over my face. "Look here, I've only been asleep for about two hours and that sun is hurting my head. I don't want weird conversations right now. I want a pleasant, empty, cloudy kind of sleep. Preferably nice, fluffy, cumulus clouds. And preferably one that lasts for ten hours. At least."

"You are right, my dear," says the falcon relentlessly. "You are asleep. But not—in the way you think you are. Not in the corporeal sense. As it were." It lets out a miserable squawk. "This—life form— is really extending—my range! But not a pleasant—experience. Now. Quite soon, you are going to wake up—that is, *it* is going to wake up—and when it does—you will find that the world is a different place—from the one you thought it was. So here's what I've come to say. Get your feathers in order."

I make a muffled, unhappy noise.

"Now my dear—I suggest—that you take advantage of this beautiful day," says the falcon. "Before you return—to the site. The Tuileries, perhaps? Shut-eye won't—help you now."

I pull the pillow from my face. Once again the window is revealed: brilliant, sun-glazed, cruelly transparent. Through it is a pane of cerulean sky, devoid of avian life. I touch my sleeping bag suspiciously, and pluck a hair from my arm. It hurts. I decide not to inflict further pain upon myself. Then the bile rises. The throbbing at my temples intensifies. I roll off the bunk, fight my way out of my sleeping bag and feel my stomach contort as I stagger down the corridor. The bathroom is occupied. I hammer on the door, restraining tears as I curse whoever is on the other side. When the door opens I throw myself headlong inside and collapse, narrowly avoiding cracking my jaw on the rim of the toilet. I pray to deities I do not believe in. I whimper and compare Angel, arbiter of my downfall, to a disease-bearing bacterium. In the toilet basin, a slurry of regurgitated milkshake with indefinable lumps of matter piles up and up. It is beyond revolting.

From the bathtub comes a rhythmical sound: *click-clack, click-clack.*

The window is open. Wings, at the edge of my eye.

"No, no, no, no," I moan.

The falcon continues to walk along the side of the bath. Its toenails *click-clack.*

"The Tuileries," it repeats. "This is—the last day of sunshine in October. There will be no more until after the rains."

"How do you know?" I manage, before another ghastly retch pulls me back to the toilet basin.

"We will meet—soon. In a better—vessel." It lets out a shrill cry. "A good day for preening!"

Only bile is coming up now. When I look back, the bird is gone. I have never hallucinated before this weekend. Perhaps the bird was actually here, and it was just an auditory hallucination? Because that, clearly, is *fine.* Maybe it lives here. Someone in the hostel has a passion for falconry. Or my drink was spiked last night. That would explain my current state and—oh, Jesus God—my imbecilic introduction to Gabriela. Some malevolent client inflicted this poison upon me, probably because I can't speak French.

I flush the toilet, clean my teeth three times and wander miserably back to the bunk. I don't dare look at the window in case my feathered stalker is there, so I pull on my jeans and sunglasses and crawl out of the hostel. I check the métro map and almost choke. The Tuileries are miles away. Who does the bird think it is? I go around the corner to Sacré-Coeur instead. I buy a can of Coke and find a secluded patch of grass on the other side of the hill, away from the tourists and the white glare of the Basilica overlooking the eighteenth, smug and resplendent. I spend the rest of the day with a scarf over my face.

At seven o'clock, I get a call from Kit.

"Job's yours, babe. You start tonight."

CHAPTER FIVE

THE FALCON'S FORECAST is correct: the rain lasts all month. It's blinding rain, a monsoon that disgorges over the Basilica and splits like lava down the steep cobbles of Montmartre. Past the boulangeries and the groceries, the brasseries with their stubborn patrons shielding cigarettes on the terraces, past the late night alimentations, past the Amélie cafe, past the cars parked nose-to-tail with scooters jammed between, the Chinese traiteurs which have become my breakfast staple, over the boulevard with its prostitutes and vagrants, past the Sex Emporium, where Angel's arse is captured in a discreet black-and-white portrait, and onward; over the border of the eighteenth, racing towards Saint-Lazare and the Tuileries. Incessant rain that turns leaves to mulch and jeans to a chafing second skin, rain that wriggles inside your ears and your mouth. People say they've never seen rain like it.

My life becomes very simple, very quickly. Five nights a week I tramp down the boulevard to place Blanche, my DMs squelching in the gutter rapids, the first cigarette of the night clamped between my lips. Sometimes I see a streak of grey at the corner of my eye. I twist, expecting to see the bird, but when I turn there's nothing there.

I learn that the hierarchy at Millie's is political, and honour is earned by survival. Kit has the final word, and what Kit says is enforced by

Eloise. After the managers in ranking come the bartenders. Angel, who works days, is the exception. Of the night staff, the boys comprise old hands Victor (French, a cycling fiend), Bo (Swedish, and correspondingly tall, egalitarian and universally beloved), Yogi Millis (Australian, possibly not his own name, but if he has another nobody knows it) and relative new kid Mike (American, self-professed history geek). The girls are Dušanka (Russian, student of philosophy and misanthropy), Isobel and Simone (both French, gentle and inseparable; they insist on working the same section of the bar and always go on break together, but they work hard and are dedicated, efficient drinkers, so nobody minds), and Gabriela (Colombian, and the bar's amphetamine). Below the bartenders are the lowly floor slaves, where everyone begins. Where I begin.

And then there is Millie. The boys think of Millie as a femme fatale, dangerous but alluring. Millie is Jessica Rabbit; she is Faye Dunaway in diagonal rain. The girls think of Millie as a distillation of feminist power: Millie is Daisy Ridley taking up the lightsaber in the falling snow; she is Serena Williams smashing her way to her twenty-third major title while eight weeks pregnant. We call upon Millie in times of trial. We ask ourselves: what would Millie do?

Millie, we know, would not put up with insolent clients. Millie would carry a mojito stick in her back pocket and bash the knuckles of client hands that transgressed the boundary of the bar. Millie would rinse tips from punters as honey from a hive. Millie would shoot wisecracks from the side of her soft-lipped, slightly crooked mouth, as she prowled the heights of the back bar, hosing the night crowd with soda water.

Millie would do all of these things and more, if only she were real. That she is not, and never has been real, I discover after a month of waiting patiently for her return from holiday. Angel explains it to me one afternoon in the bar, drinking lemonade and sirop de menthe whilst Janis Joplin's voice slinks around the pillars, cracked with melancholy. Millie is a construct, he says. A figment. In this place, says Angel, it is necessary to use one's imagination. We are creatures of the night (he delivers this line with an entirely straight face) and we need protectors.

Gabriela gives me a hug. Now, she says, I am Millie's for all times. My initiation is complete.

I adore them all too much to be annoyed by the deception. I understand that I belong. Millie's staff have become family in the way the word should be understood. They are family in the way that *Transfusion* is family—messy and layered but inextricably connected. Happy in my routine, I quickly banish any lingering doubts about my decision to defer my third year. I'm in Paris now, and Paris is, and always has been, a city of reinvention.

CHAPTER SIX

THE TEXT FROM Gabriela contains three words and an old-fashioned emoji: I FOUND IT! :D

I text back: Where? She sends me a photo. I stare at the image, my chest tightening. Yes—yes, it could be. It could be the place. I take the Polaroid out of my wallet and compare the two images. The colours in the Polaroid are faded but the backdrop is the same. There's a wall, that creamy sandstone so characteristic of Paris; formed forty-five million years ago when île-de-France lay at the bottom of an ocean, mined and cut locally, built to Haussmann's regulation six storeys. There's a blue street plaque, out of focus in the Polaroid but clear in the digital image. To the right of the frame, the serpentine edge of an unidentified entrance to the métro.

I ask Gabriela which métro, and wait. I'm in her tiny studio, surrounded by her many things. The bottom layer consists of two leaning cupboards, a double mattress folded up against the wall, a sofa, an unlikely-sized single-leafed avocado plant, a standing lamp and a chest. Stacked on top are precarious piles of textbooks, headphones, cables, laptop, notebooks, stationery, magazine clippings, an SLR camera, photographs, bits of film, jeans, jumpers, odd socks, scarves, several pairs of ballet shoes whose significance I am yet to decipher, blankets, an empty bottle of Jack Daniels with a light bulb in it, a print I recognize as Dalí's *The Disintegration of the Persistence of Memory* and a five-foot-tall model giraffe wearing a fez.

It is here that I've been crashing for the last few weeks, whilst looking for a place of my own. It is here that I showed Gabriela the Polaroid, and here that she vowed we would discover its provenance. As in all things, Gabriela was supremely confident about our chances of success. I was less confident, and now that the day had arrived, less certain that I wanted to be successful at all.

My phone chimes. I get my things.

AS SOON AS I see the place I know it's wrong. Gabriela must see me before I see her, and my disappointment too, because she comes up and takes both my hands in hers.

"No? This isn't it?"

I shake my head.

"Sorry."

"I was sure. So sure!"

"It looked right. It could easily have been the place."

"You still haven't told me why it is important."

"It's just history." I glance back at the métro map. "Isn't the cemetery close to here? Père Lachaise?"

"Yes. Do you want to see it?" Gabriela points. "This way."

Leaving the wall behind, my initial disappointment fades to relief. What on earth would I have done if we had found it? What would it have meant?

AT THE ENTRANCE to the cemetery I pick up a guide, but Gabriela takes it out of my hands.

"We wander," she says firmly.

On the other side of the gates, the graves lie quiet under an overcast sky. The main path leads inward, lined with monuments of stone and overarching trees, their leaves turning slowly to gold. Ahead of us, a young couple are strolling arm in arm.

We turn left. The ground rises, uneven with sunken steps and tree roots, and we quickly leave behind the orderly avenues and sightseers with their guidebooks. On higher ground we find the unattended graves, crowded together, overgrown with moss and weeds, their residents much older, deeper, entangled in their occupancy below the earth. I stop to catch my breath. We are the only people up here. I can hear the wind rippling through the treetops, shearing leaves from their branches, and the sound lifts me for a moment right out of Paris, into a more nebulous space, borderless and strange. I am reminded of field trips to study strains of rock, the unsettling feeling when one of my companions stepped out of sight and for a moment I feared the openness of the terrain would swallow me whole.

Gabriela steps from grave to grave. She crouches by a small headstone, reading the inscription.

"This one was so young," she says. "Only sixteen years old. The age my—" She bites her lip. "My niece. She would be sixteen."

She doesn't say anything more and her choice of words confuses me—has something terrible happened to Gabriela's niece? Or is it just a linguistic mix-up? Gabriela's face, closed where it is usually so open, deters me from asking questions. Instead, I tap her shoulder lightly.

"Come on."

This time I take the lead, up a steep set of steps and along a narrow walkway. A white cat slinks out from inside a hut and rubs against my legs before proceeding on its way. Another is asleep on a mausoleum roof, triangular throat exposed to the sky.

"Somebody feeds them," says Gabriela. I think of the-cat-who-does-not-belong-to-us, curled up on the bass keys of the piano in blissful sleep, unaware that they have been tuned for the first time in a decade. It was the last thing I did before I left.

"It must be a strange home, among the dead," I say.

"I like to come here. I never feel as if I am alone. It is like houses, there are always traces in the air. It is just we don't always see them."

From up here we can see the cemetery spread out below, a jumble of grey stone and restless green. I watch the white cat wind its way between the graves with small, delicate steps.

"Do you think they'd mind us sitting here?"

Gabriela ponders.

"No. I don't think they would mind. I wouldn't mind. I would like to think that people would come, maybe they would wonder about me, about the things I did with my life."

"Yes," I say. "I suppose it would be worse if there were nobody."

"But you have family," says Gabriela. "In the photograph, they are there. You must miss them."

"We're not close."

"Not your brother? Your sister?"

"Not really, no." I select my words carefully. I know that Gabriela, who spends hours Skyping her mother in what are occasionally fraught conversations, with frequent references to the importance and vibrance of Bogotá and the irrelevance and mundanity of Paris, has a particular view about family. "You choose your friends. You don't choose your relatives. If you could, maybe you wouldn't choose the ones you have."

"It makes me sad, to hear you say that."

"But we're very different. Your family are desperate to have you back. My family won't even have noticed I'm gone."

Gabriela looks at me, startled.

"They don't know you're here?"

"Not unless they're psychic."

"You haven't spoken to them?"

"No. They haven't tried to speak to me, either. And I know that, because I check my English SIM card every few days."

"You should call them. They will worry. Promise me, Hallie."

Her eyes meet mine, radiating concern.

"All right. I promise."

It's a promise I have no intention of keeping. I've prepared my exit far too carefully to blow it in one moment of weakness.

"Family is important," says Gabriela, undeterred. "And you must think so, or why do you look to find this picture?"

"Because it's bugging me." I pick up a stone, a reddish piece of chert, brushing away the dirt. "I don't know. It's just something I have to do."

"Okay."

I watch her push aside the conversation, albeit reluctantly. We head back downhill, through the clusters of graves. Gabriela removes the lens cap from her camera and takes a few photographs, checking the results in the viewfinder. I peer over her shoulder.

"You know, you're really good."

"You think so? It is the only thing I ever wanted to do. My true passion."

"I wish I could be that certain."

"Is it not this way with your geology?" She flicks left. "Ah, the light is very nice in this one."

"I considered a few different careers," I say. I watch Gabriela editing her photo reel, wondering how it must feel to have such self-conviction. Not for the first time, I wonder if I'm drawn to people like Gabriela because of a fundamental lack in myself. I try to work out the difference between my friend's self-belief and my mother's, how it is I can accept one but not the other, and I think the answer has something to do with generosity. I'm lucky to have met Gabriela.

"Gabriela?"

"Mm?"

"How long has Léon worked at Café Oz?"

"Oh, some years now. Five? Maybe six."

"What's he like?"

Gabriela lowers her camera and gives me a penetrating look.

"Hallie. You should not get involved with Léon."

"I thought you guys were friends?"

"Yes, a good friend, and he is a lot of fun. That is why I know he is no good for any girl who is my friend."

"How so?"

Gabriela frowns. "It is all too easy for him. It is like he does not need people."

"That doesn't have to be a bad thing."

"Everybody needs people," says Gabriela. I want to push further, to find out exactly how and why Léon does not need people, but Gabriela moves off, making it clear that the conversation is closed. "Come on. If we head back now, there's time for an episode of *Transfusion* before work..."

I let her pull me away, unwilling to push at the boundaries of this new friendship. Is Gabriela interested in Léon herself? And why am I even asking? It's not as if I am.

We head back down to the main pathway. On the way out, I notice a plaque on the wall with single stems and wrapped bouquets placed beneath it. Several people are posing and taking selfies with the aid of a foot-long stick.

Aux morts de la commune 21–28 Mai 1871

I point it out to Gabriela.

"Was that during the siege of Paris?"

She stops, frowning. "Yes. A terrible day."

I think of Gabriela saying she never feels alone when she comes here. I agree with her now: there is nothing finite about a graveyard. It's a halfway house; a battlefield between the living and the dead.

First to go is the flesh, skin and muscle and blood, but bone will eventually begin to compress and transmogrify. This is how stone begins. What we were feeds into the things that will become, and after the last memory of us has faded from the world, it is stone that remains to tell what stories it can.

Looking at the monument to the Communards, it occurs to me that if I were to die in Paris, nobody back in England would know. The anonymity of the thought should frighten me, but it doesn't. I've made the break.

CHAPTER SEVEN

MIKE AND I have agreed the parameters of our competition. Rules and players are sworn in by a surprisingly adamant Isobel ('An agreement is an agreement, anglaise ou americaine'). Jägerbombs and Australians score the lowest points, top-shelf cognac and French the highest. It's Friday night and in addition to the usual crowd we have five coach-loads of Contiki under our roof, a fact which has driven Eloise to play 'Down Under' by Men at Work no less than six times in the last two hours and, consequentially, Dušanka to the edge of mutiny.

By midnight I'm drenched in an acrid cocktail of sweat and Jägermeister but am clear of Mike by a full fifteen points. Eloise sends me down to change the Carlsberg. I'm anticipating the sanctuary of a few cool minutes in the keg room, but someone has failed to check the thermostat because the air inside is warm—warm and malty. I wonder if the Australians have noticed they are drinking warm lager. I wrestle with the cap on the offending Carlsberg line, which doesn't want to loosen. It finally pops off; I must hit myself in the face, because the next thing I know I'm inside a column of red, swirling darkness, rushing up to the surface, and a voice says, "My dear, you made it! How marvellous!" Then I find myself lying on the floor feeling very peculiar indeed.

I get up slowly. The line's connected—did I replace the keg before

I blacked out? I check it once again: all done. I head upstairs and launch myself back into the fray. Angel's on the bar, evidently pulled in for emergency cover.

"Didn't know you were working tonight," I say. Angel gives me an odd look.

"Remember the first rule, my Anglaise," he says, and walks airily away. I look for Mike, wondering how many points he's scored while I've been downstairs, but I can't see him. If he went on break, then he's missing peak orders, and my star is about to ascend. Thank you, Eloise. I'm about to step onto the bar when she appears, a tiny golem blocking my path.

"Oy, new girl! I need a bottle of Get 31 and I need it now."

"New girl?" I say disbelievingly, but Eloise is already turning to serve someone. She must be even more riled than usual, if she's reverting to old insults. I push through into the back room, looking for Mike to tell him the competition is temporarily suspended, or at least that the last ten minutes don't count. Did we agree rules about off-bar time? Then I see him doing the rounds on the floor. We're more short-staffed than I realized.

Eloise's bidding it is. I about turn and see, a few metres away, the impossible sight of myself pushing awkwardly through the crowd.

I freeze. For long seconds I remain rooted, my mind blank with shock. Refusing to acknowledge the irrationality of what I'm seeing. Then I relax. I've spied a lookalike. A good one, admittedly, perhaps even a distant relation. My breathing resumes. Yes, the Angelopoulos genes have gone walkabout. I always knew my mother had secrets.

I move stealthily behind and start to stalk her. My doppelgänger's head is darting from side to side, searching for something; she looks flushed and harassed. She looks like me at my most stressed. The doppelgänger is wearing jeans and a T-shirt, whereas I'm in cargos and a spaghetti-strap top, but we have the same face (something has happened to her nose), the same unruly hair, the same mole on the jawline and—I look down—the same purple Doc Martins with a Pikachu sticker on the left heel.

My body heat drops away.

There's a tingle as the neurones fire in my brain.

I stop thinking, because thinking leads to conclusions, and conclusions without substantive evidence are dangerous. I'm in a dream state, immersed in the subconscious, a place of memories lost and cached, of information absorbed but unaccounted. Not thinking, I go downstairs. The door to the alcohol room is open; inside is Simone, who yesterday was sporting a new weave, but miraculously has braids again, loading bottles of Smirnoff into a crate.

"You got a Get 31 there?" I ask. "Eloise asked for it."

"Bon oui," she says. "Eloise asks, we give. My name is Simone, by the way."

"I'm Hallie."

"Enchanté."

She passes me the Get. I wait until her back is turned, then nip into the keg room and place the bottle in a prominent position on top of a keg of Kro. I hear Simone locking up the alcohol room. Her footsteps retreating. I pull my hair out of its tie so that it obscures my face, go upstairs and immediately have to dash into the bathroom as Dušanka stalks past, the top of an Akhmatova paperback sticking out of her back pocket.

My heart begins to race. This is too strange, too impossible. I edge back out, chin down, hair falling over my eyes. Concealing myself behind a group of football enthusiasts, I watch the doppelgänger— the *me*—from afar. As when listening to a familiar song, I know the chord progression that follows. The me approaches the bar. Eloise yells at her. The me looks like she's about to cry. Poor me. I empathize (I've been there) but I can't deny she's creepy as hell. Does my face really make those expressions?

The me goes downstairs first. I sneak after her, but misjudge the last two steps, raising a horrible clatter. I leg it around the corner. I hear a shout—"Hey!"—and dive into the keg room. Where I'm trapped. Cornered. *Fuck.*

I turn helplessly on the spot, panic rising, pulse accelerating, because she'll come in here, I know she comes in here, and the last thing in the world I want to do is face her, but then there's a rush of dark red and a sensation of swimming and a voice says, "Oh, well *done*, dear, a terrific start," and I'm on my back.

I SIT UP dizzily. The keg room is cool, my bare shoulders numb and slightly damp from the concrete floor. What a surreal dream. I hook up the new Carlsberg keg, stack the empty by the door and head upstairs. Mike informs me he's done a Legolas on the Australians and would I like the dregs of a Long Island Iced Tea, for he has made a dozen of them for the Contiki manager while I was taking forever to change the line.

At the end of the night Isobel confirms the scores: I have lost to Mike by forty points. Mike does a victory dance. Over staff drinks I ask Isobel, as casually as you can ask such a question, if she has ever seen a ghost in the building? Isobel says no, although she has felt the presence of her deceased grandmother. Not in this building. Elsewhere. That's nice, I say. But Isobel's brow creases. She says no, her grandmother squandered the family inheritance on gambling and mediocrities (Isobel's word) and left Isobel's parents destitute in Le Havre.

Silence follows.

"We came to Paris to escape her," says Isobel at last, and with considerable satisfaction. She steeples her fingers, faces me. "So, Hallie. *You* have seen a ghost here?"

"Oh," I say. "I'm a scientist. I don't believe in ghosts."

PART THREE

Green Bowler Hat

CHAPTER EIGHT

I GET BACK from my break at midnight to find a group of Contiki have just left and the place is a debris of empties and unwashed cocktail shakers. I slide in a dishwasher rack, kick the door shut, nudge the green button with my knee and listen to the rumble as the washer starts its cycle. When I turn around, Eloise is standing a foot away, staring at me intently. I jump.

"Jesus, do you have to do that?"

"There's a woman sitting at the alcove in section two," says Eloise. "She's asked for you."

"For me?"

"She pointed you out."

My first, panicked thought is that it's one of the family, that somehow they've tracked me down. I glance across to the alcove. There's a small party settled in there, three guys and two girls, drinking cocktails. The girls are in lipstick and platform heels, and dressed for an occasion. I sag with relief.

"Why do they want me?"

"Not them. *Behind* the pillar. Japanese woman, green hat. Go on, you'd better serve her."

Eloise makes a shooing motion. It occurs to me that she is acting oddly, it isn't like Eloise to bend to anyone else's will. The thought leaves me vaguely unsettled.

I have to squeeze past the group of cocktail drinkers to get behind the pillar. Sure enough, there is a lone woman sitting at the next table.

She's dressed neatly and rather conservatively, a green bowler hat and a matching, double-breasted jacket over a cream blouse and pencil skirt. Her skin is taut and smooth, her eyes curious, and defined by subtle make-up. I've never seen her before in my life. But she asked for me.

The feeling of wrongness amplifies.

"Can I get you a drink?" I ask hesitantly.

The woman tilts her head, listening carefully, and lifts a finger.

"Ahhh. There—she is."

I notice she is wearing rings on almost every finger, intricate gold bands inset with expensive stones: emeralds and sapphires. She is wearing expensive smelling perfume too, but underneath it a peculiar aroma clings to her, something musky and animal.

"Would you like a drink?" I repeat.

"What—would *you* recommend?"

Her words come slowly, haltingly, as though her tongue has never had to twist around the sounds before. Just a tourist, Hallie, I tell myself firmly. She's probably been reading her phrasebook all week, the same as you and your French.

"How about a gin and tonic?"

I want to make this order as straightforward as possible, and get the hell away from her.

"Yes. And—something for you. Will this be—sufficient?"

She extracts a handful of crisp new notes from a Dolce & Gabbana purse, and fans them out before me. I extract twenty euros.

"That'll do it."

"Hey, hello there? Can we order too?"

"Sure." I turn to the American party on the other side, a weary smile pasted on my face in readiness, though I am secretly relieved to be accosted. "What can I get you?"

They squabble over the shots list. Behind me, I hear something keen.

"You got that?" asks the party spokesperson at last. "You want to write it down?"

"One mojito, one Long Island, one cosmo, one caipiroska, pint of Kro, three slippery nipples and two flatliners," I intone.

"Wow, you're good. She's good, isn't she?"

I pick up the tray from their last round of shots. There's that sound again—a definite squawk. My neck tingles.

At the bar I relay my orders to Dušanka. Eloise hurries over.

"Well? Do you know her?"

"No, but she's fucking weird."

"Is she on drugs?"

"Not that I can tell."

I decline to add that unless she was shooting up smack, there isn't much she could be on that half the clientele, not to mention the staff, don't sample most nights.

"We can't refuse to serve her." Eloise looks pointedly around. "If we kicked out every crazy that came through the doors, this place would be a wasteland."

Eloise returns to the music, and I look back at the alcove. The woman is sitting there, almost motionless. She does not check her phone, or get out her handbag, as most people do when left alone for a few minutes. She is looking around with an air of quiet appreciation you might expect to find in a museum.

Dušanka slams down shot glasses onto a tray and floats a centimetre of Baileys over the sambuca. In the alcove, I am sure I see something move inside the woman's jacket.

"Slippery nipples," says Dušanka, making it sound like an offensive crime. Dušanka had come to Paris for Christine de Pizan and Olympe De Gouges. She had pledged to visit the country of origin of every renowned philosopher (and several who would be renowned, if Dušanka had anything to do with it) in order to ascertain whether there was meaning within the cosmos and whether she, Dušanka, had un raison d'être. She had not come to Paris for slippery nipples.

I deliver the tray of cocktails and take green bowler woman her gin and tonic.

"Thank you—my dear," she says. "And now—to business!"

"Business?"

I glance desperately in Eloise's direction, but she has her back turned. Green bowler woman seems unperturbed by my discomfort. She pats the seat beside her. I take a reluctant perch and a sip of rum and coke, which Dušanka has made mercifully strong. I see the woman's jacket bulge again. My stomach turns. She has something in there.

Something alive.

She sees me looking, and her mouth curves in a secretive smile. She pulls back the collar of her blouse. Tucked against her breast I see the narrow head of a falcon. It is swaddled in bandages, pinning its wings to its sides, and cotton wool has been taped around its beak. Looking at that bird, I feel a horrible prickling spread all over my body.

The woman switches her coat back into place, concealing the bird.

"It is so nice—to meet you—properly," she says, inclining her head confidentially. "You have been here—a couple of months?"

"Y-yes."

My mouth is dry, sour-tasting.

"Then it is—about time." She strokes the cape where the falcon is hidden. Where the falcon is captive. I know this without knowing how I know it.

"Excuse me," I say. I take a gulp of rum to wet my throat. "That bird—have you had it long?"

"My dear. You mustn't worry. About this bird. A mere

experiment—to test my range. I am keeping him close for the time being."

"But I just saw—"

"Yes. I know. Nothing for you to get your head—in a flap about." She gives me a wink. Her English is evening out, becoming more fluid with every sentence. "Now. Do you know why I am here?"

I shake my head mutely.

"The world turns at one thousand and thirty-eight miles an hour and we barely blink—in the rush through space. But here you are! Do you know how long I've been waiting down there? A long time. A very long time. I was beginning to despair. They said you would come, I had to be patient, they said, but I almost gave up. I admit it. But then *you* appeared. My salvation! Because, my dear, as you have no doubt worked out given recent events, you're sitting on something of a hotspot. Temporally, I mean."

I stare at her. With every second that passes, my unease grows. She's talking about temporal hotspots. She's delusional. A fantasist. But it's more than that.

She isn't right in her own skin.

"I don't know what you mean," I say.

"Oh!" She regards me curiously. Her make-up is immaculate. Robotic, I think, and once the thought has seeded it's impossible to reject. "My dear, I thought you'd realised. That little episode, with the Get 31? You must have known what was happening, or else why did you complete the time loop?"

"That was a dream," I say, frightened now. How the hell does she know about the Get? How could *anyone* know about the Get? "I fainted."

"You fell," she says firmly. "Through the dimensional chasm. And that is where I come in—your friendly local incumbent, summoned, as it were, by your excursion into the recent past. If you want a name, and you seem the type that would, I'm the chronometrist."

She beams at me. I want to get up and walk away, put as much distance between us as possible, but when I try to stand nothing happens. Schizophrenia, I think. Borderline personality disorder. Whatever you do, don't alarm her.

"The energy here is incredible," she is saying excitedly. "They vary, you know, though of course so much of it is dependent on the incumbent themselves. I suppose you could compare my particular expertise—I'm the only one with a frame of reference, after all—to that of a volcanologist."

Of all the things she has said, Get 31 included, this upsets me the most. It's as if she has burrowed into the deepest recesses of my brain.

"Why do you say that?"

"Well, the sciences are very similar. The, ah, fields differ, but the activity patterns are the same... cold and dormant, and then a sudden flare..."

"Flare?"

"The flares are when we travel, my dear. As you did, the other day."

"I didn't—I don't know what you're talking about—"

But in my head is the unshakeable image of a girl who looked exactly like me, wearing my boots.

"Then you aren't listening," she says, and her tone has sharpened. She taps her breast; I hear a faint, plaintive squawk. "Didn't I tell you to wake up? Didn't I tell you *it* would wake up, now that you've arrived? What did you say your name was?"

"It's Hallie. Are you saying—are you saying that bird—"

"Ah, a glimmer of understanding... Hold that thought, dear."

I stare at her. Her face goes slack.

"Now, Hallie—"

The voice comes from the region of her chest. I look down. Look back up. The woman stares at me. Her eyes are wide with surprise. She begins to speak very fast in Japanese. I shunt backwards.

"What the fuck is this?"

The woman's features slump. Her face shifts again. She stops talking, mid-sentence, then resumes in English.

"Just a little experiment of mine, don't mention it to anyone now, will you? In any case, I'm not convinced by the avian brain. Now. Hallie."

Once again I try to stand. I manage to lift myself a few inches from the seat, then collapse back. "I need to go," I say. "They need me on the bar—"

"Hallie. Your colleagues are currently cleaning and sending—where are we, let me think—*WhatsApp messages.*" Her tone softens again. "My dear girl. Don't be alarmed. You are in a most fortunate position. Truly, there are people who would *kill* to be you. Or me, for that matter! But words are insufficient. Let me show you. If you listen carefully, you can hear it. Listen—go on, listen now."

She folds her hands in her lap, very precisely, geometrically, and puts her head on one side. Her face bears an expression of acute concentration.

I listen too, but I cannot hear anything other than the normal ambience of the bar on a quiet night. Dušanka, dragging a crate of Corona to the fridge. Yogi Millis, deep in flirtation with an Italian tourist. Eloise fading the music from Beyoncé to Rihanna.

"Can you hear it?"

I shake my head. I don't want to hear it, whatever it is. Anyway, it won't be anything. I'm dealing with a lunatic.

"Try again," she urges. "Close your eyes."

I obey without thinking; and once shut, my eyes won't open.

I hear customers chattering, the clink of glasses. Beyond that, the white noise I have always associated with the speaker system. As I focus in on that sound, I begin to hear multiple notes unfolding within it; layers, dimensions, the foundations of a song slowly writing themselves upon a stave.

Now my eyes open, as though released. I stare at the chronometrist.

"Ahhh—there you go. Now you can hear it, can't you? It takes practice, and awareness. Eventually you will hear it all the time."

"How do you know?"

Her hand closes over mine. Her touch is chilled wax. Coldness takes my fingers, spreads to my palm, my forearm, bicep, working up to my shoulder.

"My dear, my dear." Her eyes search out mine. She is scanning me. I have the sense of an intelligence far beyond my own. My uncanny valley is off the scale. "It's who you are, as simple as that. Every anomaly has an incumbent. And this one is yours, how marvellous! It is what you might call a symbiotic relationship. Without us, they cannot thrive. And they long to thrive, they really, deeply do. I still visit mine very often, though I can go anywhere I like. You're one in a million, dear child. Do you see what I mean?"

"I—no?"

She leans forward and sniffs, her nostrils dilating.

"You will. I'd say you're ripe."

A spasm runs through my body, and she releases my hand. I hold my numb fingers in my other hand, curling and straightening each in turn. Sensation returns in painful spikes. Ripe? Who *says* something like that?

The woman's eyes are mischievous now.

"Now, how do you feel about eighteen seventy-five?"

"Eighteen seventy-five? What's that got to do with anything?"

"Next time you visit the anom—the keg room, I want you to think very hard about eighteen seventy-five. *Very hard indeed*, my dear."

The light dips abruptly. I look up. Dušanka is standing there, hands on hips, blocking the alcove entrance. The party of cocktail drinkers must have departed some time ago. I don't blame them.

"Are you all right, Hallie?" says Dušanka pointedly.

I open my mouth. *Get me out of here*, I want to say.

The woman rests her fingers on mine. The chill spreads instantaneously, this time reaching as far as my throat.

"I'm fine," I say. I can't feel my tongue.

"Could you bring us some more drinks?" The woman offers more notes. "Please, keep the change."

Dušanka's mouth sets in an uncompromising line, but she nods and retreats to the bar. She delivers the drinks without comment. I don't know if I thank her or not—I no longer know what I am saying. The woman has me mesmerised, trapped in the mesh of her words. I try to tell her that what she is implying did not happen, that I dreamed a ghost even though I don't believe in ghosts and anyway, you shouldn't see your *own* ghost, but she keeps talking. She talks and the evening is sucked away. She speaks of the House of Janus, a bureaucratic, pedantic order; she sighs despairingly over the code of practice, she mourns the alternative histories which might have been. She speaks of transmogrification, of consciousness in the cloud, of anomalies no more than shrivelled husks and anomalies alive as magma. She tells me the tale of basilosaurus who roamed the oceans thirty-five million years ago, *perhaps in this very room*. She speaks of accelerated mortality. She uses her frozen hands to describe it: death, she says, is the texture of ice cream, cold and delicious. She says she is over eight hundred years old. She's been waiting for me, she says. And so has *it*. She leans forward, her smooth, unblemished face very close to mine, and she whispers,

I am so very glad to meet you, Hallie.

CHAPTER NINE

volcano: noun (pl. *volcanos or volcanoes*) a mountain or hill, typically conical, having a crater or vent through which lava, rock fragments and hot vapour, are or have been erupted from the earth's crust // a state or situation which is liable to erupt into anger or violence

I FIND MYSELF on the sofas in the back room, discombobulated and alone. Something prompts me to check my phone. It is half six in the morning.

I hear whistling. Victor comes through the doors.

"What's your staff drink, Hallie?"

"I'm good," I say. Victor gives me a stern look.

The others come through one by one, settling on the sofas. Victor returns with the staff drinks, and places two fingers of scotch in front of me.

"Are you still staying with Gabriela?"

"No, Simone's friend came through on the Lamarck studio."

"That's good. It is getting harder and harder to find a place, especially with the low wages. By the way, I did not know you spoke French so well."

"What?" I laugh, self-mockingly. "I don't."

"Don't be modest. I heard you talking with that funny woman in the green hat. Even your accent was not so terrible—so no excuses in the future, non?"

"But I wasn't—" I stop before the rest of the sentence can come out. I look at Victor. He seems solid enough, but I feel strangely detached, almost dizzy.

"Actually, your conversation was worth the effort. She left a one-hundred-euro tip."

In my head, I complete the sentence.

I wasn't speaking in French.

I don't want to be around people, but neither do I want to leave the bar alone. What if that woman is waiting for me? What if she's formed some kind of obsessive attachment? I wait, without joining in the conversation, until the dregs of the night. People stretch, stand, announce imminent departures, carefully avoiding Eloise's eye for fear of being caught for the final dishwasher run. A silence draws out where everyone realises the music has stopped. Someone asks the time.

I check my watch. "Coming up to eight."

Gabriela yelps, leaps up and sprints across the empty back bar. Dušanka, ruffled by the abrupt exit, shrugs on her coat and yanks her laces tight. She presents her face to a select number of recipients to kiss and slouches out into the day.

It is left to me and Yogi Millis to load up the dishwasher and wait for its final spin, which we do perched on the work surfaces, having a good bitch about French customers who click their fingers in expectation of service, the curious disappearance of all the mojito sticks and the fact that the bar floor is peeling from its foundations again.

"When you were a kid, what did you want to be when you grew up?" I ask.

Yogi Millis considers the question at some length.

"A croc wrestler," he says finally.

"Crocodiles, really?"

"Maybe not salties."

"You've probably got a longer life expectancy here."

He nods. "What about you?"

"I wanted to be a volcanologist."

"People die in volcanos too," says Yogi Millis, which is irrefutable, though also arguably a case *for* volcanology.

"You know there's a super-volcano under Yellowstone that could take out the entire United States if it ever erupted again."

"No way, mate."

"What brought you to Paris anyway, Yogi?"

The dishwasher rumbles. Yogi Millis debates his answer. Finally, he concedes that he cannot remember why he came to Paris.

There was a girl.

There were Jägerbombs and someone's house, no one Yogi knew or had even met, where the floors sloped unevenly and the walls too and it wasn't because he had taken pills (though he had) it was just how the house was. Rotting. Sinking. It was New Year's Eve. This was in Venice.

At the party he had gatecrashed after the midnight crowds in St Mark's Square—there were bells, chanting, it was mystical—there was a projector on the wall. The projector was relaying a film, flickering images and music on a loop: frost formed on a lake, a dead deer, its eye in close up, reeds waving, a night sky filled with stars. It was cosmic. It was as if Yogi had fallen into the canal outside, and believing himself underwater, suspended in the arms of the ocean, Yogi Millis had a revelation.

He must go to Rome.

That was three years ago.

Yogi Millis could not remember why he had come to Paris.

THE BACK ROOM doors bang open and Gabriela struggles through, dragging a suitcase behind her.

"Front doors are locked," I yell, before she slams into the glass. Gabriela brakes, about turns, and sweeps back the other way.

"Gabriela, I'm leaving too—wait up."

I grab my coat and bag and follow her out of the fire doors, puzzled by the suitcase, and by her haste. She hasn't said anything about going away. Outside, the alleyway is bright with low winter sunshine. I squint, blink, adjust. The wheels of Gabriela's suitcase rattle along the cobbles. She has a scarf tied to its handle and is hauling it awkwardly behind her.

"Gabriela—wait!"

I catch up with her as she hikes the suitcase onto the pavement, narrowly missing a waiter setting out tables for the brasserie next door. She wheels right.

"No time, no time," she mutters.

"You want a hand with that?"

Gabriela looks at me. It is a funny, sidelong look, as though she is seeing me for the first time and does not necessarily like what she sees. That look is such a shock it is almost enough to make me walk away, but then she unwinds a second scarf from around her neck, feeds it through the suitcase handle, and gives me the ends. The scarf is made of eyelash wool, and Gabriela has a cotton one through the waistband of her jeans which would have been a more practical solution. But it is what I am given, so I take it, and with it my part in this unidentified mission.

As if the night hasn't been strange enough already.

We turn left on to the roundabout junction. Gabriela speeds up and the case swivels erratically between us. I mimic her, infected by her urgency although still unwitting as to its source. We begin a haywire dash downhill between pedestrians, bicycles, scooters and cars. I hold my breath as a lorry screeches to a halt less than a metre away, before we arrive on the traffic island.

Ahead are the steps that lead down to the métro, but the way is barred. A sign over the metal gate proclaims:

En raison de travaux de renouvellement, la station de métro Place de Clichy sera fermée le 20 novembre.

Gabriela sucks in a breath. Wordlessly, she veers left, down towards the taxi rank. A couple with three bulky cases and a girl in grey leggings form a queue. Gabriela pushes past.

Leggings girl gives her a filthy look.

"Petites salopes."

A taxi pulls up; the girl and Gabriela move at the same time. Gabriela is faster. She leaps forward and opens the door.

"C'est la crise!"

"Excusez-nous," I mutter, hoping to appease the girl.

"Moi, j'ai attendu trente minutes. *Trente minutes,* salopes! Sors de la!"

Gabriela grabs my hand.

"Hallie, get in the taxi."

I am bundled into the back of the car with Gabriela and Gabriela's luggage. Leggings girl puts her face to the window and screams.

"*Vous êtes des vraies putes—*"

Gabriela winds down the window. "Va te faire foutre!"

The driver glances at us in the mirror, unconcerned by this exchange.

"Où voulez-vous aller?"

"L'Aéroport de Roissy CDG, vite!"

The taxi shoots away from the kerb. I catch a glimpse of the vanquished leggings girl in the wing mirror, her cheeks flushed with rage. The taxi accelerates across Clichy roundabout, hops a red light and takes the second exit, honking any cars that dare to slow us down. Caught in the exhilaration of our flight, it's a minute before I realise that this is not actually my expedition.

I ask the driver to pull up.

"No, don't stop," Gabriela snaps.

"Hang on, I'm not the one going to the airport. He can just drop me at the next red light."

Gabriela's fingers grip my wrist. For a second I feel a shadow coldness. "Ne t'arrête pas!"

"Gabriela—"

"Hallie, we cannot stop."

Her fingers tighten. In her face I see something more than panic—I see desperation. The airport is the last place I want to go, but neither do I want to leave Gabriela in distress. Nothing fazes her; that's the essence of who she is, the friend I know and love.

"Why not?" I ask softly.

She shakes her head. "I cannot."

I slump back against the upholstery. The taxi moves dextrously through the traffic. I watch as Parisian stone slips away. Sandstone, Eocene. Bits of grit and silt swirled in alluvial waters and compressed through time. Now the road is lined with steel and concrete. The buildings grow wider, longer, industrial. We turn down an underpass onto the Périphérique and move into the fast lane.

Gabriela and I say nothing to one another for the remainder of the journey. I watch the scenery, the cars streaking by.

I remember the platform at St Pancras echoing with my footsteps, the Eurostar cutting through open fields as the sky lightened with dawn. The woman next to me on the train asked why I was going to Paris; I said I was an ERASMUS student. I said my name was Persephone, after my grandmother.

I prepared so carefully. Changed bank accounts, deleted my social media, deferred my final year at Aberystwyth. I remember waiting for the cab at the end of the road at four in the morning, a soft mist coating the air. My shoulders twitched, but I didn't look back. This was always about self-salvage.

And now we're heading north. Backwards. Trapped in the car, escape denied me for the second time this morning, I begin to feel the panic creeping in. Sweat is gathering in the lines of my palms. Breathe, I tell myself firmly. Just breathe.

Gabriela is bunched up on the other side of the cab, knees drawn to her chest. Her forehead presses into the window. We have been in the car for forty minutes when the Périphérique grinds to a halt. Cars line up end-to-end. We stop behind a Range Rover. Gabriela puts her head in her arms.

"What time is your flight?" I ask. She does not respond. A late November sun is breaking through clouds as it rises. I check my watch. Nine o'clock.

It takes us another forty minutes to reach Charles de Gaulle. The driver pulls into the drop-off point and announces our fare is fifty euro. I look at Gabriela. She palms me a handful of coins and gets out before the driver can lock the doors. Even before counting the money, I can feel the nausea rising, the tingling in my legs.

I empty out my pockets. A pile of one, five and ten cent pieces. I pick out the euros and the two euros and with increasing desperation, the fifty cents. That with a single note—my spoils from the hundred euro tip—gives me seventeen euro. The taxi driver drums his fingers on the steering wheel and revs the engine.

"I've got seventeen." My heart sinks. I count up the ten and twenty cent pieces, and add Gabriela's earnings. "Make that twenty-four thirty."

I offer my card. The machine in the car is not working. I say I'll go to the cashpoint. The driver says I'll do a runner, like my friend. An unhappy altercation follows. After a few minutes, people begin banging on the window. We are bottlenecking the queue. The driver swears at the window bangers and me. I swear at the driver. My mouth feels strange, not my own, rubbery. I force my twenty-four euro through the hole in the window divider and the coins shower into the driver's compartment. Finally he unlocks the door. I cannot translate the parting shot, but I can guess its meaning.

I get out of the car, wheezing by now. *Here we go again, Hallie. Here we bloody go.* People in the queue are staring. I can feel their eyes boring into me as I cross the pavement, head down, and duck through a set of revolving doors. I can breathe, but there is no air. My vision is tunnelling. There are people everywhere. I blunder through the crowds half-blind, searching for the universal sign for toilets. Arrivals, departures, baggage reclaim: every sign but the one I need. At last I see it, suspended at an angle, an arrow pointing into the ground. A distant part of me knows that it's not the sign that's wrong, it's me. I'm skewed. Distorted in space. My legs are shaking, treacherous; I urge them one step further, and another, and another, ignoring the fact that there is no air, that every molecule of oxygen has been leached from the atmosphere, that I am suffocating in this toxic not-air. I am going to die. Here in the bathrooms. I lock myself in a cubicle and sit with my head between my knees, terrified and trembling and convinced of my imminent death, so very close now.

After a time, the attack passes.

I tear off a wad of toilet tissue and wipe the tears and sweat from my face. It comes back black with mascara. I sit there, waiting for my body to still. I feel drained.

Fucking Gabriela.

Where is she, anyway?

I FIND MY wretched friend on the floor by a magazine unit, the picture of dejection.

"Well?" I demand. "I guess you missed it."

Gabriela does not look up.

"What the hell were you playing at, leaving me back there with the taxi driver? That fare was fifty euro!"

"That taxi driver was not the problem."

"Are you kidding me?"

"I had to catch the plane."

"But you didn't catch it, did you? You knew you'd missed it, and you left me there anyway, to deal with your mess!"

"I might have taken the plane," says Gabriela quietly. "I might. What does it matter anyway? It is only money."

"What does it—it matters to me! You have no idea what I had to put up with at home. Every day it was some shit like this, bailiffs, debt collectors—that wasn't even my taxi, I wanted to get out—"

"*You* have no idea! You do not understand how it is, my home hundreds of miles away and every time a fuck-up, you understand nothing—"

Gabriela gives the case a vicious kick. It shunts into the magazine rack and sends it toppling to the floor with a crash. Magazines and newspapers cascade out over the floor.

"I was not meant to stay in this country," says Gabriela furiously.

The cashier comes running out.

"Que se passe t-il ici?"

I glance around. Not only have we gathered a small audience, airport security are now moving in our direction. It strikes me very forcibly that Gabriela is Colombian.

"Christ," I mutter. "Gabriela, help me pick this thing up. If you're not careful you'll end up in questioning with the immigration people."

Gabriela sniffs. "Let them try. They can try and deport me!"

"For god's sake, you'll get arrested."

"Deport me!"

Gabriela has evidently lost it, but we can both see that the two approaching security guards are viewing her suspiciously, and this time it is a quieter protest. I replace the last magazine on the rack and steer her away to the nearest brasserie.

"And you'd better hope my bank card works."

We order overpriced café crèmes from a sad-eyed waitress. The visibility of misery other than her own seems to raise Gabriela's spirits somewhat. She lets out a long sigh and pulls her hair into a band. The tannoy calls a final check-in to Rome. Overhead, I hear the drone of a departing plane.

"Maybe you could change your ticket?" I suggest.

"There is no point." She bites her lip. "I left too late. I did it again."

"What do you mean?"

"I am not a bad daughter, Hallie. I do not mean to be a bad daughter."

"Of course not."

"It is not that I do not wish to go back. But every time I make plans, something happens. This is the thing about Clichy. People come, and they stay. It is like they get stuck here. It is like there is something here that will not let them go."

CHAPTER TEN

GABRIELA CAME TO Paris because she had decided at age fourteen to join the Surrealists. A dead movement, yes, but that did not deter Gabriela, who had subjective views on death. For a long time it had seemed to her that life could not be explained by words and mathematics, although the mechanics of society appeared to demand that it should. Words and mathematics did not explain the Sol de Lluvia, or the appearance of a young red frog at Gabriela's window in the aftermath of a meteorological event. They did not explain the transformation of Gabriela's sister, Ana Lucia, from a happy, outgoing child to a woman of so many phobias that she was no longer able to leave the house, believing the very air outside to be poisonous with radiation.

Gabriela found consolation in the work of Frida Kahlo, and from Kahlo to Picasso, Magritte, and of course Dalí, whose melting clocks spoke more purely to Gabriela's perception of time than anything she had yet encountered. A burgeoning photographer, Gabriela's work was inevitably and deliciously influenced by these masters, and in the aperture of the lens she found her rationale for a chaotic world. The next step was clear: she must retrace the steps of those who had gone before. She must go to Paris. Even Kahlo had gone to Paris, although her opinion of it had not been high. Unfortunately, Gabriela was not a famous artist liable to be invited to exhibit abroad, and she needed a visa to enter the country. Further study beckoned.

Everything was in place when Ana Lucia announced the news. She was pregnant.

There was never a question of Gabriela abandoning her sister. She watched her niece, Lorena, grow from a mewling kitten into a sunny-tempered child with a talent for dance that could bring strangers in the streets to tears. It was Gabriela who took Lorena to her ballet classes and waited outside the studio, listening to the strident chords of the piano and the footfalls of girls landing grand jetés and pas des chats. Gabriela attended the competitions (Lorena had a wall of gold medals), filled in the application forms, massaged alcohol into toes blistered by pointe work, banged shoes against the stairs until their backs broke.

She didn't mind at first. The truth was, Lorena was special. Anyone could see that. But as the years went on Gabriela had a lurking feeling, a sense in her heart that was becoming more and more robust. Parents of other dancing progenies assumed Lorena was her child, but they were mistaken. Gabriela was living a borrowed life, one that at any point might be reclaimed, should Ana Lucia recover. When she watched Lorena perform an arabesque, the child's little face ablaze with joy, everything made sense. But when she went back to her apartment, with the prints of Dalí and Kahlo and Magritte on the walls and her own fledging photographic efforts pinned between them, Gabriela knew she had forsaken her own ambitions for someone else's without having been consulted.

Before she knew it, Lorena would be a teenager, bound for a ballet boarding school—perhaps even an international school. Whether her sister recovered or not, Lorena would be gone, and Gabriela would remain in Bogotá, with nothing to show for the last decade but a certain dexterity in breaking in pointe shoes.

She was my sister's daughter, said Gabriela. But she was mine too.

And I had already lost her.

It is hard to explain the feeling when you discover your life has been stolen, even when it is by the people you love the most.

Gabriela regrouped. She submitted her portfolio to a number of institutions and was accepted on to a masters programme. She promised Lorena she would visit the Paris Opera House and bring back a pair of Parisian ballet shoes in her size. By the time I'm back, she told her niece jokingly, you'll be a prima ballerina.

On her last day in Bogotá, the city experienced the phenomenon known as Sol de Lluvia, intense sunshine followed by intense rain. The heat was biblical. The city was silent; people retreated indoors, animals took refuge in the shade, even the traffic had paused. As she walked uphill, the air seemed to shimmer, and Gabriela could feel the heat of the road through her soles. She imagined Lorena crossing the street in a succession of fouette turns, and winced at the thought of the tarmac burning against that delicate satin. But Lorena was in class, with air-conditioning.

Within the short distance uphill, the sky had clouded. The rain hit hard and fast, and Gabriela was drenched. She took shelter in a doorway and watched the drops striking against the pavement. When it finally ceased, she looked up. Among the parting clouds she saw, quite perfectly, the image of Dalí's melting clock, and in that moment she knew she had made the only possible decision.

CHAPTER ELEVEN

"AND SO," CONCLUDES Gabriela, "I took the flight to Europe, travelling in the footsteps of all the artists I admire most in the world. You see, Hallie, sometimes something happens that is a game-changer. And when it does, you have a choice. You can ignore it and pretend it never happened, or you can follow it, and see where it will take you. I enrolled at my school. I went to the Opera House, and my god, it is beautiful. I took many photographs. I bought the ballet shoes. But I have not kept my promise."

Gabriela hesitates. She glances around. Surrounding us are the just-arrived and the about-to-depart. The sad-eyed waitress leans against the bar and slips first one foot out of her heeled shoe, then the other.

"And this is the strange thing. Every time I try to leave, something happens. You might laugh, but it is the truth. I try to book a plane, there are no more tickets. The flight is cancelled. The taxi is delayed." Gabriela reaches forward and clasps both my hands in hers. "You tell me, Hallie. How do I explain to them, to my mother and my sister and my niece who are thousands of miles away, how do I explain that I have not abandoned them?"

"I—I don't know."

"You wonder why I push you to call your family. You think I don't guess that it is complicated. All families are complicated. That does not mean you give up on them."

"Our situations are totally different, Gabriela."

We sit back, assessing one another. I wonder if I believe Gabriela, and I wonder if she cares whether I do or not. What is belief, anyway? To be certain about a truth you cannot or have not yet proved. The green bowler woman believes she is a chronometrist. *The* chronometrist. Gabriela believes she is stuck in Clichy. Coincidence, or something more? Were my sensory perceptions deluding me when I thought I saw myself, or am I denying evidence?

On the runway, a plane builds up speed and launches into the sky. While I can see it, I know the plane is real. In a moment it will be gone. The emissions tail lingers, a brief stripe against the sky, before that too dissipates into the stratosphere, and soon enough there is nothing to show the plane was ever there.

CHAPTER TWELVE

IN MY TINY studio, fifteen minutes' walk from Millie's, I put on some music, pour a glass of wine, and lie back on the not-quite-comfortable futon. My empty suitcase is propped against the wall. I can almost see, glowing through its plastic shell, the small token of my English SIM card.

I imagine the landline in Sussex ringing right now. I imagine my mother, after about thirty rings, running from her studio shouting, "Busy, busy, busy!" and snatching up the receiver.

"Ioanna Angelopoulos, what is it?" she says in her worst Eurovision-style accent. She deploys this indiscriminately to deter visitors, salespeople and the could-have-been friends of her offspring, despite having lived in the UK all her life and our closest link to Greece being Grandpa Dimitris, fifty miles away in sheltered accommodation and still in mourning for Granny Persephone.

"Hello, mother, it's me."

"Which one?" she says, because she claims she has never been able to tell the difference between my voice and Theodora's.

"Hallie."

There is a long, tense silence. Then an intake of breath.

"Hallie?" Her voice is uncertain. On the brink of tears. "Is it really you?"

"Yes, it's me. Why, did you actually miss me?"

"Where the hell have you been?" she yells. No trace of an accent now. "Have you any idea how *worried* we've been? Running off in the middle of the night, not even a text message or a bloody fridge magnet note? Have you any idea?"

There is a discordant clash as she hits the piano keys with her free palm. The cat-who-does-not-belong-to-us rises in outrage and hops through the open window into the night.

"What about my letter?" I say.

"Letter? There was no letter, Hallie. There was no fucking letter." Her anger is fading. Relief rolls in, overwhelming. She feels exhausted. "We kept calling, but it said your number was out of service. Theo and George said I shouldn't worry, you'd turn up in a few months. But you don't do things like that, Hal. I've been lying awake, night after night, imagining you dead or hacked to bits in a ditch."

Her voice breaks. I hear it as though I'm standing next to her. I feel the same tightness in my throat. Tears pricking the backs of my eyes.

"I'm sorry," I whisper.

"It's all right. It's all right, you stupid goose. We love you. You know we do. Just come home."

My mother slams down the receiver. She sits, bewildered, on the piano stool. The tear that has been threatening all through our conversation trickles down her cheek and a streak of clay on her chin. Then she leaps up, yelling my father's name.

"Busy!" he yells back.

"It was Hallie!"

A moment of silence. Then a crash of footsteps as he runs downstairs from his studio. Oils on his face and his hair. My parents stare at each other. They are remembering volcano day. They are realizing their own culpability in everything that went wrong. It devastates them.

*   *   *

I OPEN UP the suitcase, retrieve the English SIM card, and switch it with my French one. I turn the phone back on and wait. Nothing.

I will never make that call, although I've imagined a hundred variations of it. Gabriela is wrong. You might not give up on family, but sometimes they give up on you. Sometimes that happened a long time ago. The SIM card, I realize, is holding me back. I extract it from the phone, reach across to the window and pull open the shutters. For a few seconds, I hold the SIM aloft between finger and thumb. Such a tiny thing.

I lob it as hard as I can out into the night.

Next I take out the polaroid. The picture contains four figures: my mother, my brother George and my sister Theodora, and me, aged two and a half. We're clustered together. My mother is crouched, one hand resting on my shoulder, the other pointing to something outside of the frame. Theo is holding an ice cream which is dribbling down its cone, George is standing on one shoe lace. So far, so average. What is extraordinary about the photograph is me. It's my expression: happiness, even glee. It's evidence of a previous era; one accessible only through artefacts, the way the Eocene immortalised its lifeforms as fossils. I have no memory of what we were looking at, or of the photograph being taken.

I pause by the window, the polaroid trapped between my fingers. Then I stuff it back into the suitcase.

My sleep is fitful. I have strange dreams about my mother's sculptures. I dream of sea creatures forged from lava. Fossils set in Paris stone wriggle out of the shapes they once were and are reborn as caterpillars. A falcon is perched on the steps of the Basilica, offering guided tours. I try to hide, but its beady eye sees me and somehow through the dream I know that the bird, the little falcon, is here in the room with me, waiting.

CHAPTER THIRTEEN

I STAGGER PRECARIOUSLY backwards with a sofa chair in my arms. It falls to the floor with a crash. One of the overhead lights flickers.

"Fucking boys," I mutter.

Millie's is so quiet tonight that Eloise has set me the unenviable task of cleaning all of the table and chair legs in the back room. The chairs and tables are stacked on the stage, and whoever stacked them was clearly male—or Dušanka—because they are almost impossible to get down. The sound system is off, the room silent except for me. I keep thinking about that night. Green bowler woman, the airport, the panic attack. Like an idiot, I thought they'd stopped. I thought I was finally free of them. And then Gabriela's story. I'm almost relieved she isn't working tonight—I need some time to regain my equilibrium.

Eloise's head pops around the doors to the front bar, releasing with it a cloud of eighties anthem.

"Hey Hallie! We need ice."

I hold up my cleaning products, unimpressed.

"Now," says Eloise.

The head disappears, and I emit a long sigh to no one. As it fades, I hear something else—a scuffling, up in the roof. No, not a scuffling; a fluttering. The rush of feathers. My heart jumps. I refuse the temptation to look up and instead cross the empty dance floor and head downstairs to the ice machine.

The scoop is missing, which means it's buried under several loads of ice.

"Fucking boys," I say again.

I dig about in the ice cubes, searching for the plastic scoop. My skin starts to turn numb. I burrow deeper. Why the hell can't people leave the scoop out? At last I touch something firm and I yank.

What comes out of the ice is not the scoop but a human hand. Its fingers are curled and smooth; a mannequin's hand, lightly frosted and horribly realistic.

I yelp and let the hand go.

"What the fuck kind of joke is this?" I yell, but nobody replies. They are all upstairs, cavorting with Eloise to 'Ziggy Stardust.' "For fuck's sake."

I reach back into the ice machine, intending to pull the hand out and toss it into the boys' vestiaire for whatever joker put it there to stumble across later tonight. I seize hold of the fingers. A coldness runs through me that has nothing to do with the ice. A familiar, paralysing coldness. I look closer. The hand is female, the fingernails painted with green nail polish. I want to drop it, but I can't, so I tug, expecting the hand to spring free of the ice. It comes up and a wrist follows it, then a forearm, covered in a silk sleeve.

"Funny," I mutter, but my voice comes out pinched and reedy. Now I can see the hump of a shoulder—yes, there's a shoulder— and, pushed back at an unnatural angle, the shape of something round, a roundness that with hideous inevitability is going to be the crown of a head. I try again to let go of those fingers, to shout for help, but my throat is a dry husk. My tongue waggles and nothing comes out. The arm is almost entirely free now, and I can see it—her—emerging, the neck, the collar of a cream blouse, the face rising from beneath the ice. My heart is pounding in my chest with my rising panic and I know what it's going to look like before it appears.

She comes free. A black shell of hair, features set in rigor mortis, eyes open wide, frozen irises staring up at me.

I look at the collar of her blouse, its top two buttons undone. Her eyes watch me. And because I have to know, in spite of every part of me screaming to leave, get out of here, get away from her, I reach into the ice machine and prise away one corner of her blouse. The material is stiff and resistant with frost.

The bird is gone. In the hollow of her neck, above the collar bone, I see a scribbling of red scratch marks. The sort of marks that might be made by the claws of a small falcon desperate to escape.

There's a sudden rattling, a disturbance in the ice. I scream and push the head away from me. Staggering back, I trip over something, fall on my arse, crawl frantically backwards. The hand is sticking out of the hatch. Any second now those fingers are going to wriggle and stretch. She'll rise, claw her way out of the ice machine, lurch towards me, shedding slivers of frost. Rattling, again. It's not her resuscitating, it's a new load of ice shunting into the machine. But I must still be screaming, because suddenly there are people, Eloise and Dušanka and others following I do not recognise, people from the bar come to stare and exclaim. Dušanka grips my shoulders. She is half-hugging, half-shaking me. People say *oh my god*. People take out their phones.

ELOISE ACCOMPANIES ME to the police station. She stays with me, lighting my cigarettes, translating in her meticulous French as I tell them about the strange woman with her green bowler hat and her gin and tonic, the woman who told me she was a chronometrist, who carried a bird inside her blouse, who left such an extravagant tip. The last question is routine.

"Where were you at the time of death?"

I was in the back bar, cleaning chair legs. CCTV cameras show me there all evening.

There is no footage of the woman coming into the building at all, on any of the cameras. Not on the night she died, and not on the night I met her. She has no fingerprints, no ID or matching DNA. She is the invisible woman.

"Go home," says Eloise. "You've had a shock. You did well to hold it together. Get some sleep. Come back tomorrow. We'll keep you upstairs, you don't have to clean."

This, from Eloise, is about the biggest concession anyone could receive. I nod mutely, trying to do what she says I have done; to hold it together.

I'M AT HOME in my studio when the buzzer sounds. The noise makes me jump. I go to the comm reluctantly. I'm not sure that I want to talk to anyone.

"Hello?"

"Hallie, c'est Léon."

I step back, surprised.

"Hello?" he says again.

"Yes, I'm here."

"I heard what happened at Millie's. Can I come up?"

"Um, okay?"

I buzz him through, and look around the studio. It's a mess. The bed is unmade, empty bottles and dishes are piled up in the sink. I shove my pyjamas under the pillow and pull the duvet straight. There isn't time for anything else.

Léon appears with a bottle of Brouilly and an entire roast chicken from the roti on rue des Abbesses.

"I thought you might need a drink."

"Thanks. Come in." Feeling horribly exposed, I add, "Sorry it's such a mess, I wasn't expecting anyone."

"You should see my place." He looks around. "You travel light, don't you?"

"I'm not a great one for belongings."

"That makes two of us."

"To be honest, I wasn't planning to stay this long."

"And there I was thinking you needed a job."

"I did. But it was meant to be for like a month, then I was going to Rome."

"Clichy got lucky, as they say."

"*You* mentioned Millie's," I say pointedly.

"Guilty." He lifts the bottle. "You have...?"

"Oh, here."

I hand him a corkscrew. He pops the cork and pours us each a glass. I roll two cigarettes and pass one to Léon. I'm almost out of baccy—again. It's alarming how quickly I have adjusted to becoming a smoker.

Léon lights up.

"Dušanka said it was that strange woman who was in Millie's the other night."

"Did she come to Oz too?"

"No, but Victor was saying she tipped like crazy."

"Yeah." I sip the wine. It's good. I take a larger mouthful. At least with Clichy bartenders there's no danger of being thought an alcoholic. "I think she was mentally ill. She was obsessed with eighteen seventy-five."

"That's... unusual."

"Like there was something significant about that year."

"The Basilica was built then."

"Sacré-Coeur?"

"Oui. That's when they laid the first stone. Although it took until nineteen-fourteen to complete."

"I didn't know that."

"I don't know much more myself. It was shortly after the Siege of Paris, they're linked somehow. You should ask Mike, he'll know."

"Of course. I saw the tribute to the Communards in Père Lachaise."

"Pretty brutal times," Léon says.

There's a pause.

"Anyway," he says. "I'm sorry you had to go through that. Finding her."

I hesitate. "Have you ever seen a dead person?"

"A few."

"A few?"

"I worked in a hospital for a bit. In Australia."

"Ah."

"Yes."

"What's it like? Australia?"

"It's the most beautiful place in the world."

I wait, and after a while Léon continues.

"I don't know. That country is special to me. But when you see the beaches, the colour of the sand and the sea and everything beneath the waves, the sunsets… You watch the sun setting over the sea, and the entire world is reduced to you and this blazing ball of gas, and the water has turned to gold—actually, perhaps then you understand something about yourself and your place in the universe."

I stare at him. I can imagine; yes, I can imagine. The desert, the soaring rock, begging exploration. I can see myself standing out there, feet coated in red dust.

"Go on," I say.

He grins. I lose myself for a second in that smile. "What, waxing lyrical?"

"If you like."

Léon talks about snorkelling on the Great Barrier Reef. He talks about adolescent crocodiles in Koorana, their solid, scaly weight. He talks about the Ghan train route through the shimmering outback, surfing and swimming, the menace of sharks, the beauty of coral. I imagine my body suspended on the surface of the ocean. I imagine Léon floating at my side, the gentle rise and fall of waves.

I realise he's stopped talking. We stare at each other for a moment in silence. It should be awkward, but it isn't.

"I should probably go," he says at last. "I just wanted to make sure you were okay."

"Thanks. For distracting me."

"De rien."

THE NEXT NIGHT I go back to work. I don't want to be alone. On Friday night the place is heaving by eleven. It is jungle theme and the staff are feathered and furred for the occasion. Gabriela hugs me tightly. I'll be here, she says. I'll be here with you all the way. I have your back. She paints the camouflage on my forehead and cheeks, holding my face steady as you would a child's, and I think of Lorena. I am too shaky to hold the brush myself. As the queue for the bar deepens I can feel the threat of an attack edging closer. I glance sideways at every customer I serve, wondering if they have heard the story of the mystery corpse, if that is what they are discussing in their shrill, agitated voices.

Eloise says she'll keep me upstairs, but inevitably one of the other managers forgets and asks me to change the lines. I don't think to refuse. The events of the past few days are swilling around my head. The chronometrist in the ice machine, scratches at her breast. The falcon in the rafters. My head is a broken projector spitting out one image after another. They blur and fuse. Gabriela looks morose in a green coat. The chronometrist whispers in my ear but the voice is Gabriela's: *I'd say you're ripe.*

Going downstairs, the fear takes over; I dive past the ice machine and practically hurl myself around the corner to the keg room. Something pops into my head. 1875, the year of the Basilica. The moment I enter, I feel a shift in the atmosphere. From the heart of the concrete chamber, by the Kronenberg kegs on the second set of taps, a pool of heat emanates. My panic dissolves. I move into the warmth, curious. What is fuelling it? I feel heat, incredible heat. An eruption. I hear a high-pitched noise, stronger than I have ever heard before, and bright with soprano notes of the first melody ever sung.

Then I lose time and self and everything between.

PART FOUR

The Folies

CHAPTER FOURTEEN

HER BODY FEELS warm and heavy; her eyelids refuse to lift. She is floating in a bowl of syrup. The liquid heats gently, glooping as a spoon stirs, and the girl, cupped in the curve of it, is swirled about the bowl. She can smell the maple. No, it's not that, but something culinary. And something else too. Something that makes her sneeze. She does, twice, and her eyes open.

She is lying on wooden boards covered in a fine coating of sawdust. In front of her, a ladder leads up to an open trapdoor, yellowish light filtering through the aperture. She is still underground, but everything that was here before—the kegs, the crates, the beer lines—has gone. In their place are wooden barrels banded with metal.

She climbs groggily to her feet. Hunger. She is so very hungry. She checks the barrels: some are corked and slosh when she moves them. Others contain food: earthy potatoes, apples, dried peas, cured meat, white granules—she dips a finger and licks; this one is salt. The next one is sugar. She takes a handful of rough grains and crunches on them. The rush of sweetness snaps her awake and her stomach gurgles again. She takes an apple and eats that too. The dried pork accompanies it nicely. She eats a lot of it. Instinct prompts her to cram another apple in each pocket.

Hunger sated, she climbs the ladder to find out where on earth she has arrived, and emerges into a storeroom stacked with more barrels and a large trestle table dappled with flour. There is one exit, through a threadbare curtain overhanging the doorway. From the other side, she can hear the sounds of a bustling tavern, people eating and drinking or ordering food and drink. Someone yells: "Anne-Marie!" and a woman laughs, loud and ribald.

The curtain twitches; a woman comes through. She is broad and pink-faced. Her hair is squashed under a cap and her girth swells beneath a floury apron.

"Hello," says the girl.

The woman stares. Her cheeks grow redder. Then her lips pull back, revealing a row of unfortunate teeth; one is black and two are missing altogether.

"Unbelievable!" hisses the woman. She is speaking in French but the girl understands her without effort, and reaching for a response, she finds the words come readily.

The girl tests a step forward. "I'm sorry, I got stuck in your cellar—"

"Unbelievable, the insolence of these thieves!" The woman grabs a broom from the corner. "Out!"

She levels the broom in front of her, the bristling end pointing towards the girl. Alarmed, the girl retreats.

"But—"

"Out, thief!"

The woman and her broom charge. The girl leaps to the right to avoid being speared by bristles, the woman stumbles as her broom meets the wall. The girl whips aside the curtain into the main room. A rumble of excitement greets her appearance—the drinkers have heard the shrieks of wrath. She is aware of their gaze: the patrons, surprised and curious; the eyes of a moustached man behind the bar, narrowed; the eyes of a young woman in a bonnet, shrewd.

Behind her, the curtain bulges. The woman with the broom is

giving chase. She gets tangled in the curtain and the girl wastes no more time. She runs through the tavern, dodging legs too surprised to try and trip her, jumping up and over a table, saying, "Shit! Sorry!" when she steps on a plate—a nice pâté, by the look of it.

"Get her!"

At last the woman's roar provokes movement. Two men move to block the entrance, but the girl is too nimble. She ducks under their arms and out into the street.

Daylight—

Cerulean blue sky, what a day—oh, what a day!

There is a horse pulling a carriage down the road. Inside the carriage is a woman wearing a tall hat beneath a parasol; in front of the woman a liveried driver holds the reins. More carriages, ahead and behind. People walking along the boulevard, also in period costume. The girl looks for cameras, but there are none. Perhaps this is an aerial shot—she looks skywards once again. The sky is empty. Scraped clean, without a wisp of cloud or a tail of fumes. Not a blinking airborne light. Not—

She hears a shrill neigh just before several hundred kilograms of muscle and bone crash into her and she is knocked flat on her back, the air sucked out of her, as the horse lurches to the left.

That's when the disassociation ends. I am the one laid out in the middle of the boulevard, aching and airless and very much awake. Or someone remarkably like me. Have I split in two, like a cell undergoing mitosis? Either way, I am the one who needs to move quickly to avoid being crushed by another set of hooves.

I roll. Out of the street, into the gutter.

A woman approaches. Her narrow grey dress nips her waist and descends to her ankles. She stoops, brings her face close to mine and hisses, audibly:

"Whore! Get off our streets!"

She bustles away.

For the first time in quite a long time, I consider what I am wearing. A sleeveless tank top, cargo pants to below the knee spattered with every alcohol under the sun, filthy trainers, and if my memory is not impaired, the remnants of camouflage makeup. Last night was Jungle Night.

I look back at the door I came through. Millie's canopy is gone; the boulevard is flat-faced and grey. The road is a current of carts and carriages and top hats and bonnets and pursed lips and averted eyes and people staring right at me and people pretending not to stare.

There is no sign of the Moulin Rouge.

I gawp.

An approaching carriage driver yells a warning. I move just in time and the horse careers past, nostrils flaring. Its coat is sleek, glistening with sweat. I scramble to my feet and dart into the nearest alley; by some mercy it is just where it was in the twenty-first century.

The twenty-first century. The back of my brain fizzes. *I'm the chronometrist. This is a hotspot and I'd say you're ripe.*

Whatever this is, green bowler woman is in it up to her very dead neck.

From the cover of the alley I watch, rubbing my spine, as people pass. They are also dead, these people, even if they don't know it. They are atoms in the ground and in the air—I have breathed them in, trodden upon them, swallowed them—and yet here they are, walking around like real people, as if the twenty-first century never happened.

I place both palms against the wall, embracing its solidity, its mineral density, trying to stave off the shakiness brought on by that thought.

"—the time, Anne-Marie is incensed by it."

"It's understandable. Giving out kitchen scraps is one thing, but urchins openly thieving... it's not as if these are times of plenty, is it?"

I smell cigar smoke. The voices are male, drifting back from outside the tavern. All at once I have a terrible craving for a cigarette. I slip my hand into my pocket and feel the plastic pouch of Golden Virginia.

I'll just wait until they've gone.

"Not at all. And I am not suggesting that we are an open house, far from it. It's only that—" The voice lowers. I inch closer to the alley entrance. "Sometimes I look at these children and I can't help but imagine that their parents were probably Communards, are probably dead, and they have no one left to care for them. It is going to become a problem."

"It's already a problem. Urchins are raiding your wife's larder, in broad daylight, fearless as rats. Don't let your kind nature get the better of you, Henri."

"That child today—she looked as skinny as a rat. I don't suppose she had eaten in days."

I put my hands to my cheeks. Child? Skinny?

"She looked insolent. She looked like a regular little thief. And Henri—don't forget, we have all eaten rats."

"Never again. My God!"

"No. Never again."

"Henri!"

The screech is a woman's and I recognize it. Henri is being summoned, doubtless by Anne-Marie. Anne-Marie will not be happy to find me lurking nearby.

Which, assuming the way I got here is the way I'll get back, is going to cause me difficulties. I close my eyes, letting my consciousness reach out for a sense of it—that strange warmth, the beautiful song. There is nothing. The anomaly (careful, Hallie, you're using her words now) is silent. The way back is shut, at least for now.

A young girl exits the gates of a house off the alleyway, carrying a basket of laundry in both arms. I step away from the wall.

"Excuse me? Sorry to bother you, but what year is this?"

The girl gives me a queer, frightened look. "It's... it's eighteen seventy-five."

Of course it is.

"Eighteen seventy-five." I repeat it quietly, as though this is a perfectly reasonable response, and not the outcome of a probable brain tumour or previously unsuspected mental illness.

"Yes." She shrinks back.

"Thank you," I say. "That is exactly what I needed to know."

The girl stops. Her face goes blank. Then her features twist. Her mouth works grotesquely, opening and closing, opening and closing.

"Hey, are you all right?"

The girl blinks, twice. When she speaks again, her voice has a different tone.

"My dear—you made it. What a perfectly—fantastic jump!"

Coldness. My vision narrows, goes black. In the dark, seconds stretch into minutes, and with each minute I feel my body temperature dropping another degree.

A pinpoint of light. I grasp for it. Focus on that light until the darkness recedes and I can see again. The girl stands there, watching me with interest.

"You," I whisper. "You were dead."

"Me? No, no, no, no. Not—*me*."

I remember the frozen hand I pulled from the ice machine and I can feel it against my fingers now.

"That woman in the freezer, was she even you?"

"For—a time."

"And now she's dead."

"Collateral," says the chronometrist regretfully. "Most—unfortunate, but time was—ticking. I needed—to shock you into action."

"You killed her. Fucking hell, you murdered her."

"Would it make you—feel better—if I said she had an incurable brain tumour?"

"Did she?"

The girl giggles. "Perhaps."

"You're deranged."

"How cruel—you are!"

I stare at her numbly.

"You wanted me to come here. Why?"

The girl sets down her basket of laundry and sits in it. She fluffs up the dirty clothes around her, tucking in her legs and arms as though she is nesting.

"My dear, I am just so sick—of looking at that hideous basilica. I thought perhaps you could have a word with the architect—whisper in his ear, put your *considerable* charms to work. Dear Monsieur Abadie, such a lovely man, such a terrible instinct for design..."

"The basilica? What's wrong with the basilica?"

"Sacré-Coeur, yes, basilica, cathedral, it has many names, but whichever way you look at it, it's a monstrosity, don't you think?" The girl simpers.

"I think you're insane. Talk to the architect yourself."

"I would, but I haven't got the range, my dear. I simply can't get that far, even in a bird. Whereas you—you can go anywhere you like!"

"Then I'm going back to the twenty-first century."

The girl's expression turns sly.

"Oh, but you can't."

"Watch me."

"I would, with pleasure. But your efforts will be futile. You need a return flare, you see. And who knows when that will be? It might be days, weeks, months..."

"You tricked me." My hands bunch into fists. "You tricked me into this."

The girl lifts a hand to her mouth, tittering. I take a step towards her. I can feel the heat in my face, my anger rising. Whatever the hell this is, she is responsible.

The girl raises her hands in a show of fear.

"Oh! She's angry! I do like an angry one..."

My vision is beginning to blur again. This isn't happening. This can't be real. The girl is laughing. She won't stop laughing. She's pointing at me, tears gathering in the corners of her eyes and she won't—stop—laughing. I'm stuck here, stuck in 1875. *She's done this.*

I lunge at her, lock my hands around her throat and squeeze.

All expression disappears. The girl's face goes slack. She gurgles. Then her eyes widen in shock.

"Please," she gasps. "Miss, ple—"

I release my grip and back away, horrified. Still sprawled in the laundry basket, the girl is holding her throat, wheezing. Tears—real ones this time—are streaming down her cheeks.

"Oh, my god—I am so, so sorry—"

I feel sick to the core. How could I have lost control like that? I start to apologise again, stumbling over words, but when I look up, the girl's face has altered once more. A snide expression occupies her features.

"You should be. Such a violent spirit in there. Who would have thought?"

Tingling in my legs and palms. My heart rate begins to pound, a bomb lodged in my chest. I'm in 1875. I'm in 1875 with a non-corporeal psychopath and I can't get home. I can't get home. I can't get *out.*

I'm trapped.

"Breathe, my dear," she says. "Do keep breathing."

"You stay away from me," I say shakily. "And leave her alone!"

She flicks the hem of her skirt, eyes me saucily. With my vision tunnelling she looks distorted, a Picasso figure.

"I might be persuaded to let her go. But I really am very upset about that basilica."

My chest clamps tight.

"I can't help you," I gasp.

"No? Then I'll just have to stay in this body. We'll have some larks, me and she. Does she like to dance, I wonder?"

She starts to jig, hopping from foot to foot, moving faster and faster until the girl's face turns a deep red and I feel dizzy watching. The girl loses balance, but keeps dancing. Now the chronometrist has her leaping over the basket. She's going to fall, break her ankle. I sit where I am on the cobbles and put my head between my knees, struggling to regain control of my own body.

"Stop it," I manage. "Please—"

"Or—sing?"

She throws back the girl's head and howls. It's a terrible, strangulated noise. If she keeps this up the entire population of Paris is going to come running.

"Stop it!" I hiss. "Stop it! I'll speak to the architect!"

She pauses, one foot raised, mid-jig.

"You will?"

"On one condition. That you leave her alone."

"I give you my word."

"Forgive me if *your word* doesn't inspire me with confidence."

The girl's face turns solemn. She whirls to a halt and gathers herself, standing with heels together and hands clasped behind her back.

"I swear," she says. "By the code of practice. What will you swear by?"

"By—by Millie's."

"A tolerable deal, my dear."

"Where will I find him?"

"Oh—well, on the hill, I'd imagine."

She bends to pick up her basket of laundry.

"Wait—"

"Yes?"

"In there, in the tavern, I was speaking French. And I understood it too."

"Ah yes, the language acquisition. Think of it as a gift. From the anomaly—to you."

"But how—"

The chronometrist shakes her head. "You know, in my day—a long time ago, I admit—people would show some *gratitude*."

She settles the basket on one hip and walks slowly away. I watch her go, pathetically grateful that I don't have to face the owner of that body. I can feel the trembling in every muscle of my body. The horror that I could have hurt her. What was I thinking?

I wasn't.

I bite down on the last of my panic. I can't let anxiety take over. If I'm going to survive this, I need all my wits.

And a smoke. That will help. That will calm me down.

I extract my Golden Virginia. Inside the pouch are a few measly threads of tobacco. I'm out of Rizla.

"Oh, shitting *fuck!*"

I was intending to replenish on my break. And now I'm in a different century being blackmailed by a murderer and I can't remember if cigarettes have been invented yet or if we're still in cigar-country, but in any case I have no local currency to purchase either. What I have is a bottle opener, a Clipper lighter, a pencil, a strawberry glitter lipgloss, a handful of euros, and the Millie's weekly schedule. I don't even have my phone—it's charging in the vestiaire—not that I could call anyone. Alexander Bell won't obtain his patent for another two years.

This isn't happening, I tell myself. None of this can possibly be real.

Still, I think. If it *isn't* real, if it's all some mad delusion in my mind—then whatever I do next can do no harm.

CHAPTER FIFTEEN

ONCE MORE I brave the boulevard. Back in the public eye, it's my trousers that appear to be causing the greatest offence. Women in this century do not wear trousers. Which means—I spy, on a side road, a sign advertising potential salvation—I have to become a man.

There are two men in the barber's: one smothered in shaving cream and the other wielding a pair of scissors. I watch through the glass as the barber snips and shaves, then takes up a knife and scrapes it under the customer's chin. The barber has deft hands and a bald head himself, which from time to time he scratches. I wait until the customer's head has been cleansed and pomaded. He twitches his collar into place, squints at the mirror, nods. The barber stands back and wipes scissors and knife on his waistcoat. A bell tinkles as the customer leaves.

I eyeball my reflection in the glass, wipe away the last of the jungle makeup, and slip inside.

"Good morning. I wish to sell my hair, please."

The barber looks at me and acquires an expression of surprise sprinkled with revulsion, which seems to be the standard reaction thus far. He leans over and lifts a tangle of my hair.

"It is very long and extremely clean," I say. "It will make a good mattress. Or a wig."

That's what they use it for, isn't it?

"It's like a nest of birds," says the barber. A note of wonderment creeps into his voice. "And I don't mean little songbirds—this is like eagles, or, or falcons!"

"Enough about birds, if you don't mind."

"I've never seen so much hair on any woman..."

"Exactly. It's strong, thick hair. That's the Greek in me. Will you buy it?"

"What price are you offering?"

"What is the standard rate?"

He narrows his eyes, appraising. My first error. Now he will offer me a low rate and I will have to bargain.

"I can give you ten francs per ounce," he says.

I feign shock.

"Ten francs! This is theft, pure and simple. I might consider it for twenty, but not a cent—a centime less."

"Now who is the robber? Twenty is an outrage, you'll bankrupt me."

"I'll settle for eighteen."

"Sixteen!"

"Done."

I am already thinking about the tobacconist's.

The barber seats me in the chair and throws a cape around my shoulders. The counter in front of me contains an array of gels, shaving creams, horse hair brushes, talcum powder and metal combs. To my left is a bowl of water upon a stand, the surface opaque with scum and clippings. I turn my gaze to the mirror as the barber lifts a handful of my hair. Something falls out. He bends to pick it up.

"What is this?"

"Just a glowstick. You can keep it, if you like."

The barber frowns, as though I have offered him something deeply offensive, and drops the neon glowstick into my lap.

"Anything else in your hair I should know about?"

"I don't know," I say. "There could be. I lost a bottle opener a while back."

The barber's frown deepens. I shouldn't have said that. Now he'll think I am a drunk, and probably a prostitute as well. Oh, Hallie. You never did manage to think before you speak.

He lifts the scissors in one hand, takes a rope of hair in the other. My reflection meets me: dark-eyed, solemn faced. My skin is pleasingly smooth and glowing, but that could be the effects of gas lighting and a mirror that hasn't been polished in a while. I stare at the mirror until my vision blurs. If this *is* a dream, this is the moment I will wake up.

"Ready?" asks the barber.

No. But I will need money if I am going to survive here. Hair always grows. I clasp my hands together.

"Do it."

The scissors open and shut close to my scalp. Nothing comes away. Again, the barber snips. He checks the scissors against his thumb for sharpness, tries again, selects another pair.

"Sweet Mary mother of Jesus, it's tougher than I thought," pants the barber. "Have you put something in it? Egg yolk? Pomade?"

"No, no. Only a bit of conditioner."

I squeak as the hair tugs at my head. It hurts. It hurts the way it hurts in the real world. The barber wipes trickles of sweat from his pate. Finally, a chunk of hair comes away. He holds it aloft.

"Doesn't look like I've taken any off at all."

The ordeal continues. Three times the bell tinkles and a customer enters. The barber turns them all away. Four pairs of scissors are blunted. My hair claims a comb which is never rediscovered. The barber pants with exertion. He is sweating freely; rivulets run down his neck and under his collar, a sour aroma permeates the room. But it is a matter of pride now. He will not let my hair defeat him.

The last lock falls away. The barber collapses on a stool.

In the mirror, my head seems very small. I gulp.

"My payment, please."

The barber is too exhausted to speak. He points to a wooden box. I extract my fee. I suppose this counts as a successful transaction—I have no hair, but I have some money and I look like a boy.

"Now, can you tell me where I can buy some cig... cigars?"

He gestures in a vaguely uphill direction.

"Thank you," I say. "It's been a pleasure."

The barber gazes at me, bemused. The bell tinkles as I let myself out.

I wait for the scene to dissolve or evolve. Nothing happens. It appears my subconscious wishes me to make my own way through this curious territory. I raise my newly-shorn head and begin to climb.

CHAPTER SIXTEEN

THE BUTTE MONTMARTRE is teeming with activity. There are men in caps and overalls, frenziedly digging, leaning on spades, shouting at one another, chewing tobacco. There is no evidence of building works having begun, except for a hole in the ground and one large travertine boulder, wedged precariously in place with struts of wood. That's something.

Scanning the occupants of the hill, I fix upon a morose-looking gentleman slumped on a wooden crate beneath a tree. He is short and rotund, bearded, dressed in a dark coat, waistcoat, chequered trousers and a bowtie, his top hat on the grass beside him. Absorbed in his thoughts, the man is repeatedly flicking a finger against the hat, rocking it back and forth.

The gentleman does not notice me until I am stood right next to him.

"Hello," I begin. "I hope you don't mind my coming to speak to you. I thought that you looked very sad, and it does not seem to be a sad day."

"Sad?" replies the gentleman. "Not sad. Disappointed, yes. Frustrated, one could say. Such is always the way when one's work leaps from the paper to the stone."

I offer him one of my newly acquired cigarettes (they exist!) but he declines. I light up, remembering just in time to extract the box of matches, not the Clipper. The sensation of smoke blackening my lungs is heavenly.

"Are you with these people?" I enquire, indicating the workers gathered around the giant boulder.

"They are the implementers of my design. How I shall trust them to do it justice…"

"A fair point," I say. "It is highly possible they will mess it up entirely."

The gentleman looks at me for the first time. A startled expression captures his face. Perhaps it is the sight of me; perhaps it is merely the shock of being pulled out of his reverie into the present. Whatever the reason, he is interested enough to put the question:

"Who are you?"

"A visitor. I came to see how the church was progressing."

The gentleman snorts.

"As you see, there is not much of a church to view at present. Though there will be. One day, ah"—he peers at me—"young man, there will be a magical sight upon this hill. Magical! People will come from far and wide to see it. They will marvel at the white domes, gleaming in the sun, the statues, the interior, gracious yet commanding…" The gentleman's voice tapers away. He appears to be having trouble convincing himself.

My nineteenth-century doppelgänger, whose command of French I can't deny is proving decidedly useful, says, "Forgive me, sir, but you seem doubtful."

The gentleman continues to look glum.

"You have a particular interest in this place, do you not?"

"It means something to me, it's true."

"Humour an old man and allow me a hypothesis." He lowers his voice. "You were one of the Communards?"

I think of the Communards' Wall in Père Lachaise, one of the first places I visited with Gabriela. Brutal times, said Léon. 1875. It's barely four years after one of the bloodiest civil wars in France's substantially blood-splattered history. What were those men talking about outside the tavern? Eating rats? That would be the Siege of Paris by the Prussians.

The architect continues.

"I will not hold it against you if you were, although they say this church is to be built to expiate those crimes."

"Is that why *you* say it is to be built?"

The gentleman shrugs. "Young man, I am not interested in *why* it is to be built so much as *how* it is to be built. That is, after all, my brief."

We assess one another cautiously.

"And what have you devised?" I ask, at the same time as he comments:

"That is a remarkable haircut you have acquired, young man. Shouldn't have let the rascal get away with it. Never trust a barber, myself. Now, I could show you the design, but my notebook was thieved only this morning. This area is becoming disreputable."

You have no idea, I think. I delve into my pocket and discover the Millie's schedule, crumpled and furred at the corners. In my other pocket is a propelling pencil. I unfold the paper and offer both to the architect.

"You could draw it for me?"

Paul Abadie eyes the pencil suspiciously.

"What is this contraption?"

I click the end. "There you go."

"I see." He tests the pencil. "Remarkable," he says again. On the back of my schedule, he begins to sketch out the familiar contours of the Sacré-Coeur. "Some people do not like it," he says. "They abhor the Byzantine style."

"I would think very carefully about pursuing this route," I say. "I mean, technically it's cultural appropriation."

"Excuse me?"

"If you must go ahead, couldn't you go for something more... French?"

Once again he looks gloomy.

"French, you say? Who can say what is French anymore? Half the city is Belgians, Spanish, Italians..."

"Precisely! Italian architecture is particularly fine," I suggest. I am hoping that I will get my paper back, now that it has become a historical document, but the architect turns it over and examines the schedule curiously.

"This is a very fragile material. Which printing press did you employ?"

"I'm afraid I can't remember."

I had better retrieve my pencil. The last thing I want to do is give him any entrepreneurial ideas. That wasn't in the psychopath's brief.

He points to the Millie's logo in the corner.

"The windmill! Now there's a design for you."

"A symbol of freedom," I say.

"Freedom?" He smiles for the first time, and doodles something on the paper. "The sails, yes, there is that illusion. A design with momentum in it. And yet constraint, also; ever tethered. As we all are."

"Exactly!" I say. "Exactly. You can't beat a windmill. I really, truly think—"

We are diverted by a commotion on the building site—the stone is threatening to roll from its moorings. Five men pit themselves against it, their feet sliding in the muddy foundations.

The architect leaps up, finally knocking over his hat.

"God in Heaven and all the sacred saints!" he shouts, my schedule still clutched in one hand.

The propelling pencil has fallen to the ground. I pocket it quickly, and set the top hat upright. About to leave, I notice my beloved Doc Martins and sigh. I pull off the Pikachu sticker and stuff it into my pocket, then scoop up a handful of mud and smear it over the purple uppers. The mud is thick and cool and gritty. Something about its touch and smell goes the final way to convincing me; this is not a dream or an extended hallucination. It's not an elaborate projection. I am in 1875. I have travelled through time.

As I leave the scene I hear the architect calling to me. I hurry over.

"Be careful, young man." He scrutinizes me once more, hesitates, weighing his words. "As I said, this area is not what it once was."

I have the feeling he might have said more, but there is a shout, the boulder is stuck. He is distracted. I can't do much more to convince him today. The chronometrist will just have to wait. And the afternoon is wearing on, I need to find a place to stay. I know now I have arrived in an uneasy city.

CHAPTER SEVENTEEN

ALL AFTERNOON I walk. North of the river I find myself a pair of trousers and a shirt, which have blown down from someone's washing line (any qualms I might have about theft quickly vanish at the thought of covering my calves and arms). Gradually, I am looking the part. At Bastille I buy piping hot chestnuts from a man in a threadbare coat and a Russian hat. For over an hour we talk. His voice is slow and scrapes in his throat. I tell him I'm from Marseilles, come to make my fortune in the capital. I ask about the siege and he tells me tales of hunger and bonemeal whilst he stirs the chestnuts with a wooden spatula, slowly, carefully, around the spitting stove. His frame beneath the coat is as spare as a scarecrow.

Twilight falls and with it my worries return, and my hunger. The wealthy of Paris languish in elegant cafés, bright and cloistered, places that are closed off to me in my dishevelled, impoverished state. As the gloom deepens before the gas lamps are lit, it becomes harder to read people's faces. I recall the architect's warning and walk faster.

It is completely by accident that I stumble upon the Folies Bergère, tucked away on rue Richer. The poster outside shows a woman swathed in diaphanous material, appearing to float on one improbable toe, and the evening's entertainment is listed below:

Acrobats! Dancers! Operetta and Comedy Song!

I could cry with relief. At long last, evidence of debauchery in Paris. I am saved.

I join the queue for the Folies. The young man at the ticket booth eyes my hair with visible anxiety, but I ignore him, taking my slip and pushing through the barrier accompanied by a sea of hats. Everyone else is far too concerned with getting a good view of the stage to notice the slim androgynous figure amongst them.

My idea—the only idea I have—is to make my way backstage and mingle with the performers. They are my best chance of camouflage. I could even get a job. (Will I need a job? A frightening thought. I push it away.) Addressing the more immediate of my problems, there are bound to be costumes and spare clothes lying around backstage, perhaps even a pair of shoes.

The hall inside is filling up with eager spectators. Gas lamps cast a soft, entrancing light, the chandeliers overhead lending a sense of grandeur to the bustling scene. Women flow up and down the staircase to the balcony, skirts billowing, décolletage encased in square necklines and offset by flashing stones. Are they real or fake? Who comes here, given the nature of the entertainment about to unfold? The Moulin Rouge does not yet exist, although its advent is not far off—but Montmartre has not yet become that famous den of iniquity, and Paris has barely emerged from years of war and famine. You can see it in the damage done to architecture. You can read it in the eyes of people on the streets. No wonder they flock to the Folies. The theatre air leaves a malty taste in my mouth, the odour of packed bodies and cigar smoke and palpable need.

In the orchestra pit, musicians are tuning their instruments. I slip through the crowd, intent upon my own mission. Moving out of the main hall, I spot a gaudily-dressed acrobat trailing a pair of wings. He opens a door and disappears inside. I am at the door, ready to follow, when a voice accosts me.

It is a smoky, syrupy, sinuous kind of voice, and it says:

"Will you look at you. Bold as polished brass."

The owner of the voice stands a couple of feet away, watching me. She sports a glossy, preposterous coiffure and an array of bright jewels, and is standing in what is evidently an established pose, hand cocked at her waist, head tipped to one side.

I let go of the door handle.

"This isn't the ladies' room?"

The woman waggles a finger.

"No, it's not honey, and you know it. I've been watching you since you got here. Now I've got no quibble with you sneaking backstage, but what I don't understand is this: why are you going backstage? You know the money's out here. Them artisans got nothing."

"I'm not sure what you mean—I'm looking for the ladies' room?"

The woman winks.

"Darling. You're not from round here."

She shimmies closer. Her perfume is heady, floral, and through it I can smell the warmth of her skin, treated with powder and creams.

"There's two reasons why I said that. One, I'm talking to you in English and you answered sharp as a regular Thames brat, and the Parisians don't do that. Two, you're a girl dressed as a boy, which to my way of thinking means you're operating some kind of disguise. Hair's a bit overlong for it, too."

I touch my hair. The ragged tufts have grown a centimetre since I talked to the architect on the hill.

I make a feeble attempt at defiance.

"And what if I am? In disguise?"

"It's nothing to me, 'cepting what you might call idle curiosity. I'm not from around here either. That's why I said hello. Couldn't let a fellow miscreant fall into trouble now, could I? Or did I get it wrong? Are you one of the trapeze girlies after all?"

"I'm not a trapeze artist. I'm here because I hope to... to audition."

"I see. Well, you're a skinny thing, so I suppose you'll fly easy as pie."

It's clear that the woman doesn't believe a word I've said, but she is playing along anyway.

"So, what's your name, honey?"

"It's—" Who do I need to be in this situation? Who would remain unfazed in the face of utter surrealism? "I'm Gabriela. What's yours?"

"My name? Fleur, cabbage. Fleur Chaubert. At your service."

She delivers the last line with a little curtsy. I remain unconvinced, but I cannot stand here talking all night. The show is about to begin. An usher is standing at the entrance to the main hall, and at any moment he might turn and glance this way. I need allies. But who is she?

I decide to take a leap of faith.

"Look, I'll be honest. The problem is, I sold my hair because I thought I'd be safer as a boy, but now my hair is growing back rather faster than expected, and I need a skirt to look like a girl again. You're right, I'm from out of town—from the country. My belongings were stolen on the journey here. I have no clothes of my own and no friends in the city to ask."

"So you're going to nick some clothes backstage? Why didn't you say so in the first place? Go get 'em, I'll watch the door for you."

"You will?"

"Promise. Here, take my fan as a token. I love a joke, me. Or a good theft. That's a joke! Well..." She lifts my hand and slips the loop of the fan over my wrist. "Be quick and quiet, they'll never see you."

She gives me a firm push. The usher is still at his post, but I am masked by Fleur's copious skirts and her hive of hair. I open the door and slip backstage.

It's darker and danker back here, a warren of corridors leading on to rows of shabby dressing rooms. The doors are open, the performers within exchanging idle gossip whilst warming up muscles or smearing their faces with greasepaint. A singer cycles through arpeggios. I pass a room of ballet dancers flexing their feet in woodblock shoes. They wear tutus and tiaras. At the next door, a contortionist bends over backwards and peers at me through his legs. I follow the corridor round until I find what I'm looking for: a room full of clothes rails. All manner of things are hanging up: spangles and chiffon, bonnets and boots. I am about to filch a set of petticoats when a grey head pops up from between the rails.

"Hello, chicken. I don't recognize you. One of the new lads, is it?"

"Er, that's right." I curse inwardly. "It's my first day."

"Don't be nervous, I'll get you kitted out. I've been here since the beginning. The very very beginning." She laughs, but it turns into a fit of wheezing. "Excuse *me*. Second act, I suppose? Corsairs? Here, take one of these." She hands me a pair of breeches. "And these." A shirt follows, stockings, a tricorne hat, an eye-patch, a pair of boots. "Sweet Jesus, you're a skinny thing. Could do with a few dumplings inside you."

I thank her and change into the bundle of clothes, hiding behind a rail. I wrap my own clothes around my DMs and tie them together with two trouser legs. The wardrobe mistress gives a nod of approval.

"Don't you make a lovely pirate? Just watch out for the ladies with that pretty face. Coline in the ballet troupe's a minx, she'll have your breeches around your ankles before you can say parrot."

There is no denying that this is worse than the ragamuffin garb I started out with. Maybe I shouldn't fight it, but accept my fate and become a pirate in the second act, whatever that entails. I can foresee a life of theatrical banditry, myself as a not-quite-modern-day Viola trapped in the circus. But first, I need to return Fleur's fan.

As I head back the way I came, stuffing the eye patch into my pocket, a procession of clowns approaches down the corridor. Their chalk-white faces and cross-hatched eyes loom strange and solemn. I move to the wall to let them pass, but one of the clowns turns to me, grinning. With a flourish, he pulls a small yellow bird—a canary—from between his teeth and presents it upon a silver platter. The clowns convulse in silent, pantomime hysteria. The bird twitches. It's alive, moving. The clowns gather around the bird. I push forward.

"Don't hurt it—"

They shuffle closer, joining hands over the platter, obscuring my sight. When they part, the canary has vanished. The clown who produced it mimes his surprise. The others shrug. One wipes a tear from his cheek. They continue, bearing their empty platter aloft, oversized shoes slapping the floor until they disappear around the corner.

From one of the dressing rooms I hear a scream, followed by a burst of laughter.

CHAPTER EIGHTEEN

I FIND MYSELF alone in the corridor. All at once I feel the weight of it, how isolated I am in this alien Paris, decades from home. What do I call home now? Another city? Another century? I have an overwhelming urge to put my head in my arms and weep.

Instead I return to the stage door. It is a shock to be back in the hall of the Folies, under the shifting glow of the chandeliers. Mystery Fleur is waiting.

"What in heaven?" She appraises me. Do I look ill? I feel ill. "I thought you were after a skirt?"

"Oh. That. I was. She gave me this instead. Here's your fan, I'm going to join the show, I think it's best if I become a pirate—"

"No, no, no. If you're staying as a boy, you can be my escort. I'll call you Gabriel, like the angel. Come on—if we're quick, we can steal a spot on the balcony."

"What? No, I—"

Going with Fleur is a terrible idea. I'm wearing a corsair's costume. I look like a complete fool. Again I feel the urge to weep. Fleur tugs my hand. I can hear the string section tuning. The show is about to begin, and I must see the show. It's too late now anyway. Fleur is whisking up the stairs and I am in her wake.

"Thank you, thank you, so kind," says Fleur in that syrup-and-smoke voice, nudging her way to the front, and people smile graciously at Fleur and ignore me. I stash my bundled DMs at my feet. I've had these boots for too damn long to lose them in another century. Below us, I can see the pressing crowd, the black stripe of the conductor above the orchestra pit.

"Isn't this the most exciting thing?" says Fleur.

A sudden hush takes the audience. The conductor's arms rise and fall, a wall of sound surging up to meet us. Two figures are climbing the ladders to platforms on either side of the stage. They are identical in height and build, dressed alike in green shoes and feathered headpieces. Only the slight curvature of breasts distinguishes the female artist from the male. Reaching the platforms, they dust chalk on their hands, and each takes hold of the bar of a trapeze.

A drum rolls. Fleur nudges me with the end of her fan.

The aerialists plummet. Loosed arrows, their bodies flash in the light from the chandeliers, gaining height with each muscular beat, until at the apex of their swing they seem to disappear into the rafters. The female artist drops, somersaults through the air and catches the hands of her partner. One swing, two, and she's back to her bar. Hanging from her knees, now from her feet. The crowd gasps with every trick. What if one of them were to fall? What if they break those fragile, gleaming bodies? What if—

The orchestra reaches a climax. My skin is tingling, my heart in my mouth. The aerialists cross mid-air. There is a long, terrible moment where it seems that they must crash and fall, that their outstretched bodies cannot possibly pass this distance, before they catch the opposite bar.

A roar of applause. I bring my hands together. What a display!

Fleur does not clap. She is tugging at my sleeve, agitated.

"Gabriel. Gabriel!"

"What, what is it?" I cannot take my eyes from the stage. Blink and it's over; this will all dissolve before my eyes. All at once I'm glad that I saw this night.

"Valleroy is here! This is not good, Gabriel."

"Who's Valleroy?"

"Lord Valleroy! You must know him. He's my first patron. And my other patron is here too! I saw him earlier, with his hussy of a wife. And if Valleroy talks to me, the other one will see, and I won't be able to explain, see? Because of the wife! Oh, this is a royal cesspit of a disaster."

Fleur snaps open her fan and raises it in front of her face, flapping fiercely.

"Maybe you should choose one or the other?" I suggest. The aerialists are descending and the clack of ballet shoes now fills the stage. "If they move in the same circles."

"And limit my income? Two is nothing, two is the minimum, but neither should ever know the identity of the other! It's all about the mystery. A girl loses her mystery, she could be any old brothel whore. Gabriel, we have to leave at once."

"But the show's just beginning—there's the fire breathers and the chansons to come—"

"I'll introduce you to the fire breathers later. I know them all and everybody knows *me*; that's the problem, don't you see?"

She pulls me away from the balustrade, rustling down the stairs, hurrying us past the ushers at the doors.

"Out early tonight, little Fleurie?" says the one on the left. The other coughs, but it might have been a snigger, suppressed. Fleur hisses in my ear, "Ignore them!"

"Do you have a carriage?" I ask hopefully. There's a chill on the night air.

"Oh, you're funny. Keep an eye out for purse snatchers, little 'uns are the worst of the buggers. And—" She hesitates.

"And what?"

"Not now." A tense, almost frightened look passes over her face. "Not here. Come on."

She sets off at a brisk walk. I cast a longing look back at the Folies.

"Where are we going?"

"Back to my garret, I suppose. Unless—" Fleur looks at me thoughtfully. "Now here's an idea. You could occupy one of my patrons?"

"I'm dressed as a boy—a pirate!"

"Won't bother them—oh, come on then. But honestly, it's not a bad way to live—not bad at all. Most of them don't want any fancy stuff doing—I mean that one, the lord, he likes being tied up with my stockings, but I've heard far, far worse. And I could be persuaded to share, if you spotted one you liked. For a percentage, of course."

"Thank you, but I'll try some other ways to make money first."

"I'm low on candles, though, and there's no gin. Say, do you want to go to l'Éléphant?"

"A tavern?" The thought of public spaces raises fresh anxiety. Tiredness sweeps over me; I am hungry and exhausted, emotional, befuddled, and if I think too carefully about where I am, I can feel an attack hovering. I want nothing more than to sleep.

"It'll be fun! And the acrobats will be there later. The fire breathers. They all come out after the show."

"Well—if you can introduce me."

"Merveilleux! Hold this, will you?"

With a deft gesture, Fleur removes the hive of yellow hair from her head. An abundance of black curls tumbles to her waist.

"You're a brunette," I say stupidly.

Fleur smirks. "I get my way more when I'm a blonde."

She stuffs the wig inside a muff. We go to l'Éléphant, which is full of raucous women and men and the smell of warm beer. Fleur orders absinthe and I find us a small table and a couple of stools. Fleur has her arm round my waist and introduces me to her admirers as Gabriel, her new friend from the country who has joined the

Folies and doesn't she make a lovely pirate (so I'm a girl again), to a chorus of appreciative *oohs*. The admirers draw up a circle of chairs. Fleur, her former skittishness abandoned, tells stories and soaks up adulation. She squeezes my waist and kisses my cheek. I drink absinthe, which magically replenishes itself every time I look away. I assume somebody is picking up Fleur's tab.

"They ate elephants, you know," Fleur is saying. "From the zoo. Castor and Pollux, they were called, and in the siege them rich folk on Haussmann chopped 'em up and ate 'em, every last scrap, along with the kangaroos. I wonder who got the trunk and the ears? Imagine that in front of you, a bit of elephant ear."

"Dog gigot with baby rats," says one of the circle. "I'll never forget it."

"I caught rats when I was a child."

"The squeaking, I can't hear the squeaking without a shiver down my spine..."

"Why didn't you go back to London, Fleur?"

"I was too well known in London," says Fleur mysteriously, to a round of hoots and whistles.

"Are you from London as well, Gabriel?" asks one of the admirers.

"From near London," I say.

More hoots and whistles. I smile fuzzily.

It is past midnight when the performers from the Folies spill through the door, some still in their costumes, glitter stuck to their cheeks.

"A display!" shout the admirers. "Give us a display!"

"A round of your fire breathing malarkey!" shouts Fleur.

I wake up to watch the fire breathers. They upend the batons, bringing the fire close to their lips, and blow. Jets of flame spout from their mouths. I turn to Fleur, who is mesmerised by the absinthe and the spectacle before us.

"You were going to introduce me," I remind her.

She catches the eye of one of the jugglers, a slim young man with dark curls and gold-flecked eyes.

"This is my friend, Gabriel." Fleur produces her luxury smile. "She wants to learn some tricks. This is Fabian."

The juggler regards me solemnly.

"What do you want to learn?"

"Fire batons," I reply. "A skill, something I can perform."

Then the juggler does a strange thing. He places his fingertips at my temples and leans close, close enough that our foreheads and noses almost touch. He closes his eyes. I mirror him.

The world behind my eyelids explodes. I see fireworks. The fireworks become humanoid figures on their hands and knees, all clambering across the black backdrop of the sky, or space, or some other bleak landscape I cannot identify. Sparks strike at the figures. They cower. Where am I, where is this? I have no weight, no body, no physical matter at all. Fire all around, a Catherine wheel with eight green arms, revolving faster and faster until it blurs into a single green star. Then it vanishes, and everything is cold and dark and infinitely alone.

My eyes open. I am in the tavern. Around me laughter, the clinking of tankards. My heart is racing. The juggler's gaze meets mine, and for a moment I think he is as afraid as I am.

"Yes," he says. "You can learn. Come with me."

We extract ourselves from the circle and go out into the cold night. The juggler hands me a baton and shows me how to line my mouth with spirit and hold it there without swallowing, how to set the baton alight so that its flame will burn steadily, how to blow plumes of fire into the air. I burn the inside of my cheek, singe my eyelashes. Late night pedestrians pause to watch: the drunken gentlemen leaning upon their canes, the prostitutes with their smudged rouge and dirty petticoats, the man with his ladder who douses the gas lamps, the ballet dancers trudging home to massage their aching feet.

Now the juggler takes up two burning batons, and twirls them around and about his body. I've seen poi artists in the park with the same, effortless grace. He hands over the batons, instructs me in a figure-of-eight pattern. The rushing noise of the fire is frightening, disorientating, as it passes my ear.

"Close your eyes," instructs Fabian. "Listen to the flames."

I screw my eyelids tight, sensing the pathway of the fire, the heat of it tracking through the air.

"Good," says the juggler. "Very good. Tomorrow, we go back to the basics. You have much to learn."

"I might not be here for very long."

He does not reply.

"What did you see, when I saw those lights, those visions?" I ask.

Afraid of the answer, I wait whilst Fabian collects up the batons. He spits a mouthful of spirit on the cobbles.

"I saw your future," he says.

"I don't believe my future is preordained."

Fabian says, "You have already made it."

CHAPTER NINETEEN

IT IS LATE into the night when Fleur hurries us home, a new alertness in her face.

"I'm so tired," I say. "I can't walk as fast as you."

"You can't walk slow at night," she says. Again I sense that whisper of fear about her, and I force myself to keep up, ignoring the soreness in my soles and toes.

Fleur lives in a garret at the top of an apartment block in Bastille. As we climb the six flights of stairs she shudders a little, and tells me that some nights when you hear the wind howling it's not the wind at all, but the ghosts of prisoners who starved or were tortured to death in the old fortress, screaming for mercy.

"Folks say," she adds, "if you listen carefully enough, you can hear *exactly* how they died, like they was sobbing direct to your ears. And it were never pleasant."

I think of Gabriela and me, sat on the gravestones in Père Lachaise. *They wouldn't mind.* Back in the twenty-first century, will people be wondering where I've gone? Will anyone be out there, looking for me? Gabriela, Angel? What about Léon, who came by specifically to make sure I was okay?

A rickety set of steps leads up the final flight to the garret. Fleur lights a candle, revealing a cold, mean little room, the floorboards warped and the plaster peeling. The furnishings are a narrow bed, and a dresser with a mirror set on top of it. Fleur's belongings are scattered over the floor, petticoats and pieces of costume jewellery and pamphlets, a pair of stockings draped over the end of the bed.

"Don't mind me knickers," says Fleur.

I perch on the bed. Fleur sits on an embroidered cushion in front of the dresser.

"Valleroy gave it me," she says, poking the cushion. "He got my initials done in pink. It's watered silk."

"He doesn't come here?"

"Oh, no. He has a place."

She twists a length of black hair around her hand. When she pulls, the head of hair comes away for the second time this evening. Beneath it her real hair is cropped and copper. She sets this second wig over the mirror and the blonde one on top of it. I have to laugh.

"What's got you?"

"Look at the pair of us," I say. Fleur grins.

"Funny thing is, my real name's not Fleur at all. It's Millie."

"Millie?"

"That's my name."

"You're Millie!"

"Why, what have you heard?"

"You're Millie!" I repeat.

"What I said, isn't it? Millicent from the Wharfs. You know London at all?"

"Bits of it."

I stare at her, tiredness and hunger forgotten, enraptured. My attention does not bother Millie; I suppose she is used to it. She dampens a cloth in a pail of water, flicking away the spider spinning a web across the handle, and wipes the cloth over her face. Gradually, the rouge and alabaster powder disappear, replaced by freckles and a mole on her left cheek. Without the cosmetics, she looks ten years younger.

"I haven't been back for a time. Might have all changed. Doubt it."

"Where I'm from, there's a bar—a tavern called Millie's."

"Well, what do you know? Maybe when I've got myself a proper patron with a cold heartless wife he can't stand and plenty of riches, and he buys me a nice little apartment instead of this hovel, I'll get him to buy me a tavern as well. That'd be a hoot, wouldn't it?"

My head reels with implications.

"A hoot," I agree.

Millie flips through the Folies programme, lingering over advertisements for corsets and suspenders. Also for sale are remedies for various bodily afflictions—which I read with a horrified fascination—alongside the services of clairvoyants, hypnotists, cartomancers, palm-readers: everything, in short, that might soothe the troubled soul.

"Look at them stockings!" sighs Millie, whose desires appear to be firmly rooted in the material world. "Proper silk. You know how hard it is to keep your legs nice in the winter, cold gets up your nightgown and makes your skin red raw. With a pair of stockings like that, you can keep a man sweet for months. Last time I had proper stockings, I got a diamond pin."

I look at the overflowing jewellery box on the dresser, but there is nothing obviously diamond or pin-shaped.

"Sold it and drank the money," says Millie solemnly. "I'll tell you the tale if you like, though it's a sorry one."

"Go on." I ease off my shoes, massaging the arches of my feet and wincing at the blisters. Somehow through the evening I have managed to keep hold of my original clothes and my DMs. I retrieve the Pikachu sticker, smooth out the wrinkles and return it to the heel of the left boot. Something about the small action is reassuring.

"Well," begins Millie. "It was the gin was my downfall. God only knows it's the Devil, and when I say God knows, I mean that's *all* He knows. You may have noticed I'm not much of a Christian. I don't apologise for it, I think a girl needs higher protection than the Lord if you don't mind me saying so. Look at that church they're building on the hill, sacred this and sacred that, and who's paying for it? Poor folks, that's who.

"Although if I ever went under the knife I might change me mind. About God, I mean. It's not the blade, it's the chloroform. I've seen cats lying stiff as boards outside them places they practise it, their little feet stuck up in the air like they were saying, I never made it to the rooftops in the eighteenth and there's birds living that wouldn't have seen the light of day if they'd only met my needle paw. And now I won't see the light of day. Gives me a turn, it does. Anyway, it only happened once so far and that's when I had to sell the diamond, pawned it that is, but I knew I'd never get it back. I have instincts. I drank a tankard of gin and a measure of something a fellow girl of mine got from an old witch who's known to be reputable, and I sat in a tub full of steaming water, made my legs go pink as a slab of ham, sat there for two hours by which time the water had gone cold and I was out cold. Nothing happened that night. I woke up in a tub full of freezing water with my head like it was hit with a shovel and first thing I thought was, damn thing's still in there. I howled loud as a kitten.

"But then, what do you know, a week later I had my milliner chasing me for the bill on account of a fancy hat purchase, and I got angry and I'm afraid I said some things he didn't like and we screamed at one another like a regular pair of pigeons, and when I left I was still angry and hit the gin again and at the end of the night there was a brawl in the tavern and I got punched in the stomach by a baker, and you never did see a baker with scrawny arms. It hurt like buggery. I was sitting on the floor blubbing and blubbing, and everyone thought it was the pain and it was, of course, but it was relief too, because I knew what had happened straight away, I could feel the blood trickling down my drawers, and I thought either I'll die or I'll get rid of the damn thing but either way I won't have to worry about childbirth, and that's something. I didn't die, as you see before you. Though it was a nasty business, and I had to burn my favourite petticoats.

"After that, I had a time of feeling the world was not my friend, and every morning I woke up in a terrible dreariness wondering if I should just put myself out of my misery. You find, once you get to thinking on it in a serious fashion, there's no end of ways to kill yourself. Your last act in the world might as well use a little imagination. I knew a girl who killed herself by walking under an elephant in a circus ring. That's a true story. I'd think thoughts like that while I was sat in the tavern with the gin firing up my belly. Had me in the gutter in a month, did the gin. Lucky I've got a strong constitution, or that might have killed me too. But it didn't, as you see before you. And though I spent all the money from the diamond pin, one day I walked past a puddle and I caught a glimpse of my face and I said to myself, 'Millie my girl, you may look like you've been in the earth for a month with the worms having a guzzle, but there's good bones under that skin, and I remember when you had a spark in your eye and you weren't pulling a Mrs Clagg on life. You still know how to turn a few tricks.' And that's when I decided to join the demimondaine, and make my way in the world. As you see before you."

I wait, expectant, but nothing more is forthcoming.

"You've had an exciting life," I say.

"You could say that." Millie yawns. "I'm sleepy now. Takes it out of you, telling your life story. That's not the whole story, of course, there are other bits. You'll have to tell me yours some other time."

Millie curls up on the wall side of the mattress, leaving a space for me.

"What's out there?" I ask. "On the streets? You were nervous, before."

"Shouldn't talk about that," says Millie.

"But I need to know. I'm not from Paris, remember?"

"There's a murderer," she says abruptly. "After women. They can't catch him. He wears a rat pelt for every woman he's killed, and there's twenty pelts or more, they say. He hunts at night. That's why we don't walk slow."

"That's horrific."

Millie does not answer directly, but after a moment she asks, "Did you see anything, with Fabian?"

"What do you mean?"

"That head thing. I saw he did it to you."

I remember the crawling figures, the green-armed wheel. The sensation of unaccountable terror.

"No," I say slowly. "I didn't see anything."

"For the best," she says. "He's got the Sight. He's seen some things. Get the candle, will you?"

Millie is asleep within seconds. With her shorn head and freckled skin, she looks vulnerable, barely out of adolescence. I watch her breathing slow, the steady rise and fall of her chest, and I know why Millie has brought me home. She's lonely. Her gentrified lovers can give her jewels and clothes; they can put a roof over her head. But they cannot give her a meeting of minds, or the straightforward warmth of a hug. They cannot give her a family.

I recognise that loneliness. Until Paris, I'd known it all my life.

The candle gutters and shadows skit across the wall. I blow out the flame, and the room tumbles into darkness. I shiver, at once aware of the biting cold. Of the other thing. All day I have tried to put it from my mind, but now the day is gone and Millie is asleep and there is nothing to place between me and reality. Was the chronometrist telling the truth? How long will I be stuck in 1875? And is there any guarantee that the anomaly will return me to the twenty-first century, or might the next time be some time else again—the Revolution, the Napoleonic Wars, the Sun King's reign? What if I keep going back in time forever and ever, what if my last breath will be taken at the bottom of the ocean, in the Eocene?

I nudge open the shutters, suddenly desperate for a view, however unfamiliar. But there is nothing to see. The street lamps have been doused and the sky is dark with cloud. My hands before my face are invisible. Only the murmurs of a city at night offer reassurance that I am still alive: small creatures scrabbling in the roof, footsteps, a restless soul pacing.

There are other, darker possibilities. I could be dead in twenty-first century Paris. This might be a parallel dimension, or I'm a copy of the original Hallie, a replicant, a consciousness, doomed to languish in this century until her death. This might be a quantum world, where with every decision I take another me is born.

I close the shutter and feel my way back to the mattress. It is scratchy and full of lumps, but better than the floor. Or the streets, where—if Millie is to be believed—a murderer is walking, dressed in the furs of rats. I have been lucky, if you call it luck. Coincidence, perhaps. Inevitability.

I put an arm around Millie, covering her like the wing of an albatross, remembering Theo's hug through the duvet, my mother's screams fading as Dad dragged her downstairs, the ache in my jaw, the mucus in my nose and throat. For a time I tried to bury that memory, then I retrieved it, kept it fresh, a constant reminder. It became seminal. A thing I could not escape even if I wanted to.

"I'll look after you," I whisper to Millie. "I've got your back."

Her breathing is even; she gurgles. I hug her tight. The two of us feed off one another's warmth. It's good, so far away from home, to hold another heart so close to your own. Sometimes, it's the only thing you can do.

CHAPTER TWENTY

MILLIE CAME TO Paris because it was not London.

Millie was a child of the Thames. Her oldest memory is of the river, the stench of it, and the glint of the water, at once alluring and repugnant. Her father worked in the shipyard and her mother at the granary in Canary Wharf, or did until she became sick, and died shortly thereafter. Of cholera, says Millie, matter-of-factly. Millie was eight. Millie's father said everything happened for a reason and no one could know God's plan, which was the first shaking at the foundations of Millie's faith, because as far as Millie was concerned, if God's plan was remotely pragmatic, then He would have struck down Mrs Clagg who lived next door. Mrs Clagg, renowned for hitting both the bottle and her children on frequent occasions, before emerging drunk into the street, wailing her misfortunes, was surely a deserving recipient of death, unlike Millie's mother Alyce, who did none of these things and was by comparison a very paragon of virtue.

Millie's mother died on a Wednesday. Her father said that Sunday was too soon for the burial, and they must wait another week. For the next ten days Millie's mother remained in the house in her wooden coffin. The sides did not quite join, and some fundamental essence of Alyce was seeping through the house; with them at their breakfast and supper, with them while Millie lay in bed at night, with them when she crept downstairs and put a hand to the wood and felt the warm heat of decomposition. Perhaps this was also part of God's plan. If so, it didn't seem as if kindness was much in His nature.

After Alyce died, there was not enough money, so Millie was dispatched to a matchmaking factory to supplement the family income. Millie had always been a talker, but after Alyce's death she became ever more voluble. The more you talked, the less you thought, including about the bad things. This made her popular with other children but not with her employer, and her tenure at the matchmaking factory was regrettably short. Other placements followed, with the same outcome. Millie's father pronounced her lazy, feckless, a good-for-nothing wharf rat. He began frequenting the company of Mrs Clagg, despite or perhaps because of the gin, and Millie, now twelve and with an infallible eye for trouble, saw Newgate looming. She decided not to wait for it. The time had come for her exit strategy.

A travelling company were performing at the Victoria Theatre; she had seen the posters. Millie had always had an eye for glamour, however manufactured. Night by night she waited outside the stage door, accosting every performer who passed through until one of them succumbed to her pleas and gave her employment mending costumes. For three years she traipsed around England. She worked with suede and leather and lace and muslin. She grew taller, prettier, improved her letters and numbers, discovered other talents more profitable than sewing.

Yet still the stink of the Thames clung to her. Still the estuary sang through her voice. Even the rest of England was not far enough away from London. Even Scotland.

When a young patron about to embark upon the Grand Tour fell in love with her, Millie heard the golden call of Paris. And she answered.

"AND YOU'D NEVER go back?" I ask.

"Are you pulling my leg? Not in a hundred bloody years."

CHAPTER TWENTY-ONE

MILLIE IS EAGER to introduce me to her city. When we inevitably end up in Montmartre, I steer us towards the tavern where the anomaly—I hope, I assume—is biding its time down in the cellar. In my new clothes, it's possible the vengeful Anne-Marie won't recognize me, but barely have we set foot inside when the broom appears.

"I know your face!" shrieks Anne-Marie. "I won't have hussies in my tavern!"

She chases us half-way down the boulevard.

"What did you do to her?" asks Millie. She is gazing at me with new found respect.

"It was a misunderstanding," I say. "She thinks I'm a thief."

"You are a thief." Millie pokes me. "*Gabriel.* Oh, will you look at those hats."

She hurries over to a shop front, and I follow at a more sedate pace. I haven't gotten used to my borrowed petticoats. Millie stands with one hand pressed to her heart, gazing wistfully at the contents of the glass display. In the window, I see a small sparrow alight on my reflection's shoulder. It ruffles its feathers.

"Good to see you—alive and well. My dear."

I jump.

"Fucking hell!"

Millie turns.

"Gabriela?"

"It's nothing—"

"Oh, a little bird, how sweet!"

The sparrow cheeps.

"Millie, I need to... I need food. Some bread. I'm so hungry. I'll meet you back here in just a second—"

I stride away, the sparrow's tiny claws digging into my shoulder through the woollen dress.

"I am not doing this, I am not talking to you like this—"

"But, my dear, you already are—"

I ignore her. Keep walking. The sparrow extends its wings and flits away. A moment later I see a woman in a green cape walking purposefully towards me. A silk-lined bonnet encases her head.

"Better?" she asks.

"No! I can't talk to you right now. I'm *with* someone."

This chronometrist has an older face. Brown eyes, broad cheekbones, the complexion ruddy and porous. Her hands are covered with silk gloves. Her cape is fastened at the neck with a green brooch, masking her throat. She follows my gaze slyly to where Millie is standing, oblivious to the rest of the world.

"Oh, what a pretty skin..."

"Don't you dare. And don't pull that bird shit again."

"But I can't resist the feathers. So light! Delicious! Now why don't I go and get us a table and you can join me for coffee?"

It turns out I needn't have worried about Millie. When I return, she is still fully occupied by hats.

"Honey! Are you all right?" She grabs my elbow. "You've gone all perspiring. Do you need to sit down?"

"Millie." I clutch at her. "Do you see that woman sitting outside the brasserie over there?"

"In the green cape? Yes, I see her. What funny clothes she's wearing. Nobody's into green this season."

"Yes. Yes, her. *Her.* You can see her?"

"Of course I can see her. Why, do you know her? What is it, do you owe her money? Do we need to run? I know a back route."

"No, it's not that. I have to talk to her. Alone. I can't explain but it's important."

"I'll keep a watch, like the King's guard." Millie is excited. "I'll be right here. If you need me, you just holler."

"Thank you."

"But nice and loud," says Millie. "In case I'm distracted by the ribbons."

My feet are icy as I cross the road and join the chronometrist on the other side of the table.

"Any progress?" she asks.

"I'm working on it."

I pick up a menu, pretending to peruse its contents, but mainly because I cannot bear to look at her; I cannot bear to believe she is real. She *isn't* real, not in the way people are real. Human. She is something else.

"Time is ticking," she says. "Tick-tock, tick-tock."

"What exactly *are* you?"

"I used to be like you," she says. "Constrained to physical matter. Now I am free."

"Doesn't look like freedom to me."

"You're a gosling," she says affectionately. "You don't yet understand the power of the anomaly. What it can give you."

"You said each anomaly had an... an incumbent. So are there others? Like me?"

"There have been," she says. "There will be. I don't believe—there's anyone else in your early lifetime. Not active. Most are not so lucky as we two. They never meet their anomaly."

"Why do you want me to do this?"

Her gloved fingers tap idly against the table.

"I told you. Aesthetics are—integral, to me. Bad aesthetics—they pain me so."

"I don't believe you. I'm not sure I should be doing this. What if it affects something? What if I accidentally change history?"

The numbness is expanding. It's hard to keep my focus. But I've watched enough science fiction in my time to know that meddling does not end well. You end up killing your grandparents, or enabling tyrants through some diabolical side effect. It never works out how you intend.

"Well, my dear, if you don't—I assure you there will be *other* consequences." The chronometrist turns her head, looking once again in Millie's direction. There's a covetous expression on her face.

I stand and push back my chair.

"What are you doing?" She hurries after me.

"You said you had a range. I'm testing it."

"Don't be rash. We need to talk!"

She reaches for my arm but I brush her off and keep walking.

"Hallie—Hallie, my dear, wait—"

I keep walking.

After a while the calls cease. I stop and turn around. A woman in a green cape is standing on the pavement, looking about her in a very confused manner.

"That'll be it," I say to myself.

I make a mental note of the distance between here and the tavern—about five hundred metres. Now I know where to avoid.

CHAPTER TWENTY-TWO

IN THE EVENINGS, we go to work: regular citizens of the Third Republic. Millie goes to the Folies, or some other hall of entertainment, or to the secret apartments where her lovers stash their mistresses. I go to l'Éléphant, where I serve absinthe and perform fire-breathing for the after-hours crowd, while Millie's admirers draw up their seats. Back in Millie's garret, the two of us sleep back to back or curled up for warmth. The patterns of her breathing grow familiar, anticipated. I avoid the region surrounding the tavern and the chronometrist does not appear again.

Fabian gives me a set of training balls, traditional stuffed leather bags, because he is uncertain about the newfangled rubber variety. As my tuition progresses, I introduce other tricks to my act. I learn to use my face when I drop a ball. Accident, or intent? It's all a part of the show. Juggling is a constant series of readjustments to create an illusion of serenity: as long as you focus on what's going on above, you can't see the chaotic manoeuvrings underneath.

In a place where there are no smartphones, no digital clocks or ubiquitous references to the date, the days slip by faster than I think. I've been here for a month when something happens to shake me up.

* * *

MILLIE HEARS ABOUT it first. She comes into the tavern after a night at the Folies and I greet her with surprise, knowing she has an appointment with Valleroy. Then I look closer and see the distress in her face. Her admirers crowd around.

"What's wrong? What happened?"

It is a while before she can compose herself to speak.

"There's been a murder."

"Another one?"

"A woman," she says. "Stabbed, like the others. They found her outside the hat shop on boulevard de Clichy. I'd gone to get a bonnet. I saw... I saw her there. There was so much blood. On her arms, and her clothes. She had a green cape."

Her eyes meet mine across the crowd. Around me, the tavern seems to shrink, and the voices grow distant and jumbled. There's a rushing in my ears. Something is in motion. The anomaly, I think. I'm being pulled back in. My name's being called, from a long way away—*Gabriela!*—and then the scene steadies itself, the rushing subsides, and I'm stood behind the counter in l'Éléphant, a dishcloth in one hand, a tankard in the other.

A customer is calling for me. I ignore him and focus on Millie. She doesn't need to say anything else. She knows I have understood.

AFTER CLOSING TIME we sit in a corner of the tavern, a bottle of absinthe and two glasses between us.

"You knew her," says Millie. "You spoke to her."

"I didn't want to know her," I say, which is the truth, but does not answer the underlying question.

"Tell me."

"There's nothing to tell."

"You *knew* her. And now she's dead."

"Do you think I was involved?"

"No! I think you might be in danger. *I* might be in danger. What if it was the Ratter? What if we're next?"

"That won't happen."

"Then why can't you explain? I tell you things. There's nothing you don't know about me. But you've got secrets, Gabriela."

"Listen." I choose my words carefully. "I knew her from... back home. I didn't know her well. We had acquaintances in common. She was trouble. I hoped I'd never have to see her again."

"You won't now, will you?"

There's a sickness in my stomach when I think about what the chronometrist has done; the scene that Millie described, the lingering horror of it in her eyes. She'll carry that with her for the rest of her life. I don't know how the so-called murder was perpetuated, but I do know this: the chronometrist is not playing clean. This is a warning. Did she know Millie would be passing by that way? Did she engineer her finding the corpse?

"Millie," I say. "You know how in Bastille, you think you can hear the prisoners that were there? Like, their spirits?"

She shudders. "Don't."

"That woman. She was... haunted. As if she carried more than one life."

Millie looks at me. I can tell she isn't satisfied with my explanation. I think she is going to ask more questions, but instead she gives a hard little laugh, and raises her glass.

"To the dead," she says.

I clink. "To the dead."

UP ON THE hill, another four stones have joined the original boulder in the mud. The architect surveys his site with despairing eyes.

"Doesn't seem to be going too well," I comment.

"What's that? Oh, it's you. This project has been a ludicrous proposition from the start. One day we're building it, the next we're not. Now the money is there—now, there isn't enough money. Archbishop says go ahead, people say we don't want it. This is a city of madmen. It's no place for an architect."

"You really do need a change of direction," I say. "Think about it. These delays are a chance for you to reimagine the entire project. Come up with something truly magnificent."

The architect lowers his voice.

"As it happens, I have been plagued of late with visions for something a little... alternative."

"You have? What kind of visions?"

"It is of little consequence. The Archbishop will not brook any further delays."

"Don't give up so soon. He might be open-minded about it."

The architect frowns. One of the beautiful white stones, manoeuvring into position amidst grunts and swearing, has become caked in mud.

"You believe this is worth pursuing?"

"Everything is worth pursuing in the name of art," I say firmly.

"Perhaps I shall request a meeting."

"That sounds like an excellent plan."

The architect peers at me. "Weren't you a boy before?"

"These days I'm Gabriela."

I almost believe it. Try someone on for long enough, can you not become them? Occasionally I feel a flicker of guilt, remembering the real Gabriela back in the twenty-first century, but most days I am absorbed in the fascination of discovering another era. There are things I miss, things like hygiene and proper sanitation. Tooth paste. Hot showers. But these inconveniences are eclipsed by the novelty of my situation. However I have come to be here, I cannot deny there is something wondrous about finding myself in another century. I cannot pretend I am not glad for having come.

The next time I see the architect, he tells me a new design has been approved by the Archbishop.

"So what's the plan?" I ask.

"Oh my dear young—woman," he says. "Would you have me spoil the surprise? I'm afraid you'll just have to be patient."

"It's okay," I say. "I've got time."

CHAPTER TWENTY-THREE

A STREAM OF flames about me, the fall of the batons—one, two, three, four—into my waiting hands, regular, rhythmical, immersed in the hypnotic state of it. A soft sigh at my back. I turn slowly, my focus still with the tumbling batons, the subtle adjustments required for their safe return. Fabian is gone. A new presence fills the street, cold and watchful and malevolent. A man stands facing the tavern. Dress coat and hat, gloved hands curled around a cane, thin little greyhound at his feet. Lord Valleroy, Millie's patron. The man and the racing dog, as silent as one another, their eyes fixed on the door to the tavern.

Which has just closed upon another figure: this one stocky and heavyset, holding a club. Inside the tavern are Millie, the acrobats of the Folies, and the barmaids and regulars. I douse my batons in the nearby water barrel and follow the club bearer through the door.

I see him approach Millie, who is perched in the lap of a boy she was fluttering her lashes at earlier tonight. I see the club bearer lift his weapon and swing it. I hear a crack, a scream, see the boy's head snap back, the force of the blow tumbling him and Millie to the floor. I can't see anything else, I can't see how badly the boy is hurt, or if he will ever get up again, because just then the place erupts.

In the moments that follow the attack it is as if I am still juggling, a step removed from the events unfolding in front of me. I see it in detail. A retaliatory fist glances off the head of the club bearer and lands on an adjacent shoulder. The victim yells and swipes at her assailant, and her friend joins in, and the club bearer is staggering, trying to sight the one who struck him in the first place, mistakes his quarry and swings again. A man lifts a chair and hefts it in the club bearer's direction. The chair crashes down upon a table, smashing a dozen glasses.

A sharp, eerie ringing. The smell of aniseed soaks the room.

The fight resumes.

A tankard flies toward me, breaking the spell. I duck. The missile skims my hair and slams into the counter behind my head, denting it. I crawl under the nearest table, frantically scouting for Millie. I have to get her out. Millie is the target. This is Valleroy's doing. I have to get her out.

I crawl out from under the table and plunge into the melee. Blows catch me as I shoulder my way across the room. I see Millie whirling a candlestick holder above her head. Her dress is spattered with blood. I don't know if it's hers.

"Millie!"

"Gabriela!"

We fight our way towards one another. A hand lifts me by the neck, fully clear of the floor. I reach overhead and jab my thumbs into my attacker's face and he drops me at once. I scramble up, grab a tankard and bash the man over the head. It is the club bearer— the henchman. He reels back, temporarily dazed. I have seconds. I squeeze between two wrestling men, dart around a woman clinging limpet-like to a man's back whilst beating him with an ornamental bust, and find Millie's hand. Her palm is wet, sticky.

"The back door! Quick!"

Millie glances behind her. I see the boy, inert on the floor, a section of his skull inverse to its natural shape. The sight freezes me.

"Killed," says Millie hoarsely.

I tear my gaze away and pull her through the brawl. Behind us, the landlord roars for order. Small fires are starting where candles have been knocked over.

We slip through the back door. Outside the night is cold and empty, the alley black as pitch. I put a finger over Millie's lips and lead her deeper into the alley. They are out there somewhere, the man and the dog, and the dog can smell.

As we move away from the tavern, the sound of the brawl fades and the silence grows more colossal. Every noise causes my heart to clench. Millie's breathing is laboured. She is struggling not to cry. I squeeze her hand, tug, quicken both our footsteps.

Is that the skitter of claws on cobbles, the tap of a cane?

If I die in 1875, no one will ever discover what became of me. I'll be as anonymous as the Communards piled into their communal coffins. I won't be remembered.

Suddenly that matters.

We reach a stone wall, and I stirrup my fingers and hoist Millie up. Her petticoats rustle when they snag. She steadies herself, and reaches down to give me a hand. On the other side I feel safer. Still we creep, through the lightless night, the air a chill silk against our bare arms and necks, the fear of pursuit at our heels like ghosts or goblins or some other thing without name from below the earth. A dog barks. We start to run, fingers interlocked. We run blind, fleeing through winding streets and narrow alleys, running all the way until we reach the Seine. The river glimmers beneath a waning moon that flows in and out of cloud. We run over a bridge. Murmurs follow us, homeless and night dwellers roused from their slumber. I tug Millie's hand. *Come on. Come on, my Millie. Not far now. Not far.* The words, low and urgent, for both of us. Millie stumbles through her tears. They fall unchecked, hot salt splatters down her cheeks.

I lead us home. Now I can hear nothing behind us, and this

frightens me more: what if the man and the dog have gone ahead, travelling swiftly by carriage, and even now they lie in wait? There is no light from the building. I shush Millie, give her a handkerchief to wipe her dripping nose. I motion we should take off our shoes. We tiptoe up the flights of stairs. We can hear moaning from visitors to the brothel next door, but from the occupants in this block, there is nothing. All sleeping. All unaware, nestled in the coils of their dreams.

Outside Millie's room we stop, and I run my hands over the door. No signs of a forced entry that I can detect. I put my ear to the wood and listen.

"Give me the key, Millie."

I let us in.

I hear a scrabble of claws across the floor. Millie screams.

"Millie, it's all right. It's a rat, just a rat."

I light a candle. I cannot bear to remain in the dark. Millie throws herself on the bed and lets her sobs flow freely. I hold her. I say something, I don't know what. Her breathing clogs with mucous and sobs. I hold her. Eventually she is still. I think exhaustion must have lulled her to sleep, but then she says, "I should see who I like."

I wait.

"I should see who I like, shouldn't I? It's like you said. My lovers are my concern. I'm not a thing to be owned. But now he's dead. Luc."

"I'm so sorry, Millie."

"Maybe it was Valleroy killed the others. The women."

"I don't think it's him."

"Why not? He killed Luc."

"Try and get some sleep."

The candle gutters. I see again the boy's head, blood and matter, the shocking intrusion to the skull. I think I will be awake through the night, but I must doze, because the next thing I know, a pale grey light is creeping through the shutters, and birds are calling on the rooftops.

I lie still. Beside me, Millie's face is half buried in the pillow, the visible side blotched and crumpled. Something has changed. I think it is the violence of last night, a boy Millie barely knew murdered for a rich man's whimsy. But it is more than that.

Then I realise. The anomaly is awake, and it is singing to me.

CHAPTER TWENTY-FOUR

"YOU CAN'T LEAVE me, you can't! Valleroy is crazy, you saw what he did to Luc!"

I hurry towards the boulevard as fast as I can walk in these absurd nineteenth century skirts. Millie runs after me, clinging to my arm.

"Millie, I'm sorry, but there's nothing you can say—"

It's humming. I can sense it. In the air and through tremors in the earth. Running in rivers beneath my feet. A flare, seismic, a volcano about to erupt.

"Gabriela, this isn't fair! I helped you out, now I'm in trouble—"

"You're going to be fine. You're strong, clever... I'm not worried about you. I know you'll be all right."

"Gabriela—"

"My name's not Gabriela. You shouldn't call me that."

"I don't understand—"

This is it. This is the cornerstone of Clichy. Here is the highway of carts and carriages and pedestrians and servants scuttling with heavy loads, where in a century or so there will be a monument to Marilyn Monroe. Across the road, the tavern: my final obstacle. I am responding to a call, an instinct, something primitive in its simplicity.

I'm coming.

Wait for me.

Millie tries to hold me back as I cross the road. A horse and carriage veer away from us. The driver's whip snakes out and catches our skirts; he yells, "Imbeciles!"

In the alleyway by the tavern, a woman is waiting. Narrow, aristocratic face, pointed chin, a flash of green in the lining of her bonnet.

"You," I say resignedly.

The chronometrist twirls her parasol between two gloved hands. Her lips part in a wide smile, displaying her teeth. The expression looks uncomfortable.

"Good to see you, my dear. I would have warned you—about the flare, but you've been avoiding me."

"I did what you asked."

"You did. You did. And now—it's time to go."

Millie stares at us.

"Gabriela? Who is this?"

"Gabriela?" The chronometrist lifts one delicate eyebrow. "That's what you go by, is it?" She turns to Millie. "I'm deeply sorry—for your loss, my dear. Would you like me to kill the perpetrator?"

I jump. "What?"

But Millie at my side is straightening, peering through her tears.

"Yes," she whispers.

"No! What the hell are you saying?"

"He's a murderer," says the chronometrist.

"Yes." Millie is nodding. So is she, I want to say, but cannot, because what kind of questions will that raise?

The chronometrist edges closer. I place myself between her and Millie, but she reaches past me, wipes a tear from Millie's face. Millie shudders.

"Just say the word," says the chronometrist. And to me, "She wants this. You can see that. She wants revenge. Will you deny her?"

"Enough," I hiss.

The chronometrist looks as though she is about to respond, but something stops her. She tips her head to one side, listening.

"It's almost here," she says. "Better hurry."

Abruptly, she turns and bustles down the alleyway, her parasol tap-tapping the ground as she goes. I stare after her. My heart is knotted in my chest. But then it returns in force. The anomaly's song. She's right. There isn't much time.

"Millie—"

"You can't go, you can't," sobs Millie, but her protests are quieter now.

I take both of her hands in my own. Millie's tearstained face before me, her brunette wig knocked askew. I reach to straighten it.

"My dear Millie. I can't explain. You've got to believe me when I say there is no choice. Something is going to happen now. I'll walk into that tavern, I'll go down into the cellar, and I won't come out again."

"What is it? Is there a tunnel down there?"

"It's like a tunnel."

"Are you a revolutionary? Are you going back into exile? I'll protect you. I can protect us both. I can come with you!"

"That's not possible. You've got your whole life here."

"I'll be on my own."

I pull her into a hug.

"No..."

I remember something Gabriela said, once upon a time; that houses are full of traces. Like dust motes in sunshine, these traces are only visible at certain angles. They are the shadows of people who lived before us. The fingerprints of visitors who passed by for an afternoon, the material on a favoured chair worn to a shine. Each touch leaves its trail of atoms. And houses harbour, too, the premonitions of things desired and things that are yet to come; the families we may create, the friends we may meet, the lovers whose bodies we may one day embrace. And so, says Gabriela, a house is never really empty, and you are never truly alone.

Don't be afraid, I say to Millie. Don't be afraid of the traces.

"But—"

"I should go now. If you want to help me, I'll need a distraction. And there's no one better than you at distractions."

"True." Millie swipes a defiant hand across her eyes. "I'm mighty good at that."

"I'll miss you, Millie."

"Will I ever see you again?"

"I don't know."

As I sneak through the tavern, I am aware of Millie covering my tracks: standing on a table bold as brass, shooting wisecracks from her soft-lipped, slightly crooked mouth. Her large, raucous laugh echoed by the men drinking, by Anne-Marie's indignant wrath.

Millie is Jessica Rabbit. She is Faye Dunaway in diagonal rain.

I slip behind the curtain. I climb down a wooden ladder into a cellar that smells of sawdust and apples. I can feel the anomaly closing around me. My head throbs. My vision blurs to red. The flare is due, any minute it's going to take me, coast me out of 1875 and into—

I sit up. I feel terrible, cold and clammy and racked with tremors. I check the line on the keg, just to be sure. It's Kronenberg. Definitely a keg, definitely the twenty-first century, and that's the line I was sent down to change, so I haven't even been gone—

"Hallie! Bring a crate of Smirnoff Ice when you're done in there—and move it!"

—very long. Very long at all.

"J'arrive!" I call back to Eloise. I need a minute to recover, more than a minute, but Eloise is not interested in what I say, only in what I do. Shakily, I hoist a crate of Smirnoff Ice up on my hip. On the stairs I pass Kit. He looks me up and down. He winks.

"What's that get-up in aid of, Hallie? Rehearsing for Dracula?"

I glance down. Looped around my waist is the little leather pouch I always carry, with its five juggling balls. I am still wearing petticoats.

PART FIVE

The Moulin Vert

CHAPTER TWENTY-FIVE

"THE FACT IS in ten years' time the only people who can afford to live here will be Russian oligarchs and billionaires who piss oil."

"In ten years' time?" Dušanka scoffs. "You are the optimist, Angel. Already half the city is empty for ninety per cent of the year. The rest of us, we live in broom cupboards like skinny rats hoping for a crumb of cheese."

"You should come live in Sweden," says Bo. "There is plenty of space in Sweden."

"Bon oui, but you're all white there," says Angel.

"Actually there is quite a high Middle Eastern population these days, even before the crisis in Syria."

"And it is fucking cold."

"Cold, yes, though summer on the coast is very pleasant. But think of the sledging!"

"When the earth's temperature rises past two degrees and all the snow melts, you will have no economy from your winter sports, and what then?" drawls Dušanka.

"I will show you a good time in Sweden," promises Bo, and Mike says, "I bet you will," which is a foolhardy response given Dušanka's current levels of antagonism, but it's Christmas and everyone is very merry, and for this reason Mike escapes unnoticed.

"I don't want to talk about Sweden, I want to talk about the fact that this country is going to shit," says Angel.

"Oui, oui, c'est vrai." Victor nods, and drains another glass of Malbec.

"Can't be worse than England," I volunteer.

"Yes, let us have a competition," says Dušanka, becoming excited. "Who has the most shit country?"

Mike groans. "Man, seriously? You call that a competition?"

"Don't be too sure of yourself, Mike. Hallie's country, for example, is currently engaged in the act of economic seppuku. But it is true that the orange pussy-grabber gives you an unfair advantage. We will remove national leaders from the equation. You, Hallie, go."

"Me? Okay, um—where do I start? The NHS is being torn apart, austerity is literally killing people, we've got a government full of delusional clowns who hate anyone under twenty-five, we refuse to pull our weight in the refugee crisis, and we're the laughing stock of Europe—in fact I've probably got about a year before France kicks me out. How's that?"

"Quite shit. Angel. Victor."

"Bah, this is hardly a competition. France has Front national at one end, radicalisation at the other—"

"Refugees camping in tents this very moment and the government it is pretending they do not exist—"

"Children can't read or write, though they are probably lazy too—"

"And fat—"

"Taxation laws are complètement fou—"

"Corruption—"

"Homelessness—"

"Vineyards failing—"

"Mon dieu, the vineyards!"

"Yes, yes, vive la France, that's enough from you two—"

"We have more!" shouts Angel, but Dušanka overrules him.

"Mike. Keep it short, we all know your country's sins are many and diabolical."

"Chicago's a great city," Mike protests.

"Incorrect."

"Yeah but, Illinois, it's like a totally different country to the south."

"What a shame you didn't notice that before you federalized yourselves," says Dušanka sweetly.

"Okay, okay. Jesus. If you have to include the south, hell, I got creationists, abortion rights, white supremacists, kids shooting up schools because half the country's in the pocket of the NRA. I got the surveillance state. I got police with a free pass to murder anyone who looks like me or Angel in case we're terrorists, though that's like, everywhere. War, helluva lot of war."

"A fuckton of war," agrees Angel.

"Man, I miss Obama."

"Don't we all, poulet."

"Yogi!"

"We've got crocs and snakes and spiders and shit," says Yogi enthusiastically.

"That is not the point, Yogi. You should have said your country is full of racists and has recently deified coal. Bo. Forget your default Sweden-is-the-greatest-democracy setting, we all know you get better paternity leave than anywhere else."

"Actually the rise of the right in Sweden is quite frightening. Here it is Front national, at home we have Sweden Democrats. The government's refugee policy has stirred things up."

"Gabriela?"

Gabriela shakes her head. "My god. You ask about Colombia?"

"All right, you are excused. However, Russia wins because fundamentally we don't believe in human rights. Shots!"

*   *   *

ALL OF THE bartenders who haven't dispersed for Christmas have congregated at Bo's. Mike says the air fares are too high to justify a trip to the States, and Gabriela is staying for the same reason. Simone would have preferred Christmas in Clichy, but was sent a Thalys ticket and a financial ultimatum in the post. Léon is in Montpellier. Eloise has gone back to Amsterdam to gaze upon the face of her beloved canals and decide whether her life has gone terribly wrong or terribly right. At the last minute Dušanka, crackling with anti-festive glee, announced that she too would be remaining in Paris, and who was going to be cooking?

Bo has been sent a parcel from Sweden. He unwraps the foil package with a flourish, and we all peer at a round lump of meat.

Dušanka pokes it. "What is this?"

"Tjälknul." Bo is triumphant. He rotates the plate, displaying its singular contents. "In English you call it elk." He looks at Mike. "That's moose to you. The dish was invented by mistake. The chef put the meat in the oven on low heat to thaw, and forgot about it. The next day he remembered again, and discovered a delicious treat."

Angel shudders. "Surely this is inedible?"

"No! Just tear bits off or eat it with bread." Bo leads by example, licking his fingers. "Ah, I have missed this."

Bo had been in Paris now for a year. One night, between manoeuvres, on his year of military service, cold and bored and raked by the Scandinavian wind, Bo had stared up at the skies and had an epiphany. For too long, he had lived his life in safety. The time had come for wild abandonment. Since then Bo had travelled frenziedly, amassing a considerable carbon footprint that occasionally, but not always, caused him great twinges of guilt. But there were still occasions when he missed Sweden. And elk.

One by one we sample his offering. Angel refrains from spitting, the rest of us chew with enthusiasm. Then the cooking commences. Gabriela prepares tamales, Dušanka makes kutya. Mike brings unbaked cookie dough and Victor is dispatched with a fistful of euros to the local cave on wine sourcing duties. I bake scones, to be served thick with jam and cream. As I slide them off the baking tray, admiring the perfect golden glaze, created by the exact amount of egg white (pastry, after all, is a science), Dušanka waves a copy of *A Brief History of Time* in my face.

"Hallie, Hallie. Why are you reading this shit?"

"Did you just take that out of my handbag?"

"Of course not," says Dušanka innocently. "It must have fallen out."

Dinner is followed by cards and whisky. The air in Bo's apartment grows close and heady, and we crowd on to the balcony, where the cool night tingles against our faces. We shout at people passing in the street below and they shout back:

"Joyeux Noël!"

Back inside, slumped variously on sofas, beanbags or the floor, Angel passes round a spliff.

"Poussins. What are we going to do about the state of the world?"

"This is the internet generation," sighs Dušanka. "Sign a petition, Angel, it will appease your conscience for at least a week."

"I'm serious. There's a Moulin Vert rally in a fortnight. I will go. You should all come."

"Moulin Vert?" Victor scratches at his jawline. "That's not a proper party."

"Just give them time."

"Aren't those guys communists?" asks Mike. "Don't they want to pull down the Eiffel Tower because it's like an ode to the patriarchy?"

Dušanka's eyes light up, ready to respond, but Gabriela places a gently restraining hand on her arm.

"Just come to one," Angel persists. "Listen to what they have to say. We can joke all night, but Paris is a tinder box. We need people like them, and more than ever since the attacks."

Everyone falls silent for a moment.

"Where is it?" asks Bo.

"At the Moulin Vert, of course. Right on top of the hill."

Across the room, I catch Gabriela's eye. Now she is sending her calming vibes in my direction, but all I can feel is growing panic.

"I'll come," she says. "Hallie?"

I glare at her. What the hell?

"We must all of us face our fears," says Gabriela, cryptically—to everyone in the room except me. I think of the conversation we had just a fortnight ago, in the keg room.

"So." Gabriela raps the metal door. The sound is dull and flat. "This is the place?"

I nod. Touch my fingertips to the door.

"Sometimes, it feels kind of warm..."

Not today. Today it is cold.

Ever since what I term in my head as 'the 1875 incident', I have avoided changing kegs or bringing up stock. I make excuses to the managers, or I'm quick to volunteer for other tasks. I don't know *what's* lurking in the keg room, and I don't know how I feel about it. I haven't seen the chronometrist since she bid me farewell in the alleyway.

Gabriela knows. I told her I was good with secrets, and I wasn't lying, but one of this magnitude? I can't keep this to myself. She wants to investigate. For a while I fended off her curiosity, but Gabriela is stubborn, and she knew that it was only a matter of time before I succumbed.

I lift the bar across the keg room door, push it open and step inside.

The rush of cold air brings goose pimples to my arms. Gabriela gives me a nudge to propel me further inside and then steps past, eager to look around.

I force myself to survey the room scientifically. A dank, concrete cavern, just as I saw it on my first day. To my left, crates of lager and alcopops stacked on shelves. Further along, the door to the lift, metal and rusting. To my right, the room opens out to encompass the beer posts, each station comprising five or six opaque tubes hooked up to their kegs. Spares in front, empties by the door. Somewhere in the room there is a leak; a shallow pool of water spreads from one wall. I can hear dripping.

I climb up on a keg and put my ear against the wall. Silence. This is definitely concrete. Mixed by a machine and poured into the ground, stifling the hum of earth and stone and fossil. We're sealed off down here, I think. Sealed in.

Drip drip. Drip drip.

"What are you doing?" Gabriela's voice, bright and curious, interrupts my chain of thought.

"Nothing. Just listening. For clues, I suppose."

I rub my arms. "Can you show me how to change the Guinness again? I always struggle with that."

Gabriela obliges good-naturedly. I watch as she turns off the gas, gives the cap a wrench and disconnects the line.

"Always remember to close it first. Otherwise the beer will jump at you."

She drags the empty out the way, and I manoeuvre a full one into its place.

"Now twist it back on." Gabriela perches on an upturned crate and watches me in turn. "Open the line. Check the little ball in the measure—see that it floats to the top. That is it."

"Thanks."

Gabriela stays put.

"Did you see anything?" she asks. "Any... clues?"

"Not really." I pause.

Gabriela looks at me expectantly.

"You?" I ask.

"No. It is the same keg room."

"You don't notice anything different?"

"No." Gabriela taps her fingers against the keg. "But I believe you."

I shiver. Recently I have been struggling to sleep. I lie awake with the shutters open and the winter sun bright and strong, listening to the street below, to my neighbours moving about the apartments around me, thinking about 1875. Sometimes I wake and the warmth convinces me there is someone beside me, that Millie is here, that I never left 1875. Did I really travel through time? If my attacks have taught me one thing, it is that I cannot trust the machinations of my brain. Surely it is more likely that I am the victim of a psychological delusion, that I fell into a coma and dreamed it, or more simply, that I made the whole thing up? Yet Gabriela believes me.

"The anomaly can't be a singularity," I say. "And it's not a black hole. I've been thinking about multiverses..."

"What if there is not a scientific explanation? What if it's..." She hesitates.

"What?"

"Magic."

"I don't think so."

"You know, Hallie, sometimes you are too English for your own good."

"And you've read too much Márquez."

"Actually, I prefer Borges."

"You really don't remember the Sacré-Coeur?" I say, for the hundredth time.

For a moment, Gabriela looks thoughtful, even confused. Then her expression clears.

"Only the Moulin Vert," she agrees. "It has been there for over a century."

"You know most people would think you're mad to believe me."

"I have the open mind. Anyway, it has to be linked to my problem. You travelling, me not travelling—it is all the same source. There is something about Clichy that is causing these events." Gabriela gives the keg room a final glance. "And this place, it is the key."

I nod, although I don't believe the anomaly has anything to do with Gabriela's failure to get back to Colombia. The chronometrist said there is one incumbent for each anomaly, so how could it affect anyone else? Gabriela could quite easily go home, if she really wanted to. Ultimately, it's easier for her to believe she is trapped then to face up to the fact that she doesn't want to leave. But I don't say any of this. She is indulging me, so I have to indulge her.

"Maybe," I say. "Maybe so."

LATER, DRUNKER. WE take turns inventing cocktails. Gabriela juggles ice. Two centuries ago I was juggling fire batons and a boy told me he had seen my future. Isn't this it? I look at everyone in the room: Gabriela, Angel, Bo, Dušanka, Mike, Victor, Yogi Millis. One person is missing; but I try not to think about Léon. I look at their befuddled, happy faces. Whatever our reasons for coming to Paris, all that matters is that we are here, a family. We are home.

This summer gone in Sussex was a dry, sweltering three months. The water ban turned the weeds yellow and sour whilst indoors, the house festered. Theo and George were back and forth on trips to London, embarking jubilant with schemes and ambitions and returning listless, deflated, their plans shot down by some despised capitalist with a spreadsheet. My father had given up entirely on his work and spent all of his evenings with Ray Yellowlees. My mother had begun collecting vermin for a new installation. She was in a cycle of manic production and profound despair, and refused to speak to any of us.

Over those weeks I could feel myself being slowly eroded, worn down until I could barely remember who I was or what I stood for. It was the culmination of a very long process, but I was only recognising that now.

I remember waiting outside the locked bathroom, where Theo had been in the shower for over an hour with the water running and the water suppliers threatening to cut us off, singing.

I'm light as a bird on the wing, free as a butterfly. Letting go of all those things you said on days gone by.

She has a nice voice, my sister, full and confident. At that moment I wanted nothing more than to rip her larynx out of her throat and ensure she never sang again. The shower stopped running, but Theo continued. *And now I'm flying high, she sang. And now I'm flying highhhh, oo-oo-oo-oh—*

The hairdryer switched on, drowning Theo out. I could feel the panic slithering in, the way it always did. An attack had been looming all day. I wouldn't escape it. I never could. My chest began to contract as the air around me thinned.

But there was an alternative. Theo had told me what the alternative was: I could leave it all behind. I could slough off this confused, anxious, uncertain creature I had become and leave her on the landing in Sussex.

Start over. Become weightless. Become new.

ANGEL FLINGS THE cocktail shaker over-enthusiastically and the top flies off and out the open window, a parabola of green liquid following in its wake. We dissolve into helpless giggles. Victor opens the cognac and dribbles it into our open mouths, before collapsing into Bo's lap. Bo starts to sing something in Swedish. Dušanka's arm is linked through mine. Gabriela is plaiting my hair. We all shout 'skål' at precisely the wrong time.

At two in the morning the buzzer goes. Bo answers.

"Ja?" He turns back. "It's Léon!"

"Léon!" shouts Angel. "That putain de merde. I thought he was in Montpellier."

"I was, mes petits choux," says a familiar voice. "I decided to come back early."

His eyes meet mine over Angel's shoulder; his mouth kinks in a smile. Something tightens in my chest, pleasantly anticipatory, before he turns away. For the rest of the night we barely speak. But I am aware of his presence in the room, his gestures a counterpoint to mine, impossible to ignore. And through the cycles of conversation and ribald laughter I have—not a premonition, exactly—more of a sense that I should record this moment. I should bottle it and store it safe, because there may come a day when this moment—

But it is just a moment. Like any other through time, it is here, and then it is gone.

CHAPTER TWENTY-SIX

THE MILLIE'S THEME for New Year's Eve is superheroes. Gabriela is Batman and I am the Joker, with a purple waistcoat and lipstick slashed across my face. Crates of Moët are shipped in; the managers compete over who can devise the most eclectic champagne shots. The DJ is so drunk he misses midnight and a countdown goes around forty minutes late. It doesn't matter, at least not to the New Year revellers: the dance floor is pounding.

Eloise sends me to fetch more Moët. The second I open up the keg room I know it is happening. There's a rush of amniotic warmth, the siren song floods my ears and I go under.

I surface in another timezone. The kegs are gone and there is a party underway, a wilder and substantially less clothed party than Millie's in the twenty-first century. One man is down to his underwear and a flapper girl's headdress. A blonde woman sits half-naked, her breasts jutting between a pair of red braces, smoking a cigar. No one appears to notice my astonishing appearance, but within moments of arriving I have a bottle of absinthe in one hand and a top hat balanced upon my head. The revellers raise their glasses; they holler, they toast:

"A dix-neuf vingt!"

I drink. My head explodes into stars. A whirling green spiral rotates on the backs of my eyelids.

And they're gone. So fast! I am in the keg room with a crate of

Moët at my feet. It is freezing. I hoist the crate and head back up to the bar. My head aches but I feel pumped full of energy, alive and glowing in every cell. I grab Gabriela.

"Nineteen-twenty. Nineteen-twenty!"

"You travelled?"

The room thrums with bass. I have to shout to hear myself.

"They gave me absinthe!"

"Who?"

"I don't know!"

"Cool!"

Gabriela vaults up on the back bar and reaches down a hand to help me up. A flashback: Millie and I, scrambling over the wall. Millie and I, running. But I'm not there. We stand above the sea of bodies. Lights swivel overhead, illuminating faces, dazed and beatific, arms swaying with the anthemic beat. 1920? On the bar next to me, Angel has removed his trousers and shirt and parades up and down in his boxers. Dušanka hoses him with soda water. The crowd screams. Dušanka hoses the crowd.

Four in the morning. My hearing is fuzzy, my vision peculiar and speckled with green, the bass lodged in my sternum, rattling me senseless. Gabriela croons in my ear.

"Feliz Año Nuevo!"

I inhale absinthe fumes. I can feel myself lifting, up, above the crowd, above the lights. Gabriela shouts it again.

"Feliz Año Nuevo!"

"You're the best of friends," I tell her. "The very, very best."

"And you, my Hallie. The dearest." She raises my arm. We are champions. "We are going to have a brilliant year."

In Oz at eight a.m. we find Angel collapsed over the bar, limbs improbably sprawled, head limp and nodding. He is stirring a tumbler of poison green liquid with a glowstick, regarding both the liquid and the rotating stick with equal fascination.

"Didn't make it home?" I ask. Angel gives me a confused grin. I take up the adjacent bar stool.

"This Léon is a putain de..." Angel descends into incomprehensible French. He attempts to gather up a flotilla of shot glasses and sends them rolling down the bar. I reach over to form a barrier. From the other side of the taps, Léon's hand appears and scoops up the glasses.

"Merci, chérie."

He mops up the mess in front of Angel.

"Courage, mon ami. Courage."

"J'ai besoin de toi," mutters Angel, and promptly falls off his chair.

"That is one hell of a hangover when he wakes up," says Léon. "What time is he on?"

"He's opening the bar at twelve." Eloise makes no attempt to disguise her annoyance. "What have you done to him?"

"Nothing that hasn't been done before."

Bo and Isobel drag Angel into a booth and prop him up. He gives a dizzy smile and passes out.

"How was your new year?" I ask Léon.

"About as good as it can be when you're holding up a girl's hair while she vomits into the gutter," he says. "How about you?"

I feel an illogical stab of jealousy over vomit-girl.

"The DJ missed midnight," I say.

"He does that every year. It's a lost cause."

"Every year? How long have you been in Clichy, anyway?"

"Too long."

Voices raised, a crash from behind me. I turn and see a man sprawled on the floor, another man standing over him with his fist raised. I think of Luc in 1875, and I freeze. The first man gets to his feet and lunges at his attacker. The bouncer looks over from his post by the door, but before he can move, Léon has vaulted the bar and intercepted the two men. He speaks in rapid French until the first man backs away, hands before him. The bouncer jerks his head: *out*. The man makes as if to leave, then turns and swings a punch at Léon. I gasp, but next thing I know he's on the floor and Léon has a knee in his back. The bouncer ambles over, levers the man to his feet, grabs both aggressors by their collars and hoists them out into the morning. Everyone cheers.

Léon returns to the bar and pours me a champagne shot as if nothing has happened. I stare at him.

"What was that, karate?"

"Tae kwon do."

"Are you, like, a black belt or something?"

"I trained." He looks at me thoughtfully, though as usual it's impossible to tell what he's thinking. "It's important to be able to defend yourself. You never know where you might end up."

You have no idea, I think.

"Maybe you could teach me."

"Perhaps."

"I was thinking—" I hesitate, but inebriation pushes me on. "I was thinking maybe we could go for a drink some time."

He pauses.

"That might not be a good idea. You know what Clichy is like. People talk."

"Oh. Right, of course. Sorry."

The heat rushes to my face. With every second that passes I can feel myself shrivelling with embarrassment. *You complete and utter idiot, Hallie.*

"Hey." He pushes the shot glass towards me. "Bonne année."

"Yeah. You too."

I stumble away and join Gabriela. It is very late, I realise. The sun is up, casting bright lines across the filthy floor. It must be time to leave. From outside comes the sound of petrol engines, footsteps, the rumble of a city waking up. New month, new year. The footprint of the real world. It comes to me, very strongly, that what we think of as the real world is not; that the hours of night and dreams are more real than the day. I put my arm around Gabriela's shoulders and we pick up one another's coats. Gabriela calls: "Bo, Dušanka! On y va! Eloise, you coming?" Eloise shakes her head, indicating Angel. I glance towards the bar, thinking even now Léon might give me some indication, that I might not have got it so wretchedly wrong. But he isn't looking at us as we lurch into the day.

NEW YEAR'S DAY. My studio is cold and silent. I have no memory of getting home and my head feels as blank as snow. I try to remember the last time it snowed in December. I can't. Seasons have become the trappings of another era, long ago: one less confused, more certain.

I put on my coat and woollens and go out. The wind is vicious. By the end of the road I am chilled and shivering, but I keep walking. I follow the métro south: Saint Georges, Grand Boulevard, Opéra. At Pyramides I gaze into the brightly-lit window displays, their contents glamorous and costly. I look at jewellery and couture suits, at gold-tinted mirrors and handcrafted furniture. The trappings of beautiful lives for beautiful people. For the non-resident residents of Paris. I walk past the Louvre. The pyramid glows silver-blue, reflecting stray tourists and their cameras. I walk along the river, hands balled in my pockets. Seagulls fly or are thrown by the wind; bleak, pointed, swirling shapes, their cries thin and reedy. Over the wall, the surface of the Seine is turbulent.

I walk until it is dark. I find myself back in Montmartre. My feet are taking me up, and up, and up.

Here, finally, is my proof that it was all real. Sacré-Coeur is gone. Looming over the hill, awkward and ostentatious, stands a colossal green windmill. The eight arms stretch outwards, as if seeking to engulf the residents of Montmartre. I can hear the slow, ominous creaks of their rotation, the sails struggling on century-old mechanics.

The Moulin Vert.

The chronometrist had better be happy.

To my surprise, I'm not the only one standing out in the freezing cold. A few tourists are dotted about, and a group of Parisians huddle together on the steps. Someone is plucking at a guitar but the sound is mostly swallowed by the wind.

As I stand gazing up at the windmill of my making, a young woman in a headscarf approaches. She holds out a flyer.

"Join us, sister."

"Oh, no, thanks," I respond automatically, but she pushes the leaflet into my hand.

"Take a look."

I scan the flyer. In the top right corner is a stylized logo of a little green windmill. I realize that this is the movement Angel was talking about, the movement allegedly inspired by the monstrous piece of architecture above us. The flyer is printed in bold text. I read slowly, translating as I go.

**Capitalism has created global inequality
on an unprecedented scale.
Climate change is killing our planet.
The 1% are taking our cities and growing fat.
Hatemongerers make our neighbours into our enemies.
We live in fear. We have forgotten hope.
But there is another way.
Join us.**

Then there's a date.

The young woman smiles at me, bright and fearless.

"We're all brothers and sisters in this world. Time we started to act like it, don't you think? Join us, sister."

"Yeah. Yeah, I'll... I'll think about it."

She smiles again, turns, walks away. The Moulin Vert creaks, its sails turning. Overhead, flakes of snow begin to fall, blotting the thin paper in my hand.

CHAPTER TWENTY-SEVEN

JANUARY IN CLICHY: sober and freezing. Four hours dark when I start my shift at nine, the sky still hooded when I leave at seven. My hands are chapped and numb and cannot be trusted not to drop things. I crouch by the dishwasher and bathe my face in the steam. I listen for the anomaly's friendly warmth.

I come home one morning to find Léon outside my apartment block, standing in the sleet and clutching a bag of choquettes and a bottle of Brouilly. Beads of slush are dotted over his woollen coat. He looks freezing. I stop, keys in hand.

"This is getting to be a habit," I say. I'm surprised to see him. Since that humiliating episode on New Year's Eve I've stayed away from Oz, and Léon hasn't been sighted at Millie's either. I assumed we were avoiding each other.

"I thought about what you said," he says.

"What I said?"

"At New Year."

"Look, I was really drunk, forget about it—"

"You see, I have a rule about... Clichy. Not to get involved. It complicates things."

"It's just a drink," I say.

"It's never just a drink," he says. We stare at each other for a moment. I wish I could tell what is going on behind that face.

"Come in. It's far too cold to talk out here."

The lift is broken again. We traipse up the five flights of stairs. The stairwell is narrow and I'm intensely conscious of Léon walking behind me. My thighs are burning by the time we reach the top.

Inside the flat, I put the kettle on.

"Cup of tea?"

"Do you have coffee?"

"Sure."

I open the shutters, although at this time of year it barely makes a difference. A flat grey light enters the room. Outside, sleet continues to fall, melting on car tops and umbrellas. We sit awkwardly, Léon taking the beanbag, me cross-legged on the floor.

"I brought you something," says Léon.

He hands me a book. It's a history of Paris, a beautiful hardback with several sets of photographic plates.

"I read it over Christmas. The section on World War Two is especially good. I thought you might like it, after we talked that time."

"Thank you." I examine the plates. There's the Moulin Rouge, its terrace packed with men in grey-green uniforms. "It's so weird to think this is what our grandparents lived through."

Something flickers in his face.

"Were yours…?" I ask tentatively.

"They survived the war. Well, obviously, or I wouldn't be here. But they never spoke about it. A lot of what happened… it isn't talked about much, even now."

"I can't imagine living through something like that."

"Hopefully you'll never have to."

"But it's frightening, isn't it? The attacks that happened here— Charlie Hebdo, the stadium—there's so much anger." I shake my head. "I know Clichy's a bubble. But we can't ignore this stuff."

I get up, searching for the flyer I was given on New Year's Day, and find it on the floor by my bed. I pass it to Léon.

"This is what Angel was talking about at Christmas. The Moulin Vert people."

He reads it slowly.

"Do you think they could be a good thing?" I ask.

"I think their intentions are good."

"Yes." I take a sip of tea. A car passes in the street below, a wave of music rising briefly and tailing away. "Can I ask you something? Have you ever done something that has... unintended consequences?"

"I think you'll find that's called la vie."

"I don't mean little things. I mean... something big."

"Yes."

"How did it work out? In the end?"

"I guess I'm still working on that."

I focus on his hands, brown fingers wrapped around the mug. I remember the way he took down that drunk man. It occurs to me that Léon is protecting himself in every conceivable way. Perhaps he, too, is trying to escape something.

"Why did you talk to me, that day in the brasserie?"

"You looked like good bar fodder, chérie."

"Seriously."

"I don't know. I guess you just looked a little... lost. I could see you were looking at job adverts. I wanted to help."

"Is that it?"

He gives me a helpless smile.

"I noticed you."

"You said you have a rule."

"I do."

"But you're here."

"Hallie—" I look up. I can see the conflict in his face. He wasn't joking, I realize. This is serious for him. "I don't want to screw things up. This bubble—Clichy—I've made it my life. My home. I've been happy here."

I gently remove the coffee mug from his hands.

"You won't screw things up."

"How do you know that?"

I don't, I think. I don't know what the fuck I'm doing. I don't know anything about you; and Gabriela's right, there is something different, something I can't pin down. But if I sit here any longer with us talking in circles and pretending we're not remotely attracted to one another, I'm going to go insane.

"I just know," I say.

And perhaps it's the Clichy effect, the fact that I, too, have the feeling I've come home, perhaps it's the fact I haven't had a panic attack in weeks, or the new found confidence that comes with having survived another century, perhaps I just can't resist any longer—whatever the reason, I lean forward and kiss him.

CHAPTER TWENTY-EIGHT

"SISTERS. BROTHERS. YOU may know why you are here today. You may not."

So begins Aide Lefort, founder of the Parti Moulin Vert. A Pantheon-Sorbonne graduate of French and Senegalese descent, her political credentials are a masters in law specialising in human rights, a mesmeric voice, and a new movement that has attracted thousands of members in a matter of weeks. I know this because Dušanka is muttering in my ear, determined to provide a running commentary with opinions attached. Both the plaza and the steps leading up the hill are packed. People have brought banners and picnics; there's a jovial, almost celebratory atmosphere amongst the crowd.

Lefort raises her loudspeaker.

"One thing you do know. You felt compelled to join us today. So let me tell you why. For some time now—it may have been years, or months, or even weeks—you have been *aware*. What do I mean by aware? I mean that you have perceived a truth that, once acknowledged, is impossible to ignore: the knowledge that things are not equal in the world, that something fundamental is *out of sync*."

Dressed in jeans and a gilet, Lefort strides up and down the plaza before the Moulin Vert, the loudspeaker in one hand, a placard in the other. The sides of her head are shaved, and the remaining stripe of hair is bleached to gold. The force of her personality is undeniable.

"Sixty per cent of the global population is still offline. Forty per cent of us walk around glued to portals which take us to a seemingly infinite world of information, yet many of us feel more unhappy than ever before. Globalisation has connected us, yes. But it has disconnected us too."

Heads are nodding. I hear murmurs of assent, and am surprised to discover I understand not only the words of Aide Lefort, but the snippets spoken around me, without effort. Apparently timefaring has improved my French in my home time too.

Lefort draws a breath, gathering her resources.

"For too long," she shouts, "we have been hanging on the words of leeches, oblivious to the way they feast upon our insecurities. Our hunger for instant gratification. For Facebook likes, retweets, Instagram hearts. For our bodies to appear as photoshopped idols. For each of us to surpass our neighbours, secure in the knowledge that we—are—special."

Lefort raises her placard high. There's something about her—the way she moves, perhaps—that reminds me of Millie.

"Today I will tell you a truth I have learned. None of us is special. But every one of us is a miracle!"

"Oxymoron," mutters Dušanka.

Bo shushes her.

"It is miraculous that our planet was created. It is miraculous that we have an atmosphere exactly calibrated for mammalian lungs. It is miraculous that we could be the only life in the universe. But what are we doing with the greatest piece of cosmic luck the world may ever know?"

Lefort looks slowly around her, taking in the crowds, the camerawoman kneeling to get a better shot, the gently waving banners and balloons.

"We are allowing the one percent to hive its resources, whilst we stand on the outside, looking in. We are letting them tell us who our enemies are, when our *true* enemies are those who drain the money we work so hard to earn and hand it back to bankers. We are destroying ourselves from within!"

Noisy agreement. People get out their phones, ready to convert Aide's speech into digestible hashtags and soundbites which will no doubt generate the instant gratification she's talking about. Lefort waits, the loudspeaker poised at her lips, until quiet returns. Her tone turns sober.

"You may ask yourselves what right I have to stand here, talking to you. I grew up in Clichy-sous-Bois, which if you've never been there is a parallel universe to the skyline below us now, a place where a quarter of my neighbours couldn't find work, where police harassment is part of daily life, where some people are afraid to leave their houses for fear of assault because of their religion. All I ever wanted was to get out. My parents fought to get me an education. I went to university. I learned to talk the talk, to dissect society whilst standing apart from it. For years I planned to go abroad, work in a poor country, do good. And then I realized what I should have realised a long time ago: I needed to start at home. Because I, too, had been asleep.

"So why here, you ask now? Why not give this speech in Clichy-sous-Bois?"

She casts aside the placard and throws up an arm, gesturing to the building behind her.

"You may not know that during the Second World War, Montmartre was a crucial hub for the Resistance. It was here, perhaps on these very steps, that Resistance fighters met to smuggle women and men out of the country. They had a symbol: the green windmill. They had a saying: 'Against your four arms, we raise eight.' Never again, they said. Never. Again. But here we are in the twenty-first century and we can once again feel the shadow of fascism, the politics of fear and austerity, advancing across Europe."

Now her face is entirely serious.

"The attacks on our city have only made us more vulnerable to this rhetoric. None of us will ever forget where we were when we first heard about the Stade de France, the Bataclan, Bastille Day in Nice. The terrible fear that our loved ones might be among the dead. For some of us, those fears became reality. The perpetrators of those attacks would see us divided, have us live in hate, blind to one another's humanity. Now, more than ever, we must respond with love."

A roar of approval. Someone beside me is uploading to YouTube. Gabriela leans against me woozily. Bo is gazing up at Lefort, his face rapt. Dušanka folds her arms, habitual mistrust not quite broken. But Lefort has not finished.

"Maya Angelou once said that love recognises no barriers. She also said, 'You may encounter many defeats, but you must not be defeated.' So I stand before you today in the heart of Montmartre to call for a new bohemia. For a movement that grows not outside but from within society, that will meet the real needs of real people, that embraces hope and difference, that defends the rights for which our parents and our grandparents and their parents before them have suffered, have sacrificed. We can be a way to do things differently. Take this message. Tell it to your friends, your family, your enemies, the strangers you are yet to meet. Because the world needs heroes again."

Parti Moulin Vert members in green T-shirts are moving through the crowd, handing out leaflets. I take one.

"France was once great," shouts Aide Lefort. "She built that greatness upon rotten foundations. But she can become great again, if we can only reach across the forces that would divide us. Every act, however small, is a gesture against the tide. We must embrace our neighbours as sisters and brothers. Forget our terrors. Renew our hope. Rebuild our broken world. Friends, I ask you this: will you join me?"

Lefort spreads her arms wide, encompassing the hundreds of people gathered on the hill. She stands there for a moment, a smile blazing across her face. Then she bows.

Applause erupts. People are turning to one another, nodding, hugging, talking excitedly. Gabriela's eyes are wet. Even Dušanka looks moved.

"Ah, such naivety," she says shakily. "Such belief."

"But Dušanka," says Bo. "We are siblings! It's like that show Gabriela and Hallie love so much, what's it called..."

"Oh, you are so amusing, Bo."

I flick through the leaflet. It is full of tips and chirpy advice. Helping others is psychologically proven to improve your wellbeing! Why not introduce yourself to your neighbours? Volunteer at a food kitchen. Join a carpool. Recycle everything you use for a week. Talk to a homeless person and share their story. Offer your spare room to a refugee family. Donate to a humanitarian crisis.

"Hippies," says Dušanka, peering over my shoulder.

But Gabriela looks thoughtful. "I don't know. I think there is something in it."

Aside, she whispers to me, "This is an interesting development. We should monitor it."

I nod, but I am gripped by feelings too complex to offer a reply. The thought that this could be anything to do with the anomaly— with what I've done—feels anathema. I am too small for this. Then a cheer spreads across the hill. Aide Lefort has abandoned the loudspeaker. She is stepping down from the plaza, into the crowd. With the ease of a rockstar, she moves among the spectators, smiling, shaking hands, laughing, the crowd contracting around her in ever-shifting fractals. Everyone wants to touch her, including us.

In the excitement we lose sight of her until a shout goes up,

"Aide!"

And suddenly she's there, in front of us, her face open and radiating hope, and Bo manages to touch her gilet, and Gabriela breathes her name like a charm, and despite our weary Western cynicism, in that moment I think all of us really do believe that the world could become a better place.

CHAPTER TWENTY-NINE

"YOU SHOULD HAVE been there," I tell Léon. "It was incredible. She was incredible."

"I will be, next time."

"You'll come with us?"

"Sure."

"So… you don't mind if people know?"

"People know already," he says. "It's Clichy. The Spanish Inquisition was an amateur organisation compared to the Clichy rumour mill."

I consider this, and decide I don't care. I have enough secrets. Being with Léon is something to celebrate.

"Although," he adds. "Eloise might be pissed off when she finds out I've monopolised one of her staff."

"Fuck Eloise," I say. "Fuck everyone. I just want to be with you."

Léon rolls over, looks at me straight on. That millisecond of eye contact is all that is needed. We reach for each other.

I never knew desire could be like this. It's reflex. It's beyond conscious thought. It's desperation. I want to be closer than skin, closer to Léon than it is possible to be to another human being, unless we were to transition to a different state altogether, to become gas or energy. I'm beyond tiredness or hunger, beyond soreness or thirst. I need only Léon. When the rush fades, inertia sets us apart, side by side with sweat cooling our limbs, and here in these brief moments some logic returns. I must eat. I must sleep. And then I see his body, lean and muscular beside mine, his eyes running over my skin, preempting the touch that will follow, the touch that will bring me back to the living, and I know I will pursue that transcendence again, at any cost.

For the past forty-eight hours the only time either of us has got up has been to go to the shower or the fridge. I can't imagine how I'm going to survive the next shift at Millie's.

When we venture out hand in hand to catch the boulangerie before it closes, it's twilight. The world looks like a different place. Passersby are no longer just people on the street, they are people who are outside us, electrons to our nucleus. Léon buys baguettes, cheese, cigarettes, wine (Brouilly, of course), passing over notes and coins, never letting go of my fingers with his other hand. As though I am something cherished. I watch the vendors for signs they have observed our transfiguration; surely it must show? We go back to Léon's apartment, drop our purchases on the floor, and barely has the door closed than we reach for one another again.

"I WANT TO know about England," says Léon. "I never hear you talk about England."

"It's not the most exciting part of my life."

"It's most of your life."

"Yeah. Sad, isn't it? Life begins at Clichy. Or something."

"Where did you grow up?"

"In Sussex. About an hour and a half from London. Very rural."

He lights a cigarette, takes a drag and passes it to me.

"Did you like it?"

"Not exactly. My parents were pretty self-absorbed. They were both artists."

"What kind of artists?"

I shift onto one elbow.

"Mum's sculptures and installations. Dad's more traditional painting, I guess. He doesn't work so much any more."

They had made a deal, my parents. For two years, one of them would be the practising artist, and the other would teach, and bring in a stable income. Then they would switch places. Here my father made his first fatal error—he let my mother go first. Two years went by and she was on the cusp of a breakthrough. It was a matter of months, she said. Another year and the situation was mysteriously the same. Six years on, my birth was marked by nocturnal rows and their first separation, as my father acknowledged the by-now-unavoidable truth: that it would always be *just a few more months*.

Throughout my childhood he continued to teach. He was a good teacher, or could have been, if his heart was in it. What was in it mostly was his resentment. His practice was squeezed into the twilight hours, the evenings and nights, the tired parts of his life. A part of me admired him for neither abandoning us entirely nor taking us away, and a part of me despised him for giving in to her. He loved her too much, even knowing he was made lesser by it. She didn't deserve it.

"They were hard to live with," I say.

"You talk about them in the past tense."

"Oh, they're alive." I sigh. "I'll tell you a story about my mother. We were in the gift shop at London Zoo. I must have been, I don't know, about five. Theo and George—my sister and brother—they'd chosen their toys, we were all allowed one. Dad paid, of course. One of them had a platypus and the other had a crocodile, I think it was. I chose the seal. It had a sort of squashed face, it looked like it needed a good home. And she wouldn't let me have it because some other kids had seals as well. 'Hallie,' she said. 'Those kids over there, with the seals—they're the herd. Don't be a sheep. You know there is nothing more tragic in life than to be a sheep.' That's what she said. I remember it so clearly." I take a long drag, blow smoke towards the ceiling. "She always wanted me to be more than I was."

"Is that why you left?"

"Maybe."

I pass the cigarette back. For the first time in a long time, I think of the Polaroid. Of volcano day. Perhaps the more pressing secrets of my timefaring ventures have made it easier to revisit the deep past, but I'm not quite there yet. There are layers, I think. Some of them we're never willing to reveal.

"Where did you grow up?" I ask.

"Toulouse, until I was about ten."

"And then?"

"My parents liked to travel. We moved around a lot. We were here in Paris, for a time. I suppose I learned to blend in anywhere."

"Like an octopus."

"I think I prefer a chameleon. Not as terrifying."

"You can talk, you went to Australia. They've got all the worst stuff there."

Léon taps my stomach.

"Did I tell you about the huntsman spider in the bath?"

"No, and I don't want to know! What made you go out there, anyway?"

"I had some problems as a teenager… I kind of lost my way, actually." His face turns inward, eclipsed by memories. Is that how I appeared to him, a moment ago? I run my fingers over the short fuzz of his hair. Watch as he pulls himself back to the present. "I wanted to get as far away from France as possible," he says. "Start over. You know what I mean?"

"Yeah," I say quietly. "I get that."

I don't need to dig deeper. In this moment I feel closer to Léon than I have been to anyone. We were drawn together, I think. We've both had to find the strength to reinvent ourselves. It takes something, to do that.

"I'm glad you came back," I say.

He takes my hand, wrapping my fingers around his. "You don't have to be anything but what you are, ma chérie. Remember that."

"Those thoughts are harder to remember."

"Hallie?"

"What?"

"I am so happy to have found you."

LÉON IS THE last thought in my head when sleep claims me at night. He is the first thing I think of when I wake up on my futon, sneezing at the floor level dust. I think about Léon while I'm brushing my teeth. I think about the way he speaks, the ever-so-slightly sarcastic drawl. I think of the way he looks at me, as though I'm someone to be proud of. I think of him while I pull on my clothes—only one T-shirt left, I'm due a trip to the laundrette—and exit the studio and skip down the road to the Chinese traiteur. I think of Léon whilst I wolf down microwaved sweet and sour prawns with a pair of plastic chopsticks. I think about Léon smoking a cigarette in bed, and wearing his shirt, and the feel of it, and the smell of it, and the fact that it's still in my apartment hanging over the balcony shutters, talisman of a new life. I leave the Chinese after a record eight minutes and run the rest of the way down rue Lepic. I think of Léon. I swing right and wave at the crêpe man on the corner. I think of Léon. I run past the queue for the Moulin Rouge and waltz into the bar, thinking of Léon, and Angel stares at me as though I am mad.

Which I may well be.

Down in the vestiaire I change into my work clothes, throw my T-shirt into my locker, and I think of Léon.

I emerge to find Dušanka scrutinizing me. Her grey eyes dissect my face.

"Chapped lips, stubble rash, and craters under the eyes," she comments, as if to the air. "What has little Hallie been up to?"

"Oh, shut up," I snap. "I don't care what you think."

Dušanka shrugs. "Mere observation, my petit chou."

"And I'm not a pastry."

It is unwise to offer such ammunition. "Poussin, then," says Dušanka sweetly. "And don't feel bad—we've all slept with a Clichy bartender. You'll grow out of it."

My shoulders are rigid, my face hot with anger, as we go on the bar. With her radar for trouble, Eloise picks up the tension immediately.

"Hey, hey, what's going on?"

"Hallie's in love," calls Dušanka.

"Bullshit!"

I start quartering lemons, hurling them segment by segment into the speed rack. Dušanka leans over and raps my knuckles with a mojito stick.

"You know the lions in the zoo, they eat up little lambs. They devour them for a snack before breakfast. And the lambs, they are so foolish, they never see the lion that is hidden in the grass."

"Ladies, enough! Dušanka, section four with Yogi. Hallie, join Gabriela in section one. Get cleaning under the work surfaces, it's filthy down there."

I slice a final lemon and join Gabriela, still seething. Angel, having finished his shift, is sat on the other side of the bar with a quadruple Jack Daniels and a copy of *Le Monde*. He points to the spread.

"Isn't that the Moulin Vert woman you saw?"

I glance at the newspaper.

"Yeah. That's her. Aide Lefort."

"It's a good profile. A good haircut, too. I will go to the next rally. If it weren't for that putain Léon and his diabolical cocktails—"

"I'm going to become a vegetarian," interrupts Gabriela. Angel looks pained.

"That is excessive, ma poule."

Gabriela fills a bucket with hot water and soap. "You were the one who said we needed to change things. Meat farming is a huge contributor to climate change. Lefort says it, right there. Hallie, what are you going to do?"

I look up from scrubbing at the floor. "What?"

"Did you read the tips in the leaflet?"

"Not yet."

"You were too busy, I expect." Gabriela's tone sharpens. "The last two days you have ignored my messages."

"And mine," calls Angel from above. "And I sent her the cast list for *Transfusion* season four. That hot young thing from the stripper film is signed up, but even his presence is not enough to raise it from the Z-list."

"Sorry, I was with—"

"I know who you were with." Gabriela's voice is low and furious. "The whole of Clichy knows who you were with. This is a big mess. You should not have got involved."

"Because you say so?"

"Because I am your friend."

"Then stop acting like you're my mother."

"Right now I feel like your mother!"

"Why can't you just be happy for me?"

"It is not that he will treat you badly. Maybe yes, maybe no. I don't know. It is Clichy that will hurt you." Gabriela joins me on the floor, sloshing water everywhere. "Everybody leaves, everyone except me. I have to stay. I have to be punished. Still you are this naïve new girl, still you don't know Clichy."

Her words sting.

"Bloody hell, Gabriela. Aren't I allowed to have some fun? I've got enough weird shit going on in my life."

"And we were meant to be investigating it," she snaps.

"My problem has nothing to do with your problem."

She glares at me.

"You don't know that. If something can make you travel back—"
I glance pointedly upwards.

"Angel," I hiss.

She turns her back on me, muttering in Spanish. A part of me feels guilty—about the messages, about the leaflet—but nothing she can say will change my mind about Léon. Gabriela has taken me far, as far as she can lead me. From day to day, I barely think about back home. My panic attacks have all but abated. I'm well. But Léon is about more than leaving home. Léon is the final immersion. Léon is drowning in honey, and its sweet intoxication consumes me night and day. I am happy to be consumed. I am ready.

WHEN MY BREAK arrives I go outside to smoke. I need some air. In the alleyway, an elderly woman in a green-patterned kaftan reaches up to stroke the cat on the wall. It's Eloise's cat, by the looks of it, a large ginger tom whose territory ranges between Millie's and the local cemetery under the bridge, and who is known by all at Millie's as Satan. It was this cat, Eloise told me one night, who had inadvertently brought her to Paris. Sick of tourists assuming she was a pot-smoking liberal who supported prostitution, Eloise abandoned the canals of Amsterdam (she missed their symmetry, their linear nature that spoke of a calmer, a gentler era) to cat-sit for a friend in Paris. The friend was backpacking for a year, and had an exquisite flat. The only snag in this arrangement was that the cat had turned out to be a demon. Yes, possessed. Eloise was certain of that. After a failed exorcism, Eloise had taken the executive decision to set it free, and allow its tortured soul to roam the land of the dead in peace.

Satan yowls. The old woman straightens. A turban covers her hair and her eyes are magnified behind thick spectacles, but I'd know her anywhere.

Coldness creeps through my limbs.

"Oh, my dear, hello," she says. "I was just—in the neighbourhood. Thought I'd drop by and see—how you are progressing."

"Progressing with what?"

"Your investigations—of course."

"Who said I'm investigating anything?"

"So hostile!"

I inhale too sharply and break into hacking coughs.

"Mint?" says the woman sympathetically, digging around in a bag. "Oh, I don't have any, I'm afraid. And there I was thinking I looked like the kind of person who would have a mint. You never can judge."

"Look, I did what you asked. You said you would leave me alone."

The old woman looks aggrieved. Behind the glasses her eyelids blink slowly.

"Have I hurt you? Have I hurt your friends? Have you ever considered my predicament? I get lonely, you know. It's all very well talking to strangers, but they don't *understand* the situation. Not like you do."

"I understand fuck all," I say. "What do you want?"

"Nothing. Nothing! I was only going to suggest you might want to pay a visit to the catacombs. You, of all people, ought to see the home of the dead."

"What's in the catacombs?" I ask suspiciously.

"Bones, dear. A lot of bones. Take a look, it might appeal to your geological sensibilities."

"I don't think—"

The old woman's face goes slack. Reanimates. She stares at me. A crease appears between the thin hairs of her eyebrows.

"Do I know you?"

I drop my cigarette and grind it out.

"No."

"Who are you?"

"I'm no one."

I leave the alleyway, the old woman watching me suspiciously. On the boulevard's central aisle, a team in green windmill T-shirts have set up a food stand and are distributing steaming portions of vegetarian curry to homeless people, and possibly some students. I watch for a moment, torn by conflicting emotions. The slogan on the back of their T-shirts reads:

Change the world. It needs it.

CHAPTER THIRTY

AT DENFERT-ROCHEREAU I queue for ninety minutes in the heat, idly listening to the chatter of the party in front of me, one of whom appears to be a self-appointed tour guide. The worst kind, I think, and wonder again why I felt compelled to come here.

I pay my entry fee at the little green hut and follow the procession of tourists down a narrow spiral stairwell. It is a strange sensation, to leave the known world behind. For the first few steps the outside light still filters down, but gradually its influence wanes, and there is only the low yellow glow from the wall-mounted bulbs. At the bottom of the stairwell we pass through a brief exhibition, and then into a low, sloping stone passageway. There's only one direction to take: deeper underground.

Footsteps echo, reverberations increasingly long and meandering. The tourists thin out. The passageway goes on with no indication of where it will end. The party ahead of me is hushed now. There is no noise except for our shoes on the stone, and water guzzling in a hidden aqueduct. Claustrophobia folds around me, along with a warped sense of freedom. Panic and exhilaration. Nothing up there in the lighted world can touch me; I've escaped. But to where? And what?

The party in front, perhaps feeling the same weight of the earth overhead, are hurrying, but I want to look at everything, not just the bones. I want to see what Paris is made of underground. I slow down until they turn a corner and I'm on my own. Now I can look at the rock in peace.

I run my hands over the walls. The fossils are tight, intricate curlicues, rough to touch. They have bumps and dimples where tiny spines or ridged shells once floated in an ocean millennia ago. This, I think, is the greatest form of survival. To leave an impression that will be felt and witnessed in another stratum of time. Little extinct things, your lifespan will be longer and more enduring than ours, unless we too, the dead and buried, are left undisturbed long enough to imprint our skeletons on the rock. Our bones to be mined by explorers of future millennia, new species, even life forms from other planets. I touch the fossil again, the rough cool sandstone, remind myself that I am alive. I am still real.

I hear voices catching up behind me, and move on.

After fifteen minutes or so of walking, I reach the entrance to the ossuary. The self-appointed tour guide is already there, dictating to her group.

"Here you can read the sign over the door. *Arrête! C'est ici l'empire de la mort.* Stop! This is the empire of death. Many of the bones were brought from the public cemetery in Les Halles. The workers transported the bones through the city in huge carts in the middle of the night, it was a gigantic operation."

"How many people are down here?"

The guide draws herself up impressively.

"Five to six million." A short, possibly disbelieving silence follows this pronouncement before she ushers her group through the stone anomaly.

I linger a few moments, and then I too enter the empire of the dead.

*   *   *

THE SKULLS ARE stacked in lines. They lie upon layers of bones, and more layers of bones lie upon them. The bones were once limbs: femur and fibula, ulna and radius. They had flesh attached, they were joined, they moved. Now they sit in dislocated harmony. Bone against bone, they have transcended the laws of anatomy for a new proximity with their fellow sapiens.

Thousands of pairs of eye holes gape. Some have lost their lower jaws, but their teeth still grin. Others have lost their teeth. Under the dim illumination, they are yellowish in colour, softly burnished. Who was given the task of disassembling these skeletons— hundreds, thousands of them? Who stacked the bones so artfully and systematically, who placed the skulls upon the platters of severed limbs? Did they have to experiment, assessing different formations? Does the stability of the ossuary as a whole depend upon the measurements of each individual?

The logistics of it fascinate and horrify me. There is something eerie about the structured placement of these remains. The dead are here in multitudes.

I remember something I heard from Millie. During the 1870-71 siege of Paris, when the Prussians blockaded the city for over four months, Parisians were forced to slaughter all their animals for food. It was not uncommon to find dogs, cats, rats or horses on a restaurant menu. Even Castor and Pollux, the city's sole pair of elephants, were not spared. When there were no more animals left, the ossuary was raided to make bonemeal. Unwitting, the Parisians ate their ancestors.

I MOVE THROUGH the caverns. I see hall after hall of meticulously, artfully arranged bones. Skulls embedded in the surrounding tibias form the outline of a heart. Some visitors approach the bones; reaching out a hand as if to touch, then withdraw quickly. This is what death looks like, this is how it is for us all. Our fleeting, packed little lives laid bare. Seeing it up close is a face-off with the inevitable. There are so many of them.

A child tugs at her mother's arm.

"Are *all* those dead people?"

"Yes, they're dead."

"How did they die?"

"They died because they were old."

"Where are they now?"

"Somewhere else, love."

I stand in front of a skull. The forehead is smooth and sloped. Broad cheekbones, prominent teeth. I try to imagine the face. The thoughts ticking away beneath the scalp, the hopes and fears. I find myself thinking about Millie. *Who were you? Are you down here, with these people?*

Cavern after cavern. The rows of bones do not end, they follow me through the corridors. My mind grows numb. Through barred gates, I catch glimpses of other tunnels, closed off to the public, where yet more bones are stacked. One of the doors is ajar. I glance ahead, behind, confirming I'm on my own, and slip through.

Once again, I feel that pull. A tug, towards the centre of the earth. To go down further, deeper, darker, to burrow through mulch and rock and lava, until my body compresses into pure mineral. This is what I am made of, this is what I will become. Did nobody warn you? It is dangerous to be underground. There was never meant to be light, not here. Only a silent, creeping progress. A cycle we try to ignore.

It is not only that we're trespassing on a place we were never meant to live. Madness lurks underground. The danger of forgetting, of reverting. Evolution working backwards and forwards at the same time. Stay down here long enough, and the world above will become a delusion, petty and nonsensical. Stay down here long enough, and

I will forget myself. I will believe I am one of the calcified ocean dwellers, I will find myself adrift in a vast salt sea. I will turn over and over in a surf too immense to calculate. I will be flung about the waves. I will drown underground.

Drip, drip. Drip, drip.

From the roof of the tunnel, a tiny trickle of water. I put out my tongue to catch it. I taste the components of the earth.

There. The ocean is already unfolding from above. I am sinking.

I HEAR A high pitched noise, a singing. Nausea wrenches my stomach, waves of sickness rushing up and receding. I bend double, digging my fists into my abdomen, breathless with pain. The cavern bleeds in and out of focus.

A figure lurches from the gloom, here but not here, more substantial than a projection, but not fully formed. He has a white curled wig, epaulettes, a sash across his red coat. His mouth falls open in a laugh as he raises a bottle to his lips. There are others around him, men and women, drinking and feasting. They wear wigs, some half as tall as them, the white perfumed hairpieces knocking against the cavern ceiling. Wide skirts, rouged cheeks and beauty spots, military dress. Sombrely clad underlings scurry between the revellers, plying them with sweetmeats and wine. The scent is overpowering, fecund with hot powdered bodies, the damp of the caves, thick perfume, roasted meats and foodstuffs.

I see playing cards scattered over the floor, hearts and spades. A group of women gathered around a low table, their faces sharp as witches, their fans tap-tapping in restless fingers. One of them has lost a glove, another a silk stocking. Her calf sticks out from under her skirt, pale and provocative. It's Marie-Antoinette.

The courtiers whirl about me. Dizziness fills my head. I have to sit down. I cannot feel the floor.

They are all around me but they cannot see me, I cannot touch them. The sound of their laughter is muted.

I understand that something is happening. Time is moving. Time is shifting around me and I am trapped in its mechanics, unable to move with it but caught between one plane and the next. The eighteenth-century revellers grow fainter. There is a rushing in my head. We are moving. *I* am moving. The cavern becomes a blur of indistinct shapes, time speeding up a hundredfold.

I understand that this is not good. It's wrong, horribly wrong.

Somewhere in the blur I recognise a figure, disappearing down the corridor in staccato flashes of green.

The chronometrist.

"You tricked me!" I yell, but my voice is ripped from my throat; flung into the abyss. "You wanted me to come here. You knew this was going to happen!"

Her giggle ripples back.

"I'm no one, my dear. I'm no one I'm no one I'm no one..."

Keep moving. Get up, get out. You need to get out.

I stagger to my feet, but I don't know which way to turn. An imprint of Marie-Antoinette lingers against one wall. Then she is crushed into the wall, she is part of it, her face flattened to paper. It ripples and vanishes. I am half blind.

I screw my eyes shut and abandon vision completely. From a deeper darkness comes an old memory. Theo's voice. Her arm, an albatross wing. A net of safety. I conjure that albatross now. I imagine its beak closing around the little finger of my left hand; firm but gentle. The tip of a feather brushing my hand.

"Start walking," says the albatross. "Don't follow her. Go back. Go back."

"I can't see," I whisper.

It hurts less if I whisper.

The albatross tugs my finger: this way.

Blind, I start walking. One foot in front of the other. Every step is an effort of will. I can sense things—people—colliding against me in different time zones. I've become part of a temporal osmosis. I feel liquid, a thing in flux, as if pieces of me could separate and spill across the decades.

"Where are we?" I whisper.

"We're alongside the anomaly."

"There's an anomaly here?"

There must be.

I want to slow. I want to stop, lie down and let the vortex howl around me. The albatross nips my finger. I cannot see, I can barely feel, but I know it has drawn blood.

I put my hands out to the walls to guide me. They slide beneath my palms, slick and wet and cold. The tunnel roof is dripping, like the keg room, as if the weight of the Eocene ocean lies above, waiting to burst through.

These tunnels are labyrinthine. The shape of the walls change, become smooth and rounded. My fingers hook onto something and I realize I have put them through the eye sockets of a skull.

I scream and jerk back my hand. I hear the skull clatter to the floor. And then a rumbling, a tremor that heeds an avalanche, as the stacks of the skulls and bones collapse to the floor, rattling at my feet, piling up around me until I am shin deep in the dead.

I cannot go any further. My whole body is shaking uncontrollably. I can hear the bones clacking against one another, I can hear them shivering, their long-gone tongues flickering in anticipation of the moment I fall. I'll be buried here forever, strung out through time in some other dimension that no one will ever find.

"No!" The albatross jumps up and down. "No! Don't stop here! Here they'll never let you go!"

"I can't. I can't go any further."

"You have to. You can't stop here!"

The bones rock deliciously.

"I'm trying..." I sob, my tears falling on the feathers of the albatross, "but it's so hard."

When I move my feet the bones roll, locking and interlocking, making gates to trip me up. Grimly, I plough on. I hear cartilage crunch beneath me. I keep walking.

I walk for hours.

I walk for days.

Cart bearers come towards us down the tunnels. They have torches. The men pushing them wear cloths wrapped around their noses and mouths. The carts are full of freshly dug bones, clods of earth and dirt clinging to limbs and skulls. They complain about the long walk from Les Halles. They pass us, the carts' wooden wheels rolling deep down into the labyrinth.

I glimpse the face of one of the cart bearers and beneath the dirt it looks like Léon. But that cannot be possible.

The tunnel begins to turn upward. I have lost all sensation now. I cannot see a thing. If the albatross is still with me, I cannot hear or feel it. I feel myself being swallowed, whittled until I am nothing but the tiniest of specks, a piece of grit in a vast ocean.

CHAPTER THIRTY-ONE

WHAT THE FUCK *were you thinking? She could have died down there! Or worse—*

Oh my dear, do stop—fussing. It's your anomaly, not hers. She couldn't have gone anywhere.

You know it's unstable. I told you how bad it was coming through—it felt like I was going to be ripped to pieces, I thought that was it, over—

And what other—options did I have, hm? You weren't doing anything, so I had to. She's not acting fast enough! You know how this process works. It's not enough for the anomaly to unlock. The incumbent has to respond. She has to want *it, or the flares won't come.*

What difference does it make when she does it?

Well, it's your friends out there... If you aren't bothered about saving them... Perhaps I should hop back and have a word with my dearest Inga?

No! No. We need to finish this.

I'm glad we're in agreement. Because you have hardly been playing straight either. Have you? My dear. Oh, walk away. That's right. Easy for you! Easy for... I'm sorry. Do I know you?

* * *

BLUE SKY. AN assault of light.

I screw up my eyes, open them more slowly. A residue of green, disappearing into the edge of my frame of vision.

"She's coming round—"

"Give her some water—"

"Hallie, it's okay, don't be alarmed, just take it easy."

Anxious faces, looming over me. Léon. Why is Léon—?

He looks worried. Someone lowers a water bottle. Groggily, I try to sit up. I'm on the pavement, a couple of hundred yards from the exit to the catacombs. Léon supports me.

"What happened?" I ask.

"A woman told me she saw you staggering out of there, you looked like you'd been drugged or something. Then you collapsed. You were unconscious."

"Shall I call an ambulance?" someone says.

"No, no. I'm fine. I must have... I must have fainted. It's claustrophobic down there."

"It's okay," Léon tells the crowd. "I've got it from here."

I nod. "Please, I'm fine."

Gradually they melt away, leaving Léon and I alone on the kerb. I stare at him, confused.

"What are you doing here?"

"Angel told me you were going to the catacombs—I was going to surprise you, but you weren't in the queue, I figured you'd already gone in—so I waited. And then—"

Léon waves his hand. And then. I watch his face, aware again of that uncertainty I can't pin down, a sense that there is something I have missed. My mind is thick with fog. He tears open a bar of chocolate and breaks off piece by piece. I eat it slowly. The sugar helps.

He helps me to my feet. It's a warm, sunny afternoon. I can hear the sounds of traffic from the main road.

"You fainted?" says Léon.

"I must have. Or—"

"Or?"

I hesitate.

"I used to get... panic attacks," I say reluctantly. "Don't tell anyone."

"It's nothing to be ashamed of."

"I know, it's just... I thought they'd stopped. Léon, this might sound mad, but... I thought I saw you down there."

He stares at me.

"Hallie, you know that's impossible."

"I know, I know it is—"

I look away, aware that his face is troubled, and mine must be equally so. But what can I say? I've been travelling through time? I got stuck in a temporal anomaly? I don't even consider it. Léon and I have something, and I won't endanger that, I won't have him pity me for a fantasist. Better that he thinks this is about anxiety.

No one can know about the anomaly. I'm beginning to regret having told Gabriela. The truth is dangerous, a thing alive—the truth is impossible. The only thing I can say for sure is this: the anomaly—my anomaly—is awake. And as the fog fades away, for the first time I can hear its song clearly. The melody loops in my ears, the way the noise of a gig reverberates for hours after the event. The sound is taut and beautiful and rich with joy. It's the sound of Paris in springtime; Paris rejoicing. I don't need the chronometrist to tell me this is not going to stop, and despite everything that's happened this afternoon, there's only one way I can respond.

I get to my feet.

"I have to go. I have to go right now."

PART SIX

The Cello

CHAPTER THIRTY-TWO

SOMETHING IS CHALKED on the floor of the keg room. A date: day, month, year. I stare at it, the digits looming larger and larger as the temperature climbs. Then the transportation happens. This time it is instantaneous. One moment I'm standing by a stack of Corona, cold electric light overhead, *drip, drip* on the concrete; the next there's a bright flash and I'm on my back in a dark space. My feet are wedged at an awkward angle, my heart pounding and a taste of blood in my mouth. I run my tongue around my gums and the taste intensifies.

The residues of light fade from the backs of my eyelids, leaving me in darkness.

I know at once that this is a full corporeal transportation. It's more akin to the 1875 incident than the ghostly flickering of New Year's Eve, or even the apparitions of the catacombs. I'm ravenous, for a start. But the sawdust smell I remember from the cellar of 1875 is absent. This is something new.

I push my feet out experimentally and meet a wall in front of me. I reach behind and find another wall at my back. *Shit.* What if I've landed somewhere there's no way out? I extend a hand to the left and find another wall and a tingle of fear creeps into my skin.

I force myself to think rationally. You haven't tried the fourth wall, yet. You haven't tried the ceiling, for that matter.

Wincing at the throbbing in my head, I raise myself slowly to a sitting position.

I hear an intake of breath.

Not mine.

There's someone else down here.

I freeze, listening intently, but my heart is beating so fast I can't hear anything. Who hides in the dark? Not anyone who wants to be found. Another traveller? Someone with a more sinister purpose? Sweat prickles at my back and I can't draw in the deep noisy breaths I usually take to calm myself without drawing attention—although that's ludicrous, as clearly I've been detected already.

Then another thought occurs to me. *What if it isn't human at all?*

I extend my arm to the right and encounter something soft and pliable. Something fleshy.

I yelp and scrabble backwards, feet kicking against the narrow walls to either side in my desperation to escape. The thing is on top of me, flapping at my arms, my face, making hissing noises. I push back, terrified, and then it gets a hand over my mouth and it's still hissing and at last I understand the sound.

"Shhh. Shhhh!"

I collapse, spent, breathing harshly.

"Shhhh!"

The thing backs off. Slowly, I manage to calm myself.

"Who's down here?" I say shakily.

Another "Shhh!" Almost a whimper. I make a decision: it's completely idiotic, and it's the only thing I can do to assuage my terror. I squeeze my bottle opener in one hand, my phone in the other (six-twenty pm), and I switch on the torch function of my phone.

The light illuminates the pale, anguished face of a girl about my age, huddled two metres away at the far end of a narrow compartment. I see scuffed lace-up boots, sheer tights, the hem of a skirt beneath a buttoned-up coat. The coat looks smart but worn, a patch at the right breast where the fabric has bobbled. On the floor to one side of her there's a blanket, a bag, a glass bottle of water and bread wrapped in a cloth, a torch, paper and pencil, and a bucket.

The girl inches backwards and meets the fourth wall. She looks frantically about her. Of the two of us, she is the more frightened.

"Turn it out," she whispers. "Turn it *out*."

I hesitate, wanting to see more (because if she's down here, then she got here, which means I must be able to get out). Then I switch off the torch. I hear her breathing, shallow and uneven. The thread of her voice comes through the dark. She's speaking in French, but as in 1875 I understand her without effort.

"I'm hallucinating. This isn't real. It's no surprise, but I can't let it get to me. I can't—give in."

A pause, and then she begins the mantra again.

I sit in silence, taking in what I've seen of the girl, her clothes, the little pile of provisions. Thinking about the date chalked on the keg room floor. The last thing I saw before the flare.

"I am real," I venture at last. "My name's Gabriela. What's yours?"

"Shhh! I'm hallucinating. This isn't real. I can't give in."

I'm about to turn the torch back on (interesting that the phone works at all, although as a tool for communication it's useless) and try again, when another sound distracts us both. Footsteps, heavy on stairs. The girl stops speaking at once. I sense her folding in on herself, gathering her limbs together, making herself small. Instinctively, I do the same.

The footsteps are moving down a flight of stairs, on the other side of the wall behind my head. I wait, not knowing what this is but understanding we mustn't be detected. They reach the bottom of the stairs. Two sets. Are they coming this way? I can no longer hear the girl's breathing.

The footsteps pause. I hear the sound of a key turning in a lock, somewhere to the left. The wall must be very thin.

The door opens. Two people enter the adjacent room. I hear low laughter.

Then:

"—das schönste Mädchen—" It's a male voice, young, the timbre light and pleasant.

The door shuts.

"Non..." Female.

"Ja, das Allerschönste—"

"In der *Welt?*"

"Ich sage dir die Wahrheit."

"Vous dites de la merde."

A pause. Then giggling. No words for a while. I hear the shifting of feet. The rasp of fabric. It seems to go on forever, though it's probably only a couple of minutes. My stomach growls and the sound is impossibly loud. I curl inwards, trying to suppress it. Eventually the woman speaks.

"Je dois y aller."

"Ich kann es kaum erwarten..."

"Demain, demain. *Morgen, ja?*"

At last there's the sound of the door opening and closing, and the key turns from the far side. The footsteps begin to retreat, one set the light clatter of a woman's heels, the other loud and heavy, creaking on the wooden staircase. Then silence.

"Are you there?" I say softly.

I hear the girl's breathing, taut and terrified. I wait a few more moments and then I switch on the torch of my phone again. She is slumped against the wall, the blanket scrunched around her feet, her collar upturned, hands clenched on the lapels as though she's holding in a scream and the scream is a living thing that might at any moment erupt from her throat. The effort of keeping it in is written all over her face. At her right collarbone is the bobbled patch of fabric on the coat, where the yellow star must have been torn away.

I rap gently on the wall to my left and hear what I now expect: the hollow sound of a false wall.

"What's the date?" I ask, although in my heart I already know the answer.

She speaks slowly, stiffly. "The date?"

"Can you tell me what day it is?"

"Twentieth, twenty-first of July," she says. "Twenty-second? I don't know. They took everyone. Maman. Papa. Everyone. Then you appeared. Out of thin air. Like an angel. Or a devil. Or maybe you're just a ghost."

And she starts to laugh.

"WHAT'S YOUR NAME?" I ask quietly.

"Rachel. Rachel Clouatre." She answers automatically. Perhaps she still believes I'm a figment, a hallucination. Better for me if I were. You can't capture a hallucination, but you can very much capture an enemy agent.

"How did you escape?"

"I was at the conservatoire. I've been sleeping there overnight. Not going home. Maman thought it would be safer. After the first round-ups..."

"The music school? You're a student?"

She looks at her hands. "A cellist. We moved here so I could study. I couldn't afford to live here on my own. We should have stayed... we should have stayed in Limoges."

Her eyes are brimming, but the tears when they come make silent tracks over her cheeks. She switches on her torch, giving us a bit more light in the confined space, and I put my phone away. I notice the papers by her side are covered in scribblings: words and musical notation, and heavy crossings out.

"As soon as it started I knew they'd be taken. They were dragging people from their homes—like cattle. Not German. French policemen. *French*. I wanted to go back, I wanted to go with them, I'd rather they took us all than separated us. But the director locked me in one of the practice rooms. I was in there for hours. Me and the piano. Someone had been practising Rachmaninov, the score was there. Concerto number three. At the end of the day he came to get me and there was someone with him. Madame Tournier. Our neighbour."

Rachel blinks away the moisture from her eyes. She doesn't bother to wipe her face.

"She saw them... taken."

I feel my chest tightening as she tells me her story, the headache intensifying. *Fucking hell.* I have to help her, but I feel utterly helpless. Mad ideas flit through my head. Could she travel through the anomaly? Could I get her out—to my time? To Millie's time, even? Surely anywhere would be safer than here. But I know only two things about the anomaly: it's unpredictable, and if I believe the chronometrist, only I can use it. No, that's insanity. She has to get out of Paris.

"You have to get out of Paris," I say.

"Madame Tournier brought me here. She knows the owner, there's been... others. I have to get to the Clos Montmartre. She's set it up for tonight. Someone will meet us there."

"The vineyard? It's not far. I'll help you."

"A hallucination?"

"I'm real, I promise."

"Even if you are, I can't go anywhere. I don't have the cello."

"Look, I know you're a musician. But you can't afford to wait—especially if this Madame Tournier has arranged for someone to get you out."

"You don't understand," she says. "My parents gave it to me. The cello *is them*. And when I don't know when I'll see them again—" She swallows. "I'm not leaving without it."

Her expression tells me she won't be persuaded. Not that that's going to stop me trying.

"But you can't stay here indefinitely. Christ, the Moulin Rouge is next door, there'll be Germans camping out there every night. That one just now—what if you'd coughed or sneezed, alerted them..."

I trail off. My words aren't making an impression at all. Rachel stares at her boots.

"Yes. It's ironic, isn't it. They hate us. They describe us as animals. And yet they're happy to listen to Offenbach as long as the can-can girls are flashing their underwear. Some people I know are playing with Radio Paris now." She kneads the lapels of her coat. I imagine the pressure of those fingertips on cello strings, and then I think of piles of coats, piles of glasses, gold fillings, and I can't suppress a shudder.

With sudden violence she says, "Paris makes me sick."

Even before I speak I know what I'm about to voice is a terrible idea. And I know equally, prophetically, that there isn't a choice. The last time I came through the anomaly, I fucked up. I gave the chronometrist exactly what she wanted and I left Millie behind. This time, I have a chance to do something worthwhile.

"Where is the cello, Rachel?"

"At the conservatoire. I couldn't take it with Tournier, it would have attracted attention, she said. We had to move fast. It was strange. There were people, just the same as always, but the streets felt so empty. So alone."

"I'll get it for you."

"You will?"

I see a spark of hope in her eyes.

"Yes," I say determinedly. "Tell me where to go."

CHAPTER THIRTY-THREE

RACHEL'S LIFE: GROWING up in a small town outside Limoges, an only child. There had been hopes for a younger sister or brother, but a miscarriage in the second trimester discouraged further attempts. Too young to understand or feel the impact of this early sorrow, Rachel became the centre of her parents' world, as they stood at the nucleus of hers. Her mother, a natural worrier, wished only to safeguard her from the least and worst of life's perils, whereas her father would have given her anything she wanted, as far as their means allowed.

Rachel was eight years old when the Clouatres attended a concert at the local hall and she heard for the first time the instrument that would become an extension of her soul. The cellist was a man in his fifties, wide and suave with a dapper moustache, and the revue was Bach's Cello Suites. Looking back, he had not been the most accomplished player, but nonetheless the magic of that first encounter had not diminished in Rachel's mind. Quite the reverse: it had magnified in both depth and intensity, so that now, familiar with the Suites as both an audience and a musician, Rachel could overlay upon her memory the exact positioning of the cellist's fingers and the sweep of his bow across the bridge, as she relived the sound of its plaintive voice flooding that draughty town hall, punctuated by the occasional cough or shuffle of feet.

Rachel knew at once that this was her calling, but pursuit of her dream was not so straightforward. Cellos, and cello lessons, were expensive, and there were no teachers within the town where Rachel lived, which meant she would have to travel. In the end, it was Rachel's uncle who stepped in. He had a small but successful business in Limoges, and no children of his own. A half-size cello appeared, and lessons were arranged. Once a week, Rachel got a lift by horse and cart to the station, took the train to Limoges and was met by Uncle Andre's secretary, who escorted her to her tutor's house and back to the station an hour later. Rachel emerged from these sessions transformed, a butterfly from a chrysalis, only awaiting the epiphany of flight.

Time in school felt wasted. She dreamed in crotchets and quavers, practising arpeggios against a ruler, blocking out the words of the teacher in exchange for the curlicues of Bach. Her grades, previously above average, dropped so far that her parents threatened the removal of the cello (because what happened if the cello did not succeed? Rachel could not imagine a life without it, but her parents could, and had). Rachel reformed overnight, becoming the most attentive student in class, but still it felt unreal. She was going through the motions until life could begin. She was waiting for wings.

Aged fifteen, she performed her own revue at the town's summer fête. More than one parent in the audience leaned over to the Clouatres and said, "Your child has talent," which was the kind of compliment usually delivered only under extreme duress or with the understanding that reciprocal praise should be forthcoming, and Rachel's parents began to believe it could be true.

It has to be the Paris Conservatoire, said her tutor. Nothing else is worth your time. It was 1936. Rachel would be applying for admission in 1939. She needed more regular lessons, so the family moved into Limoges. It didn't suit them—they missed the clean air and the open sky—but the tutor gave an extra hour a week for no charge. Rachel outgrew her cello. It was time, the tutor said, for a real investment.

Rachel's mother was not so easily convinced. For years she had nurtured dreams of her only daughter's wedding, a lavish but solemn affair. She could hear quite clearly the rabbi's words, the compliments of the guests; she could see her daughter's face, serene through the veil at the Bedeken, and later the circles of dancing, and the shadowy yet undeniably handsome countenance of her future son-in-law as bride and groom were lifted high upon their chairs. Year by year, they had set money aside for precisely this event. It was their life savings, and Rachel didn't want it. She had no interest in marriage, or even men.

"When I'm a professional musician, I'll have to go on tour," she said. "I won't have time for a husband, and who'll want to marry someone who's never home?"

Rachel's mother secretly agreed with this, but to say so was impossible. She had to retain hope, even as it was somehow proposed that the wedding-money could become the cello-money, and Rachel's mother could never quite describe how it happened, but one foggy morning they found themselves on the train to Paris: herself, her hopelessly indulgent husband, her daughter. There they chose the cello in which Rachel would invest the next three years of her life. This time, although their life savings had been almost depleted, Uncle Andre was not invited to contribute. There were limits, thought Rachel's mother.

For her audition piece to the Paris Conservatoire, Rachel played the prelude from Bach's Cello Suite No. 1. Nobody was surprised when she was offered a scholarship.

Nine months later, Paris was under occupation.

CHAPTER THIRTY-FOUR

RACHEL HAS A key to the storeroom so she can move around after hours, but she doesn't want me to take the risk of leaving before closing time. We argue in whispers over the logistics whilst I chew on some dry bread to assuage my hunger. If I'm to recover the cello and get back to the vineyard in time to meet her, I can't afford to wait. Reluctantly she agrees, perhaps because she still doesn't believe I'm real.

She lets me out ("Don't get caught, figment") and—dressed in a spare set of clothes from the wardrobe of Madame Tournier, neighbour and escapist accomplice—I ascend the wooden stairs of Millie's establishment. I find the door to the front of the bar and pause, listening to the sounds of the mid-evening clientele. Clink of glasses, merry laughter, conversations in French and in German. The bar is busy. Good. It will be easier for me to slip through.

I adopt a confused expression and am reaching for the door handle when it opens from the other side. A young woman stands in the frame, chic and curvaceous, a dash of lipstick in lively contrast to her waitress's uniform. Seeing me, she frowns.

"C'est privé."

"La salle de bain?"

She opens the door wider, points. "À droite."

"Merci."

The waitress's features ripple, and her lipsticked mouth drops open.

"You're on—the right track, my dear. Never fear."

"What?"

She blinks. Frowns.

"Madame?"

I step through the door, turn right for the bathroom and lock myself into a cubicle, trembling. Was that her? Can she get in and out of a body that fast? She wanted me to come here. It had to be her who wrote that date on the floor. *22-07-1942.* It appears that once again I'm doing her bidding for a purpose I don't understand. Which makes it potentially a very bad proposition indeed.

But now Rachel's counting on me.

The seconds tick by as I weigh up the alternatives, and realise there are none. I made a promise.

When I come out of the cubicle, another woman is stood at the mirror, applying powder to her cheeks. In her smart two-piece suit she looks the essence of a Parisienne. Despite Tournier's clothes, I feel as far from Parisian as it is possible to feel. I feel like a fraud, which I am. I remind myself that impostor syndrome will not help Rachel and exit the bathroom, walking through the front of the bar as quickly as my pleasure-seeking alter ego permits. Patrons are grouped around cabaret tables, engaged in leisurely discussion. Decanters of wine glow crimson under ambient lighting. I don't allow myself to look at the German uniforms, not directly, though the grey-green fabric wants to draw my gaze, to make me stare. I keep my face muscles soft, relaxed, and I don't catch anybody's eye. It's only as I exit the premises that the voice of the waitress comes back to me and I realise I heard that same voice earlier, with the German soldier, downstairs. The knowledge shakes me: there is more than one agenda at play inside Millie's.

Outside it is still light. A late summer evening, a heat on the air, though the hairs on my arms are raised beneath Tournier's jacket.

I expected shadowy streets, a furtive, even frightened sensibility about the civilians in this occupied city. But the vibrancy of the scene is astonishing. Bars are open, terraces packed, civilian women suave and elegant in red or black hats, everyone is smoking. A woman sails past on a bicycle, heading towards Pigalle. To the right of the Moulin Rouge (*SPECTACLE PERMANENT*), a large billboard above the Brasserie Cyrano Dupont declares *Tout Est Bon*. In fact, if it weren't for the queue of German troops lining up outside the Moulin, there would be no indication of the war I know is consuming the greater part of the world.

The sight of that queue propels me to move. On the last occasion I travelled through time, my French went unquestioned, but at that point in history being English didn't make you an enemy of occupying forces. If I'm caught and interrogated, I haven't a hope of making it back to safety, never mind locating the hapless cello.

Avenue Jean-Jaurès is my destination. It's in the nineteenth arrondissement, directly east of here, and if I were back in my home time I could walk it in half an hour. Unfortunately, between me and the music school lie the cabarets of Montmartre in their dozens, and each of them is brimming with Germans.

DETAILS I GLEAN from Rachel before I leave Millie's: curfew starts at nine pm, and the conservatoire closes at half past eight. I'll be able to get into the building after that because the students tend to practise late, and some of them sleep there to avoid curfew. (By this point it's already gone eight according to Rachel's watch, and the question has to be posed as to how exactly I'm going to get in. "Through the window," says Rachel promptly. She draws me a map on a clean sheet of paper, and marks the designated window. "This is getting more and more like Indiana Jones," I say, and Rachel says, "What?") Then my questions become necessarily broader ("Just to check—what year is it again?") and Rachel's answers ("Nineteen forty-two") gain a corresponding air of disbelief. I'm not from here, I remind her. And if I'm going to succeed, it has to look like I am. No, she agrees; you are a figment. Figment or not, I say. You go with Tournier when she comes. I'll come to the vineyard. I'll bring the cello.

It seemed like a simple enough plan, assuming I could survive the journey without discovery. I've barely made it two hundred paces down the boulevard when a young German calls out to me from a terrace.

"Salut, mademoiselle."

At once my hackles rise. Keep it light, I remind myself. Friendly. And as few words as possible.

"Salut, monsieur."

"Vous êtes belle..."

"Merci, monsieur."

He holds his beer aloft, waves a newspaper enthusiastically. I'm struck by the youthfulness of that face. He must be my age or even younger. I try to imagine being conscripted to war, but the idea is impossible, implausible.

"Möchten Sie etwas trinken?"

I form an expression of regret.

"Désolée monsieur, mais c'est tard..."

He presses both hands to his chest, a gesture at once comical and alarmingly endearing.

"Sie brechen mein Herz."

If this is to mark my procession all the way to Jean-Jaurès, I will never make it in time. I need a speedier mode of transport. I keep walking, a long but leisurely stride, the heat in my face feasibly due to the balmy night. There are no civilian cars on the street, although once a German patrol drives past, its occupants armed and upright, and the precariousness of my situation strikes me again with force.

A horse and cart passes in the opposite direction. Another bicycle overtakes me, the cyclist's feet pedalling steadily. I watch as, a couple of blocks ahead, the bicycle skids to a halt and the rider dismounts, a parcel under one arm. He props the bicycle in the nearest side-street and rings a bell smartly. I slow my pace. I'm a block away when he steps inside the building. I walk decisively now.

I'm turning into the side-street and am about to step forward and seize the handlebars of the bicycle when the door to the apartment block opens. The boy steps out. He gives me a suspicious look. I'll look guilty if I turn back now so I'm forced to keep walking up the cobbled street. The foolhardiness of my almost-action hits me in a fit of weakness. Stealing a bicycle when it's still light? What a brilliant way to get myself captured. Idiot.

I continue uphill and turn right at the first opportunity, making my way parallel to the boulevard. At least I'm off the main roads, though there are plenty of smaller venues tucked away in these backstreets, where a lone woman might stand out more.

I glance upwards. As dusk begins to descend, lights briefly illuminate the windows of the six-storey buildings, and then the blackout curtains go up. Some windows remain still and empty, and I can't help wondering if they are—*were*—Jewish homes.

It seems inconceivable that Paris could continue, Paris could be cheerful, even frivolous, and yet less than a week ago Rachel's parents were dragged into the street, herded together like cattle. A little voice at the back of my head mutters: And what would you have done? I push the thought away uneasily.

I'm doing something now. I'm going to get this cello if it's the last thing I do.

Then the rhetoric of *that* thought stops me cold: this could well be the last thing I do, if I get caught. Worse, if I do get caught, I have no defences against interrogation, mental or physical. No papers, no false identity. Nothing. What I do have is a packet of Luckies—I've learned my lesson from last time—and my smartphone, a piece of technology far beyond anything they're doing at Bletchley, which would not only condemn me to the status of a spy but hand the Germans the blueprint for a computer in one pocket-sized piece.

And what if, after torture and the loss of my phone, I say something that inadvertently gives the Germans a tactical advantage? I'm no expert on the Second World War, but there are bound to be facts swilling around in my subconscious—dates, place names, the existence of the Enigma machine—that might damage the Allied campaign irrevocably. My only option would be to establish myself as insane, but people suffering mental illnesses didn't fare so well under the Nazis either.

The few people I pass on the streets are hurrying now—it must be nearing curfew. The lamps remain unlit, the streets empty out and the gloom of dusk deepens. I look skywards. Sporadic cloud cover, weak patches of starlight. No visible moon. I use the light from my phone to check a street sign, reorient myself. The display time on the screen has not altered since I came through. It's still six-twenty pm. What does that mean? Does some part of me remain in the twenty-first century, suspended forever in that second of transportation?

I push the phone back into my pocket, keep going. I pass along rue d'Orsel, beneath the hill of the Moulin Vert, down to Barbès where I first stayed after my arrival in Paris. The quickest route from here is back onto boulevard de la Chapelle, following the route of the Line 2 métro. I'm walking in near-darkness but I can hear pockets of life from the various cabarets and nightclubs continuing behind the blackout. I listen for footsteps, for the rap of military boots, impossible to disguise, the softer fall of the civilian shoes of people, like me, who don't want to be noticed. A gaggle of voices, male, slurred and drunk, forces me into a side street. Once I hear the approaching rumble of an engine and retreat to the edge of the street, crouching against the wall, my heart pounding as the patrol car draws closer. I catch the flash of torchlight, a glimpse of figures. There have been attacks, Rachel told me. Reprisals. They're more careful now. At first they couldn't imagine it, that anyone might resist. Why would they, with Petain whispering in their ears?

The car passes. In darkness, the noise of the engine is audible for a long time before fading. I keep walking. Past another métro, a station that in a few years time will be renamed Stalingrad. Swing right, down to avenue Jean-Jaurès, over the canal which gleams blackly under the starlight—I hurry, alarmed that I'll be caught in its reflection. From here, it's straight up the road.

TWENTY MINUTES LATER, with some furtive help from the light of my phone (battery: sixty per cent, time: eternally six-twenty pm) I'm climbing through an open window into the bathrooms of the conservatoire, feeling less Indiana Jones and more petty criminal. As I exit the bathroom I encounter a partially lit corridor, a shock to my retinas after the darkness of the streets. Rachel was right: there are people in the building. I can hear strains of music—brass and reed, the high-pitched singing of a violin—from both directions. There's something ghostly about it, dislocated from any source. I take out Rachel's scribbled map and check her directions. The practice rooms are to my left.

I tiptoe the length of the corridor, peering inside windows until I see the unmistakable shape of a double bass on a stand and someone who matches the description of Rachel's friend Jules. He's picking out notes on the piano, peering at a score, and from the sighing and the emphatic hand gestures, it's not progressing very well.

I tap on the door.

"I'm looking for Jules," I say. "The double bass?"

He speaks without turning, apparently oblivious to any concept of threat. "Who's asking?"

"Rachel sent me," I say. "My name's Gabriela."

This gets a reaction. He leaps up from the piano stool, crosses the room in two strides.

"Rachel? Where is she?"

"I can only speak to Jules."

"I am Jules, for god's sake."

"How do I know that?"

He points to the double bass.

"That's mine."

I check the corridor, glancing up and down to ensure we're alone, before I speak again.

"What was the duet you played with Rachel in autumn 'thirty-nine?"

"I wasn't *here* in 'thirty-nine."

"And in nineteen-forty?"

"The Rossini. First movement. Are we done with the interrogation? Where is Rachel?"

"What went wrong?"

"What?"

"In the Rossini, what went wrong?"

"The D-string was flat. It was horrendous. Is she safe?"

"All right." My heart slowly recovers. What would I have done if Jules had forgotten? I push him gently back into the practice room and shut the door behind us. "You pass. Yes, she's safe, for now. I need her cello. She's sent me to collect it."

"Wait a minute. I can't give her cello to just anyone."

"She won't leave Paris without it," I say. "And she has a chance to leave tonight."

Jules slumps on the piano stool.

"I heard her parents—"

"She has to get out tonight," I repeat.

"I should leave too." He looks despairingly at his surroundings.

I can imagine what's going through his head, and I don't envy him the dilemma. "I should."

"It's been arranged," I say. "It might screw things up if you're there too."

He nods slowly. I can't tell if he's relieved or disappointed. Both, probably.

"I can't get in the way of her chances," he says. "Who the hell are you, anyway?"

"I'm nobody."

"Some kind of agent?" he guesses.

"We shouldn't talk about that."

"Don't worry," he says. "Nobody here would dream of reporting. They'd be kicked out."

He falls silent and I have to prompt him. "The cello?"

"It's in room four. Come on."

He takes me a few doors down the corridor, and we enter a practice room identical to the first: a table, a piano, a music stand, a cello case resting in one corner. I notice a Rachmaninov score open on the piano. Concerto No. 3. Jules sees me looking.

"There was a German officer in here two, maybe three months ago," he says. "He wanted a tour. He stood right there where you are, one arm resting on the piano top, listening to me play. Afterwards, he said he'd been a musician at home himself, and hoped to return to it, after the war. He said he liked Russian music best, though he couldn't say that outside of this building. Not any more. Tchaikovsky as well, which surprised me, it doesn't seem to fit with the uniforms. My tutor asked him to play a couple of bars— as a courtesy, I suppose—and he did, and it was... exquisite." Jules comes to stand next to me by the piano. He plays an arpeggio, soft, tentative. "And then he asked how were we liking their concerts outside the Opera House? Smiling. All in this conspiratorial manner, you understand, like he wanted to get us on side."

"Did it work?"

Jules turns a page of the score. "I just want to make music."

He shuts the piano lid abruptly, and goes to fetch the cello, lifting the case and laying it flat on the table.

"Wait—"

He looks about, picks up a loose sheaf of papers from a music stand.

"She was working on this. Her tutor's notes are on it."

He opens the case and puts the papers inside.

"You'll let me know she's got out?"

"I'll ask her to get in touch. When she can."

"Where will she go?"

"South, I suppose. The Resistance—" I hesitate. "They'll have places."

"She wanted to play the Dvorák. At the Opera House."

There's a tag tied to the handle of the cello case, Rachel's name and address written in neat block letters. I untie it and give the tag to Jules.

"She will," I say firmly.

Jules doesn't reply. He is staring at the address tag in his hands. I remember Rachel's face as she said, *Paris makes me sick*, and I think that there are some things music can't transcend.

CHAPTER THIRTY-FIVE

THE STREETS SURROUNDING the Moulin Vert feel cold and deserted, as though an invisible wall occludes this section of Paris from the rest of the city. The Germans don't go up that far, Rachel told me. The Moulin's not included in their *guide aryen*—too ugly for the master race. The eight arms of the windmill loom over the hill, heavy and menacing in their stillness, the way they creak in a breeze not strong enough to move them. The impression makes me shiver, and then I realise why: it reminds me of the hooked arms of the swastika. I wonder if what Rachel said could possibly be true, that the Resistance are tunnelling into the hill, creating emergency escape routes from their Montmartre base. Aide Lefort claimed it was a hub for their activities. Are they there now, laying plots in the basements, patiently fiddling with the radio to find the BBC's illicit Radio Londres?

Making my way around to the back of the mill, I understand why this makes a good site for conspiracy, but the thought is far from reassuring. I check my phone covertly, using its dimming light to navigate the cobbled streets. By the time I reach the vineyard, the battery has dropped to forty per cent, and already I'm wondering how I'm going to find my way back to Clichy. The vineyard itself presents a new problem—it's surrounded by a wire fence, topped with barbs. But Rachel told me to wait inside, so there must be a way in.

I walk its circumference, barely thirty metres on each side, running my hand lightly over the meshing until I find a place where the wire has been cut. I push the flap aside, wincing at the echoing, metallic rasp. I push the cello case through first, which only just fits, and I scramble through after. The wire snags on Tournier's clothes and I hear something rip before I tug myself clear.

Picking up the cello case, I stand completely still for a moment, listening. I can hear the faint whisper of the vines and the trees overhanging one side of the vineyard. A rich tang of earth and grape rises from the ground. I wonder if this place is tended in wartime, or if the vines are growing freely. Glancing once behind me, seeing nothing, I move deeper into their cover.

I've only progressed a few metres when my foot catches and I trip. I fall clumsily, suppressing a cry, releasing the cello. The case drops to the ground and I can hear the strings reverberating inside with the impact.

Next thing I know, something cold and hard is slipped against my throat.

"Don't move."

French. I attempt to speak, to explain myself, and the knife pushes harder. Are these Rachel's rescuers? What if it's a trap?

An arm grips around my torso and hauls me to a sitting position, but the knife doesn't move. I can feel the vines on either side of us. The intense, sweet smell of the fruit fills my nose.

"Who are you?" demands my captor. It's a male voice, low and strained.

I assess the possible answers. If this is the Resistance, they need to know I'm an ally, not a threat. If it isn't, I'm fucked anyway.

"Rachel," I manage. "I'm helping Rachel."

The knife relaxes slightly but it remains at my throat.

"My name's Gabriela. I brought the cello."

"That's not the password."

This time, I catch the edge of an accent.

"You're American," I hiss, and I feel him tense. I switch to English. "I brought the bloody cello. Rachel's cello. It's in that case."

The rustle of vines moving. Someone else is behind us.

"Who knows you're here?"

The American continues to speak in French.

"No one. Only Rachel!" The knife pushes again. "Wait. Wait!" What the hell was it Lefort said? I dredge my memory. "Eight arms! Against your four arms, we raise eight." I tip my head as best I can. "The Moulin Vert."

"Don't say its name!"

The second person steps around us and crouches slowly. I hear hands running over the cello case. Then the newcomer steps aside.

"You open it." This voice is female, and a native accent. The knife slides away from my throat and moves to the small of my back.

"Fine," I whisper. I feel for the case, find the clasps and click them open. The woman steps closer, and a tiny flashlight skims over its contents, illuminating the rich wood of the cello, the loosened strings. I hear muttering behind us.

"What if there's something inside it—"

"You can't break it!" I hiss. "I brought it all the way from the conservatoire. Her parents gave it to her."

That gives them pause, but moments later they're scanning the cello again, shielding the torchlight with their coats, peering into the f-holes, lifting the neck to give the instrument a tentative shake. I have visions of the doomed cello being hacked to pieces by agents of the Resistance, but fortunately we are interrupted by the arrival of Madame Tournier and Rachel herself. This time the protocols are observed; I hear the mutter of voices but I can't make out what they're saying, probably something about eight arms. Apparently Rachel has certified my presence, because I'm now left to my own devices. After a couple of minutes of intense discussion, I hear her move away from the group.

"Hello again," I murmur.

"Figment," she says tiredly.

"Figment with a cello."

Rachel stops. Then she drops to the ground, her body collapsed over the open case. I can hear the slight squeak of her running her fingers up and down the strings, over the wood. I can hear her breathing shakily.

"We can't take that with us," says the Frenchwoman, returning.

"Hang on a minute—"

"We don't even know who you are—"

"She's my figment," says Rachel. "And the cello is coming."

"Has Tournier not explained this to you? Our success depends upon secrecy. Secrecy depends upon invisibility. *That* is not going to make us invisible."

I hear the click of the case shutting.

"If it doesn't come, I don't come," Rachel says. "There's no point. Anyway, you can't leave it here."

"The Englishwoman can take it back."

"No way—"

"I have to go," says Madame Tournier.

"Yes, there's more than enough of us already..."

Rachel and Tournier embrace briefly. Tournier says only, "Do what they say, you'll be safe," then makes her way back through the vines. It's too dark to see her leave, and I wonder where she's going next tonight, what she has risked to bring Rachel here, what would happen to her were she caught. What will happen to her, in the years between now and 1945. The others have taken themselves a short distance away and are arguing softly. Rachel and I wait.

"You can bring it," says the American at last. The Frenchwoman remains silent, radiating disapproval, but does not contradict him. "Time to move," he says.

Rachel gets to her feet. I lift the cello case for her.

"Good luck," I murmur.

The Frenchwoman moves swiftly to my side, and squeezes my arm until it hurts.

"You saw nothing tonight," she hisses. "You did nothing tonight. And don't ever mention that place aloud again, you understand?"

"Don't worry. I'll be gone from Paris myself, very soon."

When I hand over the cello case, Rachel seizes my wrist. I can feel her shaking. In the clouded night I can't see her face except as a swirl of grey in a world of darker greys.

"Where did you come from?" she says.

"From the future," I reply, knowing she won't believe me. Knowing that of all the events of the last few days, nothing has substance. She's moving through a plane of unreality, because that is the only way this can be happening, can be survivable—if it is not real, if we have shifted to another dimension entirely.

But her grasp upon my wrist tightens. She says, "It's not like this, is it? The future?"

I think of the train taking her parents out of France and its destination. I think of what will follow: of Vietnam, of Bosnia and Rwanda and Sierra Leone, Iraq and Afghanistan, Israel and Palestine, of 9/11, of Syria, a litany of conflict that seems to have no beginning or conceivable end, and I feel a wash of despair that I know I cannot, under any circumstances, communicate to her.

"No," I say. "It's not like this."

She releases my arm.

"Thank you, figment," she whispers.

"Come *on*." The Frenchwoman is impatient.

I wait as they file away through the vineyard, the Frenchwoman and the American and Rachel Clouatre and the cello. I can hear the rustling of the vines as they push through, but it might just be the wind, and then it is just the wind.

CHAPTER THIRTY-SIX

FOR A WEEK I hide behind the false wall in Millie's storeroom, racked with hunger, waiting for a flare. Smoking might allay the hunger, but the smell will give me away. I tear apart the cigarettes, sniffing the tobacco, I even try chewing it, but the taste makes me retch. At night, when the last of the clientele have gone home and the bartenders and cleaners have packed up, I sneak upstairs and steal some sugar and mix it with water. With rationing in place, I don't dare to take food for fear of discovery, although if I have to wait much longer for a flare, I will be forced to take greater risks. Some evenings the waitress and her German lover come downstairs and flirt outside the storeroom, and the old panic laps at my consciousness. Ich liebe dich, he says. Perhaps he believes it, too. She panders to him. You're sweet, she says. Perhaps she believes it too. I become drowsy. My mind wanders. I have dreams full of violence and running, of boarded-up trains shunting through the night, of lava brimming in ovens. Day by day I feel my strength draining away. If anyone comes, will I be alert enough to hide myself? What if Madame Tournier brings another fugitive?

In any case, shouldn't I be trying to get out of Paris, out of France and over to England, to warn people about the camps, the unspeakable horrors they contain, and more, the conflicts that await beyond this war—Iraq the first time, Iraq the second time, all the mistakes that could be averted between this century and the next? Shouldn't I be trying to save the world? These dark, grand thoughts wash up and retreat. They leave me behind, alone and confused, certain of only one thing: the insignificance of a single body, the ridiculousness of the notion that I might be a hero. I'm no Madame Tournier. I'm hungry, carb-depleted, scared. The Western world doesn't believe in prophets.

A part of me wonders if Rachel was right all along: perhaps I am a figment, intruding on this timezone only by virtue of her imagination, or mine. Either way, I'm at the mercy of the anomaly, and all I can work with are the scenarios I'm given. A darker part of my mind says: or the scenarios I've been pushed into. Best not to think about that.

On the eighth day of confinement I sense it, still a way off, but approaching. I lie still, drifting and exhausted, willing the flare closer. When it takes me I am barely conscious. On the other side, I have just enough awareness to crawl to a corner of the keg room and pull Tournier's borrowed coat over me. The beer lines gurgle gently. I drift.

When I come to, hours have passed since the time I entered the keg room and the day shift will be en route, if they're not here already. I look about me, disorientated. Fruit juice. I empty a bottle of it down my throat. The sugar rush makes my body scream. Crisps. I rip through five packets. Crumbs and empty packets discarded on the floor. I'm dizzy. I get to my feet and stumble upstairs. I can hear Angel singing as he goes about setting up the bar, too high and out of tune. He's playing Edith Piaf. Edith Piaf, who sang at German gatherings during the occupation and returned to the Moulin Rouge after it. I avoid the front bar and take the back exit out to the alleyway.

Leaning against the wall, resplendent in aquamarine, is the chronometrist. Her age and appearance has altered once again:

today she is long, blonde and athletic, and wears a fitted sports tracksuit and Nikes. Standing on one leg to stretch out her quads, she beams at me.

"My dear. Well done. Really. *Well done.* What a star—in the making you are! No! Scratch that! A star come home."

I eye her wearily, hungrily.

"You've got a nerve, showing up here again. You were found dead in an ice box in there, don't you remember?"

"Not the way—you might. Other corporealities, you understand."

"You're like some sick, twisted version of *Transfusion.* But worse."

"Do you want to know how the final series ends?"

"No! Jesus."

She takes a wary step backwards.

"You're upset."

"And you're surprised? You manipulated me. You sent me to World War Two! You wrote it on the floor of the keg room."

"Me? No..."

"There was a girl down there. A Jewish girl."

"And you helped her, my dear. Go and—where are we?—*Google* Rachel Clouatre. I suspect you'll find some—quite lovely sonatas, now that she's got her cello back. She never did marry, you know."

The chronometrist steps her left foot back and flexes her right, leaning forward over her thighs. Her nose twitches.

"It's all right, my dear. It's over. Well... it could be over. That is, it's never *really* over. But I only came to offer my humble congratulations. I'm going on tour for a while."

"Good for you. I hope it's Australia."

She gives me a wounded look. "I like you my dear, but you can be very harsh. Very harsh indeed."

"You really are a piece of work—" I begin, but she straightens, smiles at me, says:

"Goodbye, Hallie, my dear incumbent. When the time comes, remember the way of Janus is not always the way to be true to yourself. Some of us were born to be more than human. I wish you good travelling."

Her face twitches. I can almost picture the chronometrist evaporating out of her. Then she blinks and there's just a woman in a sports tracksuit staring at the stranger in front of her, her mouth parted a little in her confusion.

PART SEVEN

Basilosaurus

THE ANOMALY IS growing.

With each flare a new tendril extends, teasing through the centuries, bursting into flower through moments, months and years. The anomaly is weaving a tapestry, one ever more complex as the desires of its incumbent propagate. The incumbent is a rich resource, and after so long waiting, the anomaly is greedy. It needs to feast.

The incursions of the squatter have become a rarer irritation. The squatter will never be welcome, but is more easily tolerated in this era of prosperity.

Flares come. The anomaly expands. In the wake of a flare, it is sated, but this never lasts. It cannot. The flares become more frequent, and the greater their frequency, the briefer the satiation. The anomaly can never be whole. Not when it knows the incumbent is withholding. Not when the incumbent still has more to give.

And the incumbent does.

CHAPTER THIRTY-SEVEN

THE BEST TIME to travel is after work, at the end of the night shift and before the day preparations begin. For a precious couple of hours, there is no one downstairs but me. I lie in the keg room and let the cold chill my body as I await the warmth of the flare. It rolls in, a well of sound in my ears. The anomaly scoops me up and whirls me away.

I have been to Paris at the height of the Terror, slinking around the city in fear of losing my head. I've travelled to 1661, joined the festivities in the Tuileries while Louis XIV parades on horseback, dressed as a Roman Emperor. I've witnessed revolutions and occupations, bombardments and plagues. I've drunk champagne at the height of the Belle Epoque. Seen Sarah Bernhardt perform Voltaire, Josephine Baker bring jazz to the city. I've juggled batons at the opening night of the Moulin Rouge.

Aide Lefort says we must do what we can, and so I do. I help where I can. *When* I can. Some days I endeavour to will myself to a particular time, other days I surrender to the anomaly's desires. Acts of kindness will save the world, however small, says Aide Lefort. And this will be my code of practice.

I return to the end of the nineteenth century, and I find Millie. She is older, elaborately dressed, riding down the boulevard in the back of an open carriage. As it sweeps past, her head turns and she sees me. Her eyes widen, she stands up in the carriage. She shouts, "Gabriela!"

I chase the carriage on foot, catching up with her at Opéra. She jumps from the carriage, although she has a driver now, whose hand she rests her gloved fingers upon to descend.

"Gabriela! It's really you? What are you doing here? Where did you *go?*"

"I'll tell you," I say. "But not here."

"Oh, I've got my own place now. A proper place, that is. You won't believe it, life has gone simply delirious. Only—I'm not sure he'll let you ride with me, now I'm a respectable woman of business." She indicates the driver with her parasol.

"Tell me the address, I'll meet you there."

Millie's apartment is a luxurious affair. I stroll around, admiring the gilt-edged mirrors, the heavy silk drapes and Persian rugs. Millie watches me, at first perplexed, then furious, and finally succumbing to the absurdity of the situation. She demands my story. I tell her the truth—what does it matter? Who can it harm? Perhaps it can help. Millie listens, fan a-flutter, incredulous.

"You went where? Another *century?* What happens?"

"I can't talk about that."

"You disappear for ten years and then you return saying you went to the future? I think you can."

I tell her some things. A delinquent feeling.

"Why didn't you come back sooner?"

"I have to wait for a flare. They're like waves. They wash up and carry you to another time."

"Sometimes I thought I'd made you up, or it was all a dream. I thought perhaps the gin had driven me properly mad. I kept remembering what you said about not being alone. I thought perhaps you was a ghost. But I had your boots."

"You've got my DMs?"

"You must have forgot them. When you rushed off that morning."

"I know. I'm sorry."

She brings me the boots, cleaned up and stored in a hat box.

"Here they are, good as new."

"Millie, I can't believe you kept them all this time."

"'Course I kept them! Though I confess, I did give away the yellow decoration, only the other day in fact. An artist friend of mine was suffering what you might call a drought of inspiration—Théophile Steinlen is his name—and I thought this would do the trick."

"You gave Pikachu to Théophile Steinlen?" I say dazedly. "The guy who does the Chat Noir?"

"Oh, I don't know what he does. But he seemed very pleased."

Millie has done well for herself. Valleroy, she tells me, was found guilty of fraud against the state, and has gone into exile somewhere in southern Europe. She has a new lover now, a richer and kinder one, who has bought her this apartment. She has started a small business supplying fabrics to milliners ("I borrowed your name for that one—Gabriel rather than Gabriela, that is—easier, for the books"). She is saving up to buy a tavern.

"Anywhere in mind?" I ask innocently.

When the time comes to leave, we are both crying. But Millie is hopeful.

"I'll see you again?"

"You never know."

I do see her. She ages, and I remain forever young. I see her in 1894, on the night a tavern in her name opens on boulevard de Clichy. I see her in 1901, twice-married and twice-divorced, a patron of the Moulin Rouge, a setter of trends—in particular, hats. She shows me her latest gift, an original artwork by Théophile Steinlen titled *The Yellow Devil* which bears an uncanny resemblance to Pikachu, and asks if her artist friend is famous in the future. I tell her he is, but Pokémon Go is no more. "Is that bad?" asks Millie.

The last time I see Millie is in 1913, at the end of her life, with tuberculosis drowning her lungs. The room smells of laudanum. Millie is gaunt, feverish, sometimes lucid, more often not. She whispers to herself, snatches of tangled memories and phantasms only she can see. I take her hand. I can feel the heat of it through the gloves I am instructed to wear. She is burning up, burning out. She is dying. If she has ever truly needed me it is now, but I am unable to hold back my tears, the tide of misery rising in my chest with the knowledge that I can't stop this. I can't save her. For the first time I feel anger at the anomaly. But how can I blame it for bringing me here when it only responds to my desires?

Millie's hand quivers in mine. She has seen me. She reaches up, pulls my face close to hers. She murmurs, "I knew you'd come, Gabriela."

"Yes," I say. "Yes, I'm here, Millie. I'm here."

I NEVER TOLD Gabriela that I stole her identity. Reinvention must remain a secret; it is the only way it can succeed.

One morning I come downstairs to find Gabriela waiting outside the keg room. Her arms are folded and it comes to me that she is barring the way. The thought that anyone might try to stop me travelling fills me with rage.

"What are you doing here?"

"It's time we tested this properly," she says.

"What do you mean?"

"You know what I mean. I need to try and travel. Then we will know the truth about this thing."

"That won't work," I say at once. I'm shocked by the rush of jealousy that takes me. I do not want to share my window to another world.

"How do you know?"

"The chronometrist said it was linked to me—"

"You cannot trust that chronometrist. She lied to you, she made you do things. Change things. We should ignore her, and we should try with me."

"Look, if other people could travel, why hasn't anyone already? How come it's only me?"

Gabriela regards me calmly. "If you are certain it is only you, then it won't hurt to do a test, will it?"

This logic is irrefutable. I grit my teeth and push aside my reluctance.

"Fine. Let's do it. But I'm telling you now, nothing will happen."

It's unlikely there will be a flare. I know the anomaly's moods, and it is quiet today. It has been quiet for a few days, although I don't tell Gabriela this. After Millie's death I felt strange, uncertain about its intentions, as though it had betrayed me. I took some time away from the keg room. Now I feel its loss.

Gabriela closes the door behind us, and looks around.

"What do we do?"

"I usually lie down, or sit against a keg."

"Okay."

We lie back on the concrete, our heads close to one another and our feet pointing away.

"Just close your eyes," I say. "And listen."

"For the music?"

"Yeah."

"Okay."

"You have to sort of focus on it."

Gabriela fidgets, adjusting some part of her clothing. "I can't hear anything."

Good, I think.

"Just... wait."

We lie in silence. I cannot hear anything either. The anomaly is muted. I wonder if it is because Gabriela is here. Because she is not an incumbent. Then another, less pleasant thought occurs: what if Gabriela travels and I don't? What if the anomaly will only tolerate one incumbent, and it rejects me for her?

I open my eyes quickly. She's still there. Don't be silly, I scold myself. You're acting as if this is a sentient object, conscious and capricious. Which it might be, but I prefer not to think about that.

I close my eyes again, breathe more deeply. Listen to the *drip, drip* into the puddle. I hear Gabriela's breath ease in and out. The keg room is dim and cold. We are deep, deep underground.

Underwater, in a bubble of air. A monster looms out of the gloom. Its head is crocodilian, the ovoid body steered by small front fins. Tapering away for a good five metres, the muscular tail undulates vertically, finishing its sweep with two almost delicate flukes. *Basilosaurus.* I gape. The light in the air bubble goes out. I hold my breath as the creature draws near, afraid that even a sigh might break the bubble's fragile walls.

The monster swims overhead, its sleek body blueish-greenish-grey. This is strange. I'm flat on my back on the ocean floor, naked, spine curved into the sand. The eye of the basilosaurus is round and wary. When its mouth opens, I see the rows of teeth. Basilosaurus forges on, questing, and a shoal of tiny fish skid past in the opposite direction, safe from its snapping jaws.

The bubble is illuminated once more. The air in here is warm and amniotic. A ripple lifts me up, off the sand. I'm moving. Ahead, basilosaurus's tail sweeps up and down in powerful strokes. The bubble is following. We gain speed and soon we are coasting along the ocean floor. I marvel at the deep sea denizens. Weeds and grasses wave delicate arms. Small creatures burrow into the sand and vanish.

The ocean bed slopes abruptly. We are travelling into darker, deeper territory. Here the shapes of the ocean dwellers are indistinct;

things that pulse and quiver. We approach a formation of rocks. As we draw nearer I see there are many, separate piles, with uneven surfaces.

We have come to an ossuary. The bones are stacked in small pyramids. Beyond them I see more pyramids, stretching back into the impenetrable gloom. The empty eye sockets of a million skulls, alien in form. How did they die? How did they come to be here?

I feel a sudden, forceful shudder through the water. The bones start to shake. The stacks falter, a skull falls from the top and rolls across the floor towards me. Red pigment bleeds through its teeth, swirling out.

The bubble bursts. I watch crimson water pouring in. I gulp air. I don't want to drown, but the stream is ready to immerse me. As if the cave roof has collapsed, and the ocean is seeping through, but I am not in the cave, I am at the bottom of the Eocene ocean, and it is cold.

It shouldn't be cold.

It shouldn't be *this* cold.

My eyes open. I'm panting. Dim light fills my vision. Stacks of kegs. *Drip, drip. Drip, drip.* The puddle in the keg room. It never disappears, no matter what they do. Where does the water come from? Gabriela is slumped beside me, her cheek to the floor. I can see her eyes moving behind their lids.

My head feels heavy and drugged.

"Gabriela." I put a hand on her shoulder. "Gabriela, wake up."

Remnants of the dream—or transportation—flutter. A shell on the ocean floor. I can still feel its smooth convex curve against my palm.

Is she in the same place?

I give her shoulder a shake.

"Wake up."

Gabriela's fingers twitch. I watch anxiously as she comes back to consciousness. All at once, I'm aware of how irresponsible I have been in bringing her here. It's different for me: I know the anomaly. Gabriela does not, and I hadn't even considered the possibility that it might put her in danger.

"Are you okay? Were you dreaming?"

Gabriela blinks, rubs her eyes. She looks dazed. From the other side of the wall, I hear the faint hum of the generator. Gurgling in the lines. The day staff must have started.

"Strange," she says. "I was swimming."

"Deep in the ocean?" I ask. "Were there skulls?"

"Skulls? No! Nothing like that. Very pleasant, warm water." Gabriela brushes dirt off her trousers.

"So you didn't travel?"

"No. Perhaps you are right. It only works for you."

I am ashamed of the flood of relief when she says this.

"And you?"

"No. I was just dreaming too."

"What's that in your hand?"

I look down. My fingers are clenched into a fist. When I uncurl them, sand trickles from my palm. I pinch the grains between index finger and thumb.

"Let's go, Hallie. We need sleep. This place—" She shakes her head. "It's not good for you. You should spend less time down here."

DID GABRIELA SENSE my guilty relief? She does not ask to try and travel again. On the nights when I defer going to Oz to hide downstairs, she catches my eye and I know she knows what I'm up to. Sometimes she presses me to come with the others, sometimes she doesn't. But what can I do? The anomaly calls me; I have to answer.

When I step into a different time, the world is clean and untouched. It does not matter if it is the bloodiest revolution or the dullest of mornings—in my eyes, it has just been made, and I, appearing in it for the first time, am new again. The anomaly makes me a master of invention. I pull worlds out of a hat and I slip between them, unseen. I have no facades to maintain. I can always move on.

Not far in the future, they are building towers around the circumference of Paris. Towers with shining, bluish glass, extensions of the architecture at La Défense. Paris is tall and glorious. The City of Light glitters like a galaxy of freshly minted stars. On the cover of *Time* magazine, Aide Lefort's face at age thirty-five: *A New Bohemia: My manifesto to change the world.*

"Do you remember you told me you had planned to go to Rome?"

"Rome? Oh, yeah. That was ages ago." I squeeze Léon's hand. "Before we met."

We are at his studio, watching back-to-back episodes of *Transfusion*. I'm not convinced Léon entirely gets *Transfusion*, but he watches it anyway. For me. The credits roll up. My legs are hooked over his, our fingers interlaced. A rare night off together. I try to relax. I know these rituals of domesticity should make me happy—they are the hallmarks of belonging; they are everything I ever craved—but more and more I feel that this is another realm, strange and unfamiliar. It feels as though I'm moonlighting on someone else's life.

"I was thinking," says Léon. "Maybe we should go."

"To Rome?"

"Why not?"

"On holiday?"

The idea of leaving the anomaly, however briefly, fills me with alarm. I begin to muster excuses for why I can't possibly go on holiday.

"Maybe for longer."

I mute the television and twist to face him.

"Longer? You mean... leave Clichy?" The idea is so absurd, I laugh. Leave Clichy! "You're joking, right?"

"No, I'm serious. I've been here for a long time. Lately I've been feeling like I need a change of scene." He hesitates. "Maybe you do too."

"What's that supposed to mean?"

"You haven't been around as much. You seem tired all the time. You said you get headaches. I thought perhaps... something was bothering you."

"Nothing's bothering me."

"Are you sure?"

"Yes, I'm sure. And I don't want to leave Paris. I love Paris. This is my life now. I thought it was yours too. Or was all that talk about not wanting to screw things up just some bullshit excuse?"

"Putain, Hallie—it was just an idea—"

I flop back against the sofa, my words replaying back to me. I'm being unfair, I can see that. How could Léon understand?

"Sorry. Léon, I'm sorry. I didn't mean to snap. It's just... I belong here. The thought of leaving... it makes me anxious. Panicky, I suppose. Like... like what happened at the catacombs."

Léon doesn't say anything for a moment, but I can tell he's upset. I owe him more than this.

"You never did tell me about that," he says slowly. "About the panic attacks."

"I thought I'd left it all behind. That's the thing: you think you're better, you think you're over it, and then it happens again."

"What started it?"

"I don't know. It's hard to explain."

He strokes my hair gently. Somewhere in the distance, the anomaly's song chimes. Most of the time I barely notice, I am so accustomed to it, but occasionally a note will stand out, reminding me. As if I could forget.

"Try me," says Léon.

Why not, I think. Anything's better than talk of leaving Paris. And at least I can be honest about this, even if it's hard to talk about.

"It's like... it's a feeling of being squeezed. Like I'm becoming smaller and smaller until I might... dissolve."

I slump down deeper in the sofa. Outside, colour is draining from the sky, but neither of us moves to switch on the light.

"Did you ever have something happen which changed the way you thought about everything?"

"Half a dozen times."

"That was my volcano day."

It feels odd, to finally say the words aloud. But here I am, moonlighting. Perhaps that makes it possible. Perhaps it's not me making the confession at all. It's the old me, someone I shed months ago.

Léon waits.

"There was an art project, at school. I was always shit at art. Theo and George were brilliant, of course. They take after our parents. But this project was different. We had to make a volcano, and you know I've always loved science. I thought, this is it. This is the thing that's going to earn her approval. My mother. I hero worshipped her, you see. I used to sit outside her studio with my toys for hours, dreaming about all the places I was going to take her when I was this famous explorer."

There was always a draught in the corridor, but I liked knowing that she was just the other side of the door. As if I was her secret guardian. One day she opened the door before I had time to move out of the way, and she was carrying a painting that was still wet, and she tripped over me and dropped it. The painting was ruined.

After that I was banned from loitering outside the studio.

"Anyway, I planned it all out. I got a load of books from the library. I asked Theo and George for help making it and they both said they would. George showed me this trick with a wire coat hanger, but of course when it came down to it they were both busy and I had to make it myself. It sounds stupid, but I was so upset."

"You were a kid," says Léon. "Of course you'd be upset."

I remember standing on the porch, shivering without my coat. I could feel tears of frustration welling up. George had broken his promise. Theo had gone to one of her numerous friends' houses. Dad was with Ray Yellowlees and my mother had emerged from her studio at around five o'clock with paint on her face looking dazed, smiled and told me to do my homework, put a crumpet in the toaster, eaten it with shrimp paste, and gone to bed.

"But I still had an opportunity to prove something. I was going to do the coat hanger thing, but then I noticed the door to her studio was open. She must have been totally spaced, she never left that door open."

In the light from the street lamps outside, I could see something looming in the middle of the room, a deformed shape, almost human, leaning at an angle. It cast a shadow against the opposite wall.

"I went inside. There was the clay figure, whatever it was she was working on. I remember being kind of spooked by it. And then there was some leftover clay beside it. Exactly the right size for a volcano, I thought. So I made the volcano out of clay. I got really into it with the paint and everything, left a note saying I'd take it to school in the morning, and then I went to bed."

The noise woke me up. It woke everyone up. Shouting and bangs and crashes as furniture was kicked or overturned. At first I thought there were burglars in the house. Then I realized that the shouting was my mother, and the other, confused voice was my father, and then George and Theo started yelling too.

What the hell's going on?
Ioanna, calm down—
Shut up down there, I'm trying to sleep!
It's fucking Hallie—she's fucking destroyed—FUCK! FUCK!
My stomach turned into a bag of snakes. I shook.

Footsteps pounded the stairs. My door flew open. Mum stood there, looking angrier than I had ever seen her in my life.

"Hallie, what the fuck have you done?"

I screamed and hid under the duvet. A hand seized my ankle, yanked me out. Mum grabbed my shoulders. Her face was in my face. She was shaking me so hard I could taste blood in my mouth.

"For god's sake, Ioanna—"

"Mum, stop it!"

Mum raised her hand and slapped me hard across the face. I fell sideways and slammed into the wall. I saw dots. George yelled, "Jesus Christ, Mum!"

When the dots cleared I saw her face, livid and twisted. It took George and Theo to pull her away. I dove back under the duvet. I heard Mum kick the wall, then punch it. Dad dragged her out of the room. He and George were talking, trying to calm her down. They went downstairs. My door shut. The sounds from below were muffled.

Everything hurt. I thought my teeth were going to fall out. I could feel the indents where her fingers had gripped me and the bruise coming up where my head had hit the wall.

An arm settled on me, on top of the duvet. Theo murmured:

"It's all right. It's all right. It's just... that was her gallery piece. What were you thinking?"

I couldn't stop shaking. It was a long time before I managed to reply.

"I had to have a volcano. You wouldn't help me."

I felt Theo's arm stiffen. I thought she was going to leave.

"Don't go away, Theo! She might come back."

"She won't. She wouldn't hurt you, Hal, you know that. She just... lost it for a minute. That work's worth ten thousand pounds."

"It looked like a spare bit," I whispered.

"I know. I know it did. But, you know, that's art."

George came back with some ice cubes wrapped in a tea towel. They conversed in low voices. George went away. Theo held the ice against the bruise on my head. She stroked my back while I cried into my pillow. Theo said Mum would never hurt me, but she had. I told myself a story. Theo was an albatross, a strong, beautiful bird from another universe. The albatross's wing covered me. Its eyes were alert and watchful. I closed my eyes more tightly and told myself the story again, mouthing it into the pillow. I could feel the feathers growing out of Theo's arm, brushing against my back. Her beak nudged my head, telling me it was all okay. Except it wasn't.

"The next day we were meant to hand in and I didn't have anything to show. I knew I couldn't say what had really happened, so I lied. I said Dad had had an accident in the studio. She believed me, the teacher. I didn't think she would. Obviously I was glad I got away with it, I was glad she believed me, but the thing I couldn't stop thinking was how wrong I'd been. To expect help, from any of them. George, Theo. Mum. I should have known all along—I should have known they'd let me down."

Over the years that followed I road-tested this theory with varying parameters, and I was rarely proven wrong. It was my first scientific experiment.

"Did she ever do that again?"

There's something dangerous in Léon's tone.

I shake my head. "No. She wasn't an abusive parent, it wasn't like that. It's not like that. But that one occasion was enough. Because I realised, you see. I realized the art would always come first. The rest of us were just... trappings. Even Dad."

Léon pulls me closer. I lie in his arms. I don't know what I expected, telling him this story. Catharsis, redemption? Or simply relief, to have talked and shared? But all I feel is a long-unspoken sadness.

"I didn't really answer your question. About the panic."

"It's okay."

"They started when I was a teenager. I've had them on and off since then. I thought things would be better at university, but the attacks got worse. Like being further away had just made it more obvious how far apart we really were."

"Hallie. You can't let anyone make you feel that way. You're not small. You're infinite."

I think, but cannot tell him, when I travel through the anomaly, I do feel infinite. But you can't follow me there. And I feel suddenly, desperately sad.

A SATURDAY MORNING in early June. It is ten-thirty, working up to a blazing day. Half the night team are sitting in the middle of the boulevard, drinking cans of paint stripper masquerading as beer and cheering the cars that slog past. Gabriela is wearing wings. They are white nylon stretched over a wire frame, and they poke gauzily out from between her shoulder blades. She has make-up smeared across her cheeks, green paint with bits of glitter that glint like scales instead of skin. Our faces, exposed to daylight, are red-eyed and dissipated.

Angel, who is meant to be setting up the bar for a new day but has left the chef in charge, has come to join us for a cigarette and an aperitif. He eyes the beer cans in disgust.

"Really? Poussins, you are actually drinking this?"

"Bring us some beers, Angel," begs Bo.

"Non, shots!" Victor staggers to his feet and begins to conduct the air. "Shots, shots, shots!"

"The bar is not open yet," says Angel, who is sober and, I can tell, enjoying goading us. "You must wait two hours."

"Man, they won't notice a few Coronas from the fridge," Mike cajoles him.

"Actually I am thinking of leaving Millie's," says Angel.

Unable to form coherent sentences, we stare at him.

"No—"

"You can't—"

"This is no life," says Angel severely. "Poussins, look at you."

Gabriela takes a picture of him. "You, you are not drunk!" she shouts.

"No. I am sober. And you are very, very drunk, Gabriela. So are you, Bo. And Victor. And Isobel... is she asleep? She will turn red as a tomato, with that complexion. And Mike. And Hallie—"

"I'm less drunk," I say, which is true, marginally.

"Poussins, we are all of us so good at *talking* about doing something, but none of us ever does it. Instead we rot away our lives in this minimum-wage hovel, pouring pints for connards who don't tip and cleaning up their vomit. I cannot stay in Clichy forever. Everybody leaves."

Bo sits up. "But not you—"

"Everybody."

Gabriela looks morose, and I pass her the beer can quickly. But Angel's words have cast a blight upon our party. Victor wakes Isobel, who jolts up in alarm, her brown hair sticking out in a frizz. Bo drains his can.

"I go to the library," declares Gabriela. She gets unsteadily to her feet. I should go with her, guide her back towards her studio, to sleep. Instead I sneak into Millie's and go downstairs and open up the keg room. It is cold. Goosebumps rise on my arms and neck. I have come to love this chill, its icy fingers soft against my skin.

Today the song is contemplative and soothing. There won't be a flare. I am happy just to be here, looking after the site. If it is sentient, then it knows I am here and it recognizes me. I am the secret guardian, constant and true. I curl up by a juice delivery and fall asleep. In my sleep, I hear the eternal percussion of the puddle: *drip, drip. Drip, drip. Drip, drip.*

LÉON BRINGS UP Rome again. It turns into a full-on argument, heated and horrible, shouting at one another across his studio. I've never seen him shout before. I've never seen him angry. He keeps repeating the same things. *You're not well. The nights are making you sick. You need a break.* It's unbearable. Afterwards, we apologise to one another, but the tension remains.

Léon has a point, though I can't let on. I do feel tired all the time, and fragile, as though I've left parts of myself behind where I've travelled, and now I'm stretched very thinly across a great expanse. I keep getting headaches. Dull, then bouts of sharpness. Occasionally the pain is enough to bring tears to my eyes. Sometimes it is an effort to meet the anomaly's call. Sometimes I doubt myself, questioning whether I am a worthy incumbent, not sure I am strong enough, brave enough to keep up with its demands. Fear draws close, that it might desert me, and I will be made desolate. But then I wake again in a new world, and I can see it is worth everything. The tiredness, the headaches, the anxiety—all disappear.

The next time I am in the keg room, an uncanny thing happens. The flare rolls up and I'm halfway under when my own face appears before me. A shaky rendition, pale and startled, but horrifyingly familiar. The sight is a dousing of cold in the warmth of the flare. My body contorts in panic.

This can't happen.

I focus all of my energy into pulling back to the present. The anomaly doesn't like it. I can feel the force of its resistance. There's a terrible pressure at my joints, a cold that sears my body as it confronts my resolve. The anomaly wants the transportation. It *needs* it. Is it even possible to reverse the process?

Then abruptly, the pressure eases and I lurch back. For several minutes I lie flat, my heart thumping in my chest, the sweat chilling my skin. I remember my first day at Millie's. Eloise showing me the keg room. That ghostly apparition. That was me. There's a throbbing in my nose, my temples.

It's the first time I have resisted the call to travel, and afterwards, the anomaly is silent for over a fortnight. I have the troubling sense that it is unhappy with me, even angry, over my defection. I try to appease it, waiting every night in hope of a flare, setting alarms to wake myself in the middle of the day, just in case. When a flare finally comes, the relief is crushing.

I SEE LESS of Gabriela. I see less of Léon. Several times I catch him on the verge of speaking. I see the words form, hover on the brink of his lips, as he struggles with some inner turmoil. And then he discards them. I might have pushed him, once. But the truth is we all have secrets. Things we cannot reveal. I can imagine what he wants to say: that this closeness we have formed is compromised, that my absence, physical and mental, makes a mockery of us being together. We should stop. I can see it coming. I know it will hurt when it does; I sense that hurt loitering in the distance, I sense its citrus tang, the awful aftermath of rejection. But I cannot bring myself to make the repairs necessary to avoid it. There is another in my life and it takes all of my energy. The anomaly is a part of me now. It's in my flesh.

CHAPTER THIRTY-EIGHT

I WAKE IN the early evening with the certainty that something is happening tonight, but I cannot remember what; I can only hear the anomaly. I roll over and sip from a glass of warm water. It comes to me: Angel's last night. Angel is leaving Millie's. He's leaving Clichy for good, and in a couple of weeks he will fly out to volunteer with a charity in Nepal.

I have spent the day at Léon's, the first day in a long while. It's been nice, a break. Beside me, Léon yawns and stretches.

"Evening," I say. I kiss him.

Léon pulls on a pair of jeans and shuffles, bleary-eyed, towards the kitchen, where I hear him spoon three fat loads of coffee into the espresso maker and put it on heat. Water gushes as he fills the kettle. Making me tea. Léon doesn't drink it himself, and it is never quite right. He leaves the tea bag in for too long, so a thin film develops over the surface. When he splashes in the milk this Pangaea breaks into smaller subcontinents, and when I drink it the scum coats the mug all the way down.

Ten minutes later, Léon brings me a mug of stewed, sugared tea. He always puts in at least two sugars. I usually take one, but I have never corrected him, because there are days when that hot sweetness is the impetus I need to get out of bed. Because it shows that for reasons I cannot comprehend, Léon still cares.

"Merci, chéri," I say.

He murmurs, "De rien," half conscious, half coherent, continues on his narcoleptic evening ritual which takes him next to the shower. I wonder why he is up so early and then I remember he has to train a new member of staff.

I sip the tea and think of my first night at Millie's, how surreal and huge it seemed then, how insignificant it seems in light of everything that has happened since.

Léon comes back naked, kisses my lips and then my navel. His stubble is still wet. Beads of water cling to the hair on his chest and groin, and I wonder what he is thinking as his lips move down, fleetingly, to where my hips rise then brush—regretfully? I cannot read him; I have never been able to read him, if I am honest—upward again. He stands and starts to pull on his clothes. I sit up. He waves me back.

"It's cool," he says. "You don't have to go."

"Je sais, mon beau."

Léon goes to clean his teeth. I hear him spit in the sink, ritualistically, three times. On the way out he lounges in the door frame. His lips crack around the first early evening grin. "You know, your accent—it's still fucking terrible," he says.

Then he's gone.

THE MOMENT I walk into Oz, I know this is going to be a messy night. I have had a humming in my head since I left Léon's. In Clichy it intensifies; a flare is on the way. It feels like a big one. I am itching to go to the keg room right now and wait for it while the song immerses me, but that's impossible. If I don't show my face, Angel will never forgive me.

I meet Angel at eight in Oz, when he takes his break. Most of the Millie's night team and the staff from the pub down the road are already here, piled up at the bar, singing raucously. Léon's shift at Oz does not start until midnight, but he is making free with Oz's provisions in the meantime.

"Hallie!" shouts Gabriela, spotting me. I go over to exchange bisous but Gabriela says crossly, "You're late."

She turns back to Mike and when I move to join them, she twists in her chair to face away from me.

"Sorry," I say. "I thought we were meeting at eight."

Léon's hand slips around my waist, his lips meet mine, a glass cold with condensation presses against the palm of my hand.

"Vodka tonic," says Léon.

"Thanks."

I sip.

"I'll be on the floor by midnight," I say, only half joking.

"They all will."

"Except you, because you never get drunk, no matter how much you drink."

"That's my job. Did you hear about Simone?"

"No, what happened?"

"She was at a protest with those Moulin Vert people. The police got involved. She got a baton in the face."

"Fucking hell." Guilt overwhelms me. "Is she okay?"

"As okay as you can be with a broken jaw. Isobel and Bo are with her at the hospital. Bo said it was a nasty business. It's going to be the bordel in there tonight, and you can't count on him for any help." He jerks his head. "Angel, get your arse over here."

Angel, responding to summons, comes over to us. He is still walking straight, but his face has slumped into the classic dissipation usually seen at the end of the night. The skin around his eyes appears bruised, his cheekbones prominent. He slings an arm around both our shoulders.

"Hallie, Léon. You funny pair."

"What's funny about us?" I say.

"Ahhh..." He shakes his head, smiles hopelessly. "So, this is actually my last night! You'll miss me, poussins, when you come for your coffee in the afternoon with your terrible hangover and the problems with the landlords."

"I might never have worked at Millie's if you hadn't persuaded Eloise to give me a try."

I feel a rush of fondness for Angel, but even more so I feel gratitude. Without Angel, I might never have found the anomaly.

And Simone wouldn't be in hospital right now, either. I get out my phone and text her and Bo.

"You would have ended up here sooner or later, even if you did not meet me. Everybody comes to Clichy. And everybody leaves. Now I leave. I am the escaping man."

I try to catch Gabriela's eye, but when I do her gaze is hostile. Of course, everybody is upset that Angel is leaving and there is a lot of talk about who will get the coveted day job, or whether they will, as rumoured, bring in somebody new. That would upset people. The hierarchy at Millie's is unofficial but strictly observed; you do your time on the floor, you do your time on the nights. Maybe Gabriela is just unhappy that a good friend is leaving. Or maybe she's upset about Simone. Maybe she blames me.

Clearly my presence is exacerbating whatever mood she is in, and I decide it is best to let her alone. I take another sip of vodka and feel a surge in my head, making me stumble. The anomaly is wide awake.

At ten o'clock, Léon and I support Angel back across the road and Victor and Gabriela get coffees for everyone. Millie's is a chromium wonderland, decked out in frosting and silver tinsel. I have barely downed my espresso when Eloise nabs me. She has cat's eyes, green with slits for pupils. Two silver antennae poke out of hair which is slicked flat against her head and spray-painted white. She looks terrifying.

"Get one of these on—" She thrusts a T-shirt at me. "It's Moët night."

"I thought it was sci-fi night."

"It's that too." She hands me a pair of green antennae.

In the vestiaire I find Dušanka examining her own T-shirt with the attention owed to a historical relic. Being this near to the keg room almost undoes me. I want to get in there. I do my best to ignore it. I can sense the anomaly is in a playful mood, but I have travelled before when I am drunk and it is never pleasant.

"Have you tried to put this on?"

"I've only just got here," I say. Sometimes, only sometimes, stating the obvious works with Dušanka.

"Well, try." She waves an impatient hand. I throw my Millie's tank top in the locker, and pull the Moët tee over my head. It sticks.

"There." Dušanka is triumphant. "See this shit they give us? It would be too small for a five-year-old."

"Have you got any scissors?"

We cut a wider circle around the necks and finally manage to get the tees on. They are obscenely tight. I am wearing a black bra, which doesn't help. I examine myself in the mirror over the sink. Moët & Chandon is emblazoned in silver letters across my breasts.

"We prostitute ourselves," says Dušanka. "For capitalist shitheads, we do this."

I find a pair of cat-eye contact lenses and silver body paint. I spray my hair blue. I stick on the antennae. My armour is complete.

"Did you hear about Simone?" I ask.

"Yes. Those connards."

"Bo said it was bad."

"They overreacted. That movement is frightening them."

"Frightening who?"

"Everyone." Dušanka shakes her head. "This is not why I came to France."

Upstairs, Moët reps are wandering around in skintight catsuits with bottles holstered at their hips. I am on the back bar, so I go to set up. Normally this is an opportunity for calm before the eleven-thirty storm. Tonight, however, Moët are installing a luminescent revolving spaceship in the middle of the dance floor. I can feel Léon's vodka swirling uneasily in my stomach alongside the sweet and sour prawns I wolfed down earlier.

At eleven, Victor and Angel join me on the back bar. The doors open and the hordes flood in. Within half an hour the dance floor is full. Victor and I scurry back and forth, ducking around one another, opening fridge doors, kicking the dishwasher shut, passing bottles, sour mix, crossing arms over the taps. We barely speak, and when we do, we have to yell. The music is thumping. At least, I assume it's thumping, it must be; but the anomaly's song obliterates everything.

Angel serves the occasional pint, his hands moving slowly and sleepily. After half an hour he gives up and gets up on the bar. People climb up to join him, grinding against one another. I take hold of a butterfly-tattooed ankle to anchor one of the girls and reach around to serve a pint. Foam dribbles down its sides. I can feel the girl struggling to move; the music beat in the quiver of her heel.

Three beer lines run dry at once.

"I'll go," I say, but Eloise has spotted our predicament from afar.

"What do you need changing?" she shouts, and Victor indicates the taps capped with upended pint glasses. "I'll send Mike down," she calls.

I bite down a jolt of pure rage. I am going to be thwarted at every turn tonight.

Gabriela appears at the balustrade. She hoists herself up and swings her legs over, jumping down over the bottle bin. Without even looking at me, she orders, "Take your break!" and turns straight to the nearest customer.

I climb back up the way she came down, onto the bar and up onto the balustrade, where I wedge myself against the wall. I take out my tobacco and roll a cigarette.

"There's a new guy on the floor," I shout to Gabriela. "He's good."

Gabriela ignores me. I watch her dashing up and down the bar. Her alien antennae tip forward over her face, furrowed in concentration.

I go outside to smoke my cigarette and head over to Oz for my break. I cannot bear to be so close to the anomaly and so far; it's beginning to make me feel ill. Léon serves me drinks and a bowl of chips, fat and salted, but when I get back I feel even worse. I have to work with Gabriela for forty-five minutes while Victor takes his break. She is deliberately getting in my way, opening fridge doors in my face, hijacking the bottles on my speed rack. When we collide for the third time, I snap.

"What the fuck is wrong with you!"

She responds equally heatedly in Spanish.

It's so hot. My vision is starting to go funny; I have to pause and splash cold water on my face. Gabriela yells something.

"All right!" I yell back.

Victor comes back. Gabriela goes without a word. Victor yells, "I love this song!"

I can't hear it. I have no idea what is playing, I can only feel the bass thudding at my chest, my throat, the plates of my skull.

Victor joins Angel up on the bar and they chuck their shirts into the crowd. Then I see her.

Millie, in a silken bodice and full skirt ripped to rags, lace gloves to her elbows, antennae in her gelled red hair, dancing in the middle of the crowd.

"Millie?" I shout. "Millie!"

I don't think. I vault the bar. I wade into the dance floor and find it has been invaded by androids and avatars. The swivelling lights glint on their aluminium skin. Beneath their feet, the floor is bubbling.

The dance floor is the centre of a volcano.

I go under the lava line. Down here, words are silent and lips wrap around mute exclamations. Down here, it is possible to drown. I am on the sea bed. Millie is always three people away. Hands thrown up in the air appear as gliding fish; willowing, luminescent.

There's a shrieking in my head. A howling. The vortex, and now the world really is dissolving, through time and time and time again.

Did I mistake the anomaly's mood for playful? I was wrong. It's maleficent.

MY HEAD CLEARS. I am on the far side of the dance floor, squeezed in on all sides. Angel and Victor are dancing on the bar; there's no one behind it. There is no sign of Millie. The anomaly's song has gone silent.

Blood is pouring from my nose.

I cup my hand over my face. I can feel the liquid trickling through my fingers and down my neck. I can taste mercury. I make it to the bathroom, tip my head back, apply tissue paper. It soaks through. I apply more. *Fuck*. I have never had a nosebleed in my life. It throbs painfully. I feel giddy and sick.

Women are applying mascara and lipstick. Women are snorting coke off the toilet seat. Nobody notices me.

When the bleeding stops I clean up and wash my face in the sink. There is blood on my T-shirt but it could be mistaken for Jägermeister in bad light. Heart pounding, I fight my way back to the bar.

That was a warning, I think. For the second time tonight I wonder if things are getting out of control.

The morning creeps onward. I have a terrible headache. Every now and then, squiggly lines run across my vision. Four o'clock, five o'clock, six. I start the cleaning operation, close down one set of taps. The DJ announces his last track. Victor and Angel chant:

"Ha-llie! Ha-llie! Ha-llie!"

They haul me up on the bar between them. They are both hanging onto me, their skin feverish and dripping with sweat. Angel is wearing nothing but his underpants and his shoes. Victor is holding onto an upended mop and the two boys lean into it as they belt the lyrics to 'Easy Like Sunday Morning.' I am singing too. I can feel movement in my lips and throat; I know tuneless words are leaving my mouth.

I look at the boys, who have somehow found the energy to transcend this godawful closing song into a cabaret. Their features scrunch in mock ecstasy. The lights come up. The floor team are doing the rounds, gathering up armfuls of glasses and bottles. Dirty glasses pile up on either side of our three pairs of trainers straddling the back bar. Angel wobbles. His hand squeezes my shoulder. We are sweating and filthy and drunk to a woman.

Within the last chords of the song, it is possible to imagine a time beyond my time in Paris, a time when I could look back with nostalgia on these vibrant nights, think of a sky that seems more open for being lighter, longer, think of the terrace evenings sat sipping at a sweet pastis, think of evening heart-to-hearts and muddled languages and the delights of slow intoxication. Other exes, who sometimes come by the bar, early evening or last thing at night, have told me that this is the way it goes. Everybody has their time, and everybody leaves. You feel all right about it, they say, in the end. But at seven am on a Sunday morning, watching the remaining couples circling in their last-ditch courtship rituals, I feel confused, despondent, and at a complete and utter loss.

None of those people have an anomaly. None of them are bound to this place in the way I am bound to it. Remaining faithful to the anomaly means living this life indefinitely, even if I grow sick of it, even if I come to hate it. It means an endless cycle of hellos and goodbyes. It means I might lose everything, and I'll have to live with that too.

CHAPTER THIRTY-NINE

AFTER STAFF DRINKS, everyone decamps to Oz. I go downstairs to get my things. I was planning to go home, feeling too unwell to face the anomaly, but a sound distracts me.

From within the keg room I hear a rattling and clattering. When I push the door, it resists. The metal is cold, lightly frosted. It has been shut from the inside.

I hear a crash which could be a keg toppling over.

I bang on the door. There is no answer.

"Who's in there?" I call.

Nothing.

"It's Hallie," I try. "I left my jumper in there. Can you open up?"

Now I can hear scraping. The clank of metal on metal. Someone is moving kegs around.

I bang again.

"Hi, let me in. Hello?"

I wait. The beer lines are silent; there is no one left upstairs. I sit down, my back to the door. I have an anxious—no, worse than anxious, a really bad feeling about this. The anomaly's song is keening again. Could something have come through from the other side?

And if so, from when?

"Who is that?" I yell. My voice sounds higher than normal. Taut.

"It's Gabriela!"

"Gabriela." I sag with relief. "It's me! Open up."

"No."

"What?"

"I said no. Go away, Hallie."

"What's going on in there? I can hear noises."

"You do not want to know. Go away. Leave now."

"Gabriela? If you're trying to travel, it won't work."

No answer.

As the seconds tick by, my relief evaporates, to be replaced by a creeping sense of dread. I think about Gabriela's behaviour tonight. Before tonight. Over the last few weeks she has been increasingly short with people, both friends and customers. She has left directly after staff drinks, or sometimes not taken anything, just collecting her tips and disappearing without bisous. Even behind the bar she's been quiet and sombre.

Gabriela has been brewing for weeks. How have I failed to notice?

From the other side of the door, I hear a crash and an illegible curse.

She has chosen the time deliberately. She knows it is the time I favour. There is no one else in the building: the night staff are gone, the cleaners will not arrive for another hour. She must have been planning it for a while. Gabriela has been keeping things from me. I imagined myself as her confederate, even her sister. In a crisis, I thought that I would be the one she would turn to.

But I haven't been around. Not for her, not for anyone.

This is my fault.

I bang again. "Gabriela, I'm still here. And I'm not going anywhere."

"Hallie, you must go away. Go away now, please!"

"Not going," I say firmly. "And sooner or later, someone's going to come down here—someone that isn't me—and then you'll have to open up."

"No." Gabriela's voice is urgent. "It is not safe for you to stay. I am doing a thing."

Fear touches me.

"What thing?"

No answer. I hear the gas hissing gently through the pipes.

"Gabriela, what thing?"

"I cannot tell you."

"Fine. I'll go upstairs and get the key. I'll come down in the lift."

"I have the lift key."

Of course she has the lift key. She has had enough time to consider the details.

"Then I'll get someone to help me kick the door in."

"No, Hallie. You will not do this. You will not speak to anyone." Gabriela is faint but sure.

"I'm going right now."

I stand up.

"It's too late. By the time you get back, it will have happened."

"Then let me in," I beg. "Come on, Gabriela, open the door."

"I cannot let you do this thing with me. Listen, my Hallie."

The direction of Gabriela's voice changes; she sounds nearer to me, closer to the ground. I guess that she has sat down next to the door.

"I have had a long time to think about this. All those times I have tried to go back home, and somehow, it never happened. I promised my sister, my niece, that I did not abandon them, and yet I know they do not believe me. Why should they? And a part of what they say is right, because I have a new life here. I love the people. This is my family. And so I begin to forget about the life that is lost, even if it was not much of a life. I forget Bogotá. My real family, waiting, wondering. I forget myself..."

Her voice trails away and there is quiet for a moment, quiet except for the gas hissing, and the pipes creaking. The longer she talks, the longer she is not doing whatever she has been doing. So I say nothing.

"And then you arrive. Hallie from England, who loves *Transfusion*. Hallie from England, who does not know where she truly belongs. At the beginning, you always see the things you share, is that not the way? Both of us adrift in Paris, a place that is not our city, not our home, but we have it made it a home all the same."

Gabriela's voice has become flatter and flatter. It's acting on me like a narcotic. The keg room door is chill against my shoulders. I feel as though I have been here for days, listening to Gabriela talking.

"We are connected, the two of us. Only you are not the person I met last autumn. Not anymore. This thing, this malicious thing, it has made you mad."

"No. No, it hasn't. I'm in control."

"You are not. I am not. We have no control, because of this thing. It keeps me here, and it sends you everywhere, and now it is affecting others too. Simone, she is in hospital because of this Moulin Vert. There is only one way to fix this."

I feel sick. A trickle of blood dribbles from my nose.

"Gabriela," I say frantically. "The anomaly has nothing to do with you. It's an excuse, and you know it. If you wanted to go back home, you could do it tomorrow. That's the truth! You just don't want to face up to it! Now, for god's sake, tell me what you're doing in there."

"You talk about the truth, Hallie. The truth is you do not know what this thing really is. But I can see, quite clearly, that it has changed you. For the worse. If I am your friend, I have no choice. This thing is evil, and I have to destroy it. I have made a rig—there will be an explosion—"

"Gabriela!" I pound on the door. "Gabriela, let me in now!"

"After it explodes, you will not travel in time any longer."

"Don't be an idiot! You'll kill yourself—you'll blow up Millie's—"

"Only the keg room. It is this place that is responsible for everything."

"No!" I am yelling now. "You can't do this! I'm not going anywhere until you open that door! If you blow anything up, you'll blow up me with it."

I hammer, pounding the metal with both fists, ignoring the pain. Someone has to hear, the cleaners, or Kit wandering in early—

"Open up!" I scream. "Open up, open up, open—"

The door gives. I pitch forward with a shock, falling hard on my hands and knees. Behind me, the door slams.

The noise resounds around the keg room, bleak and final.

A key turns. I look up. Gabriela stands a few feet away. Her face is set and her eyes glitter.

"I told you," she says, very calmly. "To go. Now we are both here. It is your fault. You give me no choice."

I keep very still. I take in the kegs, stacked together, the wires, wrapped around them, over them, snaking together.

"How do you know how to make an explosive?" I ask shakily.

"You can learn anything on the internet," says Gabriela. "It is all home ingredients."

"Well, that's nice."

"There is no point in joking about it."

"I'm joking because I'm scared. I don't want to die."

"I will explain one more time. I cannot let this thing continue. Now it is just you and me who are affected, but there will be others. It is already starting. And it is getting worse. You know it is getting worse."

"I can't believe you're doing this. I can't believe you take our lives so lightly."

"Shush now, Hallie. Do not distract me."

She is doing something with the wires, joining a circuit. I should be doing something, analyzing the set-up, searching for the weak spots, but I have no idea how she has put this thing together. The thought of life without the anomaly is a black hole, alien and horrifying. The chronometrist, I think. If she were here, she could take over Gabriela, prevent her from setting it off.

"Hey," I say. "Chronometrist! If you're in here, now would be the time!"

I watch Gabriela's face, hoping desperately for a sign, but there's no change, no slackening in her features. Gabriela sighs.

"That woman will not come, Hallie. She used you. She has no interest in you now you have done what she wanted."

"Gabriela, a flare is coming."

"All the better. We will take its heart."

I can hear it. If I could see it, it would be like watching a wave coming in from a long way off. First the barest ripple, then a white crest, then a galloping monster turning over and over upon itself. The vortex grabs me. For a second I'm on the sea bed in the Eocene: warm water, monster fish.

I lurch back. Blood is pouring from my nose.

"Fuck!"

"I know. I saw you go. I saw you before, you know, when we were here. You didn't realize. I watched you. Until that moment, I couldn't be sure it was all real. Don't worry, it will be over soon."

The vortex reels. This is what happened under the catacombs. I'm in the cellar in 1875, then I'm in a crawl space in World War Two, then somewhere I've never been before, cold and empty and dank and so, so alone.

Gabriela's face is over mine. I'm on my back on the floor of the keg room, incapable of moving.

"I've set it off," she says softly. "One minute."

She takes me in her arms, my head resting against the crook of her elbow. The blood from my nose trickles down my neck and pools above my collar bone. Gabriela wipes it away tenderly.

"Sixty, fifty-nine, fifty-eight..."

I lose her. Is that Millie? What's she doing down here? Her mouth drops open in surprise, then—

"Thirty-three, thirty-two, thirty-one..."

Madame Tournier, laying out blankets, food and water.

"Twelve, eleven, ten..."

I move. I move fast enough to surprise Gabriela, twisting free. I grab her arm and haul us to the lift. Gabriela fights me.

"No, Hallie, no!"

I yank the door closed. I hang on to Gabriela. I hit the up button. We start to move, the old, rattling lift creaking its way upwards as I complete the countdown in my head.

Three. Two. One.

MILLIE STANDS LEANING against the taps. Her arms are folded across her chest and her haystacked hair sits slightly askew.

"Oh, girls," says Millie. Her syrup voice has a thick, malty scent. "Girls, girls, girls. You've gone and done it this time, haven't you?"

Her smile flickers. Is it a smile?

FROM A LONG way away, a low keening. The wave washes up on the beach and retreats.

Silence.

THEY FIND US in the lift, laid out head to head, covered in a fine, pale dust. Our limbs are stiff and brittle, as if calcified. People say neither of us were breathing when the emergency services arrived. They say it was like the dead coming back to life. They say it was the strangest thing they ever saw.

CHAPTER FORTY

THREE DAYS LATER, I am sitting on a terrace near Lamarck, and my hands have almost stopped shaking. Lamarck is just far enough from the boulevard to avoid traffic, but not too far from my studio. I'm not yet ready to venture any further afield.

The scene around me is classically Parisian. Six-storey buildings, street level grocers, boulangeries, butchers, brasseries, boutiques, chocolateries. Between them are the gated doorways to the apartment blocks above. Pedestrians pass by. Scooters, pigeons, water draining downhill in the gutters. The sky is a Parisian blue, and the air has a Parisian summer glow. But the world has changed irrevocably.

A shadow falls across my table, and someone slips into the seat opposite me. Léon.

"What are you doing here?"

The question is automatic; it does not really matter to me why Léon is here. All that matters is the unanswerable call.

Léon takes out his tobacco and rolls two perfectly cylindrical cigarettes. He puts one in front of me, and passes the lighter.

"Thanks."

I inhale. With a bystander's idle curiosity, I note that my fingers are still trembling sporadically.

"You look like you need it," says Léon.

"Everybody's talking about it, are they?"

"It doesn't matter."

"I'm sure it makes a good story."

The explosion is the last thing I want to talk about. I knew straight away that Gabriela's plan had not achieved what she wanted. Léon called as soon as he heard. Don't say a word, he said. Keep silent. I'll deal with it. I'll explain. God knows what he said.

Now, as long as I keep my thoughts clear, I can continue to function. It is possible to perform day-to-day tasks like getting out of bed and taking a shower. I can even go so far as to sit on a terrace with a coffee and watch the world passing by, without remembering that three days ago I was still a part of it, without giving in to panic. But to achieve this, I need my cloud bank: a thick cumulonimbus, heavy with rain. I am on one side of that cloud, everything else is on the other.

Léon orders espressos. I am aware of his eyes resting upon me, light and cool. The thought comes to me that he is a field medic sent to patch up my wounds. I keep my gaze directed away, over his shoulder. Across the road, a woman emerges from the boulangerie with a bundle of baguettes.

We sit without speaking until the espressos arrive. I watch the woman zip up her bag, stash the baguettes under one arm, and set off down the street.

"Hallie, look at me."

Reluctantly I meet Léon's eyes.

"I know what you are," he says. "I know what the anomaly is. I've known since I met you. It's the reason I met you."

I stare at Léon for a long time.

How is it that you can know a face so intimately, and a soul not at all? I have dreamed of this kind of revelation—I have dreamed of meeting another incumbent, or of taking Léon with me and showing him another world. But all I can think of is that day Léon was waiting for me in the sleet, and that this memory will never be the same. Léon has known all along.

Something crumbles inside of me.

"You'd better explain," I say at last.

Léon, I realise, does not look well either. He looks gaunt. Troubled. There's an odd, glassy texture to his skin.

"There are two anomalies in Paris," he says. "Beneath boulevard de Clichy is one. The catacombs is another. I'm like you, Hallie. I'm an incumbent."

The betrayal. I see it approach, acknowledge the fact of it almost clinically, before it slams into me and knocks my world askew. Vertigo. I grip the tabletop to steady myself. My fingers turn white.

"You've been travelling too," I say.

Léon. An incumbent.

"No. Not like you. And I should have put a stop to this a long time ago."

Tightness in my chest.

"I don't understand."

"I'm not from this time. I was born centuries from now. I discovered the anomaly—my anomaly—by accident. I was twelve." The strain in his voice is audible. For the first time I have a glimpse of what Léon has been hiding from me, and it's unbearable. "At first it was—it was magical. But very quickly I found I couldn't leave it alone. I became obsessed. I couldn't think about anything else, nothing mattered except the anomaly. By the time Janus found me, my life was a complete disaster and so was I."

"Janus," I repeat. A memory, as if from a long way away. *When the time comes, remember the way of Janus is not always the way to be true to yourself.*

"A handful of incumbents, from all over the world, passing the code of practice down the centuries. They got me out of Paris. Took me halfway around the globe. They helped me to recover." He shudders. "The withdrawal was... a nightmare."

"Why? What right did they have to make you stop?"

"That was my response, at first. I didn't want to go with them. I screamed and fought. I did... horrible things. But they were right. Because it's not benign, this process. The anomaly changes you. It had changed me. Hallie, I know it's got you, I know what it's like, but some part of you must feel it, even if you don't want to believe. It starts to eat at you. It takes something. The chronometrist was the first of us, and you've seen what's happened to her. I was lucky that Janus picked me up in time. I'd hardly thought about the damage I could have done to history."

"But I changed something," I say. My lungs are losing capacity, the panic muscling in. Wanting a piece of me. I can see the bigger picture opening up and I am powerless to stop it. Léon's voice is relentless.

"You were meant to. There was a war, in the future. In my time. A catastrophic war. We had to avert it, or it would have been the end of the human race. The changes we needed were in Paris. There was no other way." He looks at me, and this time I can't escape the anguish in his face. It's an abyss. I turn my head away.

"Merde," he says. "I wish it hadn't been you."

I listen, cold despite the sun, as he tells me about Rachel Clouatre, the young genius who gave up music after she lost her cello during the occupation of Paris. Rachel married, had children, led a conventional life. Centuries later, it was her descendent who made the incendiary speech on the steps of Sacré-Coeur, detonated the first nuclear device, and started the war that would rip the world apart. The incumbents gathered. Agreed that for this one time they had to break the code of practice. And it worked. The chronometrist has been back to the future, Léon tells me. The war never happens.

"After that, I was meant to tell you who I was. Induct you into the code of practice. My job was to make sure you left Paris and never came back."

"Why didn't you?"

I can feel his gaze. I keep my eyes down. To meet that gaze is to look at something broken beyond repair. I don't think I can survive seeing it.

"Because of you, Hallie. Because I broke my bloody rule. I got involved. Because I'm a fucking idiot."

Tears, at the backs of my eyes.

"But it was all a lie," I say.

"Not this. Not us—"

"All those stories—everything about Australia, was any of that even real?"

"Oui. Some of it. I spent years there, after Janus got me out. But the things you have in this century are gone in mine. The Great Barrier Reef. The Daintree Rainforest. We had zoos, and aquariums. You know, part of me hoped I'd die in the transportation. Or that our plan wouldn't work, we'd all be wiped out. It might have been better, I thought. We'd done enough damage, let someone else have a turn. But I found something here, in Clichy. People who were worth something. And you, Hallie. I saw so much of myself in you: the loneliness, the need to escape. I saw you were running, even if no one else did. I guess I thought together we might be able to stop."

All these things he has never said. It turns out Léon has more layers than I could have imagined. It must change you, I think, to hold back so much. But I can't process it. All I can think about is the intimacy we shared, the trust we had, shattered.

"I told you about volcano day."

He reaches across the table, takes my hand. I pull away, but he holds on.

"I tried to tell you, Hallie. So many times. I—"

"How can I believe that? All this time you've known who I was, *what* I was, and you never said a word! You were working with that psychopath—god, that time you turned up at my studio, telling me about Sacré-Coeur—it was all a plan, wasn't it?"

"You kept secrets too—"

"Don't go there. It's not the same thing. Not even close."

"I didn't want to come here, okay." Léon sounds frantic now. "I never wanted to travel again. Janus needed me. And then I landed in this century, started living this life—this lie, okay—months and years waiting for you to arrive—and I felt normal for the first time since I could remember. I felt like I belonged. Putain de merde, I should have told you, I know that. I fucked up."

I push back my chair, my eyes blurring.

"I need some space."

"Hallie—"

"I can't hear this."

I push through the terrace, head out into the street. I'm paying no attention to where I am going. Just walking, faster and faster as my anger builds.

"Hallie—"

Léon is following. I increase my pace. He catches up, moves to block me.

"Hallie, wait!"

"Fuck you, Léon! *Fuck* you! How could you do this to me? If the anomalies are that bad, how could you let me carry on? Knowing what you know? Do you know what it's like, hearing it all the time, not being able to respond, not being able to get there—being shut out?"

"Yes," he says quietly. "I've felt the same thing every day of every year I've been in Paris. The unanswerable call. I know what it's like."

"Fucking hell!"

"I wanted us to go to Rome—"

"Rome? Rome!" I start to laugh wildly. "Some kind of idyllic paradise with both of us hiding the biggest secret of our lives?"

"It was worth trying," says Léon stubbornly.

"It was never going to work."

"I love you, Hallie, all right? Je t'aime. You understand?"

We've never said that.

"Not fair," I say. "Not fair."

"I'd have done anything not to see your face when you found out who I was."

I look at him and see it's the truth. I turn away. Keep walking. Léon follows. After a while I realize he's not going to stop until I stop. After a while, I'm too tired to carry on. Exhaustion shrouds me. I've been tired for so long and all at once it feels malignant, cancerous. *It takes something.* I come to a halt. Look about me. We're just around the corner from the Clos Montmartre. I can smell the grapes on their vines, just beginning to ripen. How ironic.

"Hallie, please listen. There's more."

"How can there be more? What else is there to say?"

"Please. This is important. It's about the Moulin Vert."

I stare at him, blinking away the tears.

"When the chronometrist came back—when she told me our plan had worked, the war never happens, now was the time to tell you—I asked her if there had been any repercussions. And she didn't give me a straight answer. So I went forward—a few decades from now."

My stomach overturns. That bloody windmill. Some part of me always knew it would return to haunt me.

I sit down where I am on the pavement. Léon sits next to me. Neither of us is in any state to care about the odd glances we attract from passing tourists.

"What did you find?"

"A disaster. And Janus won't break the code again. It doesn't matter to them if a few generations are fucked over, as long as humanity survives in the long run. But this will happen in your lifetime. And even if you leave Paris, which you must, it will affect everyone in Clichy that we care about."

I dash a hand over my eyes. Gather what's left of my faculties. A merciful numbness is descending. This is survival, I think. Evolutionary defence mechanisms slotting into place. Not thinking. Not processing. Just—existing.

"You'd better tell me," I say. "And this time, don't leave anything out."

PART EIGHT

A New Bohemia

CHAPTER FORTY-ONE

Paris, 2070

LÉON WAKES AMONG the dead. Their skeletal mass surrounds him, the rounded tops of skulls beneath his legs, his head resting upon a pile of tibia. He cannot see, but he can feel them, shifting beneath him. The fear sweeps in. Always the same terrible fear, with an underground transportation. Is the way out shut? Have the catacombs been closed? Will he be buried alive in bones and earth?

He moves carefully, not wanting to crush the remains, but it is impossible for him to get to his feet without shattering them. As his eyes grew accustomed to the greater darkness, he focusses on a patch of grey. The edge of light. Light means civilization. Light means people. He begins to wade through the piles of bones. This part of the catacombs, clearly, has been left to dereliction.

As the end of the tunnel draws near, the light increases and he hears the sound of voices. Gradually, his heart slows. People means a way out. He stops, listening. Moves closer. A crack on the floor as something snaps. Slow shuffle. The bones peter out, and now he is walking on dirt and stone. The voices come from a party of tourists. He can make out the boastful tones of the guide.

"…greatest ossuary in the world, a feat of engineering unparalleled by other civil societies. Note the intricate stacking of the bones—the strategic placement of the skulls. Forgive me, ladies and gentlemen, if I say only a true Frenchman could have combined art and mathematics in such a seamless way. Now, in the next chamber we will show you…"

The voice tails off. It is tempting to leave the tunnel and join the back of the tour as he has done many times before—join the living— but Léon waits. Something about the guide makes him wary. The arrogance, perhaps, or the shepherding of the tourists.

Léon waits.

Hours pass.

He waits.

Five more guided tours pass through, but the footfall is very different from Hallie's time. Then, visitors were allowed to walk freely through the tunnels, exploring the ossuary at their own pace.

When it is clear that the day's viewings are over, Léon leaves the tunnel and begins to make his way through the curated passages. How many times has he walked this route, waiting to emerge, newborn? Countless. And now the exhilaration of being back in the game begins to take over. His stride grows confident. He greets the bones like old friends. He used to have names for them, back in the day. It seemed unkind to leave them as strangers. *Hello, Sofie. Hello, Pierre. Henri, you've barely aged a day!*

This is a new era. A new world. He lived for this. For years, it was his life. Nothing else mattered.

He is nearing the end of the tourist route, beginning the ascent to ground level, when he hears the sound of footsteps. A distant echo, but coming his way. Another group? No, surely not. It's hours since the last. There's another sound too. A dragging sound, that reminds him of the carts. The carts! What a day that was, all the way from Les Halles to here, the bodies rich with graveyard dirt. Terrible, but wondrous.

The carts.

A dreadful transportation. He never went back that far again. Besides, when you're anything other than white, there's not much point in going back further than the twenty-first century in this city.

The sound is growing closer.

Léon retreats into one of the disused tunnels—he knows them all—and waits. He's an expert in patience.

Two gendarmes appear, dragging a heavy sack about two metres long. Every few metres they pause, grunting with the effort. The first wipes the sweat from his brow. Léon stares at the sack as it is shunted through the chamber. He has seen sacks like that before.

When they are far enough ahead, he begins to track them. The gendarmes take the body bag some way into one of the disused tunnels. He hears the crunch of bone as they sling it down, then their footsteps, making their way back out. Once again Léon conceals himself. The two gendarmes are in much better spirits now they have completed their drop. They chat amicably. One of them lights a cigarette. The smell of smoke trickles back.

Léon retraces their steps. His torch illuminates the tunnel, a branch very similar to the site of his anomaly. Only a small proportion of the catacombs are maintained for visitors. The remainder sprawl under the surface of the city, home to the bones and the rats. Here, too, the bones lie in disorganised heaps, many crushed into fragments that line the tunnel floor. The body bag has been slung up onto a stack of skulls. The material is thick and rubbery, no doubt designed to contain any smell as the process of decomposition begins.

Léon raises his torch, revealing at least thirty other bags, reaching back into the tunnel. Some of them are very small.

LÉON SPENDS THE night underground, and when the public entrances are opened in the morning, he makes his way outside. It's early morning, a clear spring day, almost obscenely bright. He does not know the date, but it must be around the year 2070. That was what he was fixing on.

He was half-expecting to find derelict scenes, similar to the one where he left Inga, several centuries in the future, if not so extreme. But all looks familiar. The city is beginning to stir. Shutters open, people lean out to greet the day. Every balcony holds plants and flowers. People are out walking their dogs, the dogs wearing bright collars and in some cases little capes that change hue as they trot decorously along. The dog-walkers wave hello to each other. To Léon.

"Greetings, neighbour!"

He returns the greeting.

A chihuahua stops to take a shit. The owner tugs at its lead, walks on. Moments later a small robot scurries out onto the pavement, scoops up the offending excrement, and retreats. Léon looks about. The streets are very clean. The six-storey facings have a buttery sheen, the street plaques are polished to a shine. There is bunting strung between buildings. A festive air. Léon feels it infect his mood. New again!

The street gives way to a larger boulevard where snail-shaped cleaning robots squelch up and down window fronts. Awnings extend, chairs and tables drop down onto the pavement in pre-set formations. The brasseries are opening. The aroma of coffee awakens Léon's hunger. His belly rumbles. He will need to find food before long. He has forgotten about the hunger. There are of course things you forget, some deliberately, some not. Strains of music spill from the brasserie fronts, cadences of accordion and the occasional mezzo voice. A crocodile of children winds down the street, dressed in uniform. Léon doesn't remember schoolchildren wearing uniform in Hallie's time. But then, as far as he knows, no one is stashing bodies in the catacombs in Hallie's time either.

The best way to uncover an era's secrets is to eat and eavesdrop.

Léon selects a brasserie, not too busy, not too quiet, and takes a seat on the terrace. Time for breakfast. As his buttocks touch the chair, a primitive holographic menu revolves into being before him. He orders an espresso, then remembers he has no method of paying for it. Well, he has something from a few centuries ahead. That might work. It has proved useful with cash and card machines in an emergency.

Looking about him, he feels disoriented, out of time in a way he has forgotten, and he can't work out why. There's that jaunty music again. His stomach churns. A rush of dizziness overcomes him. How ridiculous. This can't be right. Then the world sways, darkens. A face is suspended before him, a human face, concerned, asking if he is all right, if he can see, if he can hear—

"Can you hear me, neighbour?"

"Yes," he manages. Keeps his face carefully neutral. He's angry, not because he passed out, but because he has put himself at the mercy of strangers. Once again he has wiped out all memory of the toll a travel takes. Worse each time. Worse after rehabilitation. *An addict always forgets.* He remembers Inga telling him that, on what was left of a beach in Sydney. The sea is higher in his time. The planet is a mess, actually. That was part of the lure of going back.

When he gets to his feet, he sways again. Parisians crowd around, expressing concern. An unusually friendly era. Someone places a glass of water in his hand. He has a memory of Hallie, unconscious outside the catacombs, his conversation with the chronometrist. The rage he felt, seeing Hallie hurt.

A hand at his elbow steadies him. A man is at his side, escorting him with some difficulty through the brasserie, into the living quarters behind the public front.

He finds himself on a sofa.

Slowly, his senses recover. The initial rush of transportation is fading now, the shadow of a headache bedding in. He looks about him. He is in a fourteenth arrondissement apartment in the year 2070, or thereabouts. The apartment is large, neat, comfortably furnished. Homely. Concessions to automation are not immediately obvious. There is the smell of coffee and cooking eggs. A woman is in the kitchen, stirring the eggs in a pan. A child sits on the floor in front of an entertainment console, wearing a headset. Léon's stomach growls again.

"This poor neighbour fainted on us!" declares the man who brought him inside.

The woman—his wife, Léon presumes—gives Léon a sympathetic glance.

"I am very sorry to hear it! Are your iron levels low, my dear? You know how important it is to take your daily supplements."

"I'm not sure what happened. It might be a delayed concussion. I was mugged, you see, outside the station."

The proprietor shakes his head.

"A terrible crime. But they will catch the perpetrators when you file your memories, never fear! This is the safest of cities."

His wife reprimands him gently. "All the cities are safe, Charles."

"Yes, of course, Hélène. They are all of the highest security. We are very fortunate. Here, have a seat. We'll get you back on your feet."

"That's kind of you—"

"Of course! Who would not help a neighbour in distress?"

Lots of people, thinks Léon, but it would be impolite and probably unwise to say so. The woman finishes turning the eggs. She lays out four plates and four sets of cutlery.

"He can have mine," says the child, speaking for the first time. Her hair falls to the base of her spine in a single blonde plait. "I'm not hungry."

"But these are *republican eggs*."

"I'm not hungry."

Her parents exchange worried glances. Hélène dishes the eggs into three identical portions, and places one of them in front of Léon. He wants to gorge the whole plate in a few mouthfuls, and has to force himself to exercise restraint.

"Fantastic eggs," he says.

"Oh, my dear. You are too generous. But not the best. A republican egg is a republican egg." She beams. "You are new to Paris?"

"Yes, I'm from Toulouse."

"You must have done well in your citizenship exams," says Charles, with an approving nod. Léon offers a modest smile, as if embarrassed.

Hélène leans forward eagerly.

"Marine takes the first tier next month."

Léon swallows his last mouthful.

"That's great."

"Maman, that man is on the news again."

"What man, dearest?"

"The prisoner."

Charles's and Hélène's eyes widen in matching expressions of alarm.

"Marine, you shouldn't be watching that!"

Hélène rushes over to the child and tries to wrestle the console from her. The child hangs on, protesting.

"Who is she talking about?" asks Léon.

Charles is distracted, watching the tussle.

"Of course, you're new to the city... It's that bohemian terrorist up at the hill. He was due to go to the guillotine three months ago, but those fools from Brussels keep making threats about human rights." Charles shakes his head sadly. "No understanding of the modern world."

"None," Léon agrees.

"Delinquents must be put down."

"I couldn't agree more."

"But needless to say, we are perfectly safe on the left bank."

Hélène bustles over, brandishing the child's console triumphantly.

"Perfectly safe," she agrees.

"No one ever escapes."

"Not a barbarian soul."

"But let's not talk of that."

"No, it's not a civil conversation."

They sigh, and seem to reset themselves.

"Where were we? Yes! The coffee!"

"And a perhaps a tab of forgetting—"

"To put those dangerous bohemians out of your mind."

Hélène pours coffee from a pot decorated with fleur-de-lis, and a glass of orange juice for the child. She accepts it sulkily and drinks the contents in one go, appraising Léon over the rim of her glass. Finished, she licks her upper lip and says:

"If you want to know about the prisoner, you need the Remembrist."

"The Remembrist?" Léon repeats, and the child says, "Yes, in the métro," as her mother throws up her hands and cries, "Now, you know that's all made up, Marine! How many times must I tell her—?"

"The Remembrist is in the métro," says the child stubbornly, and earns herself a slap.

"The Remembrist is a virus. Tell her, Charles!"

"The Remembrist is a virus, Marine," says Charles firmly. "A piece of code." He turns back to Léon. "Dreadful business. These renegade bohemians keep infiltrating the games networks with their wretched avatars. Children are impressionable, of course." He takes Hélène's hand. "Don't worry, my love. We'll give her a tab of forgetting later on."

"She's too young..."

"Half a tab, then."

Léon interrupts. "But these bohemians, they're... they are on the right bank?"

"Oh, yes. The few of them that remain. And when they are caught, they will be processed. You have nothing to fear."

Léon stands.

"Thank you. You've been very generous. I won't take up any more of your time."

They nod. He has behaved correctly. Charles escorts Léon through to the brasserie. On the terrace, a young woman is scrolling through a holographic newsfeed. Footage shows a flooded town, people stranded on rooftops, helicopters circling down. A terrorist attack in Marseilles: nine fatalities. Suspected bohemian involvement. Then a man in an orange suit is herded into a building. His feet are shackled and a hood obscures his face.

As Léon turns to thank his host one more time, Charles claps a hand on his shoulder and lowers his voice.

"A word of warning, my friend. I don't know what you've heard where you're from, but here in Paris, we don't talk about the right bank. It is... impolite?" He smiles genially. "Now, enjoy this magnificent day!"

"I will. And thank you. I appreciate the tip."

Léon sets off down the boulevard. The second rule of any travel: keep on the move, at least until you have your bearings. It doesn't matter where you're going, as long as you move with intent. He thinks about what the child said. The Remembrist. The métro. He keeps walking. If he ever visited this era before, it wasn't like this. Paris is taller, cleaner. Emptier. There are fewer people on the streets. No water rushing along the gutters because there is no litter to wash away. He sees a drone sweeping the cobbles. A garden robot pruning an ornamental shrub.

A buzzing sound from above distracts him. He spots a delivery drone flying overhead, a box hanging from its claws. The drone descends to street level, drops the box, flexes its wings and takes off. A minute later the door opens and a small, wiry man with shaggy hair steps out. He sees the parcel and a pleased expression fills his face.

"Ah! Excellent, excellent!"

He picks up the parcel, looks up and sees Léon. He waves cheerily.

"Greetings, neighbour!"

Léon returns the greeting automatically. In the distance a bell chimes, deep and resonant. He counts: nine o'clock. Commuters begin to fill the streets, heading in streams towards their nearest métro. An accordion player stands on a street corner, playing the instrument with gusto, as if to herd them on their way. Léon falls in with the crowd, moving with the general stream.

The profile of Paris has changed. The majority of people around him are white, with only the occasional black or brown face. There are no headscarves, no djellabas or kaftans, no non-Western dress at all, and certainly no religious icons. There are a lot of flags. Discreet insignia of fleur-de-lis. It's a different population from Hallie's time—even with the tensions of fifty years ago—and radically different from his. Léon feels unpleasantly distinct. But he has to know more. He has to know the worst.

He is crossing a small square when the sound of an explosion cracks the air apart.

Everyone around him drops to the floor, hands over their heads. Léon does the same, belly flat against the cobbles, face to the ground, a sharp, sour taste in his mouth. He listens for the inevitable screaming, the sirens. He can't hear anything. The bomb must have blasted his hearing. He turns his head slowly to the left, bracing for the sight of rubble and smoke, bodies and blood.

There is no evidence of destruction. Of anything. The man on the ground next to Léon has a lead clutched in his hand. His dog yaps and snuffles at his shoes.

A siren sounds.

At once, everyone gets to their feet, dusting themselves off. He overhears a young woman complain. "The least they could do is leave it until the journey home. This suit was brand new this morning!"

A man in a cream blazer extends a hand, helping him up with a conspiratorial roll of the eyes and a "Fucking drills." The commuters continue on their way, now flowing up the steps to a flyover métro line. No tickets or touch-in points. State-run, Léon thinks. He stands on the platform with the rest of the commuters, watching the approaching flash of a silvery train, and as the train on the platform opposite pulls out, he sees the station name.

LePen.

The train approaches. Léon's sense of wrongness is expanding. He stands back, allowing others to board. Time to get out of sight. He's been a fool, moving around so freely. When the train pulls out and the next wave of passengers moves forward, he hears a shout.

"That's him!"

There is a shift in the crowd. Heads swivel curiously, seeking the target of the voice. Léon starts to make his way along the platform, towards the exit at the other end. A few streets away, he can hear sirens.

He makes for the stairs, now pushing his way down against the flow of commuters. He hears shouts behind him, senses pursuit.

At the bottom of the steps he finds an armed gendarme blocking the exit.

The officer appraises him. A red light is scanning down his body. *Merde.* Are people chipped here? The officer points to the vehicle behind her, where a crowd is gathering, held back from entering the métro. For the first time Léon sees something other than friendliness in these Parisians. Irritation, that their journey has been interrupted. Excitement, at the unexpected apprehension of one of their number, their proximity to the incident, ripe for translation into anecdote. Fear slides across some faces; in others there is wariness, an occasional flash of guilt, even relief. But the majority are trying not to look at him, not to acknowledge him, not to witness any element of the scene unfolding before them.

"Citizen, get in the car."

Léon keeps his voice calm.

"I'm sorry, officer. Is there a problem?"

"In the car, citizen."

"I'm not sure I understand—"

"I won't ask a third time."

Léon knows this is over. Cornered and unarmed, there's no way he is going to escape, but he isn't going to go gently either. The crowd don't try to stop him and they don't try to help. He meets a line of gendarmes, a snarling dog. The officer approaches and lifts something. A baton. Steel. It moves slowly, without force; that's warning enough. He rolls, but she's too quick. At its touch he feels coldness spreading throughout his body and he goes limp. His knees buckle. His teeth start to chatter.

Someone is weaving through the crowd. A woman, her face flushed and agitated. She is still wearing her apron. It's Hélène, who cooked Léon eggs this morning.

"Is this him?" asks the police officer.

The woman looks down at him, looks him straight in the face, and without hesitation she says, "Yes. That's the one. He wanted to know about the Remembrist."

"Thank you. You may go home. Take a brew of forgetting." The officer's voice becomes low and magnetic. "You know there is no Remembrist. The Remembrist is a lie. A story told by bohemians."

The woman nods. She smiles. A glazed, almost euphoric expression enters her eyes, as it does the surrounding crowd. One by one they turn, and begin to climb the steps to métro LePen.

The officer turns back to Léon, paralysed on the ground.

"Process him."

They sit him up. He sees the bag coming down over his head, tries to protest, but he's paralysed. I've fucked up, he thinks. I've failed Hallie. He barely feels it as they lift and deposit him roughly in the back of the car.

CHAPTER FORTY-TWO

"Métro LePen," I say. There's a bilious taste in my mouth.

"Yes."

"A fascist state."

"It seemed that way."

"How did you escape?"

I glimpse something behind Léon's face. A memory he is trying to suppress. A horror. I should harden my heart, but my instinct is to raise my hand, erase that memory for him and with it the damage that has been done. If only it were that easy to change the past.

"I was detained," he says. "But when they came to transfer me, I got away."

Léon is the solitary occupant of the cell. A sweltering concrete box. There are no windows. There is one light, dim and bluish. The light flickers. At times there is a high-pitched keening sound and at times there is not, and the cell alternates between noise and not-noise at random intervals impossible to predict, though he tries; after a while he hears it all the time. He hunkers in the corner of the cell, rocking back and forth, pushing his hands against his ears. It is so hot. The sweat pours off him. His hair is soaked. He is desperately thirsty. He asks for water, then begs. Water does not come. He licks at his own sweat, and the salt makes him gag and the thirst worsens and his tongue has swollen to a leech in his mouth. Water does not come.

What comes is a man in plain clothes and a plain face. He brings a chair and sits upon it, looking down at Léon. He shows no expression. There is nothing memorable about him. A man who makes no mark, because the world leaves him impervious. Léon has met people like him.

"Who sent you to Paris?"

Léon tries to form words, but his tongue gets in the way. The man holds out an empty beaker, pours a centimetre of water from a plastic bottle. Léon downs it, gasping.

"Who sent you to Paris?"

"No one sent me."

"Who sent you to Paris?"

"I need water."

"Not until you give me answers. Who sent you? Was it the Germans? Are you their spy?"

"No one. I'm from Toulouse."

"Don't lie to me. Who sent you?"

Léon looks at the floor.

"No one."

"The Icelandic, perhaps," the man says. "Or should I look closer to home?"

Léon says nothing.

"Where are you from?"

"Toulouse."

"I said, where are you from?"

"Toulouse."

"Where are you from?"

"Fuck you. I'm French."

"You know we will find out."

Good luck with that, thinks Léon. I was born centuries from now, I could lay claim to a dozen different heritages.

"What do you know about the Remembrist?"

"Nothing."

"I will warn you again: don't lie to me. What do you know about the Remembrist and his bohemians?"

"I don't know anything. I heard the name today for the first time."

"Were you involved in the Montparnasse rebellion?"

"No—"

"But you recognize the name."

"I've never heard it before."

The man regards him for a moment.

"Citizen, let me explain something. At this moment, you are in a privileged position. I am sitting on this chair. There is a space between us I will not breach. In this centre, we do not use enhanced interrogation. The fourth republic is benevolent. But if you do not give me the answers I need, you will be transferred to the right bank, and I cannot speak for what will happen here. Is that what you want?"

"I can't tell you what you want. I don't know anything about the Remembrist, or the bohemians. I come from Toulouse and I'm a French citizen. That's the truth."

Seconds draw out while the man considers.

"You are a good liar," he says finally. "But you remain a liar. Without the truth, there is nothing I can do for you."

He stands. Picks up the chair. Raps on the door.

"We are done here, citizen."

"It's the truth!"

Léon manages to stand, to stagger towards the door. It clangs shut in his face. He slides to the floor and puts his head in his hands. He has been in bad situations before, but this is as bad as any of those. The light flickers. The noise returns. He puts his hands over his ears.

It feels like he has been there for days, but in fact it is only thirty-six hours before the authorities come to collect him for transfer to the prison on the hill.

"AND THAT'S WHEN I escaped," says Léon.

I squint in the afternoon sun. "How?"

"Early on, when I first discovered the anomaly, I got myself into far too many stupid situations. I was reckless. I figured it might be sensible to learn some survival skills..."

"Tae kwon do," I remember.

"Yes."

"But you must have been exhausted..."

"I played it up. Let them think I was near to collapse. It wasn't my finest hour, but I managed to... render my guards unconscious."

I feel myself smiling.

"So now you're a ninja?"

He returns the smile crookedly. "I'll take that."

"And then?"

"I took their guns. The uniform. And then I had a choice. Go back to the catacombs and wait for a flare, and hope to fuck I wouldn't be discovered down there. Or find out why nobody talked about the right bank."

THE NORTH OF Paris is cordoned off by a wall. On the far side of the wall is the river Seine. Léon can smell it from streets away: a fetid stench of pollution. The wall is guarded, but not heavily—there cannot be many people who wish to leave the safety of la rive gauche. The city is dark and silent, with regular patrols. An unacknowledged curfew. For an hour, Léon watches the cycle of the guards. He keeps an eye on the air, too; there may be drones up there. But he has to take a risk.

Léon scales the wall. His arms burn with the effort, muscles heavy with fatigue from his incarceration. Up, up, up. At the top he pauses, looking quickly back, then outwards, but all is black. A faint glimmer below. The wall is a sheer slope to the river. The stench is stronger here, and Léon pauses, but only for a moment. Then he drops.

Shock of cold. Thick, glaucous water closes overhead. He keeps his mouth shut, but it gets inside his nostrils. He fights for the surface. Breaks free, retching at the smell. He strikes out for the right bank. No shout from behind. No whir of drones. That pushes him on, across. He claws his way up the bank. Slime clinging to his skin and clothes. He snorts away water. He's made it.

Everything is quiet. Only the faint lapping of the water below, his breathing as it settles. He lies flat in the mud, waiting for the clouds to clear and give him some moonlight to see.

When it does, he understands.

As far as he can see, half-demolished buildings protrude like rows of jagged teeth. Windows shattered, roofs collapsed, single sandstone walls laid bare to the night sky. In some places, entire streets are reduced to rubble. For long minutes, all Léon can do is stare at the devastated landscape, the place that only decades before he called his home. A dreadful coldness descends. It feels as though a part of him has died.

He begins to walk north, through the flattened streets, his progress hindered by deep blast sites cratering the ground. No evidence of human life except for a single helicopter, speeding in the direction of Montmartre. He passes through the courtyards of the Louvre. The shell of the building stands, but the windows are empty. He can hear the wind whispering through its hallways, slinking into pillaged rooms and out of holes in the roof, the wind like a thief, a faint hum surrounding the abandoned gallery. In the courtyard, a gaping hole where there was once a pyramid of glass.

Up through the places that were. Saint Lazare. Saint George. Boulevard de Clichy is unrecognisable. Millie's is a scar in the ground. Léon feels the hum of another anomaly. Hallie's anomaly. And with it the wrench of his own, an ever-present tug at the chambers of the heart, which feels distant now, and much harder to return to, separated as they are by the river. But he has to know. He has to know what Hallie and their friends will face.

A beacon to the north draws his gaze. He follows the light, making his way up through narrow corridors of rubble. Looking back, the left bank is a distant sprawl of electricity. He keeps climbing. At last he reaches the foot of the butte Montmartre.

Where the Moulin Vert stood is a fortress. It squats upon the hill, burrowing greedily into the earth, a low-slung building bristling with defences. Barbed wire fences encircle it, guards and dogs patrol the walls. The red dot of a drone streaks overhead and vanishes. Gone are the palatial steps. Gone are the quiet gardens, the water fountains, the carousel. The hill is stripped of lawn, and the beacon that drew him is a white searchlight roving voraciously over the no-man's-land between the fortress and where Léon is standing now.

"What are you doing out here?"

Léon has no chance to respond. Someone grabs him, clamping a hand over his mouth, and he feels himself being dragged backwards, away from the light. He starts to struggle but a firm clout to the head tells him it's best to keep quiet. He lets himself be dragged. If these were the people he has just escaped, there would be no need to remain undercover.

They have been moving for a good few minutes before his captors release him and push him to the floor. A torch shines in his face, the light shielded by the remains of a brick wall.

"Who is he?"

"No idea. Not one of them."

"Who are you?"

Léon spits blood, suppresses the urge to inflict reciprocal violence. He's fairly sure these people aren't 'one of them' either.

"I'm looking for the Remembrist," he says.

Hands move over him. Something else, a device.

"He's not chipped—"

"Armed, though—"

"Hey, where'd you get these guns?"

"The police had me captive. I escaped."

A pause whilst they assess. Then a voice says, "We'll take you in, because we can't leave you out here. But you know the drill. Keep quiet. No sudden movements."

They manhandle him to his feet, push him before them, a gun at his back. It's dark enough for him to break free if he wanted, most likely unhurt, but he makes no attempt. He has a feeling they're taking him exactly where he wants to go.

The sun is edging over the horizon as they march him down the hill. Under its benign light, the city's ruins are even more desolate. Léon can hardly believe this is Paris. That something he loved could be destroyed so quickly. He expects the bohemians to take him underground, into the abandoned métro, but when they reach the boulevard they turn left, towards Barbès.

MÉTRO JAURÈS WAS named for one of France's first social democrats, a pacifist assassinated at the outbreak of the First World War. Hallie walked past it in 1942 on her way to the Paris Conservatoire, where musicians used to train, and once a student called Rachel Clouatre sat on a piano stool in front of Rachmaninov's Concerto No. 3, knowing the world had come to an end when it should have been just beginning.

The overground section of Line 2 is gone, but the supporting pillars still stand. In the shadow of the station, a grey-haired woman sits at a small square table, studying a chess board. A single plait trails down her back, wisps of white mark her temples. A bandage covers her left eye. Her right rests on the board.

The game is in an advanced state of play, but the opponent's chair is empty.

The bohemians indicate Léon should approach.

A few metres away he stops, unwilling to break the woman's concentration. Eye fixed upon the board, the chess player beckons.

"You're looking for me?"

"Are you the Remembrist?"

"Some call me that."

"Then yes, I was looking for you."

"Come. You can take a seat."

"Am I expected to play?"

"You could. But I wouldn't advise it. I'm about to put my opponent in a very sticky position."

Léon sits.

"Why do they call you that?"

"I guard the old city's memories. Some are given freely, others are left out, and I take them in. Some need a little... encouragement."

"I need to know what happened here," he says.

"I can tell you it all, if you can take the telling."

"I can."

"Do you know what it means, to hold a history?"

"I do."

The Remembrist angles her head, her good eye towards Léon. Bright, alert, the colour of quartz.

"Where do you wish me to start?"

"There was a windmill on the hill. It was called the Moulin Vert."

A silence.

"Many would prefer to forget that name," she says at last.

"But not you."

"There was a great war in the middle of the last century." The woman frowns. "It consumed the world and many millions of lives. The city fell under occupation. The occupiers sang songs in the music halls. They played symphonies on the steps of the opera. Their music was sweet, and hearing its melodies some forgot who they were. But others did not forget."

The Remembrist's fingers flutter to the board, as though she might make a move, then retreat.

"Those who did not forget had a symbol to remind them. The Moulin Vert, they called it, a building at the heart of Montmartre, which in those days was still a magnet for people who believed in freedom, and art, and love. During the Second World War the Moulin Vert became something more; it became a code."

"And a meeting point."

"That is also true. Its symbol appeared in windows, on secret pamphlets. For a brief time, it was the most important building in Paris. But eventually, the war ended, and after the war people forgot, again, because often it is easier to forget, and that is the nature of things.

"Then came the beginning of this blighted century, when an economic crash swept the world and a new shadow of fear and hatred began to squeeze the hearts of the cities of Europe. Democracy was under attack from outside and from within. There were many senseless deaths. Once again, the windmill appeared. Now its symbol was stamped upon pavements and graffitied on walls. There were rallies on the hill. A young woman roused a new movement. Her name was Aide Lefort, and she might have saved us."

Léon waits.

"It was to be a new bohemia," says the woman. "Once again, people looked to the Moulin Vert for inspiration, and Lefort supplied it. Lefort knew her history. She remembered. She rallied the people of Paris as the climate of fear and hatred grew more insidious. For a long time she refused to enter politics directly. She felt she could make more of a difference from the outside. But eventually, she did as her followers asked. She stood for President."

She looks at Léon.

"You must have been barely a child when she died, if you were even born. This was almost thirty years ago, on the eve of the last true democratic election."

"How did she die?"

"She was assassinated," says the Remembrist abruptly. "Though, of course, that is not what we were told. We were told she had murdered her partner and her children and then killed herself. We were told she was mad, dangerous. A fanatic. The Front national rallied and won the election."

"And here we are."

"And here we are." She falls silent for a moment. "After that, the Parti Moulin Vert turned dark. They had always been a community who embraced their fellow citizens as sisters and brothers. Perhaps Lefort was the only one who could have held it together. Once she was gone, they turned upon one another. Some held for peace, others vengeance. There were clashes. Offices bombed, politicians assassinated in her name. Within a year, the names of the Moulin Vert and the New Bohemia were tantamount to treason, according to the new laws. Within another five years, they were a network of terrorist cells, determined to bring down the authorities who had killed Lefort.

"Meanwhile, the rest of the world was slowly falling apart. Oil reserves were almost depleted. Crops failing. Thousands emigrated to the cities from the flood-plagued countryside. Riots spread through the north of Paris. Today, the state calls it the last revolution. The final act of that government was to clear north of the river, where the Vert terrorists were said to be hiding. Citizens who had proved themselves loyal republicans were evacuated. Anyone questionable was left behind. Then they sent in the drones."

"We bombed our own people."

"And in place of the Moulin Vert, the government built a prison. Those who go there are forgotten also. Their names are removed from records and their bodies from society." The Remembrist sits back in her chair. Her single eye roves across their surroundings. "This city's history has always been paved with blood."

Léon tries to imagine the scene: Paris turning upon its citizens. The whir of incoming drones, the incipient terror. Or perhaps there was no warning. A clear day, and then an inferno. His country. He wants to deny it could be possible, but he knows it has happened too many times before.

The Remembrist folds her hands in her lap, observing him. "This story has troubled you."

"What if I told you there was a way to end all this?"

"I'd love to hear it."

"I'd need your help."

She leans forward, beckons Léon to do the same. She brings her forehead close to his, almost touching. Her fingertips are light beneath his chin.

"You have a good heart," she says. "But why should I trust you?"

"Because I can do something no one else can."

She leans back a little, her good eye shut. For a moment her hand hovers just above the chessboard, then swoops. Her fingers fasten around a knight and claim a pawn from the white player.

"Obvious, now," she says.

She gets slowly to her feet, palms supporting her sacrum.

"Would you mind...?" She indicates Léon's chair.

"Of course."

He stands. The Remembrist sits, settles herself, and studies the board anew from the opposite side.

"Well, that was a beast of a move she left for me. All right, my child. I'm willing to hear more. But you'll have to convince me."

Léon starts talking.

*　　*　　*

THE ABANDONED TUNNELS of the métro: dark, dank, labyrinthine, populated by rats and insects and other things that crawl or scuttle or slide. The bohemians run its highways, squat in its darkness, let their minds bend from above the earth to below it. They know where a roof has caved in and they have dug the narrowest channel through. They know the weak spots. They know the cavernous stretches that flood in a storm. They know where the mines are. They know where they can trap, and be trapped.

There are not many of them left. One is the great-nephew of Aide Lefort. Another is an insider turned outsider. The youngest were born here, underground. Their first memory was of darkness. Some of them came from the left bank. Ex-citizens, their names erased from all but one public record: the guillotine's waiting list. A green windmill is suspended in their minds. On moonless nights they have crept close to the bleak exterior of the prison, in initiation ceremonies, learning to focus their hate.

The bohemians are funded by the solar-rich states of north-east Africa. They have channels to Germany, connections in Greece, links to underground movements opposing other fascist governments across Europe. Their tactics are guerrilla. Their centre of operations moves every forty-eight hours. Their best work is done by hackers: burrowing into state infrastructure, pulling grids offline, encrypting databases, squirrelling themselves into the binary world of gaming. Their most successful raid was on a pharmaceutical amnesiac factory. They used homemade explosives and halted the production line for a month.

They have never taken the life of a civilian, although they do not include the police or the armed forces in this. They believe that a tipping point is coming when every bohemian must take up arms, and when it does, they will be ready: woman, man and child.

When Léon arrives in the tunnels, preparations are underway for the bohemians' latest mission. A prisoner is due to be moved to the hill; they plan to intercept the transport. Léon is given food and water and fresh clothes and a pair of boots suitable for traversing the tunnels. The leather is old and supple; someone has worn these boots before. Someone who no longer has need of them.

Léon sits apart from the others, back to the wall, feet wedged under the rusted rail tracks, the remnants of an advertisement for some department store or other at his back. He attracts looks, curious and guarded, but not unfriendly. The Remembrist has vouched for him. A woman, Aude, introduces herself. She will be his guide back to the left bank. He asks her how long she has been with the bohemians.

"Five years," she says. She was a university lecturer. For some time before she defected, she had been feeding her classes illegal syllabi, teaching them about democracy. Then a colleague threatened to expose her.

She still has family in the city. "Many of us do," she says.

She says sometimes there are journalists who come, from those countries where there is still a free press, like Germany or Iceland or further afield. They meet with the bohemians, ask earnest questions. They listen. Then in that other country there is an interview, or maybe a few minutes of video, and for a while the bohemians are news. Their plight is described as tragic, unconscionable, and there is outrage, until the next thing comes along, and then they are forgotten again, put out of mind with the mundanities of daily life.

Léon waits as the assault team go through their final checks. When they leave, so will Léon and Aude. Light is the final concession, a dim, reddish light; the majority of the preparations have been made by ear and touch. There are murmurs, the clicks of firearms being assembled. The bohemians work effortlessly.

They gather along the tracks, facing the platform, waiting. The great-nephew of Aide Lefort—sole survivor of her family—stands before them, an Ethiopian rifle slung over his shoulder. He addresses the assault team, wishes them good hunting. He reminds them: theirs is the revolution that will break open the minds of the people. They will liberate the prisoners of the state. They will destroy the stores of Forgetting that dull independent thought. A new era will dawn, one where the bohemians can embrace the light, need no longer skulk in the dark. Tonight, they will free one woman in the road to this end. The bohemians applaud and stamp their feet. The sound, in that gloom, is immense.

The assault team make ready, performing their final checks. Aude picks up her backpack, and nods to Léon. Time to go.

A siren blares through the underground station, momentarily freezing its occupants. Then a bohemian screams.

"Breach!"

Lights are doused, the station pitches into blackness. Léon hears the sound of weapons being taken up, safety catches clicking off. People shoulder past, running into the tunnels, footsteps uneven in their haste. Aude grabs his hand.

"Come on."

When Léon glances back, he can see a light approaching down the opposite tunnel, harsh and bright and moving at speed. The assault team, caught in its glare, are framed, ready to attack whatever emerges. Aude pulls him further into the tunnel where the others dispersed. They start to run, tracing the path of the old tracks, heading west. Behind them, Léon can hear a smatter of gunfire against the walls of the platform. It's going to be a massacre.

He stumbles. He should go back, try to help. But if he gets himself killed now, he loses the only chance there is to prevent this future unfolding. Aude keeps tugging his hand. Doesn't pause for a moment. The Remembrist has given her a mission, and she intends to keep faith with it. She leads Léon through the underbelly of his city, smuggling him through disused tunnels, platforms that were never open, boltholes and spaces barely wide enough to fit a body through.

She takes him back under the river. Under the wall. There is a place where the métro intersects with the catacombs, known only to the bohemians. Aude is sure-footed and does not falter. With each step closer, Léon can feel the presence of his anomaly amplifying, its eagerness to have him back. Time falters; begins to lurch around him as the anomaly sends out tendrils, loose strands of past and future that yank at his heart and lungs. The fabric of this world growing thinner. Dizziness toying with his balance.

"You don't have to come all the way," he says to Aude. But she refuses to leave him alone. She has her instructions, has to know that what he told the Remembrist is the truth. He suspects if he were lying, he would find himself joining the dead for good. But a flare is on the way. He can feel its call.

Through the halls of bones. The disused tunnels.

Terror, exhilaration.

The anomaly is waiting. He is ready to embrace it.

He puts all of his focus on the date in his mind. July, 2018. Hallie's time. Aude is speaking but he doesn't hear what she says. He is in a blind and deaf space. When the flare comes, he can no longer see the bohemian's face, but he can imagine the look of astonishment as she watches him disappear.

CHAPTER FORTY-THREE

Léon and I, sat on the pavement by the Clos Montmartre in the heat of early afternoon. The smell of young grapes in the air, tourists traipsing past us in flip-flops. The future Léon has just described feels impossible, but I don't doubt him for a second.

"We have to save Aide Lefort," I say.

"Exactly my thinking."

"She's the key."

"I asked the Remembrist to tell me everything she knew about the assassination. It happened in 2042. Aide was staying in the Hôtel Josephine in Bastille, the night before the election. When the polls opened in the morning, Aide, her partner and their children were found dead in their rooms."

"We have to stop it."

"*I* have to stop it," says Léon. "There's no point risking both of us."

"Are you serious? After everything you've just said? We do this together or not at all. Besides," I add, "If it wasn't for me, the Moulin Vert wouldn't exist."

"And if it wasn't for me, you'd never have gone to work at Millie's."

"So we're equally responsible."

"Right."

I give him a sideways look. "Don't think this means you're forgiven."

He smiles properly for the first time today. "I wouldn't dream of it."

He breaks off, a spasm of pain crossing his face.

"Léon, are you all right?"

"Yes. It's just... recent travels. The headaches are back. I'll be fine."

His skin still has that peculiar texture. A waxen, glassy quality. His words come back to me: *You're tired. You're not well.*

"The anomaly's making you sick," I say.

"I'll be fine, I promise. It's two more trips. There, then back again."

"And then?"

"We can go our separate ways, if that's what you want."

"Or?"

He hesitates. "Rome?"

I think about Rome. I think about Rome with Léon.

"Let's start by getting out of Paris. I have a feeling we're going to need each other for that."

He nods. I try to ignore the wash of fear at the thought of leaving. Leaving the anomaly. Abandoning it. It won't be easy. It won't want to let me go. I might have been manipulated, but the future Léon has seen is the result of my actions. He is right. I can't risk staying in Paris. I can't risk creating something worse. Neither of us can.

2042 will be our final trip.

It is almost a relief.

CHAPTER FORTY-FOUR

Paris, 2042

FROM FLOOR TO ceiling the bar thrums with bass. Jittery, nauseous from the transportation, I fight my way through gyrating bodies that jerk in strange sequences under the strobe. Sweating faces, irises dilated, fingers jabbing overhead. The dancers lost in submission to the beat. Above the bar, a digital menu flashes up special offers for the day. Bartenders lounge in sequinned vests and jeans, creating alchemy with their smoking concoctions. On the floor, an army of robots, some ferrying laden trays, others collecting empties. I eye the bartenders with envy. They haven't done a day on the floor in their lives. Then, leaning against the counter, in full flow of the recounting of some elaborate tale, I glimpse a face that is both familiar and strange. It's Angel.

He must be nearly fifty. I stare at him, transfixed. He's lost none of his charm. What is he doing back in Clichy, at this time of all times? I watch him raise his glass, cry empty. The importance of what Léon and I are about to do strikes me anew: it's the futures of our friends that are at stake.

I turn away, push with more urgency through the crowd. Shoulders brush mine, a boot crushes my toes. Someone flattens a sticker against my arm. I swat it away. As I exit Millie's, the bass gives way to a cool night, a neon extravaganza of advertisements, and the unmistakeable blare of sirens. I watch a police car race down the boulevard in the direction of place de Clichy. My forearm itches. I look down. A moving graphic, apparently glued to my skin, shows eight whirling green arms. They rotate faster, blurring into a frenzy, then vanish.

I'm in 1875 and Fabian's face is close to mine, fireworks exploding on the backs of my eyelids, humanoid figures crawling through tunnels. *You have already made it*, he said. My future. I didn't believe him then.

I shake aside the memory. It can't help me in 2042. Assuming the transportation went as planned, and this is 2042. What I've overshot, and the election has already happened?

I turn to the bouncer.

"Excuse me, can you tell me the date?"

He gives me a dubious glance. "One too many pills, hey?"

"I'm not high, I'm jet-lagged as hell and I was meant to be meeting my friend tonight but she hasn't shown... It's the fourth, right?"

The bouncer breaks into a hooting laugh.

"Lady, you are *out* of it. Today's the sixth of May. Get your arse to bed."

I count backwards from Lefort's assassination. I'm late for our assignment, but only by two days. Still time to save Aide. Still time to find Léon. As long as Léon has made it too. I remember his face clenched with pain and feel a stab of anxiety.

The wail of more approaching sirens. This time it's three cars and an ambulance. I stare after the retreating vehicles. An orange glow makes the night appear brighter than it should. That's not electric light: it's fire, not far from here. Something is burning. I catch the scent of smoke and all at once I realize there are a lot of people on the central aisle of the boulevard, far more than you would expect on a regular weekend night, even if the city's population has expanded. Some are drunk, some are dabbing holographic stickers onto people's skin, some are talking loudly and earnestly and in several cases aggressively, some are just watching.

Waiting.

Behind me, the bouncer swears.

"What's happened?"

"Another fucking car bomb. You want my advice, get yourself home and stay indoors. This shit won't stop until the election's done."

"Yeah," I say. "Yeah, I think I'll do that."

It's beginning, I think. This is where it starts.

TEN O'CLOCK in the morning. I've been outside the Clos Montmartre for thirty minutes and there's no sign of Léon. The vines are still here, though when I speak to one of the gardeners, he tells me the grapes are struggling with the brutally hot summers, and fewer varieties are grown each year.

"You've chosen an interesting time to visit Paris," he says. I want to ask him how he's planning to vote, but I don't dare.

I sit down on the pavement. The tarmac is beginning to heat with the sun, and I listen to the patter of sprinklers moving over the rows of vines. Crop yields down, pollen count up, the gardener says. A heating world is having its impact. I ask him how we are doing on the Paris Agreement. He laughs.

We need Lefort, I think. Her and many more like her.

Come on, Léon.

As the minutes tick by my worries multiply. What if he arrived too late? What if he didn't make it at all? What if something went wrong in the transportation?

"Still waiting?" asks the gardener, an hour later. "He's not worth it."

"He'll be here."

I watch people passing by. No one stops to look at the vines. Their attention is elsewhere, with devices or friends, or their internal thoughts. Between conversations in French I catch frequent snippets of Spanish and Portuguese, and I wonder if climate change in southern Europe is beginning to push people north. I wait. My anxiety grows. It's gone noon when I see a familiar figure heading up the road. The relief is overwhelming. I scramble to my feet and run at Léon, throwing my arms around his neck. His arms encircle me, tentative at first, then squeezing me tightly. He kisses me on the lips. Unthinking, I respond.

"You're late," I tell him.

"So are you," he says teasingly. "We said two days ago."

"I thought I might have missed it—we don't have as much time now—"

"It's okay, Hallie. Actually, I've been here for a month."

I break free of his embrace.

"A month? We agreed to meet a week before!"

"I wanted to scope things out."

"Bloody hell, Léon." I glare at him, furious. "You have to start trusting me, or what the hell is the point of us doing this together?"

"Okay, okay. Je suis désolé." He grins helplessly. You're not sorry at all, I think. You're loving this. Being here. "But listen, chérie. I have been doing some research."

I fold my arms, unwilling to be appeased so easily, even if this is for the greater good. But despite myself, my annoyance is fading, eclipsed by relief. I recognize a shift in my relationship with the anomaly: now I'm afraid of it.

"And?"

"Aide Lefort is meant to be staying at the Four Seasons. But that's not where she was found, according to the Remembrist."

"And?"

"So it's a bluff. By her security. They've given out false information."

"Which means the only people who know where she's staying…"

"You, me, and the assassin."

"Then it should be easier to get to her."

"Exactly. But there won't be as much security…"

"So we're on our own."

"Oui."

"We always knew that, though, didn't we?"

"We did."

"Léon, did you come through okay?"

"Fine. No bodies in the catacombs this time. You?"

"Yes. I can hear it, though. The song. It's muted, but it's there."

"Me too."

I slip my hand through his. My body still responds to his touch, the heat of his skin. I can't let you go, I think. Regardless of what you've done. I understand it too well.

"Tell me everything you've found out."

THE SEVENTH OF May 2042, the night before the biggest election in years. Allegiances over the past two decades have polarised even further. The media depicts crises of soaring unemployment and automation, rising energy costs, the ever-present threat of cyberterrorism, and an unstoppable refugee crisis fuelled by war and climate change. Voters require something radical. Once dismissed as urban hippies, the Parti Moulin Vert has gone from strength to strength, and votes for Aide Lefort are expected to dominate the left. Their greatest opposition comes from the latest iteration of the Front national. No one can predict the outcome. It's going to be close.

Aide Lefort's security detail is a visible force outside the Four Seasons, while unbeknownst to the public, Aide, her partner, her brother, and her children occupy the fifth floor suite of the Hôtel Josephine on rue de la Roquette. Nobody, human or robot, stops

Léon and I as we enter the foyer hand in hand, approach the reception desk and request a room on the fifth floor. Léon deals with the AI system whilst I cast an eye about the foyer. The place is almost deserted. It must have been smart once—in my time, perhaps. Now it has the look of an Ikea store exposed to the wrath of the elements. We are told the fifth floor is closed for refurbishing, so we accept a keycard for a room on the fourth.

In the lift we call the fifth floor.

"Apologies," says a recorded voice. "The fifth floor is closed for refurbishment. Do you require the fourth floor?"

"Fourth it is," says Léon. The lift doors close, opening again on a long corridor with a steel blue carpet and beige, peeling walls. We walk its length in silence, passing door after door. We don't see any other guests. No cleaning staff or bots. There must be people behind those doors, asleep or resting, unaware of what is about to unfold. The assassin may already be here, among them.

We climb the stairs to the fifth floor. Room number 562. As we approach the door, my perception narrows to these three innocuous digits, and a rush of deja vu overwhelms me with its violence. I stop where I am, paralysed. This has happened before—not in my lifetime, but I know it has in Léon's. Who else knows? Who else is coming?

"Okay?" says Léon.

I nod uncertainly.

He knocks at the door. We hear voices, a child's high-pitched tones and running footsteps, then another voice, sharp, calling the child back. Slower, heavier footsteps approach.

There's a long pause. I glance upward and see the eye of a camera observing us. I nudge Léon.

"We're being watched."

The footsteps subside. I hear low murmurs.

"They're calling security," I say.

Léon knocks again, louder this time.

"Aide Lefort!" he shouts.

"Aide," I call. "We need to talk to you! You're in danger—we have information!"

"Aide, please answer the door."

The voices sound like they are arguing. Rapid footsteps. We hear the electronic click of locks and the door swings open with sudden force. I anticipate Aide's partner, or a security guard with a gun, but the woman standing in the doorway is Aide Lefort herself, dressed in loose, casual clothing, exposed and completely unafraid. After the speech on the hill—just months ago, to me—it's a shock to see her middle-aged, lines at her eyes and mouth, no attempts to disguise the strands of grey in her hair, now worn short and natural. But her face has a new force.

"How did you find me?" Her voice is full of contempt. "Which of the media are you working for? Haven't you had enough work hounding my family these last weeks?"

I step forward.

"Please, you have to listen to us. Your life is in danger."

"There's going to be an attack," says Léon. "Tonight, in this hotel. I know you have no idea who we are and this will probably sound completely crazy, but we have information."

"It's not just you in danger, Aide, it's your family—"

"Your children."

Aide's shoulders twitch.

"Is that so?" she says. "You can tell it all to my security."

At the end of the corridor, I hear the chime of the lift arriving.

"Aide, listen to us! They're going to kill you and your family and make it look like you murdered them and then killed yourself."

"Issa, Sofia," she calls back. "Can you hear this nonsense?"

"If you die, the Moulin Vert will lose the election," I say. "It will be the end of Paris as we know it."

Security guards are making their way down the corridor. A woman comes to Aide's side. She puts a hand on her shoulder. Aide grips it.

"Aide, you don't have to listen to this," says the woman firmly.

"It's going to happen in this room—at least move to a different location—"

The guards reach us.

"Mademoiselle, monsieur, you're coming with us…"

One guard takes my arm, another secures Léon. I can see him itching to break free, but that will do our cause no good at all. The guards start to steer us away from the door.

"Aide!" I shout desperately. "Aide, you have to get out of that room! Please, I'm begging you! This is not a hoax, we're not the press, we don't want anything from you!"

Aide holds up a hand.

"Wait."

The guards stop. I catch Léon's eye, see him nod. We've got a chance.

"We'll hear them out," she says. "If they managed to find us, someone else might too. Bring them in here."

The guards exchange glances. Clearly unhappy with the situation, they frisk and scan us with various electronic devices before herding us inside. I look about. The fifth floor suite is as shabby as the rest of the hotel. Inside the room are Aide, a man about the same age who I assume must be her brother, and her partner Sofia, shepherding two children into the next room.

"Sit," says Aide.

Léon and I take a seat on the sofa, and the guards stand directly behind us. I'm intensely aware of a gun pointed in the region of my head.

"Tell me what you know."

"Could they put those guns down?" I say.

"I don't think so. Start talking."

"There's a plot to assassinate you. It's planned for tonight, between one and three. It's like Léon said. They're planning to kill you and your children and say you went on some kind of murdering rampage. Make it look like you're insane."

"*This* is insane," says her brother. He has a low, forceful voice, and shares his sister's strength of feature. "Aide, why are you giving these people the time of day? You need to get some rest. That's why we came here in the first place."

"Insane or not, I can't dismiss a threat, Issa. Not when it involves the children. You, what are you, British?"

I nod.

"You live here?"

"I used to."

"And you?"

"From Toulouse," says Léon.

"So who are you? Where did you hear about this so-called conspiracy?"

We exchange glances.

"We can't tell you that," says Léon slowly.

Aide indicates her brother.

"Then tell Issa, he's my chief of security. Convince him, you might convince me."

"All we know is an assassin is coming here. They may already be in the hotel."

One of the guards speaks.

"Should we evacuate the hotel, Madame Lefort?"

Aide strides angrily up and down. "Evacuate? No. That would be a media farce. Just what I was trying to avoid."

"Better that than dead," I say.

"You," she says. "You have no idea. You're a kid."

"I've heard you speak," I say. "You'd have my vote."

She comes to a halt. Looks to her brother.

"Issa?"

He gets to his feet.

"We can't take any risks. We'll move down to the next floor. Have all entrances and exits monitored. Maintain an invisible police presence. I'll alert the agencies. But let's not evacuate. If we raise the alarm, we have no chance of apprehending this assassin—if they even exist."

Aide nods. "I agree. If these claims are true, I want to know who this person is."

"You should move to another hotel entirely—"

Issa cuts me off.

"*If* there is an assassin out there—which I doubt, because God knows why it would be on your radar and not ours, especially given you don't even have an explanation for where you heard this nonsense—moving anywhere at all may put Aide at risk. We stay put until the morning."

"And you'll keep everyone together?" I say.

He looks at me coldly.

"If this is a hoax, I'll see the pair of you in a police cell by the end of tomorrow. For now, you're staying where we have eyes on you."

ONCE AIDE AND Issa have made their decision, everything happens very fast. It takes minutes to move the party down to the fourth floor. Aide's children, ten and twelve, are wide-eyed and excited and far from sleep. From the bedroom I hear the soothing tones of Aide's partner, Sofie, and Aide herself, reassuring them nothing is wrong, all will be well. In the second room are myself and Léon, Issa—stepping out every few minutes to take a phone call—and a security guard. Two more are stationed on the other side of the door, and plainclothes police are patrolling the street. The guest list has been lifted and they are running checks on everyone staying in the hotel. I should feel reassured, but my relief quickly fades. I can't help feeling that we should have relocated elsewhere. As long as Aide remains inside Hôtel Josephine, she hasn't escaped history as the Remembrist told it.

Léon squeezes my hand.

"It'll be okay," he says quietly. "They'll have alerted secret services. The whole region will be under surveillance. There's no chance of anyone getting through."

"We should have moved," I say.

The hotel has become oppressive. I can feel the denseness of its bricks and mortar, the burr of glass brittle in its frames. I look about the room, taking in each detail: the slightly loose light fitting, the smudge of fingertips on the wallpaper by the dresser, the heavy folds of floor-length curtains, muffling sound from outside. Everything seems significant, everything holds potential.

Aide comes back through.

"They're asleep, for now. Sofie will stay with them."

"You should get some sleep too," says Issa. "You need to be on your game tomorrow."

Aide makes an impatient noise. "As if that will happen."

She looks at me and Léon.

"Do you know how many death threats I receive each day?"

"Several," I venture.

"There's a conservative estimate. Yes, 'several' would cover it. A lot of people out there don't want a Moulin Vert representative in power, plenty more don't want a woman in power who's both black and gay. But they're threats, you understand? The disenfranchised, the psychopaths, the scum of the internet. Who would go to the length of assassinating me? That's a statement of intent. Even the Front national wouldn't stoop so low."

"And who's bankrolling them?" Léon asks. "You must have enemies in the international community."

Aide drops down on the sofa.

"There are always enemies," she says. "Always someone who'd be happy to see you destroyed. And there are easier ways to destroy someone than murder. My God, I'm tired."

That's why the assassin is doing this, I think. They're not just after Aide, they want to compromise her legacy too.

"Aide?" I say. "Can I ask you something?"

"You've got a captive audience. God knows who the pair of you are, police can't find a thing on you. I don't know why I'm listening to you. Probably because I'm exhausted and delusional. What do you want to know?"

"I was wondering why you decided to run for president, when you've refused for so many years. Why now?"

Aide looks at me thoughtfully. There's weight in that glance: the weight of long years, of decisions taken and sacrifices made. Then she sighs.

"I guess it was my time to stand up and be counted."

The overhead light flickers. I look up anxiously.

"It's nothing," says Léon.

All of the lights go out.

For a moment nobody moves. There's the sound of people breathing, shallow and frightened, trying to make as little noise as possible, and then we scramble to our feet.

"Sofie!" For the first time, fear touches Aide's voice.

"Aide, what happened—"

"Madame, stay where you are—" One of the guards. Click of his gun, readying.

"My comms are down—"

The door opens, closes.

"Aide—"

"Madame Lefort—"

"Everyone stay calm—"

"Madame Lefort?"

"Yes, I'm here, Francois—"

I find my phone. Dim blue light from the screen. Léon crosses to the window, stands by the curtains.

"Street's down too."

I activate the torch function on my phone, illuminating eight people: Aide and Sofie, the confused, sleepy faces of the children, Léon, three of Aide's security detail.

"Everyone get below window level," says one of the guards. It won't be a sniper, I think, but I do as I'm asked, getting to my knees with everyone else. Aide looks about her.

"Where's my brother?"

"We didn't see him, madame—"

"Issa?" she calls. "Issa, where are you?"

One of the guards checks the connecting room where the children were sleeping.

"He must have slipped out."

"He didn't say he was going out—"

I meet Léon's eyes, see the same thought dawning in his face.

"Léon, what did the Remembrist say?"

"The Remembrist? What's she talking about, what's this Remem—"

"Did she mention Issa? In the hotel room?"

"No," he says slowly. "She didn't."

Aide stares at us.

"What are you saying?"

"Why wouldn't your brother say where he was going?"

"He obviously went to get help—"

"Who knew you were staying here?"

"No." Aide shakes her head. "No, never. How *dare* you even suggest—"

Sofie, staring at us in horror, pulls the children to her. One of them starts to cry. The security guards exchange glances.

"If comms are down, someone needs to warn the police," says Léon. "I'm going."

"What? Léon, no—"

He's out the door before anyone can stop him. I want to follow but I can't leave Aide. In the torchlight, her face is a storm of emotion. I check my battery. It's down to fifty per cent. The light will only last so long.

"Madame, we should get you out of this hotel," says the guard called Francois. "Ramez will fetch the car once we're out."

"We're not leaving without Issa," she says.

"Aide," Sofie whispers. She looks down at the children. I can see the conflict in Aide's face, the struggle to process even the possibility of betrayal, the imperative to protect their children at all costs.

"The lift will be down," she says. "The stairwell's a trap."

"Secret services will be moving in, madame—"

"Not if their comms are down too." She looks to me. "Is yours working? It looks like something from the 'twenties."

I try the phone, knowing it won't work.

"It's down too."

"Maman, what's happening...?"

Aide kneels in front of her children.

"It's all right, my darlings. There's been a power cut, that's all. We need to get out of the building and find somewhere with some light. Now, listen, I need you both to be very, very quiet. Quiet as a pair of mice. Can you do that for me and Maman?"

They nod.

Aide presses a hand to Sofie's tearstained face. "I refuse to be taken like a rat in the night," she says. A look passes between them.

Francois takes my phone, as it's the only torch we have. He inches the door open, flashes the phone left and right.

"Clear," he says. "Let's go."

One by one we creep out into the corridor. My heart is pounding so loudly in my ears it seems impossible no one else can hear it. We're all in danger. Issa is on the loose, and if it isn't Issa, it could be one of the guards. I have no idea where Léon has gone. He might have run straight into the assassin. He might already be dead.

No.

I think of that look between Aide and Sofie. The resolve in it, the absolute trust. That's me and Léon, I think. Whatever has happened, we are meant to be together. We will survive this.

We make our way down the corridor, the guards, Sofie and I flanking Aide and the children. They don't make a sound. I wonder if they have done this before, if they will have to do this again. I imagine how afraid they must be, and bite down on my own fear. The torch flashes ahead, whips behind, jumps ahead again. Constrained glimpses of doors, carpet, ceiling, all made hostile with shadows. Every moment I expect the rush of footsteps behind us, a shot in the dark, a scream.

We reach the stairwell. Francois goes first. As quiet as we try to be, it's impossible to disguise our progress. Sofie moves me in front of her, insisting I go ahead. What a life, at the side of a politician, knowing you and your children are forever pawns in someone else's agenda. Every day living with the terror of losing them. We descend, the soft fall of our footsteps sounding louder with the echo. One flight. Two flights. Two to go. We keep moving. It feels as though it will never end.

Francois stops. With infinite caution, he pushes open the door to the lobby. Runs the torch up and down its length. Finally he beckons us through.

The lobby is deserted. Outside, a sea of blinking blue lights. A helicopter hovers somewhere overhead. A lone man in a suit stands with a gun in his hand, completely surrounded. It's Issa. Police cars form a road block, armed officers aiming at him from behind car doors. He must know it is all over, but he is refusing to drop the weapon.

Beside me, Aide has frozen. I can only imagine the torment she must feel at this sight, but if her heart is being ripped in two, it doesn't show in her face. I think: you are the bravest woman I'll ever meet. She looks almost preternaturally calm as she pushes past her security guards to step through the revolving doors of Hôtel Josephine. Sofie lets out a moan of distress, clutching the children. There's a shout of alarm as Aide appears outside. Arms waving frantically behind the barrier, cries of, "Don't shoot!"

Issa turns. Sees his sister.

Aide takes a step towards him.

"Issa, please—"

He looks at her, a wry smile twisting his face.

"You'll fuck up this country, Aide," he says.

Then he puts the gun in his mouth and pulls the trigger.

CHAPTER FORTY-FIVE

LÉON AND I lie side by side on the grass, the sails of the Moulin Vert creaking gently behind us. It's almost dawn. We lie without speaking, watching as gold brushes the Parisian skyline, then fades to make way for a clearer, cooler light. My hand is in Léon's, our fingers loosely intertwined.

"We did it," I say. "We saved Aide."

"And now she has to live with the knowledge that her brother was working with the nativists for years. She has to lead the country, knowing that."

"But she will. Lead it."

"Yes," says Léon. "And you'll be alive when the year comes round. You'll get to see that."

"We both will."

I watch the skyline solidifying into its linear formations with a knot of sadness. Our respite here will be too brief. Soon a flare will come, we will return to 2018, and it will be time to bid the city goodbye.

"Paris really is the most beautiful place in the world," I say.

"But Rome will be beautiful too."

"Yes. Rome will be good."

I squeeze Léon's hand, turn to look at him, and see the now-familiar tightness. He's in pain. The translucency of his skin is more evident than ever. For a moment, I think I can see straight through him.

"Léon—"

"Hallie, there's something I didn't tell you."

My chest constricts.

"Léon?"

He avoids meeting my eyes. I sit up, twist to see his face. I see him reach for words, discard them, try again.

"I can't go back," he says.

"What do you mean? We're going back together."

"No." He speaks with an effort. "I can't."

"Léon—"

"There was a reason I couldn't complete Janus's mission myself. A reason it had to be you. When I left Prague I thought I had two, maybe three travels left. Going to twenty-seventy pushed me to the brink. I wasn't even sure I'd make it here. But I know—I know for certain—I won't make it back. Not whole."

I gaze at him. A hollowness expanding in my ribcage, as realization sets in. I've been blind, preoccupied with my own problems. I've been so stupid.

"The chronometrist," I say.

"Yes."

"This happened to her."

Léon's voice is tight.

"She faded—and faded—until there was nothing left."

"Then there's no question. I'll stay too. We can still go to Rome, we can do all the things we said we would. We'll just—be a few years ahead. It's not so bad—"

"No."

"It's not your choice." My voice cracks. This can't be happening. This isn't right, this isn't *fair*. "Why should you be left behind?"

"This isn't your time."

"Or yours! Stop being so bloody noble about it!"

"But you have the chance to go back. Listen to me, Hallie. I've been out of time for half my life. The last few years, I pretended to myself that it wasn't taking a toll, that I belonged. But it does. It's not a natural state. You don't age, have you noticed that? Other incumbents have died from it, or gone mad. If you stay here, you'll be never be happy. And I... I can't bear to see that."

I shake my head. My nose is blocked, my eyes are hot with tears.

"I won't do it. I won't leave you."

Léon looks at me then, and I see he is crying too.

"I love you, Hallie. And I'll do anything—anything, you understand?—to make you go back. You have to do what I can't. You have to be free of it."

"How can I?" Taste of salt on my lips. "How can I do that."

"Because you're strong, and kind, and clever, and you deserve to live in the real world. Not with a ghost."

"But I love you."

Léon pulls me into an embrace. I cling to him desperately. He feels light in my arms, disconcertingly so. He's changed already, I think. The anomaly has done this to him. He's right: it never lets you go. And I feel a piece of my heart break.

Léon speaks into my shoulder.

"You have to do something for me."

"Anything."

"Get me on a train. I haven't... got the will... to walk away from Paris myself. I can feel it, every second. Tugging at me. Trying to pull me back. It *wants* me, Hallie. The anomaly. Can you help me do that?"

"Of course I will." I tighten my embrace. My tears are falling freely now, and I make no attempt to stop them. "Of course I will."

*   *   *

GARE DE LYON. People give Léon odd glances as they pass us on the concourse. Léon leans on me, although I barely feel his weight. It is as if I am supporting a bird, a tall, beautiful albatross, his wing resting across my shoulders, the bones within it hollow. It is true that there is something unearthly about him, something that causes people to stop and take stock of their surroundings, reassuring themselves that the ground they are connected with is real, and can be trusted to support them.

Slowly we make our way down the platform, along the carriages of the bullet service in their sleek blue livery.

"You're lucky," I tell Léon. "You get a direct train. I'm going to have to go via Milan."

"You'll go to the Colosseum," he says. His voice is no more than a whisper. Bruises under his eyes from lack of sleep. In certain lights, he seems to vanish into his surroundings. I have only his touch to reassure myself he is here.

"And the Pantheon, and the Sistine Chapel. You will too."

"Oui."

We pass a family boarding the train, two young children chattering excitedly as their suitcases are passed up.

"Hallie. Promise you won't come looking for me when you get to twenty-forty-two."

I stop walking.

"Promise me, Hallie."

"I promise." My voice trembles. "I promise, Léon."

"And after I've left you'll go straight to your anomaly."

"A flare's already on the way," I say.

"That's good. You have to say goodbye to Clichy for me. Wish it well. And Millie's. That place has been good to me."

"Yes."

Over the tannoy, the distinctive three-note chime of Parisian railway stations. A final call for Rome. I blink back tears. Help

Léon to keep moving. It takes the greatest of efforts to look up as we reach each carriage, to tear my eyes away from his translucent face.

"This is you."

"It's like *Brief Encounter*," he says.

"Oh, don't joke."

"You weren't at the premiere?"

"No."

"Nor was I. I didn't go back that far."

"Liar. You moved half the bones from Les Halles to the catacombs."

"That was an accident."

"Léon—"

"Don't," he says gently. "There's nothing left to say."

I kiss him desperately, hold him as tightly as you can hold a bird without breaking it. He takes my face in his hands, brushes my lips with his.

"Live your life, Hallie."

I help him climb into the carriage. He isn't carrying anything except his ticket. I watch, through the windows, as he makes his way down to the seat. He looks old, I think, as if all the years he has lived out of time are finally visible. He finds me through the window. Touches his fingers to the glass. He mouths something: *The Colosseum!* Smiles at me.

That smile.

A whistle sounds. The carriage doors close.

"Oh, god—"

I clamp my hand to my mouth, suppressing the cry I want to let loose. Blink away tears. I won't collapse with him watching, I won't make that his last memory of me. I wipe my eyes, stand straight. The train starts to move. I begin to walk, then run alongside it. Lift my hand in farewell. Shout, *I love you! Léon, je t'aime!*

I'm nearing the end of the platform. Léon's face, still there. Blink. When my eyes open he's gone, the train accelerating away, departed.

PART NINE

The Source of Joy

CHAPTER FORTY-SIX

Paris, 2018

I WAKE IN my studio knowing that I have had nightmares. My shorts and T-shirt are damp around me; the sheets are twisted into coils. My heart is racing. In the first disorientated minutes I remember nothing, and then his name comes into my head and the full force of memory hits me all over again. I turn into my pillow and heave dry, painful sobs.

When the storm of grief is exhausted I lie and listen to my heart contracting in my chest, its rhythm not quite settled even now, the sunlight warm and strong through the shutter cracks. I listen to Paris's siren song, lodged in the whorl of my ear. I feel fragile, not quite substantial, but I feel alive.

I have to get used to sleeping through the night again. And I have to decide what I'm going to do with my life.

TEN O'CLOCK, THE sixth of July. In two months I will have been in France for a year—if you count the clock in the present moment, that is. In other, unaccountable ways, I've been here years. I've aged. I open the shutters and light floods the room. I pad around the tiny apartment, straightening things, blowing dust away, waiting for the coffee to percolate on the detachable hob. I drink the espresso wedged into my balcony, spine pressed against concrete, knees to my chest. Watching pedestrians crossing the street below. Pigeons on the rooftops. The world goes by, with or without me.

I have a shower. I brush my teeth. I get dressed.

I wonder if the sense of missing someone ever goes away.

Since my return the anomaly continues to sing, though the song is muted, and somehow I am able to ignore its voice, or at least to pretend I cannot hear it. In fact, I feel quite detached from everything. Detached enough that I pick up my phone and call Gabriela, who I have not seen since she tried to blow up the keg room, almost killing us both in the process and effecting our banishment from Millie's.

GABRIELA AND I eat ice cream on the banks of the canal Saint-Martin. The water is cluttered with boats. It is a blazing day. The concrete paving sears the backs of my legs, and I am grateful for the arc of spray when a speedboat jets past the bank.

"So why did you call?" asks Gabriela. She has not looked at me directly since we met at Stalingrad. Hasn't forgiven me, I suppose.

"I wanted to say sorry."

"And?"

"And I'm sorry. For getting you involved. For not listening to you. For getting sucked into the whole travelling thing. All those things. And I'm sorry for what I said about you not wanting to go home..." I hesitate. "It wasn't my place."

"Hallie..." Gabriela dips one toe into the canal. She trails it back and forth. I wait until she is ready. "I accept the apology. And I am sorry too, about the explosion. It was a moment of madness. But we cannot be friends the way it was before. It is... things have changed. I need some space, at least for a time."

"Gabriela—"

"There is no point in arguing. I know my mind. This is it."

"But it was so perfect."

"Yes. It was."

My thoughts flit to Millie, to Rachel, to others I have known and loved. I spread myself too thinly, I think. I loved Paris indiscriminately, and there wasn't enough of me left to sustain the present. That's what Léon was trying to tell me. That was his experience.

"I'm not going to try and convince you," I say. "But I hope you'll change your mind, however long it takes."

We sit on the canal bank. A pedal-boat drifts down the channel and spins three hundred and sixty degrees, its occupants shrieking as they attempt to steer.

"Kit asked me to work again," says Gabriela.

For a moment my old grievances flare up: anger, jealousy, an awful fear that Gabriela will reach the anomaly where I cannot.

"Are you going to?"

"Yes." She shrugs. "It is my life, Hallie. But not yours, I think. Not forever."

"You may be right."

The pedal-boat has received assistance: two rowers are grabbing its hull and hauling it around. Their banter drifts across the water.

"Have you called your family?" asks Gabriela.

"Not yet."

"Call them. Remind them you are alive. And then go home, make your amends. One of us must."

I look at her. "What do you want, Gabriela? Honestly?"

Gabriela leans across. She brushes away a strand of hair that has stuck to my face, strokes my cheek. For that brief gesture, she is my old friend and confidante again.

"Who knows what I want?"

She hesitates, then takes something out of her bag: a photograph. She hands it to me. It is a scene I recognise, though I have not looked at it for a long time. It is the same scene as the Polaroid photograph I brought with me to Paris, only this time, the frame is wider, and I can see what lies beyond the wall where I stood with my mother and brother and sister. To the right of the photograph is a métro entrance.

"I found the place," says Gabriela.

I stare at the photograph, a lump rising in my throat, not knowing how to respond. Gabriela gets to her feet.

"I should go. I work at six."

I watch her making her way back down the canal path. She stops to say hello to a young whippet running off the lead and the whippet leaps up to greet her rapturously, as if she is the best of acquaintances. I remember Gabriela in Café Oz, the wizard at the end of the road, Gabriela in the cemetery, talking excitedly about *Transfusion*. We're all of us trying to find out who we are, I think. Perhaps some of us never do.

MÉTRO HÔTEL DE Ville. There is the familiar art nouveau sign, the green-painted metal railings housing the entrance to underground. Two men manoeuvre a buggy down the steps. A woman with a guitar on her back takes the stairs two at a time. To the right of the entrance, a newspaper stand displays copies of *Le Monde* and *Le Figaro*, with front page images of the new refugee camps that have sprung up in the forests of Calais.

I stand there for a while, surveying the scene. I go over to the wall, touch my fingertips to its rough stone. Sandstone. Eocene. I stand where I was standing, follow the path of my mother's arm, waiting for a flash of memory, a moment of revelation; but nothing comes. I was here, I think.

This is the source of joy.

*   *   *

LATER THAT DAY I top up my French SIM card and call Sussex. The landline rings. Long-short: an English tone, which I have not heard for months. There is a string of clicks and scuffles as the phone is picked up, and then my mother's voice.

"What!"

"Hello, Mother. It's me."

"Which one?"

"Hallie."

I wait for the intake of breath.

"Oh, Hal," she says breezily. "Haven't heard from you in a while. How's uni? Have you had your exams yet?"

"What?"

She raises her voice and enunciates with undue stress.

"I said, *how's university?* Hideous line, isn't it, sweet pea? I think it must be the revenge of British Telecom, they've severed some wires or something. Or maybe it's your end, are you in a field?"

"You're not with BT," I say. "Look, what do you mean, 'How's university'? I'm not at university. I deferred for a year."

"Oh."

There is a pause and a human mewing sound; I realise she is talking to the cat-who-does-not-belong-to-us.

"Mum?"

"Well, where are you, then?" she asks. "I must say, we were wondering when you didn't come back for Christmas. I suppose you had a fall-out with Theo, did you?"

I force myself to take a deep breath.

"I've been in France," I say. It's so hot. My head is spinning. How can travel through time feel as real as the skin on my hands, and yet my own mother sounds like a fantasy?

Somewhere in the room, a fly buzzes.

"France? That's rather bohemian of you. What are you doing, darling, looking at rocks?"

I cannot be having this conversation, I think.

Then again, I haven't spoken to them in months. I've forgotten.

"No, I'm not looking at rocks. Are you honestly saying you thought I was at university?"

"Where else would you be?"

"In France?" The fly zigzags around my head. I grab a tea towel, wrap it around my damp free hand.

"Well, isn't that bizarre! We might have been worried, darling, if we didn't think you were at university. But Aberystwyth's such a safe place, I never worry about you there. Whenever I think of you in Aberystwyth, I always imagine you looking at rocks. Oh, by the way, I found those binoculars you wanted for birdwatching. They were buried in the back of my wardrobe, in a mouldy old rucksack. No wonder we couldn't find them."

"Jesus Christ. That was over a decade ago."

I swipe the tea towel and miss the fly. I open the shutters. The full heat of the sun hits my face. I curl into the balcony wall, her voice tinny in my ear.

"Time flies like the birds." She chuckles. I have not heard this laugh in nine months, and hearing it now I realize I haven't missed it. I haven't missed *her*; what I've missed is an idealized version of what I've always wanted her to be, against all reason or logic or even fairness.

"Hal? Is it alright if I keep them, then? New sculpture."

"Sure," I say. "Sure, you go ahead."

"Thank you, darling. They'll be perfect."

"Are you working on a new exhibition?"

"I am. It's going to be a big one." Her voice turns confidential, girlish. "*The* big one. I haven't been so excited about a project in years. If this all goes to plan—and there's no reason why it shouldn't!—your father will be able to drop the teaching *for good*. Isn't that fantastic?"

"That's great," I say. "That will make him happy."

"You will come to the exhibition, won't you? I must say, it was funny not seeing your solemn face around in the winter. You always seem to fit winter. And then the electricity got cut off, and the man told us it was in your name. He seemed to think that was rather odd. We had to change it back again. I had to work by torchlight for a week."

She plays an out-of-tune arpeggio.

"We do miss you, darling."

I don't know whether to believe her.

"Are you coming back soon?" she asks.

"Not straight away. But I'll need to collect my stuff before term starts. I'll let you know."

A miaow.

"This cat," she says uncertainly, "is always hungry."

"It's just angling for food," I say. "It's trying to play you."

"Yes. Yes, you're probably right." She brightens. "They are such foolish creatures!"

"I'll let you go, Mum. I'm sure you've got a million things to do for the exhibition."

"That's true, sweetpea. I'm hellishly, hellishly busy."

"We'll speak soon, then. Bye, Mum."

I cut the call before she can reply.

I sit on my balcony in the infinite sunshine. My head aches. There's something pushing at my chest, compressing it, trying to squeeze me in upon myself. I lean back and reach for the pint of water on the floor inside, and upend it straight over my scalp. Water runs down my face and neck and under my clothes. I tell myself that it's all water, but I can taste the salt. I realise it's a relief to admit it, that I can cry, I can sob until my eyes are swollen and my throat is raw, I can let it all out. When the sobs subside I feel a strange calm settle over me.

She'll never be the woman I once hero-worshipped, lying outside her studio, plotting expeditions into the wilderness. What woman could be? We'll never have the implicit understanding she shares with Theo and George. But somehow the balance has shifted. I could tell her all the things I've survived in Paris; I could try to impress her with tales of chronometrists and Nazi-occupied Paris and a girl called Millie who became an entrepreneur. But I don't need to. I no longer have anything to prove.

TWO MONTHS UNTIL I'm back at university. I check my bank account and plan a full itinerary. I book my train from Gare de Lyon to Rome via Milan, and another train from Rome to Pompeii. It's time to lay the volcano's ghost. After Pompeii, Naples, and a return flight to London mid-September. I leave a couple of days to collect my things from Sussex before returning to Aberystwyth.

I call my landlord and tell him I'm breaking my contract. He's not happy, but I don't care. I throw my clothes crumpled and unwashed into the suitcase. I put the spare key to the studio in an envelope and drop it into Gabriela's mailbox, with a note saying if she's quick she can get her hands on my furniture before the landlord claims it.

Several times in those last few days I go and stand on the boulevard, opposite Millie's, and through the screen of tourists I watch people come and go. On the last occasion, Dušanka, stepping outside for a cigarette break, spots me loitering. She strides across the boulevard, ignoring an oncoming bus, which screeches to a halt to avoid flattening her. I hold my ground, expecting recriminations, prepared to fight. But Dušanka takes out a packet of Luckies and passes one to me. I offer her my lighter and think I see her mouth tweak.

"Will Gabriela forgive me?" I ask.

"Oh, she'll come round. She always does."

"When?"

"Don't wait for it." Without looking at me, she says, "You remember what I said to you, that first night?"

"That this life is a dream."

"And it is. For most of us, it is an interlude." She sucks in smoke. "Simone and Isobel have left now. Mike, too."

I feel a wash of sadness.

"I didn't get to say goodbye."

"Mike is in Chicago," says Dušanka. "You can look him up. With this internet savagery of the modern age, it is impossible *not* to find a person, even when one does not wish to be found. I will leave soon myself, but no doubt these people will find me too."

"I'm sure you'll bear it with dignity," I say.

"What happened to Léon?"

"He went to Rome."

Dušanka makes an annoyed sound. "So rude, not to say goodbye. But he always was a strange one."

"Everybody leaves," I say.

"That's how it is."

"I didn't think you'd remember. What you said to me."

"I have an excellent memory."

"And where will you go?"

"To Greece."

"For Socrates?"

Dušanka looks at me in outrage. "Do you have *any* idea how completely the ancient Greeks suppressed the female voice? Sappho. My god." She takes a long draw, holding the smoke in her lungs before exhaling slowly. "I don't know what happened in there," she says deliberately. "But it doesn't matter. Do you understand what I am saying? None of it matters. None of it is real." She peers at me. "You and I," she says. "We have other things. I have philosophy. You have rocks."

"What if it's not enough?"

"These things are important." Dušanka tosses down her cigarette and grinds it into the pavement. "You should not underestimate them. My break is over."

"I'll see you around, then."

"You might," she condescends. "But I make no promises."

CHAPTER FORTY-SEVEN

THE TWELFTH OF July, my last night in Paris. At seven o'clock tomorrow morning the SNCF to Milan will pull out of the station. I will watch Gare de Lyon recede into the distance as we rush through the outskirts, the suburbs, the open fields, heading south-east. Rome beckons.

But before I go, I have to say our goodbyes.

The heat wave broke earlier today and the air smells of warm rain. I leave the apartment wearing flip-flops and harem trousers, my suitcase clattering along behind me. Midnight. Outside, street lamps flood the roads with orange. A crocodile of tourists muddles uphill, past the shuttered fabric stores, the crepe vendors, the men with their cotton bracelets, and up, and up, to the Moulin Vert where I watched as the first boulder was laid. Where a student found her cello. Where Aide Lefort preaches for a new bohemia. I turn the other way, downhill, joining the boulevard between a kebab stall and a shop peddling discount sportswear of dubious provenance.

The road is restless, cars and scooters intercut by pedestrians, each convinced of their right of way. A warm night breeze brings the blood to my face. Instinctively I hurry my step, weaving in and out of the tourists, ignoring the wolf whistles and low-voiced *salut, mademoiselles*. Horns blare. Men slip out from red-curtained entrances, looking furtive. Bars spill onto the street, pichets of wine and cigarette smoke, laughter and music and the sound of dancing. Le Chat Noir, the Musée de l'Érotisme, La Diva, the Moulin Rouge. On the central aisle, drugs change hands and volunteers on a Moulin Vert stall hand out day-old baguettes.

HERE I AM, outside Millie's, back where it all began. The bouncers are filtering the queue. Kit and Eloise are at the doors, walkies clipped to their waists. A floor skivvy comes out to the terrace, stacks empty pints, gets out his notebook to write down a dozen orders he cannot yet remember. Someone has squashed a pink Stetson on his head.

The floor skivvy shoulders open the door and I catch a glimpse of Gabriela on the bar, a feather boa around her neck. I set my suitcase down and sit on it. I seem to have come impossibly far, and nowhere at all.

I always imagined that it was possible to cast off those elements of myself that I disliked or did not want. I had come to Paris cleansed; in my wake was a trail of the undesirable, stretching back like flotsam after the tide. I didn't plan to look back. But that's an impossible ambition. Your identity is an evolution in itself. It is sedimentation. Each new facet compresses the one before, but can never entirely erase it. Below the smooth, polished face we present to the world, we have fault lines, glitches, air bubbles. If we were made from rock, our history would be as decipherable as mineral, and like sandstone, the fossils buried in our pasts can, and will, emerge to haunt us. But it is up to us if we allow them to dictate the future.

When people ask me about Paris, what will I say? Will I talk about timefaring, eighteenth century parties in the catacombs, a man I loved but could not save? Will I tell them of Clichy, of mojito nights and Oz at dawn, of Gabriela and Angel, Millie's heroes? Which version do I give and which do I keep close? If I deny either, will it diminish in my memory, grow smaller and blurrier until I can no longer trust it as truth? Or will it remain safe, untarnished, a well to return to in times of drought, a source of joy?

IN THE EARLY hours of the morning it grows cold, but I remain where I am, ignoring the fluctuations of the night around me, the gradual exodus of revellers. The sky lightens. Birdsong. In the tunnels beneath the boulevard, the métro starts to rumble. And something else. A flare is on the way. I can hear the anomaly singing, I can feel its hum in my bones. I know that I could walk inside Millie's, wait until the bouncers are distracted and slip inside the barrier with old ease. I could answer the unanswerable call and will myself back to 2042. I could find Léon in Rome.

My limbs protest when I stand, joints and muscles stiff from hours of sitting in the cold. I take the handle of my suitcase and go down into the métro. Line 2 to La Chapelle: four stops against the wrench of my heart. A short walk to Gare du Nord. Every step an incalculable effort, the song building in my head, the anomaly unwilling to let me go, my mind captive in a place twenty years from now. Line D, all the way down to Gare de Lyon. Take the escalator up into the station. Swept along with the rush of morning commuters. The footprint of the real world. Overhead, the vault of the station roof, rows of trains lined up in their bays. Movement, ever forward. The train to Milan is boarding.

I walk along the platform, ticket in hand. Conscious now of two presents. In time and out of time. An echo of Léon walks beside me, his weight that of a bird against my shoulder, his arm the ghost of an albatross wing, here but not here, as I go on.

ACKNOWLEDGEMENTS

MY THANKS TO the generous readers who looked at early or later drafts of the book and offered their thoughts and encouragement: Nina Allan, Clare Bullock, Beth Grossman, Genevieve Helme, Dominique Larson, Chris Priest, Kim Swift, Veronica Swift, Andrew Swift, Björn Wärmedal. Thanks to the Southbank Set: David Bausor, Kyo Choi, Christabel Cooper, Jaq Hazell, Dominique Jackson and Colin Tucker, for their feedback on various excerpts and all round support. Thank you to Rooksana Hossenally and Marko Waschke who kindly checked my French and German translations—any errors in the text are my own—and to Sophie Webber who advised me on Jewish weddings. Thanks as always to my agent John Berlyne and to Louise Buckley at Zeno Agency for their editorial advice and support and for keeping faith with the book; to my editors Jon Oliver and David Moore, publicist Remy Njambi, and the wonderful team at Solaris who have given the book a home; and to Joey Hifi for the beautiful cover art. Love and thanks to the friends I met in Paris, an inspiration and a source of joy, and to James for keeping me sane along the way, this time and all the other times.